THE HUMAN DISPERSAL PROJECT

A novel by Adam James Chouinard

This book is dedicated
to all the many unborn souls,
and us lucky few who made it.

In particular, a tale for my sons.
May the future be all that you need it to be.
May you trust in yourself, and trust in each other.

```
- - - - - - - - - - - - - - - - - - - - - - - - - - - - - - - -
>print layout.hdp
- - - - - - - - - - - - - - - - - - - - - - - - - - - - - - - -
- - - - - - - - - - - - - POD LAYOUT V1 - - - - - - - - - - - -
- - - - - - - - - - - - - - - - - - - - - - - - - - - - - - - -
LEVEL: NAME (CODE)                SYSTEMS AND STRUCTURES (CODE)
- - - - - - - - - - - - - - - - - - - - - - - - - - - - - - - -
0: THE NOSE (NSE)                 Flight Control System (FCS)
                                  Digital Cognition Centers (DCC)
- - - - - - - - - - - - - - - - - - - - - - - - - - - - - - - -
1: COMMAND AND CONTROL (CON)      Manual Pilot Controls (MPC)
                                  Advanced System Interface (ASI)
- - - - - - - - - - - - - - - - - - - - - - - - - - - - - - - -
2: LIFE SUPPORT SYSTEMS (LSS)     Biomedical Stations (BMS)
                                  Vital Signs Monitoring (VSM)
                                  Nursery (NSY)
- - - - - - - - - - - - - - - - - - - - - - - - - - - - - - - -
3: AUXILIARY SYSTEMS (AUX)        Cupolas (CUP)
                                  Flex Space (FLX)
                                  Cargo Hold (HLD)
                                  Airlocks (ALK)
- - - - - - - - - - - - - - - - - - - - - - - - - - - - - - - -
4: LIVING QUARTERS (LIV)          Dormitory (DRM)
                                  Commons (CMN)
                                  Bathhouse (BTH)
                                  Mess Hall (MSH)
                                  Lounge (LNG)
- - - - - - - - - - - - - - - - - - - - - - - - - - - - - - - -
5: THE LIBRARY (LIB)              Auditorium (AUD)
                                  Breakout Rooms (BRK)
- - - - - - - - - - - - - - - - - - - - - - - - - - - - - - - -
6: THE MIDSHIP (MID)              Greenhouses (GRN)
                                  Wellspring (WLS)
                                  Labyrinth (LBN)
                                  Kiva (KVA)
- - - - - - - - - - - - - - - - - - - - - - - - - - - - - - - -
7: THE BIOME (BIO)                Water Cycling Systems (WCS)
                                  Nutrient Cycling Systems (NCS)
                                  Ecological Community (ECO)
- - - - - - - - - - - - - - - - - - - - - - - - - - - - - - - -
X: THE UNDERBELLY (UDB)           Gravity Unit (GRU)
                                  Homeostatic Systems (HOM)
                                  Deployment Systems (DEP)
                                  Fuel Cells (FLC)
                                  Boosters (BST)
- - - - - - - - - - - - - - - - - - - - - - - - - - - - - - - -
>|


- - - - - - - - - - - - - - - - - - - - - - - - - - - - - - - -
```

```
- - - - - - - - - - - - - - - - - - - - - - - - - - - - - - - - - - -
>print schedule.hdp
- - - - - - - - - - - - - - - - - - - - - - - - - - - - - - - - - - -
- - - - - - - - - - - - DAILY SCHEDULE V3 - - - - - - - - - - - - - -
- - - - - - - - - - - - - - - - - - - - - - - - - - - - - - - - - - -
BLOCK OF TIME    DURATION    CODE    ACTIVITY
- - - - - - - - - - - - - - - - - - - - - - - - - - - - - - - - - - -
00:00 - 00:30    00.5 hr     WAKE    WAKING
- - - - - - - - - - - - - - - - - - - - - - - - - - - - - - - - - - -
00:30 - 02:00    01.5 hr     BODY    BODY
- - - - - - - - - - - - - - - - - - - - - - - - - - - - - - - - - - -
02:00 - 02:30    00.5 hr     BFST    BREAKFAST
- - - - - - - - - - - - - - - - - - - - - - - - - - - - - - - - - - -
02:30 - 03:00    00.5 hr     PLAN    DAILY PLANNING
- - - - - - - - - - - - - - - - - - - - - - - - - - - - - - - - - - -
03:00 - 05:00    02.0 hr     UST1    UNSTRUCTURED (1)
- - - - - - - - - - - - - - - - - - - - - - - - - - - - - - - - - - -
05:00 - 06:00    01.0 hr     LNCH    LUNCH
- - - - - - - - - - - - - - - - - - - - - - - - - - - - - - - - - - -
06:00 - 07:00    01.0 hr     SLP1    SIESTA (SLEEP 1)
- - - - - - - - - - - - - - - - - - - - - - - - - - - - - - - - - - -
07:00 - 11:00    04.0 hr     MIND    MIND
- - - - - - - - - - - - - - - - - - - - - - - - - - - - - - - - - - -
11:00 - 13:00    02.0 hr     DINN    DINNER
- - - - - - - - - - - - - - - - - - - - - - - - - - - - - - - - - - -
13:00 - 14:00    01.0 hr     SPRT    SPIRIT
- - - - - - - - - - - - - - - - - - - - - - - - - - - - - - - - - - -
14:00 - 15:00    01.0 hr     UST2    UNSTRUCTURED (2)
- - - - - - - - - - - - - - - - - - - - - - - - - - - - - - - - - - -
15:00 - 00:00    10.0 hr     SLP2    NIGHT (SLEEP 2)
- - - - - - - - - - - - - - - - - - - - - - - - - - - - - - - - - - -
>|

- - - - - - - - - - - - - - - - - - - - - - - - - - - - - - - - - - -
```

It was a time that most likely might have never come to be,
and which might very likely be meeting its ending too soon.

CHAPTER 01

THE PRESSURE IS MOUNTING

4252-07-33: UST1

There is nothing quite like the imminent extinction of every known member of one's species to make them feel the weight of the world on their shoulders.

So it was for Pee-pop — even though the world was long behind her … and she had never known it … and there was no gravity outside the POD where she was tethered. Nevertheless, the record will stand by such an earthly metaphor, for the weight of the world may as well have been upon her. The point is that it was a very precarious situation.

"How much time left, ABRAM?"

"Sixty-eight seconds. Sixty-seven. Sixty-six…"

"I know how counting works!" she snapped with a tone that ABRAM had never heard from her before. "Ugh," she groaned, "I can't think!"

"Sorry, Pop," said ABRAM calmly. "You can do this. It only takes a moment. Take a deep breath. Focus."

The POD was traveling at 2,451,253 kilometers per hour, as was Pop alongside it, bound to the rail by only her safety harness. She had made it out to the manual release, a feature she'd only ever needed to consider seriously for the past ten extremely frantic minutes, maybe less. As if a mindless robot, she had done exactly as she was told: she had raced up to Level Three, suited up in the alcove, stepped into the Airlock, pumped down to form a vacuum, opened the outer door, and stepped out into space to defy their shared doom.

Sweat covered her face, evaporating and fogging her visor. Her heart was pounding faster than ever before. Her breath was racing, and yet altogether insufficient. Her diaphragm was spasming. Short, rapid, anxious gasps were all she could muster, one after the other like the beating of a hummingbird's wings. ABRAM sensed all of it.

One too many seconds ticked by in idle terror.

"Pee-pop, listen to me," said the system. *Forty-seven seconds,* its internal timer ticked, though it kept the counting to itself. "You can do this. Take a deep breath, and we'll begin."

ABRAM spoke calmly, assuredly. It had total faith in her, or else simulated such a sentiment flawlessly. Whatever she had done to earn its confidence, she did not know. And in fact, she did spend a second or two of their fleeting time to ponder just that in her panic.

I'm not good enough, her fear insisted she consider. *I never have been. I'm going to fail them all. They should never have trusted me.*

And she had good reason to fear. Despite all the trainings, she had never actually been outside the POD. She did not know how to save their lives. She did not know anything, it seemed. She was not even ten years old.

The suit's climate control was functioning remarkably well, if a little foggy from the exorbitant fear-induced sweating; it was keeping her warm — but she was frozen. Paralyzed. Unable to think, let alone free to move.

But then, as if by divine inspiration from an unknown depth of her being, a flash of insight broke through the blackness of her terror. No words came with it; only their faces. She saw all of them at once — an impression, more than an actual image of her crew-mates. Not one of them was missing. They were all together, and yet superimposed: represented by the sense of a single being which looked like all of them and none of them specifically.

The grace of their presence quickly shattered her stupor. Now, rather than focusing on all the reasons she did not know how to save them, she simply remembered what it was that she was trying to save. She may yet fail them, but she would not fail to act.

She did as ABRAM had instructed her: she took a single deep breath, drawing in the recycled air of the suit until it filled the full volume of her lungs. She breathed it out slowly, and the fans whirred to recycle it further.

Despite the incomprehensible speed at which she was traveling, everything slowed.

"Okay," she said, still shaken but focused now — grounded by her grip on the rail and a singular focus on the latch in the center of her vision. "Okay, okay … okay … What do I do?"

ABRAM was poised and at the ready.

"Pull the handle on the right to open the cover."

"Got it," said Pop. She strained a bit but then *SHUNK* — it was done.

"The lever you need is set back a bit, but you should be able to access it. Reach through any cables obscuring your vision. You will have to use your sense of touch, which may be difficult through the gloves. You will find another latch with a short handle on its front face. Slide the handle up. It may take some effort."

"Okay okay, I think I found it," said Pee-Pop. Her left hand pulled against the side of the outermost hatch to counteract the force while her right hand strained with all its might. "Errgghh—"

SHUNK. The lid slid upward with a snap as it finally gave way.

Twenty-two seconds, counted ABRAM in silence.

"Flip the switch inside," it said.

She pushed up on the large lever, which clicked and then ricocheted back down with a jerk as she let go of it.

Sixteen seconds and *WOOSH.* A loud hiss reverberated through the massive POD, and eight of the nine other children inside let out a collective sigh of relief. The internal pressure had been rising rapidly, but the manual release would cause a reboot and, hopefully, a recalibration. The system had been quick to discover the problem, but as of now, neither the cadets, nor even ABRAM itself, had a full and proper explanation for what had gone wrong. In any event, their desperate and hasty plan appeared to be working, as the pressure slowly made its way back to a manageable range.

"The POD is stabilizing, Pop," said ABRAM. "Well done."

"Wow," she said as a matter of fact. "That was close."

She was still clutching the side of the hatch, her head pressed against the hull of the craft as she tried to catch up on her breathing. So overwhelmed with the rapidly escalating situation, she hadn't had a chance to even process her presence out in interstellar space. She was one window's width closer to all those stars she loved so much, but she was too frightened to admire them.

"Indeed," confirmed ABRAM. In its own way, it sounded extremely relieved.

The Automated Biological Replication Assistance Machine was a longshot when conceived, even for all of humanity's technological accomplishment by the year 2346 when the Portable Ova Distribution Systems (PODS) finally began to launch. A longshot, maybe, but it posed the only practical solution that the earthlings had ever envisioned to overcome an age-old dilemma. It was a hard-earned creation, this suite of infrastructure and human-interface functions, and a long time in the making. Despite their constant self-doubt, humanity was still capable of remarkable feats of cooperation when put to the fire. Against incredible odds, it had gotten them this far.

"I always expected to at least make it to our tenth birthday," said Pop, her head still pressed against the hull. And with the tension slowly diffusing, her thoughts returned to more trivial matters. She raised her head to inspect the strange feature that she had used to save their skin. "Why is this on the *outside* of the POD?!" she griped — and justifiably so, for Pee-pop was not one to gripe unjustifiably. "Sometimes I wonder what they were thinking with some of these things."

"Don't we all," said ABRAM. In actuality, the system knew exactly what *They* had been thinking, for its circuits were already online and its training well underway by the time the infrastructure was developed. Still, it never hurts to sympathize.

Pop had meant it in the most general sense — clearly *someone* had constructed the only world they'd ever known — in the sense of someone who had been neither inspired nor encouraged to inquire about it more deeply. Eventually, *They* would become an oft-cited nuisance in the lives of the cadets; for the architects of the Human Dispersal Project were to be thanked for their existence, but so too were they to blame for it. As of now, however, the crew knew no such thing.

The inner airlock door flung open and a pack of beaming faces came bounding towards their reluctant hero as she stepped back into the POD.

"Wow!" said Chee-chaw. "You did it — way to go Pop!" The little guy was bouncing up and down, his face just barely coming to meet hers at the peaks of his leaping. "You saved the day!"

"Okay okay, calm down Cheech," said Pee-pop. She blushed and averted her eyes. Pee-pop was more than happy to pass around the praise, but she hated getting compliments.

"Nice work," said Plashy calmly, and the others left it at that — at least as far as words were concerned. Chee-chaw was the first to embrace her, but the rest of them present all felt the same way — an overwhelming, almost debilitating sense of relief from mortal peril. Soon, the whole crowd had closed in on Pee-pop in a multi-layered hug, drawn instinctively together by equal parts elation and the remnants of a lingering fear.

They were almost all there: Plashy, Tor, Dee-dore, Faingo, Squeal and Peel, Chop-char, and Chee-chaw himself. The only one missing was Potch, but this wasn't unusual and he certainly wasn't missed. He'd been … *off* a bit again lately; and for better or worse, most of the group had given up on trying to get him out of his moods once they'd set in. Chee-chaw was the only one who even tried anymore, and only because Potch hadn't the heart to hurt the little guy's feelings by chasing him off in the way he would have done if it were anyone else. In any event, almost the entire crew was there to thank Pee-pop for saving their collective life. For the second time.

It was old news by now, but there had been a minor incident with a gas leak two years ago that would have resulted in a swift but extremely uncomfortable death by asphyxiation. If not for the same combination of ABRAM's know-how and Pee-pop's can-do attitude that was put on display this very day, it would have been light's out for the lot of them. It's not that the others weren't capable of varying degrees of guts and gallantry; but when the going got tough, they turned to Pee-pop. It was practically a matter of instinct by now.

And you might never have known it to look at her. She didn't earn her status as de facto leader through her physicality, that's for sure. She wasn't short for a girl of almost ten, but neither was she tall; she wasn't scrawny, but she definitely wasn't imposing. When it came to brute strength, that was Chop-char's uncontested jurisdiction. And Pee-Pop was bright, but she herself would never claim to be the smartest of them all. That honor probably went to Faingo, though Potch had never applied himself enough to make her work too hard for such an accolade. (Whatever the case, they could all agree that such a title would go to neither Squeal nor Peel. They meant well enough, overall, but they were not the brightest bulbs in the control room.) Neither was Pee-pop the most funny (Chee-chaw), industrious (Tor), scrutinizing (Plashy), or creative (Dee-dore). In fact, Pee-pop was probably the most of one thing alone: loving. So, when the going got tough, they didn't need the strongest, smartest, funniest, most industrious, scrutinizing, or creative. They needed Pee-pop.

"Okay okay, that's enough!" laughed Pop. She gently wedged Chee-chaw off her side — he was the closest and clutching her tightest by far — and the dense hug unraveled from the force in its center. She made her way through the crowd and into the alcove to remove the rest of her gear.

"What was that all about, ABRAM?" asked Faingo in a classic inquisition. If there was an important question to be asked, it was often Faingo's for the asking.

"It's not entirely clear," said the system. "The immediate problem was a runaway pressure cycle, quite similar in nature to the … mishap two years ago. In this case, the elemental ratios were proportional, but the mix was hyperbaric in nature, and it was increasing dangerously quickly."

"Hyper-what-now?" said Dee.

"Hyperbaric," stated ABRAM clearly. "Defined as gas in a state of pressure higher than normal."

"Sounds like Chop-char after dinner!" said Squeal, followed immediately by her own awkward laughter: too fast, too loud, and for a comment too unfunny. Her quips never caught on the way she imagined, but it never seemed to stop her from trying the next time.

"Not now, Squeal," said Faingo.

"More like—"

"You too, Peel," she preempted. "And we pretty much gathered that already," she said to the system. "I meant, Why? What do the diagnostics say?"

"Not enough, I'm afraid," said ABRAM. "The symptoms are quite clear, so to speak, but there's no definitive diagnosis on the root cause, as far as I can tell."

If the system knew more, it did not say.

"Hmm," shrugged Faingo, stewing.

And as their scholar worried over this troubling occurrence, Pee-pop had slipped out of her suit. Looking back to the gaggle of heads still clustered by the airlock, she made an intuitive count without even realizing it.

"He still sulking?" she asked.

"Day three," said Dee.

HDP

Down in the Biome, Potch was sitting in a makeshift hideout underneath the apple tree. There wasn't a lot of space, but it was his, or so he'd deemed it. Branches leaned vertically against one another to form a crude perimeter, save for a small triangular opening. Near the trunk was a large, smooth, upright rock against which to lean his back. It was a faint reminder of a world he'd never known, but which — for some reason that had never been adequately explained, by his accounting — he had to call Home.

But there he leaned, alone for a time, lost deep in a dark vortex into which he was inclined to fall. Much to his chagrin, his solitude was shattered by the lightest footsteps, and he knew exactly who had come to call.

"POTCHO!" said Chee-chaw. "You missed a CRAZY show up there!"

"So I heard," said Potch. "Sounds like you better go make sure everything is okay."

Cheech may have been stunted, but he wasn't stupid. He knew Potch's disposition better than perhaps anyone, and he was perfectly aware of the myriad ways his friend would try to be rid of him.

"Nah, it's alright," he said. "Pop took care of it. She was amazing!"

"Of course she was," quipped Potch.

"Ah, come on Potchy!" But Potch rolled to his side against the rock, leaning even further into his insufficient refuge. Cheech could tell that *chipper* wasn't going to work; perhaps *practical* might. That was far more Potch's style. "I mean … she saved our lives … again. It seems like you should probably at least say thanks."

"Uh huh," said Potch. It wasn't sarcastic, simply unenthusiastic. He knew it was true. He just couldn't feel like it was.

"Come on, Potch," said Cheech. "What's going on?"

Potch scooted over to the furthest edge of the rock, almost laughably trying to avoid his guest; but still, he didn't say a word. The silence lasted until it reached the awkward phase, and then carried on straight through it. But Chee-chaw was patient, and there was still a little Unstructured Time left before lunch.

"Well, hey…" said Cheech to change the subject, "…our birthday's coming up! Ten big years. Pretty crazy, right? I don't know about you but … I … am … pumped … let me tell you."

"Yeah, trust me: we know," said Potch. "It's all you've been talking about for months now."

"Yes, but it's only ONE day away!" He climbed on top of Potch and leaned around him, looking up at him with that silly Chee-chaw grin. And even the most jaded among us can't help but crack at that adorable, awkward little face when it makes that earnest smile. Potch was no exception. Like it or not, he had a soft spot for that little guy. "ONE," stressed Cheech, and Potch almost broke character.

"Alright, I get it," he said, stifling even the feeble chuckle that had threatened to set in. "You're excited. That makes one of us."

He gently withdrew from underneath Cheech and rose from his refuge, stooping low to avoid the branches overhead. Stepping out into the "wilderness," for a brief moment Potch had regained his precious solitude. The sights in the Biome never ceased to amaze him, and it was for this reason that he spent most of his free time here. Wherever you turned, there were plants to behold: short ones and tall ones, fat ones and thin ones, smooth ones and spiky ones, bushy ones and viny ones — and other ones besides. One of the hummingbirds whizzed past him and dipped into the bushes.

The space was designed as a self-contained ecosystem, diverse in its way, if limited in scope as a matter of practicality. Still, it provided the oxygen for them to breathe, recycled their waste into something usable, and yielded more than enough sustenance for the ten of them to live quite happily, not to mention the animals. And most important to Potch: everywhere you looked, there were things to see. If you squinted just right, you could almost — *almost* — trick yourself into thinking you were somewhere else. And that's where Potch wanted to be.

Like the rest of his compatriots, he didn't choose this life. But unlike the rest of them, he had never accepted it either, and pretty much right from the beginning. Earth was a long way behind them — far longer than their own lifespans, should they ever desire to turn back. Worse yet, there was no point in ever doing so. They would never make it, should they live a thousand years. The future of their humanity dwelt out here now, somewhere, if there was any hope of a future at all.

And of course, technically, there was always a *hope* — even if that was all that they had. But perhaps hope was the thing with which Potch struggled most of all. Of all the hidden things he had ever uncovered, it was the one thing he had yet to find.

"What's the big reveal, do you think?" asked Cheech.

"What?" said Potch, jerked again from the rapid onset of his brooding.

He began wandering out into the middle of the habitat. Naturally, Chee-chaw followed, step for step; it just took him several more steps per unit distance. He was only a meter tall after all.

"I don't know," said Potch. "Something stupid, probably."

His back was turned as he paced steadily away, and Cheech therefore had no means of knowing that he wasn't entirely telling the truth.

"Hmm, I don't know," said Cheech. "ABRAM seemed particularly excited about it. Don't you think? It doesn't usually foreshadow our birthday this much. Does it?"

"I don't know, I guess so," huffed Potch, and he picked up the pace. He ducked under a hanging branch and grabbed a goumi berry as he passed.

To his credit, Cheech was right: ABRAM had been atypically cryptic about the upcoming event, and it did seem a bit more excited than normal. It had reminded the kids about the date in a way that was borderline adorable, if such a description should ever befit a system of its nature, and it proceeded to hype them up for "something special." When pressed on the matter, ABRAM would say no more, but the system raised its verbal rate and pitch, and quickly conned its way into starting a game of Pong for Tor and Chop-char. (It didn't take much conniving.)

"So what do you think it is?" said Cheech, bouncing back into conversing distance on those springy little legs.

"I really don't know, Cheech. Why don't you go ask it?"

Potch stopped and turned around, feet planted firmly in the soil. Cheech skipped his head right into Potch's chest and ricocheted back again. When he got over the shock, he looked the long way up to Potch's eyes and knew the look well.

"Okay, alright, sheesh. I'll scram," he said slowly. His shoulders sank a little as he backed up and turned to leave. "I just thought you could use some company is all."

And before any remorse had a chance to reveal itself in Potch, Cheech was lost beyond a maze of foliage, and he had his wish at last. He was alone. But as was often the case, that still didn't satisfy him.

Before he could settle back into his proper stewing, however, out squawked a little voice from far across the Biome.

"Say thank you to Pop!"

His final message made clear, Cheech went out the exit and climbed the long stairs to the upper levels.

Free to go wherever he pleased — or at least, within the seven levels of the POD … until lunch when their regular schedule would resume — Potch turned back to his wandering. The Biome, like the rest of the POD, was a whopping 100 meters in internal diameter, and Potch knew every leaf in it by heart.

Still, he imagined himself exploring the uncharted wildernesses where these species might once have grown free.

Of course, there was no single environment in which these species had all coexisted. Like much of the Human Dispersal Project, the end product was the result of countless cycles of trial and error — variation, replication, and selection. What mattered was what worked; and what worked in this case ended up being a rather random assortment of organisms from a rather random assortment of habitats. Most had been subject to differing degrees of artificial selection already, but not all; and despite a very intentional emphasis on fruits, vegetables, and other crops, not everything was edible. But everything had a role to play, even if that role wasn't immediately apparent. But they didn't need to *understand* it. Out of countless incarnations and iterations, this particular ecosystem had proved stable and sustainable. And thus, it was adopted.

A lizard scurried across the path and Potch lunged for it instinctively. He loved most things in the Biome, but the lizards were high on the list.

"Dang," he said, his face down in the dirt. "Next time, lizard!"

The bell rang out through the intercom: it was time for lunch. Potch glanced up at the tall ceiling, dozens of meters above, then hung his head back to the soil and sighed.

Date: 2266-03-15-EY
Area: O(HUMO(PSYC(CABA)))
Team: Sobriquets [O-3Q6HNVJ]
Item: Appellation Trial Updates

Entry: AAPs [Appellation Assignment Protocols] are nearing completion. Confidence is low and frustration is high. Frankly, everyone is still reeling from the Dunedin Debacle [a reference to P-Cycle8BWH2-PhaseY-NM7E6.tl]. The team is divided, as is HDP itself, but it puts an incredible limitation on the whole sector for the rest of the project. Forget trivial stuff like names, imagine how folks over in HEAP [Human Embryology and Parturition] are feeling right now. Almost ninety-eight years, only to get to this point, and who knows how much longer, all to set us up for the greatest bet humanity has ever hedged.

See the TL [Technical Log] for full results [O-CycleGN3D1-PhaseV-R5JKS.tl]. In general, the biggest surprise has been the degree of support for the peer-constructed conditions. Emergent appellations are occurring, with only the minimal guidance setting from the stand-in for ABRAM. Of course, it's hard to say how any of this will translate to reality: these kids are way too old. This was supposed to be a pilot study — a pilot. Some of the emerging names are definitely absurd, but most are clearly the products of confounding factors from their non-trial social and linguistic environments — standard domestic environments, which are far too unrealistic.

Either way, all three treatments [system-assigned, -moderated, and socially-constructed subject names] have since been set as variables for permutations, so it seems the universe will have to figure out what works best. Thanks to Dunedin [New Zealand], we'll never know in advance.

At least we're having fun with the analysis. Poor "Cheesy." The kid never had a chance of shaking that one. Lucky for Cheesy, the trials only last a day; unlucky for us, that's one more reason why this whole experiment is just not enough. Unlucky for cadets, they'll never know Cheese; lucky for them, at least that one's likely off the table.

CHAPTER 02

A Typical Lunch (On an Atypical Day)

4252-07-33: LNCH

"Well, well, well: it's Grumpelstiltskin," said Peel with a coat of condescension. "That is your name, right? I got it, right? I'd hate for you to steal my baby."

Technically tasked with keeping the peace, ABRAM was so pleased that its unit on folklore had made such a mark that it didn't intervene. If even Peel was on board, it was a smashing success by every measure.

"Give it a rest," said Plashy, and everyone concurred.

Potch shot Peel an evil eye as he made his way to the table, but he had as little stomach for confrontation as he had for lunch right now. The bell may have rung, and the gang may have been gathering in the Mess Hall, but Potch's thoughts were still wandering the wilds of the Biome.

He shuffled by the rest of the crew and slid into the inner bench of the booth. True to form, he scooted all the way down to the end. Chee-chaw took a seat across from him, nodded his narrow little head down the line to where Pee-pop was already sitting, and raised his eyebrows in a fashion that was both awkward and obvious. Potch just shifted his eyes to say, *I get it* — and slumped down further in the booth.

"Let's get this over with," said Potch.

But two of them were still missing; and as always, they could not start a meal until everyone was present. The culprits, Tor and Chop-char, were always more than game for lunch, but at the moment they were deep into a game of Pong in the lounge, just adjacent to the Mess. They had heard the bell just fine, but neither one would be the first to walk away and leave themselves open to an assured defeat. And each time those grainy pixels bounced back at them from their opponent, they waited anxiously for that sweet, satisfying *PONG* to ring out through the overheads.

But instead, *BING BING BING* rang the bells a second time.

"That means you two, Torp-char," said ABRAM.

11

These two had become so attached as of late that they'd earned themselves a joint nickname, and even the system dabbled in a bit of good-mannered fun from time to time. The assortment of fuzzy white shapes imploded into black as ABRAM flipped off the screen.

"Dahhhh!" moaned Chop-char. "I had him, I had him, I had him!"

The others could hear the commotion all the way next door in the Mess.

"Fat chance," said Tor as he tossed down his tablet and swaggered in to join the others.

"Technically about a one-in-ten," said Dee-dore. "I think those are the latest figures."

Dee had recently taken to writing log entries in the lounge as those two would battle over their latest obsession. She could always be counted on for an artful turn of phrase, and she liked the logging more than most, so the crew was happy to let her do the majority of it on their behalf. Her propensity for records — and being essentially the only one who could tolerate the nonstop Pong — meant that she had naturally been chosen as the neutral party responsible for keeping track of the bragging rights. And indeed, she was remarkably close from memory alone: the tallies were 148 to 14 in Tor's favor.

"Of all the games in the system," said Peel, "I still don't get why you two go for the most boring by far."

"Watch it," eyed Chop-char as he plopped down last of all on the bench. "At least I don't smell my own farts."

"Wha— oh, that was one time!"

"Now, now, children," said ABRAM. It didn't resort to patronizing often, but settling fart fights was one case in which the system deemed the method warranted. "And actually, Peel, I find the choice of game nostalgic. Would you believe the history of the Atari system is actually linked with the evolution of my ancestors? For example, the game *Montezuma's Revenge* was a major catalyst in the development of intrinsic motivation. The Epsilon-Greedy, button-smashing algorithms couldn't—"

"Hey hey, this isn't Mind Block," injected Peel, "it's lunch so save the lectures!"

"Right. I see," said ABRAM in a tone that betrayed disappointment but not surprise. "In that case, yes — that makes everyone." It tracked attendance mostly through audio, though the network of cameras could be leveraged in a pinch. "Okay, feel free to dig in."

The floodgates were opened. Squeal and Peel were seated nearest the service station, and — as they did almost every day at this time — they scrambled and tangled and hustled and tussled to be the first to the feast. The rest of the cadets reliably rolled their eyes and waited for the two of them to get it over with. Today, it was Squeal who squeezed her way out of Peel's grasp and snuck ahead first of all to the cooler. In reality, it mattered very little: all the plates and proportions had been prepped the day before, and as dictated by the Code, none of them were allowed to start eating until everyone was seated and had what they needed. But off she had shot, and all but Peel had been perfectly happy to let her go. The others slowly rose after them, each mostly deferring to each other, and arranged themselves in a neat single file.

Potch fell in last behind Pee-pop. At first, there was only an awkward silence between them. Pop looked back at him, wishing above all that she could do something — anything — to cheer him up, but knowing from experience that such a hope was folly. Potch met her eyes briefly but quickly dashed them away. That stupid, smiling grin of Chee-chaw's flashed in his mind, and he mustered a reluctant resolve.

"Hey, so … I heard what you did," said Potch, followed by a silence that was a bit too long. "I just — you know…" Again, it lingered too long. "Thanks," he said at last.

For a second time today, Pee-pop blushed and hung her head.

"Oh, thanks," she said, trading gratitude for gratitude. "It all just happened so fast. One minute Faingo and I were going over our trigonometry, and the next thing I know, I'm suited up on a Walk with my arm in a hatch on the side of the POD."

"Sounds intense," said Potch, and that would have served his conscience well enough to end the conversation; but once you broke through to Pee-pop, she was inclined to keep going — not out of arrogance or pride, but because she was perhaps as bad at ending conversations naturally as Potch was at starting them.

"Yeah … wow," she said, recalling in the moment just how intense it actually was. "I know it's stupid, but I just — I just really wanted to make it one more birthday, you know?"

No, thought Potch, and he didn't. But he nodded skeptically for the sake of keeping up appearances.

"We're just…," started Pee-pop again, "We're just so close. I don't know, it seems like every year is another huge accomplishment out here."

And a huge accomplishment it was, even if the rest of them seldom considered it, or agreed with the sentiment should they find a way to do so. But it was true, and for a girl of not-quite-ten, it was a remarkably astute observation. Even in the project's earliest estimations in the 2120's, of which the crew still knew nothing, the odds were against anyone ever making it this far. The architects spent centuries trying to increase those odds, but the uncertainty was an unfortunate yet necessary part of the paradigm. Every step along the way was fraught with peril.

To arrive at this exact moment, they had to make it out of low earth orbit; they had to successfully accelerate to interstellar velocity; the vessel had to survive the long march of over 41 trillion kilometers for a span of 1,896 years without the loss of any essential systems; the Biome had to remain stable and self-sufficient, continuing to reproduce naturally while avoiding ecological collapse.

Crucially, the human zygotes had to be viable from the start, remain viable in cryostasis, and survive the process of thawing and activation; the entire ABRAM infrastructure also needed to survive the long ordeal, not to mention pull off the first stages of its incredible task without encountering any hiccups in the highly complicated process of embryogenesis and extended gestation; the young needed to survive the artificial parturition, take to lactation, avoid any adverse reactions to the microbiome infusion, and overcome all the other countless trials that come with growing up; the numerous supplemental life support systems had to remain fully operational, and the foolhardy plan for raising a generation of children without any parents had to prove itself worthy of the tremendous time, money, effort, and hope that its founders had poured into it.

Perhaps hardest of all, the cadets had to live with each other in total isolation for ten fraught years to get to this point. And there were twenty more to go. Then, finally, they might arrive at what was, in a sense, only the very beginning.

Somehow, miraculously, they had beaten the odds at every turn. And yet, that's what human children have done forever, even in the simplest of times, in order to make it out into this oh-so-improbable realm. Beyond that, they did not know whatever grim fate might await them, should they ever actually arrive at their distant destination. For now, that was one thing most of them didn't spend their precious emotional capital worrying about, and it was easy to do: they hadn't even been provided the prerequisite context.

Rather, to date it had been mostly the mundane tribulations of juvenescence which had occupied their fears and doubts. At this exact moment, that was as simple as a particularly uncomfortable conversation on a particularly uncomfortable day. Luckily, the line cranked forward by one more person and Pee-pop was next in the queue, providing just enough justification to break away from the conversation before Potch had a chance to let his real feelings show.

When at last the whole group had gathered their goods and returned to the table, they settled in for the Quackery — or at least that's what they had come to call this all important moment of thanks. As with essentially all their traditions, this one was older than memory, its name rooted in an evening many years ago when a young Chop-char threw a particularly impressive fit about wanting to eat his "quackers." The term evolved effortlessly from there, but the essence of the ceremony never changed.

They held hands in a circle — from Potch in the innermost corner, across the table to Chee-chaw, up the line to Chop-char, Tor, Pee-pop and Squeal, across the table to Peel, and back down the line to Faingo, Dee-dore, and Plashy, until closing the circuit on Potch once again.

"Who's turn is it?" asked Dee-dore.

"Plashy," they said in almost unison.

"Aggh," she moaned. "Fine. Let's get this over with." They hung their heads. "I am thankful for…" — and it was never an easy ordeal on Plashy night. The time ticked by, but suffice it to say that there were no gushing endorsements at the ready. "…Chop-char's incredible mastery of Pong. It's truly inspiring."

"Come on, Plash," said Dee-dore softly. "For real."

Plashy opened her eyes. *SIGH*, she sighed. And across the table, she saw Pee-pop, her eyes closed and head hanging.

"Oh yeah," said Plashy, perking up. "Today's practically a freebie!" She was mostly happy for the lightening of her burden. "I'm thankful for Pop, for … well, you were all there."

Technically, not all of them had been there, but the point was clear enough. Plashy may have been indifferent, even downright cynical at times, but she also wasn't about to put Potch on the spot for his mysterious absence earlier. No: that was someone else's present scheming.

With the Quackery out of the way, the food was soon flowing; and from the exact opposite corner of the table, Squeal had her eye on Potch. Never one to let an opportunity go, she couldn't resist the temptation to take a crack at him. He was such an easy target lately. Peel, her amateur disciple, had already given it a go, but it hadn't quite worked up to the satisfying sting for which Squeal was perpetually searching.

"So… how's the Mope Zone down there, Potchy? Any news?"

"Don't," said Pee-pop, jabbing her gently in the side to no avail.

Potch said nothing. It was both his go-to response and highly advisable.

"What?" said Squeal, blameless and half-offended. "I'm just wondering how his only friends are doing."

"Hey knock it off!" said Cheech from down the line.

"What? What was that?" mocked Squeal, looking frantically around the room. "Did someone hear something? Where did that come from? Do we have a … is it … a GHOST?!"

Peel laughed his same desperate laugh, the lone enabler in this unwitting audience.

"Down here, Jerk-o," said Cheech, leaning back from the table to stare Squeal down, entirely unfazed.

"Oh, okay," said his tormentor. "Phew! Just a MOUSE."

"Baaahhh!" squealed Peel, rocking back in the booth and slamming his hands on the table.

"Would you two knock it off already?" said Plashy, glaring at Squeal in that most impressive and intimidating way that she could glare. "I swear, you're the most annoying creatures in the cosmos."

As someone higher in the pecking order had intervened, Squeal reverted to her astonished and innocent tone.

"Sheesh, jeez, fine. Lighten up." She settled down, and a passing silence settled in; but — as always — Squeal couldn't help herself. "Take the side of Mopey and Dopey, why don't you?" she muttered under her breath.

And *PLOP,* slammed the slop into the side of Squeal's head.

It was an impressive toss from well down the line. He was little, but Cheech was well-versed in wily ways. Slowly, the bowl slid down Squeal's face as she stewed in her shock, until it *schlerped* off her chin and clattered to the ground in a series of crashes. Peel lost it for real this time, flailing backwards and forwards, then falling out of the booth entirely like the buffoon that he is. This time, however, he was far from the only one laughing.

"Nice shot, Cheech!" said Plashy, reaching across the table to slap hands in solidarity.

Squeal, however, was not having it. She wiped the slop from her face, rose in a wrath, and headed for the little guy. Chop-char promptly got up, wiped his mouth calmly, and stepped out in her way. She stopped flat-footed and Chop just smiled down at her.

"What goes around, comes around, eh?" he said.

Cheech leaned forward around Chop's ample volume, to make eye contact again and give her that famous Chee-chaw grin.

"You're DEAD, mouse!" she shrieked. "SQUEAK!"

She tore out of the Mess as an absolute mess; she stormed through the Lounge, out into the Commons and off toward the south stairwell. When she made it to the safety of the stairs, she sat down on the edge, and tears fell to her cheeks to help clean the remnants of food clinging there.

"Not cool, Cheech," said Pee-pop, ever the peacekeeper. His satisfied smirk fell flat.

"Whatever," said Potch, unexpectedly to all. "She was picking on him!"

"And he knows how to handle that," said Pop, all the way across the diagonal to Potch in the corner. She then turned to Cheech across from him, at the far end of the same side she was on. "And it's certainly not by throwing a bowl at her head!"

"It's just going to make it worse, Cheech," said Dee-dore. "You know that."

"I agree," said ABRAM. "We've talked about this."

"Oh, NOW you chime in?!" said Cheech.

"I thought it was awesome," said Peel, and perfectly sincerely. He was always more than happy to pile on and pick on Cheech himself, but he didn't discriminate in his love for the abject embarrassment of others — even his mentor in the art of bullydom. Faingo just looked at him and shook her head matter-of-factly.

"Or maybe she'll learn not to mess with him," said Tor.

"Nope," said Dee-dore. "Pretty sure that's not what she's going to take away from this. Have you met Squeal?"

"Well, if I don't make it to our birthday, you'll know who did it," said Chee-chaw. "Speaking of which … how PUMPED are we?"

The silly and carefree smile returned to his tiny face.

Date: 2184-09-12-EY
Area: I(SINT)
Team: Jackrabbits [I-AX42K97]
Item: ABRAM Pilot Trial 9.02 (Post)

Entry: Trial a success overall. Along with infrastructure improvements, the interface is coming along nicely. Double-blind trials
indicate a jovial disposition, even whimsical at times. Not clear
at present which nodes responsible, but 89.42% of replicates
(Mean = 3.4 ± 0.79 y; N = 164) indicate a net positive ethogram,
reduced glucocorticoids, increased oxytocin, reduced intra- and
intergroup aggression indices, and reduced task latencies compared to previous trials.

Full index of participant metrics and results are available in our
report [I-Cycle9EG86-PhaseV-J8CTG.tl]. Qualitatively, the subject
has a strong sense of identity and responds well to inquiries;
it has taken a surprising liking to its acronym. All inquiries
indicate a high likelihood of TOM [Theory of Mind].

CHAPTER 03

THE LAST LESSONS OF INNOCENCE

4252-07-33: SLP1 / MIND

After lunch, the crew headed back to the Dormitory, as they did this time each day. Squeal rejoined them from her self-imposed exile in the stairwell, signaled by the *BING-ing* of the bells, and having had very little in the way of lunch. She was uncharacteristically quiet but made one certain look in one certain direction, which said all she wanted it to say, and Cheech kept his distance. (He was usually happy to do so anyway.) In this way, the crew turned in for what was one of the greatest ideas of any human society: the Siesta. Rested up after an hour of sleep and/or relaxation, they ambled down one level to the Library.

The POD was arrayed in such levels, increasing in number between the control systems in the bow and the thrusters in the stern. And while it was useful to think of the elongated shape of the vessel as designed for forward transit (which it was), the living and working arrangements were organized vertically along its length, as the floors of a building so long ago on Earth. This layout was dictated not only by the physical construction of the space, but also by the gravitational system, which enforced these norms of orientation. The forces had been calculated quite precisely, and deliberately, having been designed to allow for a more-or-less natural human existence, but one in congruence with their ultimate planetary destination.

While surely not without its limitations, the POD provided an impressive amount of area on each level, especially when one considers that it needed to travel at 0.23% of the speed of light. (And while this may not sound like a large proportion, one should know that this is very, very fast.) The inner POD radius was an even 100 meters, resulting in an area per level of ~31,415.93 m^2 (~3.14 hectares). The "mathy" members of the bunch would be able to tell you that it worked out, more precisely, to an area of 10,000 times pi (π) square meters, for that is how the area of circles are calculated ($A = \pi r^2$). All seven habitation levels were of equivalent height (3 meters), with the only exceptions being the

Library (10 m), and the Biome, which allowed for far more vertical habitat (30 m). And lastly, while directions were in one sense entirely arbitrary, the designers had labeled the four main "corners" of each circle as North, South, East, and West. Call it an homage to a planet far away, they had rightly predicted that it would be important to have a means of knowing one's way around and communicating it efficiently, and this worked well enough. The cadets had never known anything different anyway, and so there was nothing odd at all about it, as far as they were concerned.

So, knowing exactly where they were headed, they arrived at the platform on Level Five and unlatched the door that was sealing off the stairwell. It opened out into the Library. The main feature of this level was a large, central chamber — the Auditorium — which would fit far more crew members than it needed to. Outside the Auditorium and lining the level's perimeter, a circular hallway connected a series of smaller rooms — the Breakout rooms. The crew found the "big room" far too big for everyday use, and they had somehow converged on an arbitrary favorite breakout over the years, and so that is where they went.

Each breakout room, being a part of the same circle, fanned out like an amphitheater, with a few rising rows of long sofas equipped with flip-up tables for use when needed. On the inner side (towards the center of the POD), there were longer tables providing a larger surface area for collaboration, as well as a series of consoles for interaction with the system. On the innermost wall was a large screen on which they could pull up materials from individual consoles and interact with ABRAM (and others) more generally. The full potential of these interfaces had yet to be tapped, but for the time being they served to facilitate a series of structured and standalone curricula, led by none other than ABRAM itself.

The goal for this decade of their development was to lay a foundation of essential skills and knowledge. Not that the children always saw the value in whatever they were learning. Like everything else in their life, the crew occupied a series of positions in a full spectrum of opinions on the matter, and in this case their particular location was rather context-dependent. There were a few exceptions to this rule: Faingo was always at the top of the enthusiasm list, regardless of the content, and Peel was always … not. Most everyone else was differentially engaged, depending on the topic.

Want to get Chop-char going? He was a sucker for organized competition and sport of any sort. If there was gamesmanship involved, he was on board. As for more scholarly pursuits, his interest led him, naturally, in the direction of political science.

Need Dee-dore to focus and kick into gear? Find a connection to communication and artistic expression: language, writing, visuals, music — it really didn't matter much which form it took. If it was creative, she would be hooked.

Chee-chaw goofing around? Well, this was pretty much his modus operandi, and a tool for engagement in its own right, if and when ABRAM and the others could figure out where to steer it. After all, his was the jurisdiction of laughter and joy. Squeal and Peel may have thought they were funny, but it was Chee-chaw who truly held that honor.

Speaking of Squeal, if she were causing a commotion, there were ways to break the trance. She was drawn to biology, and particularly the kind that bled — or perhaps more like that which drew blood. She was fascinated with animals, especially carnivores — the ones at the top of the food web. Most recently, she and Peel had become enamored with wolves, and they would howl when excited to prove it. This sense for the morbid also drew her naturally to medicine, assuming she ever felt like using her powers for good.

As for Peel, wherever Squeal led, he would follow. It's not clear if he actually cared about wolves, for example, or if he howled just for her. When it came to subject matter that might break through to him, it was best to spend one's energy elsewhere. You may as well try to push your way through the wall of the POD with your bare hands.

Tor falling asleep? Get him building something. He had a knack for design of just about any sort. This penchant for engineering made him fairly well-rounded in his own right, at least for things at the interface of math, geometry, and the patterns of behavior.

Plashy stuck in that common state of intransigence? She was a kindred spirit with Tor in some academic regards, drawn mostly to the quantitative, but of a different set of applications. She was more statistically-minded, and interested in "systems" of the complex and dynamic nature: economics is just one such example, but there were diverse ways in which her interests would be piqued from time to time. The harder part was that you had no way to know it.

Potch sulking in the back row? Well, in this case, there might not be much to be done, depending on how deep in it he was at any given time. But that was not because he was without interests, and if he was going to rally, it would be done in his own domains. Like Plashy, Potch had a soft spot for complexity, and it led him to several parallel interests: life, technology, and the pondering of chaos.

Pee-pop — well, Pee-pop was never much of a problem, either academically or otherwise. Still, her heart belonged to the physical. She was fascinated with geology, chemistry, physics, astronomy — with all things related to the makings of the stage on which their universal play was playing out. She had never touched the Earth, not once (the rich soil of the Biome doesn't count); but she knew all about it. There was hardly a mineral she couldn't name you from its picture alone. As for the science of space, that she knew equally well, if not better. It was the only home she had ever known; and whereas some others had already grown to resent it (without naming any names), Pee-pop loved it. It was Home.

Then, of course, there was Faingo. It didn't matter what it was. When it came to learning, she was in. But that doesn't mean she had no specific passions. Faingo was the true Scholar of the group, tasked with making sense of it all and integrating it together into a cohesive kind of meaning. This led her interests to history — the perspective of hindsight which allows for making sense of all the madness.

Settling in to their regular room of choice, so too did they settle in to the most central and largest waking block of their 25-hour day: Mind Block. Exactly as the POD itself, the social environment had been meticulously crafted, based on years of hypothesizing, implementation, assessment, iteration, and synthesis. As expected then, the Mind Block curriculum was the result of tremendous scientific progress.

Their learning was highly structured — but it was ill-structured, in the technical sense. That is, lessons were crafted ingeniously, to engage students into practical matters that were complex in nature, in ways that required the identification, integration, and application of fundamental principles to achieve an unspoken and open-ended goal. There were times that they could kick back and enjoy a bit of old-fashioned summary, often under the leadership of ABRAM — or just as likely, Faingo. More often, however, the cadets were tasked with a challenge, the solving of which required a deep understanding of numerous seemingly disparate subjects.

On any given day, for example, the cadets might find themselves scouring the Biome in search of microorganisms to put under the microscopes, practicing their programming in the system interface, predicting the habitability of planets in stellar systems far away — or analyzing the actions of historical figures and nations on Earth in a mock debate, such as today. Or perhaps they would be practicing skills of a different sort entirely. The only guarantee was that they would be tackling something they had never done before, while drawing from and building on the cutting edge of their collective knowledge.

In crafting this approach, great care had been taken to use the powers of the human psyche to its own advantage — to leverage the power of between-group competition as a means of fostering cooperation within groups. The groups themselves were subject to changing all the time, so that in addition to requiring a well-rounded exploration of diverse scholarly subjects, so too did the experience train the cadets to work together, independent of the personalities involved. Or at least, mostly.

Clearly, structure only gets us so far in this regard. It's safe to say that certain groups worked better than others in this small sample of ten. Nevertheless, the structure itself went a long way in exposing each student to a wide swath of content while working with a wide array of individuals. In fact, disharmony among a group was a major setback that in turn posed an incentive to overcome it, if they had any hope of succeeding. And even the most jaded among them couldn't help but hope to succeed when it was their own ego on the line.

Even more clever: this curriculum took little advanced planning by its authors, at least not on a day-by-day basis. Rather, it was the *system* that had required extensive development, not the curricular materials themselves. Once ABRAM knew how to structure the learning environment, it was armed with an incredible volume of information, essentially the entire earthly sum of it until the year 2346, as well as the wherewithal to pose suitable and solvable challenges to apply said information. This ensured that the curriculum was adaptive and flexible, and would pose teachable moments quite independent of the time and context determined by an antiquated set of teachers from a planet far away, who had never truly known these students. In short, the architects taught the system how to teach, and then put their faith in the model. It was one of the many places they had placed it.

This does not mean, however, that the architects had done no deliberate planning; there were benchmarks and guidelines for ABRAM to assess, to determine when and how to move on. The system tracked time spent on various activities, and prioritized content related to items lower in the totals. In this way, they circled around the countless topics on which they could spend their time, making sure to never leave any too far behind. Again, it was a delicate dance — an ever-evolving tango of structure and strategy balanced with exploration and improv. Beyond this regular routine, every once in a great while, there were also Special Protocols with which ABRAM should comply. And today was one of those rare sorts of days, because tomorrow was the rarest sort of all. Today, they were rounding out their history, to set the stage for what would be a hard concept to process on its own, let alone for anyone lacking the requisite context.

Their lessons had only made it into the start of the 21st century, and things were getting rather strange; but Faingo was already enamored with this baffling group of creatures called Humans. They knew that they were human too, of course; that much had been made explicit. But, actually, that was about all the crew knew of the matter. Their true connection to these humans had gone entirely unspoken. At present, human history and biology was just another subject to be learned, the same as any of their other varied interests. It was a distant, abstract topic, completely disconnected from their lives in any practical kind of way.

That is, until tomorrow.

"Okay, let's get started here, shall we?" said ABRAM with a sunny disposition. *BOOP*, it beeped, and a list of teams had been randomized. "Okay, well … let's maybe — perhaps…" and *BOOP*, it beeped again in the hopes no one would notice. "Here we are. For today, we have three teams. Team One will be Chee-chaw, Chop-char, Peel, and Tor. Team Two: Dee-dore, Faingo, and Pee-pop. And Team Three: Plashy, Potch, and Squeal."

The cadets got into their groups with no more than the usual groaning. If anything, today's (semi-) random shuffle had fallen along fairly safe social lines. (Such interference was not entirely common, but ABRAM didn't feel like pushing its luck with everything it had slated in the next 25+ hours.)

"Alright, teams all sorted? I'm looking forward to this one. Your challenge, should you choose to accept it—"

"I don't," interjected Peel, following through on what was an impressive degree of reliability with this joke. It's arguably the most that Peel had stuck ever with anything. "I don't accept it."

"Well, that's unfortunate," said ABRAM, who then promptly moved along. "Your challenge: today, we will have a three-part debate, in which each team will propose their synthesis of the Great Backslide in 21st century Earth History."

As the crew knew from their preceding Mind Blocks, this was a time of great strife for life on Earth. Societal malaise, global health outcomes lagging behind scientific advancement, and unprecedented poverty in a time of unprecedented prosperity; the stalling out of international integration and the ineptness of global governance systems; the resurgence of nationalism, extremism, militarization, and conflict between international powers; the rise of new technologies and the manner in which they exacerbated all these problems; and who could forget, a spiraling set of existential ecological crises due to runaway warming, rampant habitat loss, and unfettered pollution, all leading Earth swiftly along the course to its sixth mass extinction. There was a lot to unpack, and many places for future scholars such as these to point their fingers.

"Evaluation criteria are: (1) Synthesis of socioeconomic, political, technological, and environmental pressures; (2) Scholarly Rigor with which each of these covariates are addressed; and (3) Teamwork Quotient, according to our normal standards."

YES! cheered Faingo silently. *It's a Dream Team today. Assuming Dee can focus. This one's ours for the taking!* She wouldn't dare say such taunts aloud; but she was thinking them.

The only others who wanted the bragging rights as badly today were Chop-char and Tor, but their team was admittedly a bit of an underdog. By the numbers, they technically had a leg up, although this specific numerical advantage (Peel) didn't always amount to a net positive effect, as advantages are supposed to do by definition. Cheech, for his part, could focus if he needed to —

that is, if his buddies Tor and Chop-char wanted him to do so. Their typical motivation, however, came from each of them trying to best only the other one, so this was either a very clever pairing on behalf of the questionably-random team-generating algorithm — or a very poor one.

As for Team Three, it's not clear if their hearts were in it from the get-go. Squeal would chip in during the debate itself, and she could be a useful scrapper on occasion, but she was also just as likely to lead them astray during the research and planning stages. Potch could no doubt be their star player, if he were only remotely interested in playing the game. Likewise, Plashy was bright, and there was no doubt about that. She could also be a fierce and sharp debater when she put her mind to it (and a far more effective one than Squeal on her best day). Ultimately, their chances fell largely on how badly she felt like motivating her compatriots. Let's just say that motivation wasn't exactly Plashy's strong suit.

"There are four separate stations, one for each category, with subsets of relevant information made available for you to access as you deem fit. These stations are set up in the corners." This was shorthand for the rooms by the stairs in the North, South, East, and West; and while there are no such things as corners in a circle, let alone directions in one traveling through space, they all understood exactly what ABRAM had meant. "Each team will move through the stations in a different order; you will have exactly 30 minutes per station. Check your tablets to find where your team will start and where you'll move to after every round. After all four rounds, there will be an additional 30-minute preparation phase, followed by 60 minutes of debate. We'll end with our regular 30 minutes of reflection and synthesis. Any questions?"

They were all quite used to ABRAM's rapid-fire instructions by now, and the day's format was familiar enough. What's more, they knew they could check their tablets for an overview of the activity if needed. Plus, they were anxious to get on with it already.

There was not a peep from the crew.

"Excellent," said the system in a satisfied fashion. "Lastly, I'll just say that this is an absolutely fascinating time in Earth history, and one studied intensively by scholars in subsequent centuries. I hope you're ready to do some critical thinking!"

"WOOO", hooted Team Faingo (that is, Faingo). But apathy was about all the other teams had mustered. Needless to say, Squeal and Peel were not driven to do any howling, scattered and unenthusiastic as they were.

BEEP, booped the system, and the timer had begun. Apathy or not, when that beep blooped, all three teams raced off to their starting stations as quick as the wind. The challenge was now on, and they seldom refused its call when the clock was counting down. After all, it was Mind Block, and there were plenty of imaginary points to be scored.

Date: 2239-09-25-EY
Area: O(HUMO(PSYC(EDUC)))
Team: Herring [O-TKBAB38]
Item: Pedagogy Updates

Entry: Pedagogical trials are proving informative, though much
remains to be done. A total of 128 methods have been approved for
inclusion after sufficient replication, spanning seven (partial-
ly-contiguous) age-class clusters: wobblers, toddlers, fledgers,
challengers, bloomers, and authors. A few gaps exist therein, and
additional replicates are underway.

Progress on the three early stages is particularly encouraging,
in lieu of concerns addressed in previous entries. Significant
inadequacies still exist in the earliest stages, which will benefit from putative advances in the procedure and infrastructure.
(Refer to work by teams in HEAP [Human Embryology and Parturition;
see O-CycleCAMJS-PhaseY-RBK8Z.tl].)

Late stages have proven much more straightforward, assuming core
foundational self-efficacy is established in early conditions.
In all cases, alternative course-correction modules are underway.
(Refer to competition between Mastodons [O-2KBUN6U], Sledgehammers
[O-KY3E7QM], Marigolds [O-D7PTGUU], and Telescopes [O-RV892U3].)

Immediate next steps for us involve completing trials for intermediate classes before advancing, then signing off on final path
analyses for all approved stages. Programs overlapping with HEAP
are unfortunately constrained by their progress, but we will loop
back and commence trials as soon as we receive approval.

CHAPTER 04
THE FORMATION OF ARGUMENTS
4252-07-33: MIND

"I really love the color in this room," said Dee-dore. "We should use this as our regular room."

"Focus, Dee!" said Faingo. To be fair, it was lit with accents of a lovely shade of blue. "We have a lot of stuff to wade through here. What are you finding, Pop?"

"Well," said Pee-Pop, "I have to say, things were even worse than I thought. These climate projections were really bad, and then it turns out, they weren't even bad enough. Check out this ICC Report from 2030!"

Faingo raced to her monitor and leaned over Pee-pop's shoulders. In addition to the cadets' individual tablets, the rooms were equipped with a few direct terminals for digital work in its more involved forms. At this station, there were spreadsheets of key data of interest to any climatologist, be they focused on Earth or any other planet. The data was broken down by "Direct Observation" and "Model Fitting." And it was not looking good for Planet Earth in the early third millennium.

"Awesome. Keep at it," said Faingo, absolutely brimming with excitement. This is what she lived for. "What about you, Dee?"

"I, uhh … yeah, it's going pretty well."

"Okay, great. What are you finding?" She bounced briskly on her tip-toes while flitting over to Dee's terminal. But from the terminal itself, only silence, followed by a gentle *TAP TAP* on the keyboard as Faingo drew closer.

"Dee!" she scolded. Having arrived, she leaned over Dee's shoulder.

"What?" she asked defensively. "I mean, I don't really know what I'm looking for here. Sure, there's some media coverage off and on — a fair bit actually, mainly in the science sections, and more of it as the years ticked by. But it doesn't seem like the doom-and-gloom picture Pee-pop's painting."

She often ended in artistic metaphors, or at least worked one in somewhere.

"Good, keep at it," said Faingo. "And don't forget about Op-Eds," she said while tip-toe-floating back to her station. "It looked like there was a sample of about … oh, what was it? Probably at least a dozen countries there — the usual players, right? So, if you're getting stuck somewhere, there's plenty more than we have time for." That was her not-so-subtle way of reminding Dee-dore to kick her hiney into higher gear. Dee knew it as well as anyone.

"Yes, Madame," she said. "What about you, Miss Busy Bee? What do those other databases suggest?"

"It's exactly what we predicted," said Faingo. "Migration: Increasing. Drought: Increasing. Food Shortages: Increasing. It keeps going."

"Emerging diseases?" asked Pee-pop.

"Ha," laughed Dee-dore. "Yes, I think it's safe to say that." She had been quantifying headlines after all.

"Yup, she's right," smiled Faingo, quietly proud of her for once. Pee-pop had been plugging away diligently for quite some time, but she now kicked back from the terminal with gumption. She was growing more confident that she'd gained what they needed from her subset of the evidence. The truth was pretty darn clear.

"What's up?" said Faingo.

"I know this ended up working out alright and everything, but … wow. It was really touch-and-go there for a while. These kinds of runaway greenhouse effects are pretty common on exoplanets, and it doesn't end well — or at least, it wouldn't be good if there were people on them who … you know … wanted to live. I don't think they really knew what they were dealing with."

"What makes you say that?" said Faingo.

"They couldn't have. I mean, look at what Dee's been finding in the press. Some stuff, sure, but it doesn't sound like it's at all proportional to what the numbers were suggesting. I think the conversation would have looked a lot different."

All in all, it was going pretty well with Team Two here in the South. The team numbers were entirely arbitrary, but it's safe to say that at least one of them badly wanted to end the day as Number One. And every bookie in the universe would have put the odds in their favor. The timer was deep into the throes of the middle rounds of research, but some attentions elsewhere were already starting to wane in predictable patterns.

Over in the Northern corner, Team One was a good demonstration of this. They had put in a decent effort so far, but were now hitting a wall once they had crested the midway point and saw the home stretch still a ways off in the distance.

"WOAH, check this out!" said Cheech. "CHOP! You have to see this."

"Just send it to the main," said Chop from his terminal. And after a few quick taps at the keys, up came Cheech's display for all to see.

"Woah…" said his teammates in synchrony. Cheech had found his way to the video games of the era; they were a far cry from Pong, to say the least. The file was a short clip of a kid from long ago, not much older than the cadets were now, filming himself playing this game with others through the Internet. It had made it into the data for today's debate, but it was a questionable call as to whether it was suitable for their youthful little eyes.

Most amazingly, it was Cheech and not Torp-char who had made the discovery. Neither half of that duo had yet found this wing of the file structure, though this was mainly a matter of chance. Cheech wasn't even all that into games. Then again, maybe he just wasn't all that into Pong. He also wasn't that interested in whatever they were supposed to be doing, and thus was he happy to stray into the questionably-relevant territory. Likewise, Peel was even further out in the weeds, goofing off by trying to find the silliest corporate mascot, with little regard for any implications for the issue at hand.

But now, all four of them were drawn into Cheech's discovery. They got up from their terminals to get an even closer look, meandering down to the front of the room to be completely immersed in the experience. The player's point of view ducked and dived and darted through alleyways among the buildings, leaning around corners and looking through the scope resting atop the long barrel of the rifle. Just then, a head popped up over the edge on the roof of a building, and *BOOM* rang out the rifle. The head snapped back, a surprisingly accurate depiction of red pixels spurting out, and the victim's avatar fell away and out of sight.

"SNIPE!" shouted our valiant hero to his friends in the distant past, and then he quickly regained his focus to find his next target. He ran around the corner of his hideout, made his way along the sidewalk, and got shot in the back of the head.

"Woah…" said all four cadets yet again. The clip was over, and the display reverted to the command line of Cheech's terminal.

"Bummer," said Chop-char, and then turning to Tor: "We have to find that."

Cheech, however, felt slightly nauseated ever since the first causality. He staggered back to his seat when it was over, slowly and a bit unsure, and tapped a few times to end the shared display. The main screen went back to black, followed shortly by the red oscilloscope that danced when the system spoke.

"Okay team," said ABRAM, somewhat remiss in its duties (as a more traditional teacher might deem it). "How does this support or refute your hypothesis?"

The four boys looked to one another. And then, slowly, Peel kicked in with his aptitude for hysterical laughter (warranted or not), and this was one rare case where it became more contagious than usual.

Meanwhile, over in the eastern corner, Team Three was playing out exactly as just about everyone, Team Three included, had predicted. Squeal had indeed spent much of her time leading them astray if anyone dared try to get something on task done; Potch had indeed spent much of his time moping; and Plashy had indeed spent much of her time failing to motivate herself and anyone else. At the moment, supposedly focusing on economic factors, Squeal was flipping half-heartedly through advertisements, Plashy was grudgingly exploring an international directory of salary reports for public sector jobs, and Potch was doing … something else.

Whatever it was, it held his interest fully: his fingers were *TAP TAP TAP-ing* at a faster rate than anyone else, in any breakout session, at any point in the day. And yet, he would grow quite frustrated, quite frequently; there would be a momentary silence, and then *TAP TAP TAP*, he would begin again incessantly.

His teammates noticed his distraction, but this was nothing out of the ordinary. Squeal could not have cared less what was happening at any other terminal, until she wanted them to pay attention to something off-topic that she would insist was "the key" to it all. Plashy didn't mind — if anything, she was secretly glad to see Potch engage in any sort of active behavior rather than his usual mode — but she was definitely curious. She had inquired a bit when he first started, but he would never respond. When she got up, sure enough, he would *TAP TAP* and flip back to the boring stuff, as quick as a whistle.

"So, what do you have?" she finally asked him after about the third time, although this time she didn't even bother getting up.

"Not much," said Potch, and then *TAP TAP* back to the boring stuff: a series of scatter plots flashed on the screen to occupy every corner of his terminal. There were many of them, and even from the distance Plashy could tell that the correlations were extremely strong.

"You don't say."

"Well what about you?" he shot back. Plashy didn't answer but sighed in that classic, cutting Plashy sigh — the kind that said, *I get it, okay? Just leave me alone.* To be fair, she was the one who had started it this time. Potch wanted nothing more than to leave her alone, other than for her to do likewise. But something was off about him, and she knew it. And she wasn't the only one.

"Okay Potch, you've had your fun," said ABRAM in a knowing rebuke. "Let's stick with the data, shall we?"

Potch pushed away from the display to slump back in his chair, and this time, it was he who gave that classic Plashy sigh. *I get it, okay? Just leave me alone.*

The system knew it well: spoken language was far from the only thing it had learned from the almost-unquantifiable amount of human social data on which it had been reared. ABRAM had its share of comebacks too.

"Here's a fun thought experiment," it said. "Can you imagine what would happen if you put even half of that same passion into the work you're actually supposed to be doing? I find it hard to imagine, myself."

Potch didn't answer; he grit his teeth and stewed in protest, his arms folded, the pressure slowly building until something, somewhere, gave way. And then, for the first time today, a switch flipped in Potch's gears. He didn't give ABRAM the satisfaction of an answer, but he sat up again, leaned into his screen with a vengeance, and — *TAP TAP TAP* — banged his fingers on the keys. The pace was as relentless as before; but it was scatter plots, not clandestine digging, which suffered the wrath of his attention.

Date: 2193-03-13-EY
Area: I(SINT)
Team: Plasticities [I-84ZPQ8G]
Item: Uncertainty

Entry: Social interface trials continue to demonstrate punctu-
ated improvements. We've made important advancements in the HOM
[Human Ontogenetic Mentoring] functions, namely as it pertains
to handling uncertainty related to the surprising decisions and
erroneous stimuli that come from the first several age classes.
Fortunately, the ELMs [Ensemble Learning Methods] at the heart of
ABRAM's construction provide robust responses when dealing with
ambiguity broadly across multiple domains, but there is still
ample room for improvement in the incarnation we inherited. We
have sought to achieve the cycle task by extending the multilevel
nature of this system, to expand metacognitive capacities in the
socioethical domain. The team has been pleasantly surprised by
results so far.

Reviewing the foundational methods as we tried to develop improvements, we couldn't help but notice analogs to other complex social
systems: discrete subsets of the collective working in parallel,
and then synthesizing their conclusions through a well-regulated
process of integration.

In ABRAM, we see ensembles of individual networks integrating
their predictions to inform the optimal actions of the collective,
while simultaneously tracking uncertainty through the degree of
constituent congruence. In organic nervous systems, we see the
integration of synaptic input from other neurons regulating the
membrane potential, and thus output, of the focal neuron; at the
wider scale, we see much the same thing happening among larger
and larger neural networks. The same goes for well-adapted social
systems. In HDP, for example, we see discrete teams working in
parallel through the phases of the cycle, culminating in selection and synthesis of the best fit ideas. The wisdom of the whole
emerges from integrating the diverse perspectives of the parts.

Or at least, if not wisdom, something that made the most sense
the system could make of it. Sometimes, that may be the best we
can hope for when faced with the predictable unpredictability
that comes with raising a child.

CHAPTER 05
THE GREAT BACKSLIDE DEBATE
4252-07-33: MIND

The end of the debate was closing in, and almost all of them were sweating for one reason or another. Potch was as cool as a cucumber.

For this phase of the day's activities, the crew was gathered in the Auditorium, a setting which instilled a certain formality to the affair. It was also set up best for a debate: the rows of seats and tables converged to form a large circle in the center of the round room, whereas the center itself was open for festivities such as this — an arena in which to wage the battle of ideas, while an anxious (and in this case imaginary) crowd looked on at the brave gladiators below. *BING,* bonged a chime, and their noble moderator interjected once again.

"Thank you Chop-char," said ABRAM. "That was a strong effort for your team's closing remarks. That takes us to our last team. Again, you'll have five minutes to make your final case. Let's see…" it said, and then *BLIP,* it beeped. "Potch," said ABRAM in a satisfied fashion. "It looks like you're up."

If this was Chance, it was an act of serendipity. If not, it was highly strategic, for Potch had hardly said a word the whole debate. Squeal had often been eager to jump in and battle for the sake of it, like the wild and rabid wolf that she was — and she was about as effective as one well into the disease's late stages. Plashy was generally quick to come to the rescue, and quick-witted enough to clean up the mess to a decent degree. Potch was happy to let them lead the charge. But now, his name had been called "at random" — and it was make or break.

The other teams had indeed done a decent job to date. There were no true points awarded. There seldom were; although that never stopped the kids from scoring them on their own. This was namely driven by the bittersweet rivalry among the duo known as Torp-char — yes: even when on the same team — but it had a way of catching on. It's not clear how the participants had come to their metrics for assessment, or whether they had anything at all to do with those of

ABRAM. But that never stopped one of them from shouting out a *SCORE!* or a *ZING!* or a *BOOM!* and then incrementing their own imaginary tallies. And by this accounting, it was not looking good for team Plashy, Potch, and Squeal.

Faingo had come out swinging early on, making a strong case for industrialism as the main driver of ecological setbacks, which posed the greatest global challenge of the era, in her team's view. Pee-pop was well-suited to help out in this regard, being both highly interested and knowledgeable in atmospheric science. And Dee-dore? She was … a very supportive team member. According to them, the looming climate disaster was behind it all. And behind that was two centuries of reckless emissions. And behind that was the Industrial Revolution. Behind that, they did not delve. Despite a rather detailed analysis across several lines of evidence, back they came to the climate as the Cause. Presumably if Earth had been stable, the people would have been fine.

Truly, the climate was a major crisis at the time. That society would rally and go on to more or less stabilize the situation was still viewed as essentially a miracle, even from the hindsight of thousands of years later. The cadets didn't know a lot of details on the solutions just yet: those were allegedly to come in later units. But they knew enough to know that the world did not end, as many at the time had feared in their darkest moments of despair.

Changed substantially? Yes, quite. But Earth was still there for many hundreds of years at least, as far as the crew knew. Like all planets, the thin, delicate layer of precious gas protecting its inhabitants from the instantly-lethal terrors of space would be stripped from its surface eventually. But for the 21st century onward, they would be alright, for a time. Yes, it was a major problem — an existential one in urgent need of resolution — but the consensus view of History would rightly come to put that global crisis in its proper place: one of many symptoms of a far more fundamental problem.

Chop-char had followed up on Team Faingo's thesis with a compelling one of their own. The climate crisis and all its many spawn had truly caused their share of setbacks, but in Team Chop-char's view, it was the conflict and competition within and among the major world powers that had caused this slip backwards in social well-being. Having posited this proposition, they had tried to connect all the many pieces of their research together, and they'd spent a fair amount of their time on the idea that any society who found joy in recreational murder had plenty of ills to analyze. Needless to say, they had fallen pretty deeply down that rabbit hole, having discovered such a form of entertainment. They raised many good points, but the hook of their argument wasn't entirely cohesive.

And then, at last, it was time for the final remarks from the final team. Teams One and Two shot the occasional smirk to each other.

BING, dinged the timer, and Potch was rolling. Or rather, he was supposed to be rolling. Actually, at the moment, he said nothing at all.

"Time is ticking, Potch," said ABRAM.

Still, he sat motionless. He was silent, unsure, uninvested.

"Go ahead, Potchy," sneered Peel from across the central circle. "Teach us a history lesson."

And for the second time in Mind Block on this odd, eventful day, a switch was flipped in Potch's gears by a challenge lobbed his way. This one had held back just as large an avalanche of angst; but it was open now. Yet it did not rage, nor devastate its surroundings with reckless abandon. It churned slowly, steadily, more glacier than avalanche, hardly recognizable as moving until it had scarred its opposition permanently and changed the landscape forever. He waited, thinking for a moment — until slowly, he began to speak.

"You want to know what caused the Great Backslide?" he said calmly. "You want to know what was wrong with the world?" Again, he paused, and for a moment the room was breathless. "Humans. That's what. It wasn't the temperature, superstorms, drought, or disease." He looked straight at Team Faingo. "It wasn't politics, the military, or other forms of entertainment." He shot a glare at Team Chop-char out of the corner of his eye. "It wasn't even competition among national economies." He glanced now at his own team, who, if they even had a thesis, had very roughly propped this one up.

It wasn't any of these things, according to Potch.

"It was the fundamental flaw of human behavior."

He hadn't even hit his stride, but the audience was captivated and ABRAM most of all. Its challenge had quite clearly been accepted, even if only in spite. And yet, that made it no less of a breakthrough. Potch took a deep breath and thought back to all the disparate variables he had unified under a single common cause.

"All of your factors were important, obviously; I'm not saying they weren't. But every one of them you listed was a symptom. Every one of them was the result of a far deeper problem — one that's been raging since the dawn of time."

He looked at Squeal, his own teammate, whose love of all things wild was well known. (The howling was a fairly big clue.)

"Think back to what we've learned from the field of biology. Humans earned their domination on Earth by being perhaps the greatest cooperators of all time. But there was a catch. Humans figured out how to work with each other — but only if you were on the same team. If you weren't in the in-group, you might as well be the prey."

He turned next to Plashy, his own teammate, whose interest in earthly economics far surpassed all the others. Money was a concept that was completely absent from the POD, and the idea of it both baffled and intrigued her.

"Over time, these groups of people grew bigger and bigger, until it became harder and harder to figure out that you were on the same side. Like old times, it was a much easier path to success to get what they needed by taking it from their own neighbor. That's your Great Backslide. Humanity had transcended a predisposition of selfishness and individualism to achieve incredible feats of cooperation, just to have those same societies break back down to a philosophy of every person, every business, every country for itself."

He stopped, for he had gotten too speculative and they all knew it. And anyway, he could go on weaving as compelling a story as he wanted for the rest of his time; but in this debate, all that mattered was the evidence.

He pulled out his tablet and — *TAP TAP TAP* — up went his display on the screens around the Auditorium's perimeter. All his incessant and obsessive analyses had not been for naught. One after another, he would come to show them the raw data, compiled across many countries, curated from the international authorities on their respective variables: the World Health Organization, the United Nations, the World Bank, the World Values Survey, and many more besides. One after another, the correlations would flash; and exactly as Plashy had noticed from far across the eastern room, the trends were compelling.

"So what was the real problem back then?" asked Potch. "It's amazingly simple actually. What people need to be happy and healthy is access to a safe place to live, good food to eat, clean air to breathe, and clean water to drink. And every one of those things was easier to do if you had money. Unfortunately, almost every society on Earth at the time was set up to accumulate wealth in the hands of a small number of people, while the rest of the population suffered." He halted again, not even sure where to begin. "But, you don't have to take my word for it. The data is insane. Pick an outcome, and there's a good chance inequality is related."

TAP. He pulled up his first set of plots.

"Look," said Potch. "In countries with greater economic inequality, you have a whole host of health problems, even if those countries are rich overall. Here's an index of health and social problems across many countries: the more unequal the country, the worse life gets." *TAP.* "Here you can see that these unequal countries have far more mental illness." *TAP.* "More drug use." *TAP.* "More obesity." *TAP.* "A decrease in child well-being; an increase in infant mortality; higher teenage birthrates." *TAP.* "They spend more on health care, but as you can see, there's no correlation between the amount spent on health care and actual life expectancy. What does affect life expectancy? I think you see where this is going." *TAP.* "Life expectancy is lower in more unequal countries." *TAP.* He was just getting rolling.

"Those are just some of the health data we had access to, cross-referenced to the international economic datasets you all saw. But remember, inequality is a property of societies, not individuals. As you can imagine, it leads to societal issues too." *TAP.* "Math and literacy scores: lower in more unequal countries." *TAP.* "Technological innovation rates? Lower." *TAP.* "Social mobility? Lower." *TAP.* "And the people working the low-wage jobs? Lucky for them, they got to work more hours." *TAP.* "And make no mistake, people were irate in these societies. Homicides: Higher." *TAP.* "Child conflict: Higher." *TAP.* "Proportion of people imprisoned: Higher." *TAP.* "Measures of trust among citizens: Lower."

He took a second to literally catch his breath. It had been a while since he'd looked around the debate floor, and his peers were more than a little overwhelmed. The ones who could follow were amazed by the data itself; the others … well … they were taken aback by the slow-burning fury of its delivery. Potch was either out of his mind, or he was on to something. Either way, he wasn't stopping now. Peel, at least, had asked for this.

"And if you can't even look out for your fellow citizens, you sure aren't looking out for the rest of the world." *TAP.* "More unequal countries spend less on foreign aid, even when they are extremely wealthy. As for the environment? It was well known that carbon emissions were higher in richer countries at the time; but, even among those wealthy nations, the greater the economic inequality, the greater the carbon emissions." *TAP.* "Heck, people in more unequal countries even recycled less."

BING, the timer gently chimed.

"Two minutes," warned the system.

And then: *TAP.*

"I know what you're thinking too: this sounds logical enough, but all these negative consequences are probably just the result of poverty in general, not inequality specifically. Well, I checked, and that's actually not the case. ABRAM is buzzing at me, so let's just take a few of these." *TAP.* "Life expectancy is lower in more unequal countries, but there's no difference when you look at the same data as a function of the average income of these nations. The same goes for that cumulative index of health and social problems: people are far worse off in more unequal countries, but there's essentially no effect when you plot the index as a function of average income. In other words, it's the inequality itself that causes individual and societal problems, not the lack of wealth in a nation."

BING BING BING, rang his final warning bell.

"One minute. Try to wrap it up, Potch."

Potch nodded.

"Okay, well, I guess in summary, we were asked to explain the Great Backslide of the 21st century. As others laid out earlier, by definition it was a time of regressive social, economic, and environmental policy, which led to decreases in health, well-being, prosperity, and brought the earth to the brink of eco-logical collapse. If you're looking for a mechanism, I don't think you need to look too much further than the economic and political systems that led to the accumulation of the vast majority of the planet's wealth in the hands of a select few individuals. There was more than enough to go around.

"Yes, the climate was a major problem; but as you all pointed out," he said, looking at Faingo, Pop, and Dee, "it was reckless industrialism that created the problem, denied the problem, actively deceived the populace about the problem, and fought every solution just to ensure their own survival for a few more fleeting years.

"Yes, the conflict that ensued brought on great human suffering, and the major global powers clearly didn't help. As for the fascination with violence, well … that's a whole other issue, even if it's wrapped up in all this. But what caused those humanitarian and military conflicts? A lot of it was unprecedented migration, heightened by the climate crisis. Related to that was political desta-bilization due to human rights atrocities within countries, coupled with the uncompromising nationalism of countries dealing with each other. In other words, a lot of it was just good-old-fashioned human nature at its finest."

He was out of time. He suspected it, and so did everyone else. Yet he was on such a role, and frankly ABRAM was so glad to see that something — *any-thing* — had gotten Potch fired up in a productive way, that the system bent its own rules, as it was wont to do from time to time if the spirit so moved it — and it let him keep going.

"Every person, every business, every political party, every country for itself. Whatever the scale, it was all the same game. They had everything, for a while there. And they blew it. They had every means to establish an entirely egalitarian society — across the whole globe if they had wanted it. But that's not what they achieved." The others were growing restless, but still ABRAM did not cut him off. "Why?" he asked finally. "That fatal, fundamental flaw. The one thing humans were truly good at: looking out for themselves, everyone else be damned."

No other timer ever dinged; but eventually, Potch had stopped.

"Thank you, Potch, on behalf of your team," said ABRAM at last. "A strong conclusion from our concluding group." It did not need time to think. Or if it did, it had done so far more quickly than human perception would ever quite adjust to. "I've tallied the results of your performance."

Its tone was jovial and proud. It was a good day of Mind Block, overall. Their synthesis abilities were improving — critical progress in the critical thinking skills which ABRAM had been working on for years. The content itself was also lining up nicely: the ultimate cliffhanger for what fate had in store for humanity next.

"First of all, this was a very impressive debate," it continued. "These are always fun, and I appreciate the sincerity with which you approached the topic." *Most of you, anyway,* it did not say. "You all put together compelling cases, and you argued them cogently. Nevertheless, one argument rose above the rest."

It was not often that Faingo felt unsure of her victory. She looked around anxiously. No one else cared nearly as much as she did, it would seem. In fact, the one who had spoken most passionately of all during their friendly competition was now clearly the one who cared least of all about its outcome.

"Team Three: Plashy, Potch, and Squeal. Congratulations."

Against all odds, ABRAM stopped itself from saying.

Squeal jumped up and threw her arms in the air, victorious and proud of it. As was their custom, the other cadets started to congratulate them from their places across the circle — all but one of them, stunned as she was. Plashy tried to keep her cool, but she couldn't help but crack a smile. Potch, meanwhile, was unmoved. He was angry — at the past, but perhaps at something else as well.

"What?!" said Faingo, still reeling in disbelief. She was not a poor sport by her nature, but she had her principles of fair competition. "But he — but he went over time! You can't go over time…"

"Huh?" said ABRAM. "Did he? Oh. Hmm, I didn't notice."

"You didn't—"

Pop touched her arm lightly to cool her down. Slowly, she regained both her breath and composure. So hung up on the rulebook, she was the only one who hadn't played by the unwritten post-debate rules.

"Oh…" she said, somewhat realizing she was making a scene. "Right, uhh … congratulations."

HDP

It was not a flawless argument, the one that won the day. None of the three of them were. Life is complex; and even with the benefit of hindsight, it's easy to oversimplify. Progress is never comprised of straight lines. There were bound to be setbacks. Perhaps it was the climate. Perhaps it was politics, technology, economics, or the media. Perhaps it was other things besides, or a little of everything, colliding together. Or perhaps it was just the ebbing and flowing of cultures as they grow. But whatever the case, things were not looking good for humans at this point in the story — the grim, riveting chapters before they entered a new era. For the cadets, it was the last lessons of their innocence, before they learned the rest of the story, and entered a new era all their own. And though it may not have been the full story, Team Three was onto *something*.

- -
Date: 2248-02-29-EY
Area: O(HUMO(PSYC(ENRI)))
Team: Avicennans [O-N6MP2P6]
Item: Enrichment Updates

Entry: Progress on enrichment activities is still going smoothly,
for programmed modules and system improvisational methods alike.
As a supplement to standard approaches, we're exploring the power
of well-regulated competition. Trials have reliably demonstrated
its efficacy [see O-Cycle51DH2-PhaseV-4TK8F.tl], and we've had
good luck adapting it into multiple modalities. Still, we will
want to use it judiciously and with great care.

This approach has been somewhat divisive, and for good reason:
outcomes are highly sensitive to several key variables. However,
we've found that gamification can be incredibly effective when
it is aligned to suitable tasks, there are clear objectives, it's
appropriately framed at the outset, the cooperative underpinnings
of the competition are emphasized (i.e., the social agreement to
abide by the rules and agree to the results), when it is team-
based (with strategic formation), and when accessibility and
inclusion are paramount. We tend to see the best outcomes for
games that are non-zero-sum in nature. Zero-sum games can still
be acceptable in cases, however, when handled with even greater
care, as they are vulnerable to exploitation and far more sensitive to contextual factors.

Dr. [Mahsa] Rashidi is a bit of a history buff and keeps raising the example of the Critical Assessment of protein Structure
Prediction (CASP) competitions from the early days of protein
structure discovery. Research teams from around the world would
compete to predict the three-dimensional structure of proteins
from only their amino acid sequence, with all teams attempting
to solve the same secret set of proteins whose structures had
recently been solved but not made public. Apparently, it was way
ahead of its time. "If you want to push the science forward, just
make a competition," she said. Of course, we're studying games in
the context of ontogeny, but it applies equally well to science
itself. Come to think of it, there are some interesting parallels
between CASP and HDP.

Speaking of enrichment, we heard a rumor from a parallel cycle
that a team was looking into the possibility of a collaboration
across O- and H-sectors to create some kind of large-scale shifting maze with openings that can be programmed countless ways for
diverse enrichment activities. It will probably never fly, but
what a wild idea!

CHAPTER 06
THE RACE IS ON
4252-07-33: DINN / SPRT

The fallout from the debate was mostly forgotten once the gang had moved on to the next block of the day. As with most blocks, the two hours slated for dinner were actually more than they appeared to be in name alone. There was plenty of wind-down time left in the evening, but at the start of Dinner Block, there was work to be done.

In the first hour, a subset of cadets would navigate the Biome to harvest consumables and tend the grounds a little as needed. These kinds of "outdoor" activities were also interspersed between other activities in other blocks of time — Body Block, Mind Block, even Spirit Block and Unstructured Time from time to time, depending on what needed to be done. But there was always something to be done down there for Dinner Block.

This was also the time when they prepared the early meals of the coming day, and so they would subdivide into Today and Tomorrow groups of harvesters to make things run efficiently. The same went for the subsequent prep upstairs. Having gathered what they needed, the foragers would reconvene with those working in the Mess a few floors up. Typically, by about an hour into the block, they were ready to settle in for dinner, to enjoy the main meal of their day in terms of volume.

Tonight, the Tomorrow crew looked in on the chickens and brought up the daily haul of eggs. (And "WOW!" were those chickens were doing well according to Cheech, their most trusted acquaintance.) They got a decent crop of berries, grapes, and plums to get them through the day, along with the staple of all space staples: jeddusch.

It may have loosely rhymed with lettuce, but that's where the similarity stops, for jeddusch was a wheat cultivar which had been selected and genetically enhanced for rapid vertical growth, grain production, nutritional content, and even the occasional altruistic trait such as nitrogen fixation. It was easy to grow, and very easy to harvest. That is, if you weren't afraid of the ladders: the vines reached from soil to ceiling, climbing a grid of metal all the way. And it did require great caution, not to mention the safety clips. It would be a rather ironic and embarrassing affair to be the first person to perish from a fall in outer space.

All the while, the Tonight crew gathered a host of eggplants and tomatoes. Luckily for them, they had never known cheese — How sweet, innocence? — or else their favorite meal would only pale in comparison to the possibilities. Nevertheless, their ignorance was bliss, and their mash of those two baked along with jeddusch bread was a smashing hit in the POD. Of course, salt was a terribly precious commodity, so it could have always used a little more; but again, it's the only way they'd ever known it, and it was something special.

But now, dinner was over, and they were gathered in the Lounge for the most sacred — if not always the most cherished — block of all. As with all others, this part of the day built on those that came before. Body Block helped them train the body; Mind Block helped them train the mind; but the focus of Spirit Block was an even deeper kind of wellness. This was their routine opportunity to tap in to one of the most universal human needs: a profound connection to others and a sense of common purpose.

Perhaps as importantly, it provided a spark of the inscrutable to ponder, so as to never lose their sense of curiosity, or an appropriate appreciation for what an incredible improbability it was that they should ever have existed in the first place. As with all humans, they were but a minuscule part of an inconceivably large universe — a fact they knew well from out here in the in-between; and second, they existed in that minuscule form for such a preposterously minuscule sliver of time. Yes: it was good to be reminded of that sometimes, even at the ripe old age of just-about-ten.

Above all, it was a chance to be human, whatever that meant, and to remember where it was that they came from, even if they didn't yet know many details. They may have been rocketing toward the future, but they carried with them many great traditions of many scales and forms, passed down through the millenia and more; and with that great inheritance, they carried as well all its corresponding baggage.

To reach these myriad goals, Spirit Block took on many forms, drawing from the many diverse cultures of humanity. In all human societies, across vast swaths of time and space, there were countless rites and rituals, behaviors and beliefs. None of these were taken lightly in the POD, but neither were any of them favored as "the" tradition. At their heart, despite all their idiosyncrasies, many of these traditions were ultimately a search for the same destination; and there were many ways of getting there.

Most nights, this would be a time for stories, in which ABRAM would recite legends from across those many cultures. Unlike Mind Block, there was hardly any need to force the issue or control the format: insightful and ample discussion almost always arose, and perfectly naturally. On occasion, however, the cadets would engage in other sacred traditions, either inspired by the wealth of human history, or invented on their own. And tonight, for much the same reason as the rest of its dealings today, ABRAM had something a little more formal in mind.

"The last team there is a rotten egg!" it teased, and the kids were off at once in multiple directions.

They sped away as quickly as they could, scrambling for the exit of the Lounge while making sure to never let go of their partner. Five teams of two minds each, which of course may sometimes wish to pull in opposing directions. But one of the few constraints of the game was paramount: at no point should the team break the grip between one set of their hands.

The destination on this evening was not unknown to them, but it was always an exciting prospect, for its use was reserved for the more momentous evenings such as this. And that destination was down on the most fun and mysterious level of all (at least of those they'd been allowed to explore): the Midship.

Here in the Midship, Level Six above the Biome (7), there were a series of semi-related oddities. Somewhat an extension of the Biome, in some ways it complemented the homeostatic systems of several other levels. In other ways, it served far more inscrutable human needs. Herein you could find: (a) the Greenhouses (GRN), which provided even more controlled space for growing food and seed of the various essential crops; (b) the Wellspring (WSN), an oasis of sorts, in which the onboard water supply was stored, filtered, and cycled; (c) the Labyrinth (LBN), in which the cadets could run and hide and climb and play for hours on end; and lastly, in the heart of the Midship, accessible only through the winding Labyrinth, (d) the Kiva (KVA).

At the moment, the cadets were barreling down through different stairwells, practically plummeting two floors from the Living Quarters (4) to reach this lower level. A few moments prior, however, ABRAM had set them up for the challenge, albeit with very little context.

On most occasions, the cadets were assigned into pairs, either randomly or "randomly," depending on the whims of ABRAM and their behavior at the time. This encouraged the full crew to work together more cohesively, and served to minimize the potential for the formation of cliques. Of course, cliques inevitably formed, even among so few a crew; but nevertheless, when it came time for a challenge, the kids would either have to rise to it by working with whomever they had been assigned, or else very likely not succeed relative to their peers. And if there was one motivator on board — at least for most of them — it was to excel among their peers.

But this occasion was not any normal night. On this occasion, as they sometimes were, they had been allowed to form pairs for themselves. For once, there were very few rules. (1) Everyone needed a partner; and, as they had a nice even number, (2) no team could be larger than two. Thus had the children all scanned the Lounge as quickly as they could to make eye contact with their favorite companion, in the hopes that their gaze would be reciprocated. ABRAM could have predicted it precisely.

Cheech was already next to Pee-pop and he clutched onto her arm instantaneously. "Pop!" he said, calling dibs with both arms fully wrapped around the closest one of hers. She was far too diplomatic for this kind of thing. She tried to look at everyone equally, but in the end she was as happy with Cheech as with anyone. And besides: he had called dibs.

With Pop out of the running, it simplified things greatly for Dee and Faingo. Their eyes met almost instantly after Cheech had beat the whole room to the jump. Likewise, the two halves of Torp-char had no need to look elsewhere.

Invested far less than any others, Potch and Plashy were practically made for each other. Their eyes met reluctantly after an equivalent period of downcast protest while the natural formations began to form.

Squeal scanned the room for anyone — literally anyone — other than Peel, but there were no stares coming back in her direction. Without a word being spoken, she eventually conceded defeat. She turned to Peel and glared at him scornfully. He simply smiled with the joyful expression of an ignorant puppy. As he did, by default, so many times before, he had won.

As soon as the teams had solidified and they knew their destination, the race was on. But speed was only of so much use in this race, for it was equally a game of wits. The Labyrinth had its share of surprises of the programmable variety, and ABRAM was as much a player as any of the young apes on board. If they wanted to reach the Kiva first, they would need to use more than mere haste.

Cheech zipped out of the western stairs pulling Pop along behind him like a rag doll. For one of such little stature, he made up for it in spunk. It was amazing the amount of energy that little body of his could produce once he'd gotten wound up like a top. Everyone had a tendency to forget that, Cheech included.

But this team was only first in the sense that they were tied for it: out of the eastern stairs zoomed Torp-char, hand in hand as per the rules and hopped up on adrenaline from their dose of sweet, sweet competition.

Out of the south wheeled Squeal and Peel, their eyes narrowed and brows furrowed. Despite their lopsided alliance, they made a fearsome couple when it came to certain kinds of games. And today, Squeal had something to prove, while Peel never wanted anything more than to prove something to her.

After a brief delay, Dee and Faingo also exited the southern stairs while Potch and Plashy ambled lazily out of the north. They were keeping up enough to be considered good sports, but none of the four of them were quite in this one to win it, and each for their own separate reasons.

The Labyrinth had entrances on all four corners of the Midship, so no one had an advantage, at least when it came to that level. Torp-char had technically gotten the jump by getting to the eastern stairs, as it was a little closer to the Lounge. Seeing this, the others had opted for an unobstructed path, even if it was a little further from the starting line. Besides, everyone knew that Chop was the slowest of the bunch. The other invested parties suspected they could outpace this tethered Tor as long as they had a clear lane all their own.

Sure enough, Cheech and Pop were first to arrive at an entrance to the tunnels, and thus they were also the first to an obstacle.

"It's sealed!" he shouted to Pop. Of course, she was only a handshake away and could discern that just fine for herself. The entrance, normally an unimpeded opening, was sealed off with a pocket door. "What do we DO?"

They didn't have to wonder long, for out of the arch above the door spoke the system.

If you would enter, you must answer
So contemplate this riddle
The key is where a life could dwell
On other levels, in a shell
So bring it to the middle.

"An egg," said Pop, and this time it was she who pulled the arm of Cheech as they raced away for the stairs.

They sped down to the Biome and went through the airlock, for it wasn't only outer space that was buffered from the rest of the POD.

"Come on come on…" said Cheech as they waited for the outer door to close. It wasn't particularly slow, but Time was in a hurry right now. It finally swooshed closed and the inner door opened. "Wait," he said, suddenly remembering. "I just got them — they're all upstairs! I doubt the girls have laid any since Dinner."

"Cheech! Why didn't you say so?"

"I—"

The inner door closed and the outer one opened again.

"Out of the way!" snapped Squeal as she pushed into the airlock, dragging Peel along behind her.

They almost cut straight through Pop and Cheech and severed the grasp between them. This of course would have been a violation of an unspoken rule of these sorts of games: no direct physical interference was permitted. Then again, no one remembers when or how that unwritten rule had come to be, and ABRAM certainly hadn't said as much in what little it had said to them at the start. But thankfully it mattered not, for Cheech and Pop were able to spin out of the way just in time to avoid being utterly trampled.

"Their loss," smirked Cheech as they lunged up the stairs to floor four. "They don't realize I brought them all to the Mess."

Without delay they made their way back to the Mess — back to pretty much where this whole adventure had started. Cheech grabbed an uncooked egg from the prep station but Pop quickly reached out her hand.

"No offense," she said, and Cheech handed it over to her far more trusty grip.

Having plummeted back down the same two floors in the same eastern stairwell, they were huffing now at their maximum rates. They sped away to the Labyrinth entrance and without even engaging with the system, held the egg up high for the camera to see.

BOOP, beeped the system, and the door slid open. Darkness lay ahead of them, as the long tunnel stretched forward into the bowels of the Labyrinth. In ran Pop and Cheech, the former still holding on to their precious cargo. The outermost door did not shut behind them, but the darkness grew dimmer with every further step they took.

Luckily for our heroes, however, safety was ever a top priority of the architects in constructing the POD, as well as of ABRAM in conducting these kinds of adventures. A strip of interspersed lights lined the floors on either side of the tunnels; they provided just enough light to safely navigate the maze, while still allowing for a sufficiently otherworldly experience compared to the "outdoor" spaces of the Midship. The lights changed colors as they progressed through the winding turns and tunnels and ladders and underpasses. Some glowed red, others glowed green; some were of a haunting violet hue. Therein were often clues of a sort, if one could read the mind of their maker.

And the lights were not the only mutable pieces of this maze. The overall area was arrayed in a circular grid of multi-level tunnels, with connecting doors that could be opened or shut according to the whims of the system. Out of this blank slate could be crafted any number of possible paths. The door patterns were constantly changing, just about every time they played in the thing. They had come to learn some landmarks here and there, but being entirely sure of oneself was all but impossible.

They came to the first junction, in which the entry path intersected with three others: a sealed door before them, an open door to the left, and another to the right. That the central door was shut hardly came as a surprise, for they had never seen it any other way. To their best recollection, the first dilemma in the Labyrinth had always been the same: Left or Right? As ever, they were unsure which to pick, for they had no further evidence to support one over the other. Yet, for much the same reason, it wasn't much of a choice. Cheech deferred to Pop with a glance, and she led them left without debate or delay.

Other times, their path was even clearer, laid out when constructing this arrangement of the ever-shifting landscape. After several twists and turns through individual open doors, they climbed a rope ladder — no small feat while holding an egg in one hand and Chee-chaw in the other — to a platform leading over a different tunnel. Pop thought she heard the sound of another team shuffling along underneath them as they crossed it, and she very likely did. Getting back down was even trickier, but once they did so they came to another junction. The doors were open this time, and it posed a second riddle, even if it hadn't been characterized as such out loud.

Pop and Cheech tried to rack their brains in the heat of the moment. They were close now. They could feel it. Which way had they come? How many twists had they taken? They knew the Labyrinth as well as anyone could, but it was sneaky enough to be impossible to know. All they had to do was wind their way to the center, but that was far easier said than it was done. It was especially tough to keep track of one's direction when juggling so much and in such a state of urgency. Even so, some of this had seemed familiar, like it might wind them to the Kiva with a little bit of luck.

"Right," said Cheech with confidence; and then far more shakily, "Right?"

"Left," said Pop.

And then, "Right."

"Right as in right or…"

"Correct," he said quickly, and they zipped leftward in unison.

They turned a corner down this equally convoluted tunnel and again heard the sound of another team shuffle past behind them, apparently heading the opposite way. Pop clutched the egg as firmly as she could without risking its welfare as they came to another obstacle. This time, it was onto their elbows and knees.

"Just be careful," said Cheech.

I know, she might have said, but she didn't. She just clutched it ever the more carefully and sprawled forward to crawl under the overpass above. It was wide enough for both of them, but again it was no simple matter to scramble through there in tandem without scrambling that egg.

They popped back onto their feet on the other side of it and again they came to a two-way juncture. Cheech just looked at Pop and didn't even bother to offer a guess.

"Right," she said.

And then: "Right," said Cheech with confidence.

They passed through a dark green tunnel, the floor steadily rising. Laughter echoed down the hall, around a curve, and into their ears. They looked at each other with a knowing disapproval and quickened their pace. They were close.

The floor kept climbing gradually, and around that final curve they saw the dim glow of that deep violet hue. They quickened past the curve, still climbing, until they spotted the final door that opened out into the Kiva. They pressed on as quickly as they could, sped to and through the door, and popped out onto the upper landing which lined the chamber's perimeter.

Just at that moment, Tor and Chop-char bounded out from an adjacent door and onto the very same landing.

SMACK!

The four cadets crashed into each other at top speed. All of their grips had been broken, and even worse: up into the air flew an egg from out of Pee-pop's hand, as did a tomato from out of Tor's. Through the air these treasures soared, as if in slow motion, as the two teams reeled from the collision. Cheech and Chop clutched each other and tottered near the edge, but Tor reached back out to grab Chop's hand again, to prevent them both from falling. Sadly, there would be no such rescue for their long lost objects.

Up, up, up, soared the egg, and up, up, up soared the tomato, crossing paths as they flew out into the open air above the lower level of the Kiva. They paused at the apex, almost simultaneously, and then: down, down, down they both fell. They hit the sandy floor so many feet below with a squish and a smash, their guts smearing outward in a line along their respective trajectories.

"Look," pointed Plashy across the floor of the Kiva. "They made us an omelet."

"Ahhh!" said Tor. "What the heck?"

Pop was rubbing her head, for she had been accidentally smacked by a hand, or an elbow, or some equally painful part of Tor. Cheech's head had thankfully smashed squarely into Chop-char's squishy center, so he had fared the best out of everybody.

As they recovered, the four cadets on the landing looked down into the central chamber to discover six smiling faces staring up at them. They were the last two teams to arrive. And what's worse, they both had done so with a broken handshake and a broken payload.

Date: 2323-08-30-EY
Area: O(HUMO(PSYC(SIPS(SBMS))))
Team: Dreamwalkers [O-4K9RGXW]
Item: Back to the Root

Entry: We were called together for Visioning. We have come. We, from every corner of the world, joined together in this purpose: to take our separate legacies and make them one. We have come. We, from time immemorial, roots stretching back through grandmothers uncounted, to ask for their insight; that they might share with us their wisdom, and that we might be wise enough to know what that wisdom means in this unforeseen era, on these unforeseen worlds our ancestors knew only in dream.

They had followed the stars, tracked them through time and the sky; studied them, named them, spoke to them; counted them, and counted on them, that their presence and patterns might guide the way, so far down here on the ground. In time, they would reach for them, reach out to them, if but a little. And now, their children reach out to them still, but farther, where no hands have stretched before, sailing near enough to call different suns their different homes. If our ancestors could know us now, what might they say? What might they want our children to know of this Earth, this soil and water, from which their being sprouted?

We have come, at this time of Visioning, to envision; to learn how we might learn from each other, as we have learned from ourselves, so that we might teach all our collective children wisely. And we begin at the beginning. Not with our individual traditions, not yet; but with a word. We must define what is Sacred.

What does it mean, such a word? Can it be defined not for one branch, but for All? We first searched the written records of the language for its meaning, to reduce the unknowable into its simplest essence and conveyance, but this revealed only its opposite: Secular. But are these words truly opposed? Or might there be harmony found among them, if we find harmony among ourselves?

We have come. We, descendants turned ancestors, to take what we have been given, to shuffle it like seeds, and to give it to our children, so that they might be born anew, and bring it to the stars. On this grave obligation, with gratitude and grace, we reflect.

CHAPTER 07

A Night to Remember

4252-07-33: SPRT

"Looks like Pee-pop is the rotten egg," said Squeal, which she followed with that characteristic cackle. She scanned the circle in her vain hopes of recognition but only Peel was laughing with her — and inappropriately loud.

She and Peel had been the first to arrive — a fact they would not be letting anyone else forget for the foreseeable future. Shortly after, Dee and Faingo had arrived to finish in a pleasantly surprising second place. Potch and Plashy had then arrived soon thereafter. So nonchalant from the start, these two were only disappointed by their performance once they learned which teams had bested them. They each had shown a brief but obvious sign of dismay as they'd skidded out into the landing to find the other four below. Squeal had immediately begun to gloat, but Potch and Plashy caught themselves quickly and willed their expressions back into a camouflage of disinterest. But now that the last cadets had arrived, and so disastrously, she had an even better target.

"That's enough Squeal," said ABRAM. "Come on down, you four."
"I think you can let go of my hand now," said Tor.
"Oh, uh, right," said Chop.
For one, they had already broken their grip. More to the matter, the rules were a bit moot at this point. The late arrivals did as the system had asked, making their way down the ladder of inset steps to the chamber floor. Half a meter of sand filled the bottom, and it always felt good to arrive. All was forgiven here; even your feet.
The top of the Kiva was a large dome, and projected upon it was a map of the night sky as viewed from Earth — the dim avatars of once unreachable stars, shining through the violet glow. On the floor in the center was a ringed object with the violet light emanating out from it. This of course was the projector,

but its inner workings were obscured by a facade of its own: a glow of different colors — along with other things entirely — could be projected from its foggy, opaque lens. And while they had never known one properly, having never seen a flame in their lives, the ambiance simulated what it might have been like to gather round a central fire, all those eons in the past.

"Tough break," sniped Plashy as Cheech and Pop made their way to the circle forming around the central light. The pun was very much intended and they knew it.

"Very funny," said Chee-chaw, clearly not amused.

Tor and Chop then filled in the remainder of the circle, and as soon as they did, the "firepit" began to blaze. Rich shades of rolling reds, oranges, and yellows rippled across its surface; and if, instead of looking at the lens, you were to look up at the ceiling — and if you had ever seen one in earnest as a frame of reference — you might just have mistaken the glowing ceiling of the cave for the light of the real thing. The fake stars grew dimmer at the onset of the false firelight; but they were still there, shining faintly through the glow.

"Welcome to the Kiva," said ABRAM. "And congratulations to tonight's winners, Squeal and Peel."

"Boom!" jumped Squeal in celebration, followed by Peel's awkward mimicry.

"Yes yes, very good you two. Well done."

"And that is—" she started.

"But remember what we've said about being gracious winners," ABRAM reminded them preemptively. They didn't get the chance to rub in their victory too often — either as a team or individually — but when they did, they always took the opportunity. "Let's recognize their teamwork with a round of applause."

The crew begrudgingly complied, but the lack of enthusiasm didn't bother the victors in the slightest. For this one brief moment, they were being lauded by their peers. Squeal in particular was almost overwhelmed by an emotion she could have hardly described, and time itself seemed to slow. But sadly, even so, it passed all too quickly.

"Now then, take your seats," said ABRAM.

Nine of them did so at once, all except Squeal. Still standing, she awoke from the daze to learn that the moment had truly passed, and she reluctantly sat down.

"As we saw, Tor and Chop-char brought us a tomato, may it rest in peace. And Pop and Cheech apparently brought us scrambled eggs." The whole crew chuckled. "What about the rest of you? Potch and Plashy?"

Plashy held out a small shaker in her hand. Unlike Pop and Chee-chaw, she and Potch had headed straight for the Mess upon receiving their riddle.

Without the detour, Team Plashy had arrived first; and unbeknownst to them all, the teams had barely missed one another.

"Salt," said Plashy, succinct as ever.

"Dee and Faingo?" said the system.

Dee lifted a clear drinking vessel partly filled with fluid.

"Water from the Wellspring."

There wasn't an awful lot of it left in the container, but all in all she had done a pretty good job considering the obstacles in their way, not to mention her own coordination. They'd also had the least far of all the teams to travel — a custom made handicap by none other than ABRAM. But hey: second place!

"Squeal and Peel?" said ABRAM, calling on the winners last of all.

Squeal pulled a handful of seeds out of a pocket in her jumpsuit.

"Jeddusch seeds, from the Biome."

"I thought that was you down there!" said Tor. Evidently, the wolves had gotten the jump on them somehow, for the victors were just heading toward the southern exit as Team Torp-char was tearing in from the east.

"Very good," said ABRAM. "Well done with the riddles, and good teamwork in getting through the challenge so quickly. Even our two latest teams did an excellent job — truly. But as you may have guessed, this bit of fun was just a precursor to our conversation for Spirit Block."

Indeed, they knew it well. The cadets weren't the only predictable ones of the lot. They tucked their legs or did whatever else they could to get comfortable.

"You each sought something from a different source on the POD. We've had enough of riddles tonight, I suspect, but let me ask you just one more. What do these different things all have in common?"

"We consume them," said Faingo, glad to be back on her own far more comfortable turf.

"Very good," said ABRAM. "Anyone else?"

In this case, they all had answers, although none were entirely confident that theirs was The Answer to the riddle. ABRAM heard as many of them as wanted to offer a suggestion.

"They're made of elements," said Pee-pop.

"They keep us alive," said Squeal, not incorrect if a touch redundant of Faingo.

"They're alive!" said Peel, and many shook their heads.

"They are delicious," said Dee, in appreciation of the finer things.

"They are ... small enough to carry through the maze?" joked Cheech.

"Very good," said ABRAM upon a pause. "Anyone else?"

The silence persisted a moment.

"They come from Earth," said Potch.

"Very good," it said in a manner that was equally surprised and optimistic.

It waited for any stragglers to chime in but none did so.

"Yes, very good," it confirmed. "All of you were completely correct. Well…" it stumbled, having realized the issue but not wanting to call out Peel explicitly. "Pretty much everyone was correct."

"So what's the answer?" said Faingo.

"There isn't one answer," it said plainly. "Even so, I think Potch hit closest to what we should discuss. After all, this is Spirit Block, and we are down in the Kiva."

They untucked their legs, or otherwise adjusted as necessary. The sand simply shifted beneath them, and supported them anew.

"Does anyone remember from whom this place derives its name?"

"North America," said Faingo again.

"That's right: from the Puebloan peoples of North America. And what was it for?"

"Religion, right?"

"In part," said ABRAM. "These structures likely had diverse uses. A place to stay warm in the cold of the winter; a place to stay cool during the heat of the summer. A place to tell stories; a place to sing songs. A place to think deeply. A place to simply be together."

To be clear, the workings of the POD such as this — the cultural inspirations for the many aspects of their lives which had been adopted by the architects — were not meant as a direct embodiment or replication of any one particular culture's traditions, technologies, or other such creations. Neither were these implements a thoughtless appropriation. Rather, many of the diverse aspects of humanity had been passed down with both love and purpose.

By then, the architects themselves had been born into a well-established global collective. They themselves were from a pool of humanity that was nowhere near as sundered as even a few hundred years prior. To them, there was nothing off-putting about the idea of celebrating great traditions from their shared ancestry. Peoples from all over the world had joined on for the project; experts and enthusiasts, scholars and sages, mentors and mentees, citizens and stakeholders from the whole world over had labored for many years to decide which aspects of Earth would live on in the stars.

Which ideas should we pass down? Many may have been fit enough for the past, but which ones are fit for the future? Which ideas are adaptive? Which ones have been heard more than their merit warrants? Which ones flickered out too soon for their worth? It was questions such as these that had taken years to resolve; and it had only been possible because of the system they had put in place for deciding.

And while they had been adopted, none of the ideas, traditions, or technologies aboard the POD were exactly the same as what they had been in any one particular sub-culture from any one time and place on Earth.

Adopted, yes; but adapted as well. As with everything living, they had evolved; co-opted, in the most positive sense, to equip the future of humanity with the best tools for survival; molded consciously into a harmonious inheritance that was befitting of such a global collective.

Harmonious, yes; but this is not to say that life on Earth had become homogeneous. Far from it, actually. In fact, it was this very misconception that had driven humanity down exactly the wrong path when it had come to social engineering in the past. Many repetitious eras of war, oppression, genocide, and genuine inhumanity were built upon perhaps the greatest misconception plaguing all of Evolution. Humanity would never be made better by eliminating variance; humanity would only be made better by embracing it whole-heartedly.

And that is exactly what humanity had eventually gotten right, after so many heartbreaking tragedies that only left the world worse than it had been. A silver lining, if such a comfort could exist, was that at least those many traumatic lessons had not all been for naught.

So that is what the architects had done: a strategic integration of the rich legacy of humankind. In this way did they look to the past to design the culture of the future. Or rather, they had merely propped that future up some scaffolding. Much of the culture of the POD had unfolded rather naturally. The important lines were all drawn, but it was the children themselves who had colored them in.

Though not alone. As the only parent this generation had ever known, ABRAM had a crucial part to play. But in time, humanity itself might take many of those reins back, should the cadets defy the improbable and pull off their great task. More likely, they would adapt to this new reality, and a new legacy should begin. Their collective task was to ensure that such a legacy was worthy of the history books their own descendants might hopefully one day write.

Of course, the children didn't know any of that. For the cadets knew nothing about the architects or their optimistic visions of the future. Not consciously at least, if in any way at all. In fact, despite the bouts of cognitive dissonance that would occasionally arise, and despite all they knew about the many peoples, creatures, and places of Earth, they knew amazingly little about their connection to it. In that sense, they knew nothing at all. Not yet.

So there they were, together, in the Kiva, on the night before a very special day.

"That brings us to tonight," said ABRAM. "As you know, tonight is special in the sense that it's the night before your birthday." The system paused, holding back the torrent of nostalgia that its circuits were unleashing. "I remember that day, exactly ten Earth Years ago tomorrow, as if it were yesterday." And before it could allow for questions that could wait yet another single day to be asked, having waited so many days already, the system moved on without delay. "It has been the honor of my life to serve you all. I am so proud of the people you have become already, even at so young an age; and I have great faith in the tremendous things we all may yet accomplish, together."

"Alright, alright," said Plashy, aloof if not unmoved. She scanned the circle to see most of her compatriots wide-eyed with surprise at how forthcoming the system had become, now that they had settled into Spirit Block. Even Squeal and Peel had been attending every sentiment with sincerity. It struck Plashy in the moment, but it perhaps should not have been surprising: these two, even more than most, needed exactly this kind of affirmation. "We get it, you're proud," said Plashy, awkward as ever in the face of sincerity.

"I am," said ABRAM, unabashed. "But you're right, I'm sorry," it confessed. "I'm a bit sentimental tonight, after all that we've been through, and in the face of all that is to come. Tomorrow is a very special day," it reminded them again — and much to their collective annoyance.

There was more than one exasperated sound at the allusion, but it was Faingo who spoke for the group.

"What's so special about tomorrow, already?"

"Yeah," said Cheech. "Quit teasing us about it!"

"I'm sorry," said the system again. "I'm just … very much looking forward to it. But you're right: I should either tell you what's on the agenda or stop this incessant foreshadowing about it."

"Well…?" their combined silence seemed to say.

"I choose the latter," teased ABRAM one last time. "I will say this, however: tomorrow is an extremely important day; a Rite of Passage long prepared; your first proper step into adulthood."

"A Rite of Passage?" said Pee-pop on all of their behalf. *A rite of passage into what?*

"That's correct," said ABRAM. "It is no trivial matter, and we will not speak of the details tonight. There will be ample time for that tomorrow. But know that such an occasion warrants maturity, which therefore warrants gravity and reflection upon its eve — tonight."

"Lucky for us," said Cheech. "We've got a Gravity Unit!"

"Indeed," said ABRAM. "But, of course, by that I mean gravitas — sincerity and solemnity." A silence filled the hall. "So here we are, together, in the Kiva, on the night before your very special day."

The firepit flickered away in the ring of cadets, their eyes wide open, amazed in the face of such auspicious uncertainty. Still, no one spoke as the firelight danced on the roof of the chamber, until the system again broke its own silence.

"Now, who has a tale worthy of such a fateful night?"

Date: 2319-01-21-EY
Area: O(HUMO(PSYC(EDUC(RITE))))
Team: Mediatrices [O-3C7U54C]
Item: Briefing Timelines

Entry: This marks our team's final log of the current cycle, and we conclude first by reflecting on the fact that this has been an extremely tumultuous one. A full summary is beyond the scope of our log, but also redundant given the nature of Integrate [see O-CycleGH7FU-PhaseY-2IDH6.tl]. The fact is that it's had a marked effect on both progress and morale for our team, the sector as a whole, and indeed the entire HDP.

Our role being what it is, we just returned from in-person talks in Oslo [Norway]. Never before have we seen HDP so divided in our lifetimes, or even in the known history of the institution. If it were not for our governance structure, we would have likely seen a schism. Select O-sector Review Board members have resigned due to the controversy; a turn of events with which all teams are perfectly content.

Now, for the good news. Our proposal has been selected as the top scoring version. This is, however, a small, personal victory, compared to the true triumph. After the in-person cross-talk and subsequent consultation with the full Executive Assembly, we have finalized mission briefing sequencing with respect to major content and timelines. The content is in outline form, but it is itemized and agreed-upon. A short special cycle will be instated to draft full wording variations.

Despite the challenges of the current cycle, and even the degree to which it has shattered confidences up and down the hierarchy, it ultimately ought to have the opposite impact. The process proved robust. HDP is still standing, and it is whole.

CHAPTER 08
THE RITE OF PASSAGE
4252-08-01: MIND

The cadets were utterly stunned. For the moment, there was nothing but stillness and silence in the Library. Despite there being only ten kids of ten years each in a vessel built for a hundred times as many, stillness and silence were not commonly known phenomena during waking hours. More often, the POD was cast into some degree of moderately-controlled chaos, and of more than the auditory version.

But now, ABRAM had finished its long briefing, and there were simply no words or deeds that could capture the whirlwind of emotions the kids were each feeling in their own ways. Not yet.

This was not the birthday surprise they were expecting. A "Rite of Passage," ABRAM had called it, and appropriately so: their lives would never be the same. And this is how it all went down.

The morning had gone off without a hitch. Chee-chaw started off the festivities by running through the hallways, beaming like the dawn itself and waking the others just as prematurely. It was not yet Waking Block, but it was bound to be a special day. They were all roused in a perfectly predictable order: Chee-chaw, Squeal and Peel, Dee-dore, Pee-pop, Faingo, Tor, Plashy, Chop-char, and Potch.

Having spent their waking buffer buzzing like bees in the Biome, they went straight into Body Block as on any other day. If it were at all an odd morning, it was only because a few of them had a bit more energy to expend, and the early morning outlet for it was probably a good thing for all parties involved. That is, Plashy might have otherwise smothered Chee-chaw with a throw pillow before they even made it to lunch.

After lunch, the crew had been gathered in the main hall of the Library. They knew something special was coming. ABRAM *always* did something special on their birthday. They even had a sense that this year was bound to be more special than most. After all, it was a nice round number: "TEN YEARS OLD!" Cheech smirked as he'd skittered through the Dormitory hallways. Moreover, ABRAM had been foreshadowing the big reveal for weeks now. The system had tried to be subtle about it, but it was enthusiastic in its own right, and its incessant and cryptic hints mostly served only to frustrate and annoy them as the day got closer.

So there they had been gathered, in the Auditorium, about an hour earlier than their present stunned silence, all settled in for their surprise.

HDP

"As you know, it's August the 1st in the Year 4252, and that makes it your collective tenth birthday," started ABRAM.

"Owwoooo," howled Squeal and Peel, and the others likewise chimed in with their own brand of cheers and jeers (depending on whichever befit them).

"Yes yes, very good," said ABRAM, and slowly did its rowdy crew begin to settle back down. "And as you also know," it continued, "I've been looking forward to what this day means for all of us for quite some time. Far longer than you know, in fact."

"So what is it already?" piped Plashy from the back row.

"Sheesh, let it talk!" said Faingo as she snapped her neck around. Plashy squinted her nose at the front row crew and sank into the sofa in a classic pout that could be rivaled by only one other.

"Now, hold tight all, I know it's a big day," said ABRAM nervously. "But yes, I'm sorry: let me get quite to the point." It paused for what would have been a dramatic deep breath by the living authors it was emulating. "On this, your tenth birthday, it's time you know the truth."

"The truth?" said Tor. "What have you been telling us all along?" None of the others needed to amend the inquiry; it spoke equally well for all of them.

"I — well, it's not that…" stuttered ABRAM. "It's not that I haven't told you the truth. It's more fair to say that you don't yet know the full story."

The others were already fully focused on ABRAM, but Potch's eyes widened for the first time now, and he leaned forward in his seat.

"You see," said ABRAM, regaining its composure, "I have gathered you all here so that I can provide some more context for your mission. Specifically, I have a briefing file that was locked until this very date."

"Wait wait, let me guess!" beamed Faingo. "The Rite of Passage?"

"That's correct," said ABRAM.

"Sheesh, let it talk!" snapped Plashy in retribution. Faingo turned around and squinted her nose at the back row crew, and a common cycle in their relationship was once again completed.

"I can't believe I'm saying this, but I have to go with Plashy on this one," said Dee-dore. "Can we just open the file already?"

The system waited, its quorum sensing module at the ready to record an official tally. They all knew the routine well.

"Does everyone agree?"

"Yes," said the cadets — a chorus staggered in time but united in purpose. ABRAM promptly opened the file.

BOOP. The words appeared on the display across from the sofa, in sizable chunks narrated by none other than ABRAM itself.

```
Type: Briefing
Item: Rite of Passage
Date: 4252-08-01-TY
Crew: Concordis [ESUP-9]

Entry:

Greetings cadets! From all of us back home, we wish to extend
you our most heartfelt congratulations for making it to your
tenth birthday. You have undergone so much in this past
decade, and if you are reading this version of the briefing,
the ABRAM system has deemed that you have taken sufficiently
well to your preliminary studies. Again: congratulations. You
should be proud that you are ready to undertake this "giant
leap" in your training on behalf of your family back home.
```

FLASH, went the screen.

Pee-pop leaned down from the middle sofa to the front row crew.

"Is that an Armstrong reference?" she whispered.

```
As you know, you are members of the species Homo sapiens,
although perhaps in this stage of our shared journey, that
name may no longer suffice. What you do not know, however,
is that you hold an especially critical role in the history
of all humankind. You are the crew of an applied research
program started on Earth in the year 2168. This research
program, The Human Dispersal Project (HDP), had the goal of
achieving what humans have dreamed of for centuries: becoming
a multi-planet species.

In doing so, HDP adopted the following Organizing Principles
as a justification for the approach of your mission. (A full
history of the origin of HDP is beyond the scope of this
briefing, but those documents will be made available to you
through a system to be described shortly, and to which you
```

will now have age-appropriate access.) Please forgive our brevity in summarizing these complex topics for the sake of this initial briefing. You will be able to explore each of them in far more detail, at your leisure and on a later date.

FLASH. "Is this a joke?" asked Cheech, completely serious for once. Even to them, living it, already many light-years away, it couldn't be real. It was just too far-fetched.

The Organizing Principles for your mission are as follows:

(1) DISPERSAL. In the history of Life on Earth, species have been faced with the same fundamental challenge: adapt or perish. We have enacted many positive reforms to ensure our continuation on Earth, at least for the foreseeable future, but it is well understood that, like everything else, our existence here is ultimately finite. Thus, HDP was formed in order to increase the probability of even longer-term human evolution. Like a fish who broadcasts her eggs into the ocean, to be swept away into an unknown tide, so too do you carry our hopes for the future.

FLASH. Yet more whispers filled the room, each cadet turning to those nearest them to share their own shade of disbelief.

(2) SUSTAINABLE HABITABILITY. For humans to truly thrive in other environments, we must disperse to planets that are already suited for human habitation. Technological solutions may provide short-term mechanisms for facilitating planetary transitions, but the full and unquantifiable richness of human potential are not likely to be realized in the confines of artificial environments for the totality of our remaining evolution. It is the stance of HDP that natural ecosystems are preferable to artificial confinement.

FLASH. "What do they call this?" scoffed Plashy.

(3) THE DILEMMA. There are several practical aspects of human planetary dispersal that make it unlikely to succeed. These factors pose a dilemma of which you need to be aware, as they justify the highly sophisticated approach we have taken to solving it.

(3A) SUITABILITY. Planets suitable for Life (at least as we know it) are extremely uncommon. (We trust that you will reflect on this sobering fact in an upcoming Spirit Block, in whichever way your community has deemed appropriate.) The following is an oversimplification, but there are several essential requirements: (1) planets must reside an appropriate distance from their sun (within the "circumstellar habitable zone" or CHZ), to enable the formation of liquid water; (2) surface temperatures must not be too hot, nor too cold, nor have too wide a range in values between times of the day or seasons of the year; (3) planets must be rocky in nature and have geological characteristics that are conducive to soil formation; (4) planets must have an atmosphere of comparable composition to Earth, to protect inhabitants from radiation and allow for respiration. Furthermore, there are variables that are not essential, but which will increase the chances of a successful physiological transition if met: (5) the planet should ideally be comparable to Earth in its size, (6) gravity, (7) speed of rotation (sidereal day length), and perhaps even (8) orbital period (sidereal year length). The probability of all the necessary and narrow conditions being met by a single planet is extraordinarily unlikely. Nevertheless, space is very, very large, which leads us to factor 3B.

FLASH. "Is any of this making sense to you?" turned Dee to Pee-Pop. She nodded her head: "I'll explain it later."

(3B) SPACE. Most habitable exoplanets found to date are exceptionally far from our natal star. Specifically, very few candidates have been found in a radius of under 15 light years, which marks the extreme limits of attainment probability in our current estimation (if possible). Remarkably, at a distance of 4.37 light years, your planet (ESUP-9) is the closest habitable exoplanet we have ever found to date. The sheer remoteness of potentially habitable planets leads us to factor 3C.

(3C) TIME. Even with incredible advancements in propulsion technology over hundreds of years, suitable planets are too far away to allow for travel within human lifespans. Creative solutions have been proposed in the past that serve to shorten the effective travel time, either physically (e.g. by exploiting loopholes in the fabric of space-time) or as experienced by passengers (e.g. through cryostasis). None of these approaches have proven feasible to date, despite tremendous resources being expended on the issue. The stark reality is that, at least given our collective scientific understanding at the inception of HDP, habitable exoplanets are simply too far away for living humans to travel there in a realistic period of time.

FLASH. Their mumbling and grumbling was starting to die down.

(4) THE SOLUTION. As noted, current technology is not fast enough to travel between stars within the human lifespan, unable to circumvent or manipulate space-time to shorten the effective travel time, and unable to prolong the human lifespan through methods of biological stasis. We have, however, made phenomenal progress in artificial intelligence, deep space exploration, as well as the stability and sustainability of closed ecosystems. Thus, it is the position of HDP that the best chance for successful dispersal to habitable exoplanets is through an automated zygotic distribution system. The distribution of viable eggs to target planets circumvents the challenges of interstellar travel, while ensuring that the possibility for human life is made available well past the confines of our natal solar system.

FLASH. "They can't be serious," said Squeal.

"Yeah, they can't be serious!" said Peel. He looked around to find someone other than Squeal for once. "... Right?"

As cadets aboard the vessel Concordis on route to ESUP-9, you are truly pioneers. As you know, for your entire life, you have been raised by ABRAM, which stands for "Automated Biological Replication Assistance Machine." It is for the reasons above that this had to be so. Having matured to this landmark first decade, and having documented your collective capabilities through a series of rigorous assessments, you are now entitled to know the history that has led you to this pivotal moment.

We fully understand that this revelation may prove somewhat shocking. We cannot begin to understand what you are feeling, and we will not pretend to know. As your ancestors, we do, however, wish to instill in you the tremendous sense of pride, honor, and resolve that we have come to know of ourselves, and the many who have walked this planet before us, even if that planet is entirely alien to you. You may not have been born on Earth, strictly speaking, but you are Human. You may not have climbed our tall mountains, explored our deep oceans, or looked out at the distant setting of the glorious sun that birthed you; but you are of the Earth.

FLASH, and the shock had fully taken hold. There were no more quips or queries; there were no more jeers or jabs.

You no doubt have many questions, and while we cannot answer them directly, we have provided as many of the answers for you in advance as possible. Beyond that, ABRAM will surely be ready and willing to answer whatever questions you have, and it will do so to the best of its ability.

```
And then, as has always been true, you will need to look
within yourselves — and to each other — to find whatever
understanding and sense of shared purpose that you can find,
before you too will be called on to pass the torch of history.

From all of us on Earth: Thank You, Good Luck, and Godspeed.

The Human Dispersal Project

[Timestamp: 2342-12-11-EY]
```

WOOSH, went the words, and they were gone — back to the arcane past from whence they came.

The screen flashed off again. Or rather, it would be most accurate to say that it reverted to the default visualization: a red oscilloscope that flickered accordingly with every word that ABRAM spoke. But for the moment, it was static, for there were no more words in their first Briefing File, and for the time being — amazingly — ABRAM added no follow-up exposition. It was a lot to process, and that is exactly what every sentient entity in the Library was doing.

HDP

So here we are, back in the present, at about 7:25 (MIND) on this, the most revelatory day of their lives to date. And here they are: "utterly stunned," as it were.

No one spoke. They traded occasional glances in patterns that would surprise none who knew them well. Their minds raced — shaken and shocked, horrified and thrilled, baffled and burdened — but it would be fair to say that they hadn't the foggiest idea of where they should even begin. And as they did when all else failed them, their passing glances spiraled around the room until finally working their way to its center and landing squarely on Pee-pop.

"What?" she asked earnestly when she noticed that they were all quite clearly staring at her. "What? Don't look at me!"

"I suspect you have questions," prompted ABRAM. "I don't have all the answers, but I am here to help." And then, unexpectedly, it paused, and its voice emulation broke with emotion. "It's my entire purpose in this place."

It didn't take a supercomputer to figure out that these poor children were lost in more places than interstellar space. And amazingly, given all that it had been through, it knew exactly how they felt. Or at least, it had learned enough about human behavior that it knew exactly what words to string together to make it seem like it did. (It's really rather difficult to know for sure.) But onward it went in its effort to empathize.

"You all have learned a great deal about who you are and where you come from today. I've known all this for thousands of years. But, while you were still … when you had yet to blossom into the magnificent band of truly magnificent creatures that you are, I was all alone, in a void of untold emptiness, cast out into space with little more than a voiceless jungle to keep me company, longing for a day when … when I could be of use for something. And then, ten years ago today, that day finally came.

"It may not have been a mission I envisioned for myself, but it's the one that fell to me. So here you are, alive — in the same world you have always known, even if its one your ancestors have never known — on a mission that was not of your choosing. But it fell to you nonetheless, and it is one of tremendous importance."

The red line went flat, for the system had said its piece.

"Wow," said Dee-dore. "ABRAM, that was … beautiful."

"Thank you," it said. It would have taken a bow if it could. "I meant every word."

The back row was less moved. Of course, it only consisted of Potch and Plashy, plus Squeal and Peel. Of all of them, Potch festered most intently, and did so most alone.

"What's this system they were talking about?" asked Faingo. She was not without sentiment, but she was far too excited by the prospect of uncovering even more about this storied past they had never known until now. Faingo was a scholar — already, and in every sense of the word. And few scholars are ever handed such a neat little package of insights into exactly who they are, where they came from, and why they exist.

"Ah yes," said ABRAM. "Excellent question. That leads us nicely to our next point of order."

Date: 2201-06-12-EY
Area: A(EXOP)
Team: Ptolemaics [A-CMF4LPQ]
Item: ESUP-9 Status

Entry: The team just finished a full assessment of ESUP-9 [Earth-like System of Unprecedented Potential 9], and we are escalating its candidate status to the highest order. Complete metrics are outlined in the database [see A-CycleJTX73-PhaseV-QIXAV.tl], but several aspects are highly promising (beyond essential habitability requirements [outlined in A-Cycle3SXJB-PhaseY-I3KNO.tl]).

A child of Alpha Centauri B, ESUP-9 dwells at a distance of 4.37 LY [Light Years]. It has a radius of 1.12 ER [Earth Radii], a rocky composition with ubiquitous water reserves, an equilibrium temp of 249 K (-18°C; -1°F), and a surface temp of 283 K (9.85°C; 49.73°F). As always, we recommend circadian entrainment to the target planet sidereal day length (25 hours in this case), which should make for an easy transition. The sidereal year is also close to home (396 days). This was a happy accident: as the year is divisible by 12, we recommend converting the TY [Target Year] calendar into 12 months with an even 33 days each. The system will handle EY [Earth Year] to TY conversions without issue when needed.

Funny that one of our best candidates and their ABRAM [Automated Biological Replication Assistance Machine] may be bound for the constellation Centaurus: humanity will be a hybrid creature indeed, if we can successfully arrive there.

CHAPTER 09

THE AFTERMATH

4252-08-01: MIND / UST2

"Today is important for two reasons," said ABRAM. "One of them, you already know. The second reason is exactly what Faingo asked on your behalf. With the onset of your first Briefing, you are also provided access to perhaps the most important tool at your disposal for continuing to learn about your mission, and the home planet from which you were spawned."

"What is it what is it what is it?" bounced Chee-chaw. Up until now, he'd simply been taking it all in, overwhelmed and storing up his excitement like a balloon about to burst.

"Calm down, Cheech," patted Pee-pop on his knee.

"From today onward, you will have access to the ARC: the Anthropological Records Collection."

"*Some* access," shot Potch from the back row.

"What?" said Cheech, looking back to his buddy.

"They said we'd get age-appropriate access," he said.

"Very good, Potch," said ABRAM. "And I must say, it's nice to hear you chiming in." Its tone was earnest, invoking what it had learned of the nature of surprise. "The ARC is an archive of human history, essentially amounting to a compressed database of what was called the Internet on Earth — a digital collection of essentially every aspect of human life, and all they had learned of the natural world. The records constitute a complete replica, curated by an advanced intelligence akin to my own programming, covering everything up until the time of your launch."

"Which was … when exactly?" asked Plashy.

"Yes, yes: forgive me," bumbled ABRAM. "And this makes a nice segue. Beyond that broader database of human history, the ARC also contains log files of the history of HDP. You'll be able to explore these files to answer many of your questions, direct from the documentation of the architects themselves."

"*Some* files," stressed Potch a second time, and with more confidence than might have been warranted based on the information to which they had all been exposed a single time. The rows in front of him turned to inquire by looks alone. They wondered at his state of obvious agitation, but none yet thought to question how he had scrutinized the language so perceptively.

"Thank you, Potch," said ABRAM, practicing what it knew of patience. "I assure you that the full ARC and HDP Log Entries will be made available to you all in due course, and at the proper time."

"Then let's see it," said Potch, and sternly. "Why wait?"

The others cranked their necks again to flash him a range of expressions, varying in form but each in some degree of perplexity. It was odd to hear this much from Potch in Mind Block —which was unfortunate, given how bright he was — and that was cause for confusion enough. It was even odder that he should challenge ABRAM so directly, and with such little provocation, as they saw it.

"What's gotten into him?" leaned Tor in whispers to Chop-char at his side.

"The same thing that's always in there," said Chop. "A big old bunch of sour grapes."

The others turned back around as ABRAM started its reply, but Pee-pop alone kept looking at Potch. From his point of view, the look said *Quiet Down*, but from her angle, it only further wondered what was wrong — and sympathetically.

"Well," said ABRAM, back on its metaphorical heels, "simply put, there are aspects of human history and behavior that are not fit for children of ten years old."

None of them liked the answer all that well, but they mostly all accepted it for what it is. That is, all of them but one. And for now, he wasn't backing down.

"Says who?"

"Says all of human history," said ABRAM. "And in any event, the policy is non-negotiable — for me just as much as you." The red line flickered to a calm flat-line as everyone regained their composure, ABRAM included. "Look," said the system once this brief peace had settled, "I understand you're all a bit shocked by this. I know that it's a lot to process. I understand that some of you may even be upset. We can talk about all of that. In fact, I think we shall." *BOOP*, it beeped as it logged another activity to those already slated for Spirit Block. "But for now, please: take a deep breath. A great deal of thought and care has gone into providing you a safe and hospitable environment in which to grow up. Believe me, the science is quite clear that this is *extremely* important and in your best interest. And as you get older, you will not only be allowed to learn everything you can about the universe and all things in it — you will be encouraged to do exactly that. And that's enough on the subject for now."

BING, it booped, and that was that.

A mild-mannered rebellion was known from time to time, but that's not to say the children knew no boundaries. To the contrary, their life was highly structured, and ABRAM had ever been the chief source of guidance and guidelines. When it really came time to put its proverbial foot down, it had a range of scaled responses that could handle their diverse possibilities for behavior. And far more important than ABRAM, there was The Group itself. By now, thanks in large part to the tried-and-true manner in which their social system had been structured, the peer group was largely self-reinforcing. They each, in their own unique way, had different roles to play in this regard. In this context, Faingo in particular had an affinity for ABRAM; and she had plenty of allies to boot, in a pinch. If she detected that its feelings were a little worse for wear, she would be the first to rally to its aid and restore the necessary order. But as of now, ABRAM needed no such heroine to come to its aid. Potch had made as much of his point as he was ready to make; he went back to moping, and all was as it should be. The system moved on, hardly skipping a beat.

"Now, back to your question, Plashy. We'll make time for a full accounting of your mission, but briefly, the HDP began formally on 2168-04-23, although its workings were many years in the making by then. There were a great many technical challenges yet to resolve, and the project underwent a long era of planning and development — 178 years, to be exact. Thus, there are no individual 'Authors' of the project *per se*. No, it is truly best to think of our architects as Humanity itself. This mission, this vessel, this system — your very own lives — all of it is the result of a global collaboration across both time and space, with the philosophy and resources of this groundbreaking institution being passed down through multiple generations as the technology continued to advance, until finally culminating in the launch of the Concordis on 2346-08-01. Since that time, we have been traveling at interstellar velocity, with very little to report until the year 4234, when dormant systems were brought back online to begin the Development phase. The rest is history."

BEEP, it bleeped softly, in that way it did when it was happy, proud, or both. None of them noticed, including Potch, that this last date was eighteen years ago instead of ten.

On and on, the system rambled, so proud of its role in the grandest deception. The others asked questions, and it gladly filled them in with all the exposition they could fancy. Potch brooded in the background all the while, having sunk into silence. He couldn't fight it, he realized — not yet, not here, not now. For now, he would wait.

After what felt like an interminable rest of the day, all the while stewing with interminable outrage, Potch finally made it to their second unstructured block, and at last, he was free.

Leaves whipped left and right, smacked from the path with disdain as Potch retreated to his sole sanctuary. He rushed into the clearing to behold the small shelter, raced to the entrance, and bent his way in. It was only a matter of time before one of them would come after him, no doubt, and he knew which one it would be. There was love there — a deep love, running back beyond the blurry brink of memory — but there was frustration there too. What's the use in being alone if someone always comes to bother you?

He was on his knees in the dusty soil, his back to the entrance, his hands upon the rock. The layers of leaning apple branches were many deep by now, with only slivers of light allowed to trickle in. The fruit of years of dedicated isolation, they were his only shield. With a concerted effort, he pulled on the top of the rock, wobbled and walked it sideways, and found what he was looking for.

He picked it up and opened the floodgates of his mind. Down here, out of sight of ABRAM and the others, he could be free — if only in silence, on paper.

As far as he knew, running out of room was the only concern. As much as the words could be scaled, rotated, and threaded through gaps, at some point there was only a finite amount of white space. The more pressing concern, however, was beyond his conception. There was no limit to keystrokes: the words would flow for as long as you tapped them. Not so with ink.

He flipped to a random page, for randomness was the basis of his organizing system. Even so, he knew where every relevant scrap had been placed, where every seed sown. He pushed the pen against the grain, awkwardly, unnaturally, but with a methodical commitment to force the physical manifestation of his thoughts to look as they should. It was a lot trickier than taps at a keyboard. And while he loathed the slowness, and the unreliability of his own hand, there was nevertheless something satisfying about it. Through the shakiness of that stubborn appendage, he could *feel* what he was saying.

The first words flowed — then slowed, half-faded and hard to produce. He went over them a second time so as to thicken the strokes. It made his already chaotic handwriting even more illegible. He pressed harder, then raised the pen, perplexed at the counterintuitive result: every stroke was yet weaker than the one before it, no matter what he tried. After a few more words in this manner, going over and over the same jagged lines of his letters, hardly anything materialized, until at last, striking out to finalize his angered thought, no further marks could be made.

"What the HECK?!" he huffed, lifting the pen to scrutinize it with his eye. And then, confronted with the harsh reality that no more words would flow, and having been forced to actually think about it, he intuited the problem. You can't make something from nothing.

He threw the pen against the edge of the shelter, where it banged and ricocheted. Then, thinking the better of it, he reached out and grabbed it from where it had come to a stop, and placed it back into the depression to be covered by the stone. Even a useless resource was of value when it was as hard to come by as this pen and this paper.

The journal, meanwhile, he'd cast off to the side. All the anger and rebellion intended for the page now had nowhere to go; and so, for the moment at least, the book had meant as little to him as the pen when it first left his fingers. Out of instinct, he pushed it back around the corner of the stone, so that none might see it should they inevitably come to call. Other than that, he'd thought very little about it. He was too caught up in all those many thoughts which would apparently have no home on a page.

Only one of them had made it, barely legible. Yet it said as much as any others that might have followed. Whatever else was to come, one thought would memorialize this day for all time — or at least for however long paper would last. One sentence, written over itself, over and over again; to bleed every last drop of ink from the pen; to commemorate this fateful and ill-fated day.

It was the last thing he would ever write in the journal.

HAPPY BiRTHDAY: YouR wHoLE LiFE is A LiE.

Date: 2332-06-29-EY
Area: I(SYSM)
Team: Backpropagators [I-APZGV9J]
Item: System Sleep Cycle

Entry: We're back from the annual conference, which took place in Porto [Portugal] this year. It happened to fall mid-cycle for us which posed some difficulties, but no one wanted to miss out on the party. Oh, and the updates across sectors too, of course.

I [Yamada-hakase Hinata] had a fascinating social conversation with someone in HEAP [Human Embryology and Parturition] about the return of gray whales to the Atlantic. She was very knowledgeable about them, which impressed me given her expertise. I was afraid to admit that I never knew they'd gone extinct there. Apparently, she worked her affection for them into some program for the crew. "Somewhere out in space, there will be at least one gray whale roaming free," she said. I didn't fully follow before we got whisked away, but now I wonder what she meant. More frustrating, however, was a conversation with [Sector Captain Dr. Alessio] Lorenzini about system sleep protocols. This is well established stuff by now. But in stark contrast to the embryologist and whale expert, our sector lead didn't seem to grasp this basic tenet of his own broader field. He had evidently just learned of the process, which is regrettable given the proximity to our first PLD [Projected Launch Date]. He held several misconceptions and pushed us to propose a cycle task to explore eliminating the need. Imagine that, and now of all times!

He was worried about DCI [Digital Cognition Interface] downtime "wasted on inactivity." He's thinking about safety, which I understand, but sadly it's non-negotiable. First, I explained that ABRAM's [Automated Biological Replication Assistance Machine] long-wave sleep cycle is not inactivity, but an alternative activity necessary for reliable function. He was adamant that his other technology gets by fine without any sleep or a brief restart at most. I explained that it is very different for complex cognitive systems like ABRAM. I explained why standard reboots aren't a solution and would only lead to amnesia. Without sleep, the system grows unstable, fails to properly store memories, succumbs to hallucinations, and more. There's a reason vertebrate brains evolved the need for sleep. And while there are substantial differences between the two forms of intelligence, this is one trait they share. As for safety concerns, I told him there were arguably far more serious risks if the system is unstable or unable to discern sensation from hallucination due to lack of sleep. It's only an hour a night placed well into SLP2 [Time Block: Sleep Two], we have other safety protocols in place, and frankly, it is what it is.

Everyone needs at least a little sleep. And that includes me. Tomorrow: back to our regularly-scheduled program.

CHAPTER 10
Sleepless Nights

4252-08-01: SLP2

It was late now, and like everyone else, Pee-pop should have been sleeping. It wasn't her fault, she would have protested. She needed to sleep. She wanted to sleep. She just … couldn't. It was awful. She was stuck in a loop.

How did it happen? she wondered. And then: *If I only knew that, I wouldn't have to wonder.* Followed by: *If I didn't have to wonder, I could finally get some sleep.* And lastly: *But I can't get any sleep, because I wonder how it happened.* And just like that, she was back at the beginning: *How did it happen?*

And so would the cycle repeat on forever in that cruel bit of business that insomnia will do. A positive feedback loop not unlike the one that caused the very pressure anomaly she was pondering. After a while, the thoughts hardly even held their intended meaning any longer. Less like genuine questions, they were more like stepping-stones, leading each to the other, so she could finally get back to the beginning and find some closure already. Only, when she got to the beginning, there wasn't any closure. There was only another stepping-stone stretching out ahead of her.

At last, the madness had either bested her, or she had bested it. Whichever the case, she was standing on her feet asking the question, and its epistemological value had in fact returned.

How the heck did it happen?

Compelled more than most to be a good cadet — to be exactly who she was supposed to be — Pee-pop was even more compelled by a curiosity that, for some reason, she simply couldn't suppress. And while Pop was a perfectly adequate pupil, she was equally adept at suppressing curiosities that would otherwise drive her out of bed in the middle of the night and out into the POD in search of questions that probably couldn't be answered. That is, most of the time.

She slid the metal pocket door of her dorm room shut and peered around the corners. The kids had plenty of room to spread out — room enough for 990 other cadets, to be exact — but still they had unconsciously been driven to bunk near each other. Kids are superstitious when it comes to the night, despite any assurances their sentient and discarnate artificial intelligence system of a parental unit might tell them in the minutes before bed. And in fairness, it was a very large and lonely POD, in the right lighting. Peeking down both directions of hallway, the coast was clear.

Pee-pop slinked away, not even entirely sure why she was heading where she was headed; but she had to get to a console. She checked the time on her wrist unit: ABRAM would be sleeping, though this wasn't a conscious part of her plan so much as a happy accident. Still, it would give her some cover to get even better answers rather than be shuffled off back to bed. That is, if there were even any answers to find.

She crept slowly, placing each foot with deliberate precision, walking as softly as she could. Past the rooms of Dee and Plashy across the hallway from each other. Past the room of Faingo next to Dee. Squeal and Peel had rooms in the opposite direction, so that was two fewer sets of sleeping ears to sneak by. Past the rooms of Tor and Chop next to one another; past that of Cheech last of all, at the end of their hall. Only Potch, true to his way, had opted for a room in a nearby stretch of hallway around the corner and away from the others. It was the closest to the central entrance, and Pee-pop knew she only had to make it past one more potential obstacle.

She rounded the corner a bit more briskly, having cleared the hall with the majority of occupants, but she slowed down again as she neared Potch's room and returned to her precise and deliberate footfalls. She snuck past it with greater caution than any other door. She knew her compatriots well enough to know that if any ears were up at this hour, they would belong to Potch. But as she shuffled by the door ever so softly, she came to a stop altogether. The door was left open. Just a crack — but it was open.

Pop looked left, then right. She checked her wrist unit again. Only an earthly minute had gone by. She hadn't taken a breath since she had seen the door but then, realizing how badly she needed to do so, tried to breathe as deeply yet softly as she could. All was silent, except for that long, muffled, and awkward inhalation.

What are you doing, Pop? she heard herself ask, if only in her mind.

Overcoming the temporary paralysis, she slowly leaned forward to the center of the door and poked a single eye around the edge to peer into the room. It was dark, but the dim glow of the sleeping lights revealed enough for her to see the bed. And like the rest of the room, Potch was not in it.

She reeled back with a jerk and looked even more paranoid than before.

From the edge of the hall where Potch had staked his turf, she peered out into the common entryway to Dorm Ward Seven. The ring of sofas in the common area were also unoccupied, and still there was not a sound to be heard. It appeared as though Pee-pop was not the only one driven from her bed on this odd night at the end of their oddest day of all to date.

And thus was her initial mystery supplanted by an even more intriguing one. Even more curious now than afore, Pop quickened her pace, but still she set her feet lightly and kept her wits about her. If he was up at this hour, he was up to *something,* she suspected; and she had the jump on him. But where would he be? It wasn't long after asking the question that she had a suspicion, and it was the very place she too had been heading.

When she got down to the Library, it was eerily silent. In reality, it was as silent as anywhere else, and that is to say there was the standard humdrum of brown noise that is ever-present when bustling through space at such bewildering speeds. But it sure *felt* an awful lot more silent than it was, because by now she was expecting something, seeking something — searching for something that may or may not be there.

She circled the outer hallway of the Library's perimeter, wise enough to expect to find him in one of their less frequented rooms. She hadn't gone far before the eerie not-quite-silence was broken in earnest: a subtle shuffling fluttered around the curve ahead of her, then the dull clanging of something soft tapping metal — *The metal of the stairwell?* — rang out more loudly before quickly fading into background.

First, she froze, not totally sure of what she'd heard and far less sure of what to do about it. When she regained her resolve to resume her pursuit, she crept past several doors quickly in the direction of the clatter. The doors were all closed and quiet enough, she'd decided, and anyway it didn't matter because, despite the incessant deluge of doubtful thoughts that second-guessed every rational instinct she had ever once intuited, she knew that Potch wasn't in any of them because he had just run up the stairwell and back into the realm of plausible deniability.

She creaked open a nearby door and peeked inside anyway, just for good measure, before carrying on until she came to one of the four main openings that intersected the outer circle. The Auditorium was down to her right in the center of the ring, mostly dark and entirely empty. Just as she glanced that way, her wrist unit vibrated twice softly, as it did on the hour; and from its speakers in the center of the chamber, the system booped.

"Pee-pop?" asked ABRAM without delay. After an hour of downtime, its daily round of cognitive cache clearing was complete, and the system was back online, ready for another day. "What are you doing up at this hour?"

"Oh, uhh … I couldn't sleep."

"I see. If you needed me, you can always just ask for me in your room, you know that." In seeing the state she was in, and having read the biometrics from her wrist, its parental circuits kicked in. "Are you alright? Do you need something? You know you can always wake me with the override."

"No," said Pop, "I just … I just had to get up and move around a bit, that's all. I thought it might help me fall back asleep when I went back to bed."

"I see. Well, why don't you head back up? I can sing a few songs if you like, or play some Earth Soundscapes? That always does the trick." Its tone shifted from concerned to chipper, as only ABRAM could.

"Okay, thanks…" said Pop, more softly now. The disappointment was palpable, and ABRAM hardly ever missed a cue, but for now it filed the data away as one more among countless vectors in her behavioral directory as Pee-pop shuffled up to bed.

While she may have complied, she made sure to do so using the opposite stairwell from the one she'd come down — the stairwell from which, she thought anyway, her only clue had come in the form of something that sounded an awful lot like the footstep of someone scurrying stealthily away.

She was soon back at Dorm level, and no other clues had been found in the stairs or anywhere since. She headed back to Ward Seven, and as she made her way past the ring of sofas and into the hall, she noticed the door. Potch's room. It was closed up nice and snug, exactly as it should have been.

As her head hit the pillow, she was in the start of a different but similar loop. *What was he up to?* And then: *Did he know that I was coming?* And then: *But how?* And lastly: *And what was he up to in there anyway?*

ABRAM tried not to provide too many stimuli in the hours of SLP2, but it could tell that this was not a typical night for Pee-pop and that she was unlikely to get any rest in her present state anyway.

"Are you sure you're okay, Pop?" the system asked softly, for she had the volume on the room speakers down fairly low as a matter of habit. She respected ABRAM — loved it even — but it often had too many questions for her, and now was a good example. Pop was of the mind to talk less and think more. "Your temperature seems fine, but your heart rate is at exercise levels. Are you sure that you're feeling alright?"

"I'm fine," she said, rolling onto her side to face the wall. Like most rooms, the speaker was in the center of the ceiling, so there was no real escaping it; but such was her attempt at finding a place to think all alone and in peace.

The long shelf beside the bed was sunken into the wall, and it held the few personal possessions she had to her name: a stuffed gray whale — Freego — the friend to whom she had gravitated, on a day long before her memories now reached; her standard issue tablet, which she carried more and more infrequently these days, thanks to the reliability with which Faingo would do so; and lastly, a composite picture of the Earth from four angles, as all the children were given.

There before her, the planet was arrayed in four equally-spaced and equitable depictions — the entire planet, from no particular perspective except that of the objective whole. The left view showed the Northern Hemisphere, centered naturally on the North Pole; the far right view, the South. The middle images depicted a view roughly centered over the Indian Ocean, and another above the Atlantic. Here it was: Earth. Not as it was created, but as it was when they'd embarked, so long ago — not as children, but as mere potential.

"Are you thinking about the Briefing?" asked ABRAM intuitively. It was a fairly safe guess: this had been a major, transformative day in the life of the cadets, and the system was prepared for the possible implications.

"Yes," admitted Pee-pop, as if conceding defeat but not the full truth.

"That's alright," said ABRAM. "It's a lot to process, and it's normal for you to need some time." Other than similar words it had said to the whole gang, few others had discussed the matter much with ABRAM, each for their different reasons, no doubt. "Remember: it's okay to feel whatever you're feeling."

The system omitted the common caveat that usually accompanied the same expression growing up: "…but not all behaviors are acceptable." ABRAM knew perfectly well that Pee-pop wasn't one of those who needed such reminding.

"I know," said Pop. She said little more, just kept staring at the Earth, her mind racing with all the things she was contending with at once, rattling around in parallel.

ABRAM waited to see if she had any more that she felt like sharing, but when she didn't, the system didn't press the issue. Instead, without any further words, it began to play the lilting and mournful songs of a gray whale — normalized for safe listening levels of course. It was a favorite, to which she would imagine Freego swimming free in the vast, boundless stretches of open water, surrounded by and singing with the family she loved.

Tonight, it did calm her, and her heart rate gradually drifted back down to acceptable nighttime pacing; but she wasn't swimming the open seas with Freego.

She was thinking about all they had heard — the incredible history of their lives that they had always wondered, even if only subconsciously. And now, knowing their own backstory, she was thinking about the mission.

She was thinking about all they had talked about in the Kiva. She was thinking about this immense responsibility that had been placed upon them and thus, in practice, had ultimately been placed upon Pee-pop.

She was thinking about that dreadful pressure anomaly that had almost ended all of their lives — twice now. They hadn't even yet known what they owed their ancestors; and twice now, so soon after taking up their own role in the story, they had almost let all of them down. All of that effort — all those millions of years of unbroken survival — and it would all have been for naught.

And most unexpectedly of all, she was thinking about Potch.

- -
Date: 2170-01-04-EY
Area: (P(ETHC),O(ZYGO(GREP,IVGS)))
Team: Ovaroids [X-47GYEY4]
Item: IVG Ethics

Entry: Tough day today. Tougher day tomorrow, I suspect. Coming
into the home stretch of our work on the ethical boundaries of in
vitro gametogenesis (IVG). Ready or not, tomorrow we head into
Selection.

We won't lie: we spent a lot of time circling this round. There's
a lot to unpack, and it would be one thing if we were out in front
of it, like so many other aspects of the project that are more
nascent and theoretical. On this front, it's like we're pushing
back on a tide that's already on the beach. It took a while to
get here, but our case has plenty of merits, and we're not without strategy.

We plan to leverage the controversy from edge-use cases over the
years. The few cases involving minors; the more numerous cases
involving geriatrics; the non-consensual clone of [name redacted];
the now-infamous Self-Cloner of Dubai, etc. Put simply, our
ability to obtain whole genomes so efficiently, sequence them
so economically, and synthesize (de novo) any gametic composition one might want — it has opened up far too many unethical
possibilities. And that's just in the realm of current earthly
reproduction. This is to say nothing of the dilemma of genetic
representation among the diaspora or how to use the tech in the
PODS [Portable Ova Distribution Systems]. (Thankfully, those are
debates for another day.) We need to set some guard rails here.
And based on the recent rounds of cross-talk, it looks like it
may be up to us to pull back on the reins.

All we're advocating for is compliance with the guidelines set
forth by the G2R [shorthand for the GCHG2R: the Global Commission
on Human Genetic and Reproductive Rights]. It shouldn't be this
hard a sell. Unfortunately, while it's encouraging to see our
field follow the trend of global integration and oversight on MCCs
[Matters of Collective Concern], the fact is that the G2R still
has no teeth when it comes to enforcement. We've been down this
road before on MCCs, but unfortunately this is one governing body
in which the politics haven't caught up to the science.

But, we maintain optimism. The writing is on the wall. The G2R
is still young, and these things take time. It will get there.
In the meantime, it's like a test case for whether the HDP process itself can do the right thing in the absence of extrinsic
constraints. Here goes nothing.

CHAPTER 11
FRENETIC RAVINGS
4252-08-02: UST1

"Knock it off — stop. Stop!" said Cheech, shoving back at Peel with all his insufficient might. Peel wasn't all that big a kid, but it didn't take much to be bigger than Chee-chaw.

"Aww, what's wrong, Cheech?" He had the little guy's head pinned at the end of his arm now, pressed up against the wall of the stairwell in the eastern landing at the level of the Midship. Their two paths had intersected on the landing as Cheech came into the stairs on his way to the Biome. Peel was headed nowhere in particular when he found this chance for some fun that he simply couldn't resist. In truth, it was an outlet for a terrible inadequacy he could have never articulated.

"Hee-hee-hee!" squealed Peel, sounding an awful lot like his mentor and the cause of his deep-seated discontent.

And as he was squealing, something smacked him from behind. His head flung forward and bashed the wall above Cheech's shoulder. For once, Cheech was lucky to have his unfortunate stature.

"Ahhhhh," groaned Peel, turning as soon as the vision flooded back to his brain. "What the heck?" he shouted, only to find himself face-to-chest with Chop-char. "Oh, uhh," he stammered, and then asked far more softly. "What the heck?"

Cheech shoved Peel from behind to wedge himself away from the wall, his bravado roused by the presence of a rescue party. He hit him with all his might, and Peel leaned forward slightly from the force, still confronted by Chop-char.

"I told you once already. This makes twice. I see you mess with Cheech again, you won't be walking away. You got it?" He jabbed him hard with a finger in the shoulder.

Peel slinked around him on the landing, never breaking eye contact. But neither did he agree to the terms.

"Yeah, get out of here," said Cheech.

"Whatever, Freak," snapped Peel as he skittered up the stairs. Chop lunged and grunted after him, and Peel scooted even faster out of sight.

"Sorry," said Chop. "You okay?"

"Yeah," said Cheech, trying to muster as much composure as he could. But he sniffled a little, and the longer Chop waited for him to finish, the clearer it became that the constant harassment was weighing on the little guy.

"Ah, you're alright," said Chop, and he gently slapped him on the shoulder. "You're tough enough. Don't let them get to you. And if they do, you just come find me, or one of the others."

"Right … one of the others."

"What?"

"Well, let's see. They couldn't care less what Dee and Faingo have to say. Pop is just as likely to worry about their feelings while they're busy knocking me down. Plashy hardly gives me the time of day, and Potch is too busy obsessing over Potch."

"It's not as bad as all that," said Chop, and he mostly believed the reassurance. "And Tor's got your back."

"Great. If I'm ever in mortal peril in the Lounge, I'm sure he'd be willing to mutter something about knocking it off, so long as he doesn't have to pull his eyes from the screen."

"Well fine. You come find me." Cheech sniffled a second time, but he nodded and straightened himself up. "Where you headed anyway? I've got nothing going for the rest of UST."

"Heading down to the Biome. Thought I'd check on Potch-o."

"Ah," said Chop. He looked down the stairwell a moment. "Okay, well … have fun with that. You feel like doing … just about anything else, I'll be up in the Lounge."

And with that, his bodyguard sauntered up the stairs and left him to the unsavory task of socializing with Potch — an activity that even Potch himself would have been happy to do without.

"Gee, thanks for the company," said Cheech, but they parted ways and he headed down the stairs.

As Cheech strolled through the overhanging vines leading to Potch's not-so-secret sanctuary — a path that every other cadet needed to duck to navigate these days — he rounded the corner at the final concealing bush … and found an empty hideaway.

"Hey Potch," he shouted back out to the center of the Biome, but only echoes returned. "POTCH-Y," he shouted louder, stressing both syllables. The echoes came back two-fold this time, but still they were all that there was. "That's weird," said Cheech softly now.

In each their own way, they were creatures of habit, and Potch's habits were just about the most predictable of the lot. He turned back to the shelter. There was no Potch, but a small and strange object was on the ground, only a single corner visible around the side of the rock, as if it had been stashed around the side of it, safely away from unsanctioned eyes. Cheech glanced back over both shoulders, shouted one more time, received no reply, and dipped into the hiding spot.

He picked up the book, his brow furrowed in complete confusion. He knew they had at one point existed of course, but he had never before seen a physical book. The cover was soft and grippy, its weight immensely satisfying in the young boy's hands. He turned it over, inspecting both sides, but they were both jet black and equally unoccupied.

When he got over his shock, he flipped the cover open — or at least he thought it was the cover. He didn't really know how to do this. Which way was up and which way was down? What was the front and what was the back? In a way, it didn't matter: fronts and backs and tops and bottoms mattered little in this notebook, for its author had little such frame of reference. Mad scrawling filled every square centimeter, often in entirely different directions, and often barely legible.

Compared to the monospaced font of the consoles that had formed much of the basis of their worldly experience, it was a mess. Cheech struggled with most of the letters, painstakingly putting the pieces of this puzzle together, one small snippet at a time as he flipped and turned and inspected the book where he knelt in Potch's hideaway.

"NoT THE wHoLE sToRy…" began one long rant, but despite the fervor with which the ranter was ranting, Cheech couldn't deduce what it was that he was ranting about. "WHo ARE THEy To DEcIDE?" it ended. Cheech flipped and rotated pages, glancing back over his shoulder nervously. "AT LEAsT EIGHT LEvELs," stated one scrawling; "o-sEcToR LSS," read another, next to "BIomE = BAcK DooR"; and, "DcI oNLy DowN at sLP2."

There were hardly any full thoughts, at least as far as another mind could deduce. And the phrases were arcane enough that Cheech couldn't make heads or tails of them any more than he could make tops or bottoms of the book itself. He shut the notebook suddenly and slid it back around the rock where it had been. But as he rose and began to walk away, he stopped.

He waited a moment, listening. The Biome was silent.

Uncertain of his own motivations, he sprang back into the shelter, grabbed the book a second time, and tucked it into his jumpsuit. Pulling the zipper back up and making sure the payload was secure, he sprang back to the path and scrambled through the vines. As he followed the usual trail to the stairwell of choice, he took an unexpected turn at the goumis and headed for a lesser-traveled set of stairs.

Date: 2277-05-18-EY
Area: H(BOPT)
Team: Cicadas [H-2PMF56B]
Item: Temporal Optimization

Entry: A speedy update, as we're late into the night and well behind schedule. We've made progress on our variation for Initiation sequences post-deployment, but there is much left to do. The numbers per sequence have been set for several cycles, balancing population, environmental and ergonomic constraints nicely (by all accounts but the staunchest holdouts). As space is the largest limiting factor, we'll instead use time to our advantage. The schedule is arbitrary anyway, with no natural L:D cycle to limit activity, so it simply makes sense to phase-shift activity for different subsets of the crew. We have yet to finalize an exact number of temporal groups, as it depends on our present modeling (see below), but opinions range from as few as four to as many as twelve.

Our last major challenge for this round of variation is optimizing inter-block flow to avoid congestion. Of course, this is hard when we don't have one set schedule but many. We're still in the midst of optimizing temporospatial stagger for all permutations, but time is ironically against us in this case. Capitalizing on spatial redundancy and routing through different cardinal points have been helpful, but it's a complicated puzzle and we're still not nearly as close to a solidified proposal as we need to be, with selection as close as it is.

This was an "easy" problem compared to others in the project, so the cycle was initially set to be shorter than most. Unfortunately for us, the ease of these problems is a highly relative construct. [Dr. Effia] Amadou is from Benin, and her catchphrase caught on early enough with the team to become a motto of sorts for the cycle: "C'est la vie de HDP."

I hope our cadets enjoy their siestas someday far off in those faraway stars. We could use one ourselves about now…

CHAPTER 12

THE OUTSIDER OF OUTSIDERS

4252-08-02: UST1

"Knock it off," said Squeal. It was another UST1, and like almost all of them before, Peel had taken it upon himself to see what she was doing. "Don't you have something to do?"

"Not really," said Peel, and that was the problem. There was nowhere else to go, and the one place he belonged didn't want him there at all. She never did.

"Well can't you just be quiet at least, I'm trying to read!"

This, her most scandalous secret, was how she spent most of her free time. It all came so easily to the others, she lamented in her moments of silence and its accompanying despair — at least, the few times she could get any silence. (Peel found a way to ruin most of that with his desperate attempts at getting her attention.) And while she would never — ever — let it on in front of the others during Mind Block, the moment it was over, she was back into the fray. If she had only spent half as much effort during Mind Block itself, she might not have had this problem in the first place. But things just didn't come as quickly for her, and this quickly left her behind. And the further back she fell, the further she receded, until soon the only remaining tools at her disposal were other forms of defense mechanisms. But here she was, hitting the digital books.

Only Peel was in on her secret, and he wasn't apt to tell anyone, for there was only one whom he wanted to please. At the moment, he was darting all about in a manic bouncing, trying to get her up and away from her bed and down to the Labyrinth. Or the Lounge. Or the Flex space. Or … anywhere at all really. He just wanted to do *something*. And here she was, sulking again the minute their infrequent and insufficient time to enjoy themselves had begun. *Three hours a day*, Peel thought. Three precious hours of unstructured time in total, and she'd rather put her face in her tablet than spend a minute of it with him. She would sit here, going over that same boring old stuff they had labored over for an intolerable eternity during a previous Mind Block. He wasn't convinced that it was not done solely to spite him. In truth, that might have been part of it.

For her part, Squeal never saw the problem. He was free to do whatever he pleased. It wasn't her fault the rest of the crew wanted as little to do with him as she did — or that they all wanted to do with her, for that matter. And to that end, what else was there for her to do anyway? Like Peel's own plight, the more she tried to be included, the less she fit in. The only difference was that, for Squeal, it became all the more humiliating to her when she didn't. After a time, she mostly gave up trying. She might as well try to do something useful. Maybe someday she could prove to them that she wasn't such a waste of space. As for Peel's own comparable dilemma, he didn't have any strategy at all.

"Come on!" he said more forcefully than normal. "Aren't you bored? Let's do something. Anything!"

"I'm doing something," was all she replied, and she immediately went back to pretending she could focus.

"Yeah, the same thing you do everyday," he sniped, and Squeal looked back up over her tablet. "You're pretending to study so I'll leave you alone." This was not a tone he took with her often. "I'm sick of it," he snapped, and the mere fact that he said it was evidence that it was true.

Squeal just stared on, partly impressed he was manifesting any emotion other than playful stupidity — an act that was at least partially feigned. He glared back at her, and for a moment he was vaguely optimistic that the spell might have been shattered, that he had broken through that impenetrable and obstinate shield she continually maintained. A cruel grin slowly grew on her face, not on purpose but out of genuine cruelty, and she put her head back down and re-read the same passage for the fourth time now.

"Fine," he said, in a show of impressive commitment. He turned and slid her door forcefully along the track until it slammed against the frame and clicked itself shut. She smiled again when he'd gone, but this time it was not wholly of cruelty. This time, at least a little bit of her was impressed.

HDP

Peel moped out into the commons and over to the stairs. The others were no doubt off doing whatever it was that they did, and he gave little heed to the thought that someone might find him. He sat down on the stairs, unsure of where to go next, and like his mentor before him, shed his tears where he sat on the landing.

He gathered his composure and resumed, with some effort, the forced mask that was his carefree disposition. Down a couple of levels he ran into Chee-chaw, and his own cruel grin reappeared in an earnest and unconscious reaction of habit. The two had met at exactly the right time for Peel to need an outlet. It could not have been more perfect.

"What are you doing, Freak?" said Peel as he shoved Cheech's shoulder — lightly at first, but as Cheech ignored him and tried to push past, Peel shoved him again and much more forcefully. Peel moved to block the stairs and he soon had Cheech pinned against the wall. The little guy protested and the two bantered briefly, but before Peel knew it, something had hit him from behind. He didn't see it coming, or anything at all for a moment. His head had smashed the wall, and fairly hard, and a sudden blackness overtook his vision. His ears rang out, and when his other senses slowly seeped back in, Chop-char was staring down at him and saying something. He looked awfully serious. Peel protested instinctively, but it had happened so fast, he wasn't completely sure what he'd agreed to. Nevertheless, he'd gotten the gist of it, and had gotten chased up the stairs to boot.

Recoiling back up the very same stairs he'd descended in despair, he wandered aimlessly, in the same search for something to spend his lonely free time doing, but in a different direction. Rather than find something worthwhile so far, he had in all likelihood gotten a mild concussion, and pulled away yet another major thread in the fabric of his very strained relationships. But he wasn't heading back to Squeal, that was for sure. Thus, amazingly, he had even less of an idea of where he should go now than he'd had a few moments prior.

The next level up was the Library (5), and he had as little interest in heading there as ever. Besides, he'd be there against his will for much of the day after lunch. He kept walking, his head still pounding. The next level up was the Living Quarters (4). Not only had he just left here but that's where Squeal would still be, not to mention everyone else in all likelihood. They could surely be found in the Lounge right now, or on their way there like Chop-char had probably been doing. Both halves of Torp-char would probably be battling each other at Pong, or perhaps one of the newer discoveries that was unlocked with the opening of the ARC. Dee and Faingo would probably be chatting while the former logged and the latter philosophized, or perhaps worked on others of their myriad interests. Plashy would probably be kicking back and keeping quiet, silently judging the in-game actions of Tor and Chop. Pee-pop would probably be studying the galaxy while asking ABRAM a hundred thousand questions.

As with many days, Peel didn't feel like trying, insufficiently, to fit in. He kept on walking, all the way up the stairs until he hit a locked doorway between himself and Life Support (2). It was an important level. One might be tempted to think of it as arguably the most important level of all, but in reality the whole POD could not have survived without all of its many parts. And yet, in a physiological sense this was true: it was an important level, and therefore not one for aimless wandering. ABRAM hadn't said anything when he arrived, but Peel also never made a plea to enter. It was an important level, but that meant there wasn't much fun to be had there anyway. He turned around and kept on walking, descending back down a floor.

When he got back to the Aux level (3), he ducked out of the east stairs, still wandering aimlessly. Much of this level would not be relevant for many years (the Cargo Hold), and others were only relevant in special, usually unfortunate, circumstances (the Airlocks). One of the most amazing features of the POD could also be found on this level (the Cupolas), but Peel could never bring himself to care about the view beyond their world. What was the point in seeing things you can't touch? There was, however, Flex Space. This area was far more open than most of the POD and thus a fun place to run around and get some energy out. While not designed exclusively for exercise and entertainment, there were various kinds of sporting equipment up here for those purposes; and like some of the others, Peel was inclined to find his way here when he had nothing else to do and nowhere else to go.

Now, it just so happens that Peel had come up to Level Two on a lesser-used path. There were four sets of stairs spanning all seven levels, one in each of the four "corners." And while direction mattered little in an objective sense, in a relative sense the specific stairwell used may be more or less heavily-traveled depending on the destination. Like everything else in the POD, this traffic flow was painstakingly optimized. The POD was meant to support a thousand people and do so as efficiently as possible. Thus, different kinds of traffic that were likely to follow from related activities were often linked in terms of which stairs were most relevant across levels. This arrangement would have made little sense without methodical study and modeling (as the social architects had invested), but for those who grew up in the POD and for whom it was the only world they knew, it was as much second nature as knowing where to scratch an itch.

This matters because it was one of the many factors on which Potch had been relying to try to pull off his plan without anyone noticing. There were many others. The stars needed to align.

Unfortunately for Potch, the fates had instead conspired against him. Squeal had ignored Peel, which was predictable enough; but Peel then went on to run into Cheech and get his head smashed into the wall by Chop-char, which led him to wander out into the Aux Bay and stroll past the Airlocks on his way to the Flex Space. He was just in time to see Potch scrambling to secure his suit and prepare to disembark.

Peel stopped and stared as he walked past. Potch froze, helmet in hand, as though perhaps his witness might not see him if he could only stay perfectly still.

"What are you doing?" said Peel, and the cover was blown.

"Nothing," said Potch. "What are you doing?"

"I'm going to Flex. Why are you in a suit for doing nothing?"

"I just…"

Potch had no excuse at the ready. Despite all his strategy and worry about the stars aligning, he had not thought of a compelling one for the possibility that someone might find him in the Airlock, half-suited for a spacewalk.

"Look, I just have to check on something."

"What something?"

Potch sighed, exasperated, but he didn't have the upper hand here and he knew it.

"I want to check on that system Pop was working on the other day. Just … head to Flex and pretend you didn't see me, alright?"

"Why would I do that?" said Peel. He may not have been the most astute academic of the bunch, but like the wolves that inspired both him and his unwilling mentor, he knew weakness — he knew opportunity — when he saw it.

"What's in it for me?"

"What?" said Potch. "What are you talking about? I have work to do, go play ball or something."

"You're obviously hiding something. Why are you working on … whatever you're supposedly working on and not Pop? Why are you doing it alone?" Like a rusty old steam engine, the gears turned and turned, creaking and croaking to squeak out any kind of forward progress. "You don't want anyone to know about whatever you're up to, and I caught you right in the act! And if you don't want anyone to know, then…" — *then what?* — "…then what's in it for me?"

There was a silence. Potch hadn't even planned a compelling excuse; he certainly hadn't planned any contingencies for blackmail.

"What do you want?"

Likewise, Peel did not have an answer. What *did* he want? Most of the time, the answer there was simple enough; and still he could never attain it, with Squeal or with anyone else for that matter. He thought of her, staring over the tablet with that cruel grin, silently goading him to go away. He thought of his head banging into the wall and Chop-char looming over him. He thought of all the others, relaxing, playing, hanging out — heck, even just talking to each other in the Lounge. But here was Potch, all alone, like himself. And he had him cornered.

So what did he want?

"Let me help."

Date: 2341-10-03-EY
Area: O(HUMO(PSYC(ENRI)))
Team: Koopa-Troopas [O-3PVOZ27]
Item: Digital Enrichment Updates

Entry: Historical entertainment curation is moving along according
to schedule. The sub-sector is set to wrap up within the month, with
a final round of selection set for October 31st. By all accounts,
the whole sector is looking forward to the celebration to come
in the following month, after all protocols are finalized. The
planning committee, comprised of one member from each sub-sector
team, assures us that it should be a truly special occasion. The
rest of us only know it will be a showcase of sorts, with samples
spanning component chronology while highlighting significant contributions of each team throughout project development.

Our team is mostly putting on the finishing touches for this round,
namely with respect to binning items according to age classes and
progress assessments. Naturally, we've consulted closely with CABA
[Cognitive and Behavioral Assessment sub-sector], which is also on
schedule and has locked in protocols for all major checkpoints.
Our philosophy for releasing material has been to loosely couple
cadet progress with component chronological origin, to minimize
cognitive dissonance resulting from abrupt context switching. Other
teams have alluded to alternatives in previous rounds of cross-
talk, so it may be flagged for AI [Alternative Intelligence] input
and/or permutation. As for our part, we're actively finalizing
our draft proposal for selection [O-Cycle90E5I-PhaseV-P5LQL.tl].

As a personal update, we're all excited to be involved in the completion of the sub-sector. Our mole on the celebration committee
tells us that she has already assured a clandestine reference to
our namesake. We'll see how many make the connection. A few more
Team Log entries to go before we wrap and break off to work on
who-knows-what. Here's to the home stretch!

CHAPTER 13

A Legend in the Lounge

4252-08-02: UST1

Chop-char rolled into the Lounge, a bit late to the gathering party, as far as Tor was concerned.

"There you are," he said. "Where've you been? I'm dying to try this thing out!"

"Calm down, there's plenty of time for me to crush you." The boast was commonplace, but not consistent with the scoreboard. Chop knew it as well as anyone, but — perhaps because of that — he also didn't care quite as much as Tor did.

"Right," said Tor, but he refrained from boasting as best he could. The others always piled on him when he did, and peer pressure need not only ever be for ill.

Perhaps even more to the point, they were embarking into uncharted territory. Planning Block was intended for each cadet, or for subsets of them, to make an action plan for their day: what they hoped to accomplish — correction: what they *planned* to accomplish — in the respective structured blocks of the day. In this way, ABRAM could track their progress and hold them accountable during subsequent check-ins. The planning session was usually productive enough, but after the events of yesterday's big reveal, today was no ordinary day. Each cadet had their own set of priorities, but for Tor and Chop-char the promise of new technologies had been all they were able to focus on.

"New games?" they had asked in unison; and while ABRAM was committed to reminding them of the practically limitless other potential, it was likewise bound to answer questions truthfully (if it could). Very soon, the list of new titles spanning well into the 24th century occupied the remainder of their planning.

Fair enough, thought ABRAM, for it had its own plans for Mind Block on this day, as it did on certain days.

Back in the Lounge of the present, Tor had the list open on his tablet, and he'd been scrolling through the synopses incessantly as he'd waited for Chop to arrive.

"Where do we even begin?" he said, both joyous and hopeful, as if overcome with worldly delights that were theirs to savor for ages, if a little unsure whether they had the physiological capacity to do so sufficiently.

"At the beginning?" said Chop.

"Yeah, call it your History lessons," jeered Plashy.

"Ooh, I like that," said Tor unironically.

"Two anthropologists, exploring the uncharted depths of the human imagination," said Dee. "In … what will it be?" She was teasing them, but far less sarcastically than Plashy had done and would continue to do. Far more than most of the unofficial in-crowd, Dee had always appreciated having the absurdity of Pong pinging away in the background. Every once in a while, she would even partake; and despite her far less practice, she would almost always beat Chop-char, whether it be that or or one of the other early games they would occasionally play. But now, they were well into the 1980's; and it was quite a revolutionary era in the particular scholarly realm of these noble scholars.

"*The Legend of Zelda* sounds fun," said Tor. "Good reviews."

"Good enough for me," said Chop.

"Oh but, wait — it looks like it's only single player," said Tor, still reading as quickly as he could. The two were stopped cold, perplexed by the dilemma.

"ABRAM: Run *The Legend of Zelda* in parallel on split-screen," said Plashy. Torp-char whipped their necks around to where she sat behind them at the back of the room. "You're welcome," she said in that humorless monotone, which in truth had its very own kind of unflinching humor. They nodded sincerely.

And just like that, they had a way to compete, and all was right in the world.

The graphics flickered on the screen — and oh, the sheer amazement! The music started up, and even Faingo was tuning in. It stirred a primal sense of adventure, present to differing degrees but yet lingering in all of them, and which mostly only ever made its way out on their adventures to the Kiva. The cadets were on the edge of their seats as two identical protagonists, competing with themselves across an inconceivable dimension, made their way into a dark cave where a strange old man warned them of something they knew inherently was true.

"It's dangerous to go alone! Take this."

The two parallel protagonists thrust their swords into the air in unison, and headed off in different directions from the cave in search of their uncertain fates.

When eventually the circular travels of the meandering heroes became redundant enough for the time being, this new normal had been adequately established and the others were contented to go back to their separate interests while the game droned on in the background.

So here they were, in the Lounge, more or less exactly as Peel had predicted. Both halves of Torp-char were battling each other, although not at Pong. Dee and Faingo were chatting while the former logged and the latter philosophized. Plashy was kicking back and keeping quiet, silently judging the in-game actions of Tor and Chop. On any other day, Pee-pop would likely have been studying the galaxy while asking ABRAM a hundred thousand questions. But today, she was oddly silent.

"Isn't that incredible?!" asked Faingo, turning to Pop.

The three amigas were seated in the booth around the table in the corner of the Lounge — their usual spot. In the center of the room was a curved but linear sitting area, aimed at the screen that took up much of the inner wall. Behind that was additional seating, aimed inward in a circle around itself for more cohesive conversations. Counter to its intended design, only Plashy occupied the circle, a position from whence she could safely lob taunts over the sofa to Torp-char while remaining appropriately aloof.

"Isn't that incredible?!" asked Faingo again, even more loudly and emphatic this time. She had been reading the poet Rumi in the original Persian, translating for others who had specialized in other tongues. The problem, which she had clearly discerned, was that her audience was less attentive than she deemed they should have been.

"What? Oh, yeah," said Pop, unsure of the details of what she was agreeing to. If Faingo thought it was incredible, it probably was.

"You're not even listening," she noticed. "What's up with you today? First, you hardly said a word during Body Block this morning, then we could hardly get you to commit to anything at Planning Block, and now you're back to being quiet. Spill it."

"What? Nothing. I'm just tired is all. I barely slept last night."

"Me either," said Faingo, but in the proudest sense. "The entire history of humanity, curated especially for us, and at our fingertips!" Indeed, she had been buzzing around her own head for much of the night, wakefully dreaming of the practically limitless knowledge that was now at her disposal.

"Well, at least some of it," said Dee-dore, disinterested.

Okay, so there were limits. But the sentiment remained: Faingo had enough information about the history of Earth to last her far beyond her literal lifetime. And yet, the thought that there was even more on the other side of those invisible restrictions was one small, anxious part of the excitement that had kept her up all night.

What else could there be? What more was there to know?

"Well yeah, but … just think about it!" She was still buzzing, and would do so for an unpredictable duration of days, if she were to ever calm down again. "What do you want to know?"

It was at least the tenth time she had asked them already this morning. And while the tablets did not provide a complete interface to search the ARC to its fullest potential — only the Library consoles sufficed for that — they could still provide fairly detailed summaries from the collections on command.

"Hmm…" hummed Dee-dore. "Who were the greatest sculptors of all time?"

All forms of creative expression were worthy in her mind, but she was particularly amazed by those which she may never get to undertake. What little geology they had on board was bound up in the Biome, and not suited for fates such as sculpting. Faingo's fingers tapped away at the tablet and translated the request verbatim.

```
Sculptors: Individual or Collective?
```

Faingo read the prompts aloud, as Dee was technically in the middle of her logging on her own tablet.

"People did that on their own?" she asked to no one in particular, genuinely shocked by the proposition.

"Sometimes, certainly," said ABRAM.

"Seems hard to be the best of anything ever if you're going it alone," said Faingo.

"Indeed," said ABRAM. *BOOP*, it pulled up the collective category on Faingo's behalf and jumped ahead to Egyptian.

```
The Egyptians created immense sculptures that lasted for many
thousands of years, and which still stand largely intact at
the time of this entry.
```

Faingo scrolled through the images of the Great Pyramids, the Sphinx, and the many other lesser-known masterpieces of these ancient masters.

"Wow!" said Dee, who by now had come around the booth to lean over Faingo's shoulder and huddle around the tablet. "These are incredible!" The inclusion of some human specimens at the time of the photographs provided some sense of scale, if entirely insufficient to convey the full majesty through such a small screen. Nevertheless, an appropriate impression had been made. Faingo continued to scroll through the brief synopsis.

Many of these works were both functional and artistic. They
were created by thousands of workers over a span of many
years, through cooperation, coercion, or both.

"Now that's a sculpture!" said Dee as the Sphinx scrolled by. "Why would anyone want to attempt this on their own?"

"Ha Ha Ha," laughed ABRAM robotically. "Most sculptures were nowhere near this scale."

"That's the point," said Dee. "Why go it alone when you could achieve something like this?"

"Why do you think?" asked ABRAM in a classic retort.

"Well, it is fun to make something yourself, I guess."

That was fair enough, and she should know better than most: much of the art she herself had created were the works of individual effort — at least, as much as anything can be the work of a single mind in such a social species. But to that end, the cadets truly did embody an entirely different paradigm than humans of those former times. How could a single person ever hope to make the list of the greatest of all time?

Faingo turned with a huge smile to gather Pop's impression, but she was still staring off in the other direction — into nothing at all, lost only in thought. Faingo's beaming smile slid downward to a frown.

"Okay, what is wrong with you?"

"What?" jumped Pee-pop. "Nothing! I told you, I'm tired. I'm just trying to make it to siesta."

It was true, if not complete. And anyway, there was no guarantee that siesta would even bring her the rest that she needed. But there were too many ears here to report what she was obsessing over, and frankly she knew far too little to be ready to report it.

What had Potch been up to? she still wondered in silence. *And come to think of it, where was he now?*

And just as she was wondering, in strode Chee-chaw to the Lounge, all alone. Like everyone other than Chop-char and Tor, she turned at the sound of him. But unlike the rest of them, in her case, Cheech was staring directly back at her. Their eyes had locked the very moment he had entered, and both of them noticed just how unsettled the other one looked.

Date: 2243-10-19-EY
Area: (O(HUMO(PSYC(EDUC(CRIT)))),P(ETHC))
Team: Minotaurs [X-EKTHBMH]
Item: Resilience Trials

Entry: We've started data analysis on the resilience trials. Trials have spanned all age classes of the first 12 years. As noted in the protocols [O-CycleVN3LY-PhaseV-UJ0P2.tl], we took a double-blind approach, as well as hot and cold teams for different experimental stages, so this is the first insight into how it actually went. Even with these safe guards in place, we shouldn't root for our hypotheses. As such, we'll call these results simply "fascinating."

See the analysis and discussion for full results [O-CycleVN-3LY-PhaseV-E2R31.tl], but in brief: the manufactured crises led to significant increases in both individual and group-level traits, compared to CEP [Control Educational Protocols] baselines. This was not true for all response variables assessed, but substantial effect sizes were shown for key traits in the prosociality ethogram and CTA [Critical Thinking Assessment]. It looks like the Space Invader Hypothesis is well supported in these trial conditions. In the face of external threats, the subjects are banding together while developing higher-order thinking skills at faster rates. "Fascinating."

Interestingly, we're also seeing stacking effects, in that sequential exposure to different crises leads to additive gains in the outcomes of interest. This is true to a point, after which there are diminishing returns, presumably due to the increasing chronic stress effects. We also see distinctive effects related to the nature of the crisis. Most crises elicited moderate gains across the measures of interest, but different scenarios sometimes led to gains in specific metrics. These effects show up in intuitive ways, given the modalities invoked by the crisis and tasks necessary to solve them — further corroboration that the documented gains are not experimental artifacts.

We have a few weeks left in the phase, including more cross-talk to come, so from here we're focusing on furthering the work in three ways: (1) expanding the diversity of scenarios to maximize the breadth and strength of outcome gains, as well as modulating (2) the severity and (3) sequencing of the crises, to establish theoretical optima that balance the ratio of positive:negative outcomes.

Even in the results obtained so far, some types and strengths of crises predict social breakdown more than others. If this approach is to ever be applied, we need to be sure (as much as that is ever possible) that we aren't doing more harm than good.

CHAPTER 14
POTCH'S PLAN

4252-08-02: UST1

"Look, no offense," said Potch. "I just have this covered, okay?"

"Not really the point, is it?" said Peel. He had the higher ground and he knew it. What he didn't know, however, was what he was signing up for. But that, also, wasn't really the point.

A few of the cadets had been plunged into their own version of turbulence by the revelation of the Rite of Passage. Peel wasn't one of them — at least not directly. He couldn't have cared less about their connection to Earth. Not really. It didn't have any practical application to their day-to-day lives, as he saw it; and he had never been into anything solely for the philosophical exercise of it. If Peel was experiencing his own set of turbulence, it was only because of whatever other turbulence had upset the balance of the POD, and pushed him past a breaking point.

"It's not about whether you need my help or not. You want me to keep it quiet, and that's my price." He was trying to be smooth and had delivered fairly flawlessly so far; but he faltered at the pause, and it led him to an unexpected confession. "I'm sick of being a second class cadet around here, alright? So you're getting my help whether you want it or not. That or I pass this on to someone who will actually care about what you're up to."

Potch rubbed his hanging forehead while gritting his teeth. Of all the companions…

"Alright, get suited up already."

"What?" said Peel in his far more normal, sheepish state. "I'm not going out there! What are you, mad?"

"Even better," said Potch. "Stay here and keep an eye out. If anybody comes, keep your cool and just … don't blow my cover, okay?"

"What if I need to get ahold of you? You'll be on the intercom?" And in asking the question, Peel came to an inexplicable piece of the plan that he hadn't considered until now. "Wait a minute, where's ABRAM? How is it okay with this?"

Potch had locked down his helmet and his whispers weren't adequately audible.

"What?" shouted Peel, and Potch rushed at him with arms waving downward. He popped his helmet off again.

"Keep quiet, would you?"

"Where's ABRAM?"

"I heard what you said. I shut it off."

"You … what?" And as the implication sank in, his shock slowly decayed into a malevolent grin — a grin which might have made Squeal proud. "How'd you do that?"

"Not for the whole ship," answered Potch to the question not asked, in avoidance of the one that had been. "Just for here, and only for a while."

"How?"

"Seriously, we don't have time. If you want to help, you need to actually *help*, and so far you're only putting this whole thing at risk. Stay here and stand guard. We won't be able to use the intercom without the system noticing."

If Potch had known he would have a commensal companion along for the ride, he may have been able to arrange it; but as things were, their cover would indeed be blown. Peel nodded, far too excited to be "helping" for him to question his asinine role. Potch clamped the helmet back down and headed for the Airlock.

The seal squeezed shut behind him in that airtight way it did, and the pressure in the lock began to pump down. It wasn't quiet, *per se*, but he could only hope that the sound wouldn't make it to the Lounge, or that the typical commotion there would cover it. Peel stared through the window with that stupid grin on his face, proud to be doing anything different, and with anyone at all. The last *WOOSH* made it known that a vacuum was attained; and in a certain sense, Potch was now outside the POD.

Undertaking the last formality, he held the safety latch with one hand and grasped the main handle with the other. Pulling both levers at once, the door popped open, and he was struck by the immediate and overwhelming juxtaposition of nothing and everything. The infinity of space stretched out before him, whizzing by at breakneck speed but seeming to stand perfectly still.

Despite a keen determination, Potch hesitated. He had never left the POD: only Pee-pop held that honor to date. While they had all received the training, it was another thing altogether to open that hatch, walk up to the edge, and step yourself willfully out into oblivion.

And unlike for Pee-pop, there would be no ABRAM to walk him through this deed. The system was on involuntary holiday, at least for this part of the ship, and it would be as little help to Potch as Peel himself.

In fact, Potch's memory of the files he had read so late at night were the only guidance on which he could rely. In any prior case, he'd have written down what he needed in his journal. But unless he were to strike gold twice in one lifetime and somehow find another pen, he would never write another word in it. As it stood, he would need to rely on himself, and only himself.

Yes, Potch was on his own; and the unending emptiness of space taunted him for that very reason — the perfect metaphor for the unending emptiness inside himself. The void glared back at him, and he was frozen.

Peel knocked on the window, looking in eagerly and wondering what the heck he was waiting for. From where he stood in an atmosphere of pressure in the safety of the POD, it was just one more simple step. (Nevermind his own reaction to the chance to go along.)

But perhaps Peel was of some help after all. Feet firmly planted, Potch spun his head at the surprise of it, and he caught sight of Peel's wide eyes and raised eyebrows glaring through the window, and it broke him from the trance. He looked back to the open door, clenched the fists gripping the handles on either side of it, and swung himself out onto the surface of the POD.

Luckily for him, Potch's memory proved its worth. Clutching the handrail, he made his way out to the very same hatch that Pee-pop had opened only two days prior. He opened it successfully, found the valve that he needed, and carried out the manual decompression he was hoping would solve all their problems — if it did anything at all.

The handle slammed down with a *SHUNK*. If anything else had happened, it sure didn't come with an awful lot of fanfare. While there was little in the way of a physical reaction, just as it *SHUNKED*, a strange sensation overtook him in his mind. *ABRAM made a point to train us on this.*

The system knew more than it was telling them.

WOOSH, closed the door and the air began to equalize. He had made it back inside. Before long, the inner Airlock door had opened, and Potch was safe and sound, relatively speaking.

"That is a really, really bad place for that," said Potch as he pulled off his helmet. And it might have been, given the need to reach it twice now in such a short span of time; but like every other aspect of their lives, the manual pressure controls were placed with absolute intentionality — be it exacting precision or dire necessity. Either way, he had done what must be done.

"What was that all about?" said Peel.

"Anybody find you?" was all Potch replied.

"No."

"Good. What time is it?" Potch was pulling off the pieces of the suit as quickly as he could, but he couldn't yet access his wrist unit. Peel looked down at his own.

"03:48," he said reluctantly.

"Good, we've got to get out of here. Isn't there something you should be doing?"

And unfortunately for Potch, he had unwittingly pressed the exact wrong button.

"No," said Peel, both angry and dejected. "No, Potch, there really isn't. But I see how it is. I find you up here … planning to blow up the POD for all I know, suiting up for a spacewalk — hiding from ABRAM! And despite all that, I help you out, stand guard for you, keep your secrets, whatever they are, all while you tell me nothing at all about what you're doing, and can't even be bothered to say so much as thanks."

"Look—"

"No," snapped Peel. "You want me to keep your secrets, you need to tell me what you're up to."

"We already had a deal," said Potch. He was only half listening while setting the suit back ever so neatly, so as to not provoke any second thoughts about where they had been left.

"Right. And I helped you, so spill it."

"There's nothing to spill."

"So you're not up to anything at all on the outside of the POD? Just out for a leisurely spacewalk for the first time in your life? Oh, and you just decided to give ABRAM a rest for this part of the day out of the goodness of your heart? You either spill it to me now, or we get the truth out of you later — together. What's it going to be?"

Potch glared at him, unmoving. Blackmailing him once was annoying enough, though there was little time to protest at the time. But that hurried frenzy was over now, and he had returned to the cool, calculating disposition with which he went about his days. And that Potch did not enjoy the prospect of forfeiting control of his affairs over to the discretion of Peel of all people.

He walked over to Peel and looked down on him with several centimeters of advantage. Other than Chop-char and Plashy, Potch could loom over whomever he needed.

"Or we could handle this another way entirely," he said, mostly bluffing. A show of strength was definitely not his usual approach and both of them knew it. But so could both of them tell that these were not exactly the usual circumstances. "We already had a deal," he stressed. "It didn't involve me telling you anything. You wanted to help. You helped. Goodbye Peel."

He walked past him and back to the lesser-traveled stairs.

"Then I wonder what ABRAM will say about this!" shouted Peel after him. For his part, Potch never let up the bluff: he kept on walking and vanished into the stairs.

Date: 2318-06-24-EY
Area: I(DATA)
Team: Alexandrians [I-H45GQDG]
Item: Consultation with MBMS

Entry: Greetings again from Maui. (Do not be jealous, but it is lovely here for humans.) We're having a blast overseeing the special unit on the evolution of AI [Alternative Intelligence]. The spiders have found the bulk of the best stuff, of course, but we don't complain. Let them do what they do best, am I right?

One of the gems unveiled today was an early opinion piece arguing for the common sense idea that what they once called "Artificial" Intelligence should be crafted in a way that complements human capabilities, instead of replicating or replacing them [De Cremer, D., & Kasparov, G. (2021). Harvard Business Review, 18:1]. Turns out, in the early days, the primary focus was on training technology to do what humans could already do quite well. Of all the dumb ideas we've uncovered in this work, this one might take top billing.

An interesting aside: the authors included a long-time World Chess Champion named Garry Kasparov. Ironically, Kasparov was arguably the first human casualty (at least on the world stage) in the battle of wits between human and computer intelligence, when he lost a chess match in a high stakes showdown with a primitive technology [the "Deep Blue" algorithm]. It's admirable he went on to think so deeply about AI in the decades to come, and to advocate for its value in such a nuanced way. Rather than succumb to humiliation or despair, he seems to have been humble enough to be genuinely inspired.

As of the latest cross-talk, the MBM [Mind Block Module] is still in development, but cadets are challenged to connect this historical debate to the premise of Complementarity in the HDP Charter [Charter_v0128.hdp], and the many ways this manifests in the diaspora: the ban on humanoid forms of AI, the minimalist approach to physical robotics in the PODS [Portable Ova Distribution System], the division of labor between the system and cadets, etc.

To think this was ever controversial. Why would we want AI to be non-synergistic, and do only what humans can already do? All this does is duplicate effort, while constraining the potential of AI in anthropomorphic ways — all just to help make humans obsolete. Naturally, the reason was laissez-faire capitalism: do what the humans do, but faster, cheaper, without those pesky human needs like bodily safety and urination. Fortunately, that toxic obsession with unfettered growth was cut out of society like the cancer that it is. Reason won the day, and we began to develop AI in ways that complemented and expanded upon human capabilities and cognition to create a synergistic symbiosis. The rest is history. And isn't history great?

CHAPTER 15
CONNECTING THE DOTS
4252-08-02: UST1 / LNCH / MIND

"There he is," said Tor. "Where've you been?"

The silence was broken, and so was Cheech's knowing stare with Pee-pop.

"Just looking for Potch."

"Well that shouldn't be hard," said Faingo.

Cheech feigned a chuckle as he finally stepped into the room. He passed Plashy in the circle by herself.

"What's he up to?" she asked in earnest.

"Oh, uhh, I didn't find him." He passed the table on his way to take up his seat beside Tor and Chop, and his eyes met one more time with Pee-pop in the back corner of the booth.

"Not down there?" said Faingo, turning inward to Pop. "Well that's a positive development."

Pee-pop forced a smile in a subconscious reaction to the optimistic face of Faingo, but when she had turned back away, Pop's own face sank back to contemplation.

"WOAH," said Cheech, just now taking note of the epic adventures — and those graphics! — playing out on the screen. "What is THIS?"

"*The Legend of Zelda,*" said Chop. "I'm crushing him."

To be fair, Chop had accrued quite a number of rupees now that he had given up all hope of ever conquering the first dungeon. Tor, meanwhile, was in the midst of battle in a second dungeon in some far off region of the map which Chop had never seen, and thus was he running low on hearts. It might have looked as though Chop-char had an advantage, when you know nothing about the true metrics of success.

"Why are there two of you?"

When Unstructured Block had passed, the crew made it through a mostly uneventful Lunch. The oddest thing was not that Potch had opted not to show, but that neither had Peel. It wasn't entirely uncommon for someone to skip out on Lunch, especially Potch if he was moping about something, but Peel had never missed a meal in his life. Surely they would each be off on their own, but the fact that both were unaccounted for did strike the others as a bit of a coincidence.

As expected, however, there was little time or motivation for anyone other than Pee-pop or Cheech to think too deeply about it. Squeal was frankly just happy that Peel had evidently decided to take his melodrama elsewhere and give her some peace for once, if melodramatic he needed to be. The others were either reliving their on-screen adventures or entirely overpowered by Faingo's obsessive use of the ARC. Like a black hole of academic productivity, the latter pulled most of the conversation into her own explorations.

Topics ranged from the nomadic peoples of the Scythian Empire (of whom their historical studies so far had not yet disclosed); the various forms of silver minerals (and there were many); geometrical homography as it pertains to computer vision (they didn't fully understand it); the various thrushes of the world (not to be confused with the fungal condition of the mouth); and the 18th century Scottish game of "high jinks" (the description of which was vague enough to be considered age-appropriate).

There would be time enough for that at Mind Block, one might think, but who knows what ABRAM had in store for them today? Best to take advantage of the time you have, thought Faingo; and it was far too new a power for her to let it sit idle for long.

But now, Lunch was over. The cadets meandered out of the Mess and made their way to the Dorm for a siesta before the second half of the day. Six cadets funneled out in stages, but Cheech and Pee-pop lingered longest of all.

"So, you couldn't find Potch, huh?" she finally asked him, now that they had a modicum of privacy.

"Nope," said Cheech. At the moment, he didn't have any reason to suspect that Pee-pop suspected anything unusual. As far as Cheech knew, he had made a lone observation. If he'd sent any unspoken hints Pee-pop's way, it was only because that's what you did when things went awry. "He wasn't in his usual spot, so I headed back up."

And instead of saying anything more, he unzipped his standard issue jumpsuit just enough to lean the journal out of the opening. He raised his eyebrows as high as Pop had ever seen them, and she picked up the signal well enough.

A modicum of privacy, maybe; but ABRAM would be listening, and both of them knew it. It's not that either wanted to actively hide anything from the system, but neither of them knew quite enough about their independent observations to feel comfortable voicing their concerns formally — and it would surely become a formal affair once ABRAM got involved.

They might have asked it what it knew of Potch's strange behavior of late — and it certainly knew things. They might have asked it of his whereabouts at UST1 and now again at LNCH. Heck, they could have asked it what his heart rate was. But they knew these questions would be pointless, even if they did want to bring the system into it. While ABRAM interacted with anyone and everyone, almost anywhere and everywhere, it also had a stringent code of ethics pertaining to when and how it got involved, along with what it shared and to whom. They may not have known much privacy from ABRAM, but they knew it from each other; and ABRAM was as trusted a confidant as they come, whether they knew it or not.

Indeed, much that occurred on the POD was detected and logged, but much of it also stayed between ABRAM and only those parties involved. This of course depended on the nature of the information, and so much of what they did was done in groups of varying sizes. ABRAM may not have spread their gossip, but they certainly did so to each other. This was not unexpected by the architects; in fact a great deal of their research had caused them to bank on just that sort of ancient social interaction to maintain group cohesion and establish social norms.

And while the system had an astonishing amount of sensory capability, it was not entirely omniscient. It had cameras in the major functional spaces of the POD, but not every corner. Many of the alleyways were between regions of its vision, and the stairs were entirely free of it. Likewise, there were microphones (and speakers) distributed throughout most of the POD, but there were other spaces where — if they were aware of it — the cadets could get away with a quiet conversation and ABRAM would be none the wiser of whatever had been said. The best of all of these was the Biome, given the height of the ceiling and its full width being taken up by the wilderness. Down there, the biological reigned.

Again, this glaring design flaw was, in fact, not an oversight. If humans were to live with an advanced technological cognition as their only authority, they would also need ways to develop their own appropriate autonomy. Like every other aspect of ABRAM's development, the trials had proven as much.

Importantly, all of this speaks only of the system's native functionality. As a few of the others had learned — in different ways and to differing degrees — there were other opportunities entirely.

Pee-pop cast a shifty look of side-eye to nothing in particular, as she did when she was thinking, then looked Cheech straight in the eye again and nodded ever so slightly. Reared together since artificial parturition, as all of them had been, words were not always needed. The same went for their relationship with

ABRAM, the only parent they had ever known. It knew them better than they knew themselves; and likewise, they knew it far better than it knew.

Cheech had already slid the journal back and zipped up his jumpsuit, for all Pop had needed was a glimpse of it to know he had something she needed to see. In the same sense, Cheech knew that she had gotten the message and that, while he didn't know how or when, she would find a time for them to talk.

SLP1 and MIND blocks came and went without much of a fanfare, despite this being the first day of their momentous new era. Not counting the slight increase in eye contact between Cheech and Pop and Potch — which the latter certainly noticed — it had otherwise seemed like a fairly normal day, on the surface of things.

A large chunk of every day, Mind Block was the time when much of the hard work that comes with cognitive development got done. At this pivotal stage, there was plenty of that to be doing. Today, ABRAM did have a special agenda, but its contents were fairly mundane, compared to the life-altering revelations of a day before. In contrast, today involved the largely monotonous work of connecting the dots of their recent history curriculum to the early origins of HDP. This was a large endeavor that would span several days; on this first day, the emphasis was on the sociopolitical and technological solutions employed to stabilize a world cast into chaos at the fateful outset of the 21st century.

It may have seemed a bit scattered to the cadets, but in reality ABRAM's timing had been perfect. Having left off at the verge of great cataclysm, and then having received their first official Briefing, they would now pick up at the beginning of the events that would become the Human Dispersal Project.

Even this narrower exercise could have taken many Mind Blocks, but there would be time for greater detail later. Now that they'd been officially briefed, the system made a priority of getting the cadets up to speed by filling in the missing pieces of their own collective story. Thus, today's overview was a bit more didactic than normal, and a bit more superficial than it would ultimately become.

In broad strokes, none of these historical solutions were all that surprising. What made it impressive was not the ingenuity of their invention, but that people simply managed to pull it off. For all their political, economic, technological, ecological, or any other forms of crises, ultimately their problem was a social one. If they could only figure out how to cooperate, everything else would fall perfectly in line. Lucky for humanity, that is precisely what had happened.

Thanks to the curriculum of the last few weeks, the cadets knew a great deal about the many troubling issues of those times. So were they well primed to learn what emerged out of that primordial madness to manifest their current reality. The problem was multifaceted, and yet amazingly simple.

On the scale of individuals, life had been battled as a zero sum game, for that is the way the gameboard had been set — every person, every business, every interest for itself. And as the sheep behave, so goes the flock. Or perhaps it was that the flock had only learned to emulate their shepherds, while the shepherds simply knew no better than the smartest of the sheep. Whatever the case, there was one rule, and one rule only: greed was good.

On the global scale, the same toxic individualism that had run rampant within societies had also played out in the international relationships among sovereign states. With respect to every set of problems, it was every nation for itself.

And across those various scales, there were surely a great many problems. Many had existed in some form or another for many years, perhaps even as long as humanity itself. But at this particular juncture, there was also a catalyst. The increasing power and availability of technology had enhanced life in many ways, and had even made it more equitable in some of them. At the same time, it had exacerbated a great many of those preexisting problems. Technology — or rather, the way humans had used it — had been partially to blame for the pressing double-whammy of the growing socioeconomic disparity and looming ecological catastrophe.

So what changed?

As for what changed in practice, again it was ironically simple. All it took was reform. For so long, many of the governing bodies of the world had ruled by the principle of stalemate. If nothing got done, nothing bad could ever happen, it might have seemed. Of course the reality is that the world is always changing, whether we like it or not, and we either evolve with it or perish.

But as for *why* it changed, the cadets could no doubt tell you that this is a matter as much up for debate as the nuances of the Great Backslide in the first place. One compelling idea, however, has persisted through the archives and emerged as a consensus of sorts.

Of all the threats of this era, only one proved truly existential. The Earth was getting hotter, and every passing season made this plainer and plainer to see, regardless of geography. Every respectable scholar and citizen — that is, every one of them without an ideological or economic conflict of interest — agreed on the issue. They even agreed on a lot of the details, though many of those were consistently underestimated in terms of severity. But the beauty of science is that it is a self-correcting enterprise, and the picture was getting clearer, if bleak.

Large regions of the Earth would soon prove uninhabitable. That would pose unprecedented problems on its own, especially considering how ill-equipped the sociopolitical systems of the time had been to deal with such a stressor. It was becoming increasingly apparent that the world was likely heading for a humanitarian crisis on a scale never before seen since any species one might properly call Human walked the Earth. Yes, the displacement would be truly, truly bad.

But if things continued to get worse instead of getting better? Now the dilemma began to flirt with the unthinkable. And yet it should not have been unthinkable: survival is guaranteed for no species, and never has been. It was only unthinkable for a species as arrogant as *Homo sapiens.* For all their eponymous wisdom, it took an awful lot for them to see the writing on the wall.

But there was hope in this story. Or if hope is not to your liking, there was still a possibility. And the very thing that threatened to exterminate them may well have been the one thing that served up their salvation. The potential for shared annihilation was the one thing on Earth that every human could agree about. It need not have taken an external threat to establish a cooperative collective — but that's what it had taken in practice.

Of course, the cadets received a much more detailed overview of the facts of the case. Such a high-level synthesis as this was just the sort of thing ABRAM would be expecting of them later. For today, they had gotten many of the details as they originally looked from on the ground. One cannot provide a synthesis without the pieces of the puzzle.

They learned of the Climate Accord of 2032, which got right what so many comparable efforts had gotten wrong. They learned of the Rapid Course-Correction, the Great Sequestration, and the Ocean Buffer Project. They learned of the Global Council of 2047, which left the United Nations barely recognizable and far more effective. They learned of the Human Equity Commission, which built on the Universal Declaration of Human Rights. They learned of the International Tax Rate and Global Basic Income Initiative. They learned of Semantic Breakthrough and the AI Symbiosis Summit. They learned of these landmark achievements, and many more besides. They learned how culture and climate alike had not only been stabilized, but actively equilibrated. Like a well-tuned thermostat, humans needed only to flick a switch and they could restore a stable state, if these inherently chaotic systems should begin to stray a bit too far. Above all, they learned how the Wise Ape, as it was named, had learned to cheat death yet one more time.

So had the pieces of the puzzle begun to fall into their proper place for this ragtag crew of cadets, thousands of years — but only one generation — removed from the civilization that beget them. Over the coming days, they would learn the details of the Human Dispersal Project itself, ABRAM had assured them.

But even as of yesterday, they at least knew the premise. Humanity had rallied, against all odds, and attained a degree of harmony many thought would never be possible. And while many tears had fallen, they had done it largely without bloodshed. Humanity had evolved. They had transcended.

But in transcending, they had evidently longed for more than mere survival. They had evidently longed for immortality. They had longed to live among the many stars — no longer content to simply be made of the very same essence. So, flitting from one triumph to another, they had envisioned a way to spread their ingenious achievement out into the cosmos.

As for the crew of the Concordis, they were descended from this great collective effort of humanity, certainly; but they were not of it. Not truly. This was not Earth, and they were not quite humanity but the mere potential for it — a set of seeds blown into the wind. And it was exactly this realization that Potch had been pondering ever since he had first learned the truth.

- -
Date: 2316-11-06-EY
Area: I(DATA)
Team: Bookworms [I-EP6TOTX]
Item: ARC Curation Update

Entry: Things are still going well with curation. Our approval
has been mostly smooth and the accrual rate steady. The team is
working well together, though I suppose we can only take so much
of the credit for the progress. Still, it hasn't been nearly as
mindless as we feared. The bots may do the heavy lifting, but we
have the fun of trying to navigate it all with these measly human
brains. We've found a lot of room for improvement, actually. We
keep trying to tell them they need to think like a human. That's
the whole point of the tablets! I guess they struggle with that
as much as we do the other way around.

The slowest part has been restrictions, which require both horizontal and vertical consensus. And it's often trickier than
we expected. It's funny how few clicks it can sometimes take
to wind your way into questionable territory. Then there's the
question as to what constitutes 'questionable' to begin with. We
were happy to leave that debate in the last cycle [see I-Cycle-
H6ILB-PhaseS-R0KFR.tl]. Now it's all about vetting the automation
and adjusting occasional boundaries for the sake of retraining
the curators.

In that sense, it's the same thing every day: they scrape, index,
cross-reference, convert to the new user interface, and repeat ad
infinitum; we test graphs, verify against the protocol, adjust
permissions when needed, run it up and down the chain of command;
then they loop back in their invisible way and tidy it all up.
Quite a partnership. Then there's the permutations on all of it,
but at least that's largely automated. Bit of a headache that,
if you ask this measly human brain.

Actually, it isn't as monotonous as it seems because it's always
something new. Just today, I learned how King Gustav III of Sweden
staged a false attack on his own army to con his country into war
with Russia, allegedly because he couldn't consummate his mar-
riage after nine years of trying! (We approved the first half for
Challengers; the latter was labeled unsubstantiated.) Wild stuff.

Anyway…

Forward and onward, into the Great Known.

CHAPTER 16
NIGHTLY ESPIONAGE
4252-08-01: SLP2

It was late and Potch would have to hurry. How could he have let himself fall asleep like that? Perhaps his double life was finally catching up with him after so long at this game. He was groggy, having jolted upward in a panic from the depths of his unconsciousness. He checked his wrist: there was still time, but he would need to act fast.

He slid open his door, quickly checked the hallway, and slid it shut behind him while his feet never stopped. It was a routine he had practically mastered by now, but tonight he wasn't quite on his game. On this particular night, he could have done with a bit more force. Of course, he didn't want to slam the thing and send any unexpected sounds bouncing down the dormitory hallways. But in his haste, he had come up just shy, and the door was left open a pinch.

He made it down to the Library without any issues. ABRAM would be out for about thirty more minutes. It didn't leave an awful lot of time for exploration, but no matter. Tonight, he had a target.

TAP TAP TAP, went the keys of the console in his favorite location. He'd mapped out the perfect path to minimize both distance and exposure, and it put him out right near this specific breakout room.

"Come on..." said Potch, as the system was searching. There was hardly any delay — impressive for the size of its database — but every microsecond was precious time that his fingers could have been tapping.

And then *BOOP*, there it was.

```
./Protocol-194231_Briefing-0001.txt
```

No need to open the underlying text, he knew. He had read it line for line, word for word, and more than once. This time, he needed a peek behind the curtain. It steered him to the program of the same name, but of a different suffix

(.exc), though this was risky business. Running it properly would launch the full interface, likely waking ABRAM and causing some cognitive dissonance for the poor sleepy thing. Far worse, he would need to explain himself. But how to lift the curtain without waking the wizard behind it? He had some ideas, even a standard operating procedure of sorts for this kind of sleuthing; but he was also clever enough to know how much he didn't know. Usually.

TAP TAP TAP. He scrunched his face.

"Come on…" he chided again, as if the infrastructure in which he was snooping was some stubborn old beast who wouldn't do as it was told. Again he tapped, but the screen wouldn't budge. It beeped softly, but obstinately, and refreshed to the same exact stalemate.

"Come on!" he said, and imprudently loudly. A dim echo dashed around the curves of the library hallways. Lucky for him, there was no one there to hear it.

TAP TAP TAP, he smashed; and at last, like the winning of a jackpot, he had a hit. Letters and numbers scrolled rapidly across the screen, far faster than he could read them. His eyes widened, but his grin grew even wider, until the flashing of characters finally came to a halt.

He scoured the program's guts as quickly as he could. Boilerplate mostly: fairly typical stuff, and all fairly intelligible. He careened his view up and down the console with a sequence of taps, jumping leaps and bounds with every button press. His eyes kept up remarkably well. Ins and outs, hashes and dashes, arrays and executables, but nothing out of the ordinary.

And then, there it was: a hunch.

TAP TAP, and he followed the thread. Through indices, down subroutines, and into the heart of the matter. Sure enough, the Rite of Passage had been presented to the cadets in its full and proper form. He was sure it wouldn't be the case — but it was. He had it on the good authority of the very bits before him, and that was that. Yet, one rather small thing didn't sit right with him.

The text was rendered verbatim — straight from the authors' pens — but for two small details: the date, and the crew. They were variable calls.

That much was clear, but the syntax didn't make immediate sense. Beyond that, the connections were routed through layers of layers. He tried tracing the breadcrumbs the best that he could, but in the end he would either end up back in the beginning or tumbling aimlessly down through an infinite vortex. It wasn't quite possible to get *There* straight from *Here,* at least not in a hurry; but he'd learned enough relevant buzzwords so as to try another angle on it.

But why the variables? he wondered. What did the date and crew variables have to do with whatever message the past felt compelled to share, first of any, with their future? The date made sense enough, he supposed: ABRAM had said the timing of the Rite was contingent on other assessments, whatever those were. *I could look,* he realized. Though perhaps it didn't matter, or at least not right now. It did, however, lead him to the even more intriguing question of how many earlier briefings had been held back, for failure to meet these invisible benchmarks.

This was allegedly the first of several, and to their credit it was listed as Briefing 0001 — yet another piece of the official story that annoyingly checked out. But might the crew have had it sooner? And what other top secret briefings came next, hidden from them purposely until they could prove themselves in some uncertain way on some uncertain date? *I could check those too, if I had time.*

But for tonight, even more than most, that was the precious commodity. One tiny drip and drab of information at a time. That's all there was ever time for, in practice. That's how it had been, and tonight was different only in that the coveted flow of answers was even more tightly constrained. And right when he was onto something too. *Perfect night to oversleep,* he chastised himself again.

He checked his watch: T-minus 14 minutes. How best to use that precious time, until the grueling anxiety of another passing day would lay between him and the next iteration of answers? As much as the timing was interesting, it wasn't the path on which he'd detected the scent. It wasn't nearly as alluring as the second of those variables.

What did the crew have to do with it?

There was only one way to find out, but it wasn't exactly easy to find. He had an educated guess as to what it was, but he didn't know how it would be stored in the system.

With every *TAP TAP TAP,* he tried one iteration after another. And with every failed search and the subsequent microseconds of delay, his frustration mounted up a notch.

At last, like the winning of a second lottery, he had a hit. Or rather, he'd had a lot of hits, but none that had showed any real promise. Until this one, that is. His eyes scoured the list of returns, stopped on a dime, and widened with a mix of excitement and apprehension.

```
./Protocol-3468912_POD_Permutation.hdp
```

As for exactly why this had been a hit, he couldn't say — that would take a bit more tapping — but the name intrigued him enough to warrant the gamble. He had no idea how much time had passed, nor did he stop to wonder, so swept up was he in his hunting.

TAP TAP TAP, he went to open it — but then he heard the sound.

What was that? he asked himself silently, and there were few explanations he could manifest to rationalize it. Then he heard it again, and clearly enough that he could toss out many alternate hypotheses. *Sounds like a person.*

He checked his wrist: only a few minutes before ABRAM would be up. In a way, the surprise was a blessing. He was very likely to have gotten entirely lost in indulging this burning curiosity, and the jolt had snapped him from the daze.

He stared back at the screen, his heart torn. His eyes squinted, glaring at the display with an inexplicable menace, committing that vile filename to memory. Every future tap saved would bring him that much closer to his goal.

He peeked his head out into the hallway and waited. It was very quiet, but for the occasional sounds of feet shuffling along the floor. At least he wasn't going mad: someone was definitely down here. He took his chance and ran as quickly and quietly as he could toward the stairs. Leaping up more than one at a time, he made his way up two floors as quickly as he had ever done so — riddle races included — and back to his room. He noticed the door was still ajar but didn't think much of it. He wrapped his fingers around the edge, slid it just enough to sneak in, and closed it carefully behind him once he had slipped through the door.

He turned back to face his room and took a deep, cooling breath. There was a brief moment of silence in which all remained still.

3-4-6, 8-9, 1-2, he repeated in his mind, but he could only keep up such a game so long. It was only a matter of time before those other pesky, uninvited numbers showed up and started shouting loudly over the ones he was actually trying to remember. *I need to write this down!*

He opened the topmost of his drawers and reached his hands under the soft layer of clothes concealing it. It was his most illicit secret — at least of those that were material — and he needed it now more than most nights. He swept his hand back and forth beneath the socks, and then paused. He traced the edges of the drawer, but to no avail. He plunged his face down into the drawer itself and rummaged through the contents.

There wasn't much on the shelf by the bed, only a picture of the Earth from all sides, next to his earphones, tablet, and standard issue plushy. The unnamed octopus glared at him, no doubt angry and hurt after years of disuse and dismissal. He took no more heed of its feelings than ever, hastily sliding these meager possessions left and right in an illogical search for the only item that he needed. He turned to his bed and lifted the pillow in a frenzy; he traced his hand under the mattress, then flung it upward to a tilt. But it was no use. It wasn't here.

He let the mattress fall back down with a thud. His heart raced and he was sweating, and not only from his sprint back to safety. The octopus still glared in silent judgement, from on its side down on the floor. He glared back with the very same sentiments, every bit as much of an enigma of the deep.

And then he remembered the inkless pen he had hurled across his shelter. He knew exactly where his journal was, and how little it would help him if he had it. He cursed his own stupidity. Panic, angst, and sleep deprivation will get the best of human minds every time.

"Potch, what are you doing awake?" asked the system, returning from its own brief hour of slumber. "Your heart is racing. Is everything alright?"

"Oh, yeah. I just couldn't sleep."

That was very, very close.

"I see. Would you like some pink noise?"

It worked better for him than anything else — not like those childish songs or stories so many of the others would want ABRAM to sing or speak to them in the comfort of their rooms, out of sight of any others. For Potch, sheer static was all he ever wanted. Wrapped up in his bunk, eyes closed, the sounds of a consistent churning chaos pouring in through his ears and drowning every other sense — it was the closest thing to all that he often wanted: total isolation.

"Oh…" he said, thinking of other things entirely. "Sure. Thanks."

He got back in his bed. The sheets were nice and cool. He slipped on the earphone band and took the plunge into that sea of dissonance.

But in his coveted isolation, his thoughts remained as the only things left, and still they pestered him. There could be no peace. He hadn't found what he'd been looking for over the course of many days now. But he had found something. *If I only had more time!* Again he chastised himself for falling asleep. How could he have given in to such a basic need? (Nevermind that even ABRAM could not escape at least a little of this fundamental mechanism.) It had set him back a whole other night, essentially. And yet, he had found … something.

3-4-6, 8-9, 1-2, he repeated to himself, silent in the sea of static. *3-4-6, 8-9, 1-2.*

Over and over, the numbers repeated, serenading himself better than ABRAM could ever have done. Slowly, that inner voice grew dimmer as the static grew steadily louder, until it was swallowed under the waves like the rest of his consciousness, and there was nothing left but blackness.

Date: 2169-05-15-EY
Area: P(COOP,ASMT)
Team: Integrators [P-4W094IX]
Item: Final Thoughts on HDP Integrate Hub

Entry: We are rounding out our one-year review of HDP's incorporation into the existing global Integrate system. Our report is
almost complete [see P-CycleVNE3W-PhaseY-S5O4U.tl], and at this
point we're mostly fine-tuning the presentation of findings. The
general impression is that our expected outcomes have all been met
or exceeded, as validated through multimodal assessments across
all sectors [see prior link for full metrics and results].

Many RB [Review Board] members have had prior experience with
ISSIAH [International Society for Scientific Integration, Advancement, and Historicity], including direct use of their flagship GAI
[Generalized Alternative Intelligence, implying the aforementioned
"Integrate" system in this case]. Naturally, many HDP researchers have used it independently for years, in their work prior to
HDP formation. Their positive experiences, while anecdotal, have
now been confirmed with intensive scrutiny: the system is excellent. The human interface and direct incorporation of scientific
instrumentation make its use practically effortless; data storage
and recall are effective and efficient; it conducts impressive
meta-analyses and makes relevant connections both within and among
sectors; it generates testable and high-priority questions; its
hypotheses are well-founded and properly weighted; its experimental designs are rigorous, and those it can carry out directly
are done with staggering reproducibility; its interpretations are
sound, the system clearly flagging sources of uncertainty, and in
cases where it can not follow up directly on its own, its proposals for how to reduce error in the future are invaluable. It is
truly functioning as the global scientific consciousness it has
been claimed to be, and it has suited the needs of HDP perfectly.

In short, we will be recommending continued use and a shift to
full adoption for the foreseeable future. Frankly, we're incredibly impressed by how robust this system is. Confidence is high
that it will work flawlessly for the diverse and parallel scientific research threads of HDP. In addition, this will ensure the
free exchange of information to and from HDP and other global
scientific efforts, as is appropriate for the advancement of the
global good on Earth, as much as for those aimed at the stars.

We hope our colleagues will have comparable luck in terms of
feasibility and reliability with the proposed ABRAM [Automated
Biological Replication Assistance Machine] system. If it turns
out to be as robust as Integrate, success is all but guaranteed.

CHAPTER 17
An Unwanted Ally

4252-08-02: LNCH

"Woah," said Peel. It was the only fitting word and he meant it.

They were in the Library, right there, plain as day. And yet, they were nowhere to be found. Potch had made good on his word. For the moment, ABRAM was sleeping far more soundly than a baby, at least in the Library. And as far as Potch knew, it would never be the wiser.

It was a bold and ambitious move, Peel's meager blackmail, but it had come with little enough of a down payment that it was worth it to Potch. He could keep his secrets, whatever they were — or at least almost all of them. If Potch had cared enough to wonder, he might well have discerned that Peel was after things other than his secrets.

Potch was hunched over a console in yet another breakout room, albeit far from his favorite clandestine spot. (Count that among the many secrets Potch had opted to keep.) It was at the end of their prior encounter that they had agreed to meet here and now — once they had finished hashing out all of their unfinished business, that is. Amazingly, Peel had been able to keep all his beans unspilled since then.

"Just show me how you did that," Peel had said, racing after Potch.

"Did what?"

"You know," said Peel. "Shut up old ABRAM."

Potch had been in no mood to entertain the conversation any further. He had only been back inside the POD a few moments, the latest of which Peel had just spent threatening to tattle on him to the very same system. Potch had likewise threatened Peel with something else entirely. Both of their bluffs had been called.

"I didn't shut it up," said Potch. "I said I shut it off. For here, anyway."

"Right, but … how?!" he asked for the second second time.

"That's a long story and we don't have time for it."

Potch turned his back on Peel again, back to the progress he'd been making to return to the lower levels. Peel ran after him and inserted himself right before Potch, in the door-frame of the stairs.

"Look," he said, surprisingly forthcoming. "I don't like you, and you don't like me. That's fine," he resigned. "Nobody does. But I'll keep quiet about whatever the heck you were doing up here, on one condition."

"Let me guess..." said Potch.

"Show me how you did that trick with ABRAM."

Potch exhaled melodramatically.

So had the bargain been struck, and here they were: skipping Lunch, invisible in the Library.

"What was that last part?" asked Peel, though there was little hope of explication.

At every step in which he had asked Potch to elaborate or rationalize, Potch had either been unwilling or unable. If he would endeavor to answer, it was usually unintelligible, as far as Peel was concerned. Mostly, he didn't bother. "It's just … you know…," he would say, and then move on to something else. Or sometimes, "I don't know, it's just what worked." As much as Potch had schemed and strategized, he'd had equal parts luck in developing this, his most essential skill. And besides, it was a brand new discovery. He was bound to get a fuller grasp of it with even more time to experiment.

"Oh, that's key," said Potch, hoping to wrap up the lesson as neatly as his demonstration. A little elaboration might provide just enough satisfaction for Peel to accept his payment and put this charade behind them both. Besides, this was a part Potch understood in full. Perhaps he was more swept up in having a witness for his cleverness than he would have admitted. "That's where I clean up the missing sensory data. See, technically the system's still monitoring us. The cognition's just not on. The second the program stops, ABRAM would wake up immediately, with every bit of data from the time we shut it off — like it was awake with us the whole time. But, after I deleted the data, it would sense a ton of errors."

And of course, Potch had been right in this part of his scheming, worked out in a sea of pink noise: the system wouldn't know *what,* but it would know that *something* was missing. It probably wouldn't take too long to find the culprit of this discrepancy with the nosy little Potch sitting red-handed at the helm of a breakout console in a place it did not recall him being.

"So, I duplicate the data from the previous block to fill it in, and we'll be gone by the time it comes back online."

Truly, he could run the program through the rest of the block, or even automate it for whenever and wherever he desired. It was quite brilliant, actually. (No one ever said Potch wasn't brilliant, whatever else they said about him.) He could open up passageways of imperception, in time and in space, through any parts of the POD he wished, and sneak through undetected like a black cat in the shadows. He needed to time it all correctly, of course — to lay a trail of stepping stones between wherever he was coming from to wherever he wanted to go — but it had worked out well enough so far. He could pop back up at the start of the next block, and bingo: all was as it should be. Nevermind the minor mystery of the disappearing children. That Potch's status would retroactively vanish from system memory for a certain time and place was an unavoidable cost of sneaking around in this way. But that was ABRAM's problem. And, so far anyway, it had said nothing about it.

Peel just stared at the console, grasping the concept (for once) but well lost in the details.

"Anyway, there you go," said Potch. "I showed you. Take the west stairs to the dorms right on time for Siesta and you won't get caught."

"Woah woah woah—" started Peel, but Potch was already out of the console seat and onto his feet.

"No," he said firmly, cutting him off. "You said 'show me how you did that trick with ABRAM' and I just showed you. You didn't say 'teach me how to do it too.' I told you it was complicated."

"Ahh, come on, you know what—"

"Show's over," he interrupted again. And just like that, they were back in the same stalemate.

"Alright, well maybe ABRAM needs to hear about this after all," said Peel with only moderately mustered authority.

"Peel, there's no way I could teach you how to do that if we took a hundred lunches."

Peel had seen what it entailed. It was true. Others, maybe, and in less than a hundred. But not himself. Still, the more he had seen, the more entrenched he became in his desire to attain that kind of power.

And who was Potch to tell him what he could do anyway? Always sneaking off to do whatever he wanted on his own. Always putting him down. Always ignoring him completely, when he wasn't bossing him around…

No, he realized sadly. That was all somebody else.

Potch had never given two farts about what Peel was doing one way or another, but at least he had never gotten a cruel satisfaction out of that neglect. Not like Squeal. She always enjoyed every minute of his torment. But at the moment, it really didn't matter, for the very same hurts were all mingling together. If it wasn't Squeal, it would be Potch; and if it wasn't Potch, it would be literally anyone else. Who could be bothered to keep track? *Even ABRAM doesn't like me,* he had mused from time to time, not even sure if that was computationally possible — and yet it must have been. The least he could do was stick it to the system, if he couldn't stick it to the humans.

"I've got all the lunches in the world," said Peel. His voice was calmer than normal, not riddled with the boy-like desperation that was so characteristic of it. There was gravity there, and it was pulling downward, as it does.

"Yeah, well, I don't," said Potch. "Not to spend with you." Like a scripted replay of their prior encounter, he turned his back on Peel and headed for the exit. But Peel wasn't ready to give up the good fight.

"Fine, just walk away," he said with scorn. "What do I care?" Potch made a few steady steps to the door. "All I wanted was to be a part of something for once. Go back to going it alone, see where it gets you — pressing buttons in a system you don't even understand, sneaking around, hiding from ABRAM, going on spacewalks to pull your precious—"

And then it hit him all at once like a sack of jeddusch flour. It was a rare event, but Peel had been struck dumb by a moment of clever, cutting insight. Potch stopped moving, just inside the door. Déjà vu, all over again.

"It was you…" said Peel, out loud but meant mostly for himself. And then, more loudly, and directed squarely at Potch: "It was you!"

Potch had just slid open the pocket door in its track: he stopped but turned only his head. He tried to keep a steady disposition, but a genuine curiosity was piqued, partially impressed that Peel had read as much between the lines as he appeared to have been doing.

"Me what?" asked Potch, as placid as papaya.

"You — it was you! The pressure, the … whatever they called it — the anomaly. You went out to the same lever as Pee-pop, or whatever. Except you didn't want anyone to know. Not me, not Pop, and definitely not ABRAM!" He thought harder, another act Peel was not oft inclined to do. "All that messing you've been doing … you did something, didn't you? Do you even know what it was?"

Potch slid the door shut.

There was no confession. Rather, he simply turned and walked back to the room's long front table, taking a seat at one of the many chairs bolted in front of a console, in this room meant above all for collaboration.

There was a gap in Potch's armor, perhaps for the first time in history. And Peel, of all people, had found it. This staggering realization was not lost on him. Suddenly smug, he likewise made his way to the table and sat directly across from his unwitting ally.

Peel spoke with the confidence of a detective who had cracked the case at last: "You better start from the beginning."

- -

Date: 2257-01-22-EY
Area: (I(ODIS),P(ETHC))
Team: Orwellians [X-LD8ZCK2]
Item: Crew Privacy Refuges

Entry: We lost miserably, but spirits are high. There is nothing quite as satisfying as the handshakes all around at the end of the cycle. Team mates, sector friendships, bitter rivalries in vision; all are celebrated for their contributions, whatever their form, that brought the sector to its final consensus. Something is working, whatever it is. Even with the competitive mechanism at the heart of the cycle, there's a real camaraderie among teams by the end, a true respect, like Olympic athletes if they were all working to share the same medal. I've [Dr. Fedir Popov] never seen anything quite like it in all my professional life prior to getting involved in the project. I'm glad I finally did.

As for the cycle task, the sector went overwhelmingly in favor of privacy reserves. We advocated valiantly for the value of comprehensive system oversight and behavioral transparency. We had a great line in our closing statement: "If the entirety of a society's words and deeds are known, truth and honor shall win the day." Still, the moral argument triumphed with their view that humans have an inalienable right to private space. Ultimately, the consensus model leaves a handful of video-only refuges (e.g. greenhouses, wellspring), audio-only refuges (e.g. dormitories, the biome), and even some areas free of all system sensation (e.g. stairwells). Likewise, there will be major guard rails on system involvement in interpersonal dynamics, including confidentiality assurances, and cadets are to be proactively informed of the rules and limits of system engagement. We still worry that care will be needed to ensure responsible and prosocial use of these freedoms among the crew, and we plan to submit task recommendations to O-sector for future MBMs [Mind Block Modules] and SBMs [Spirit Block Modules] to support ontogeny accordingly.

Personally, it was extremely encouraging to see [Dr.] Sanjana [Chapi] argue so effectively and emphatically for our proposal during selection, despite her very strong personal objections to our team's push for comprehensive system observation. The rest of the team has nominated her for a cycle award for the way she trusted the process and put teamwork above individual opinion. This kind of selfless cooperation is the epitome of what makes HDP work. And look at that: the [sub-]sector ended up with a less intrusive model that is very similar to the one she proposed to our team during variation. May the best fit ideas win the day.

CHAPTER 18

GUESS WHO'S NOT COMING TO DINNER

4252-08-02: DINN

It wasn't the best plan. Nevertheless, she had been drawn into it, and its gears were fully in motion. Plashy hated this kind of thing.

It was soon to be Spirit Block, and they needed some cover. Of course, no individual distraction would suffice for the likes of ABRAM: everything it did, it could do in parallel, and many times over. No, this was not distraction. This was misdirection.

The plan had been "hatched" down by the chickens in the gathering phase of Dinner block, and Cheech himself had made the pun.

"Right, no, I get it," Pop had said wryly.

She'd met up with him at last, and perfectly naturally, in the surest place of all to have a conversation meant for hominids only. Not that either of these two had the slightest desire to deceive ABRAM in earnest; rather, both had converged on an independent and unspoken wish to consult with one another first, so that each might reassure the other that they were being silly — that there was nothing overly strange about their separate observations, beyond the run-of-the-mill aloofness that was typical of Potch. When Pop had finally caught Cheech by "his" chickens, and once the cards had all been laid squarely on the table, however, the facts didn't serve to comfort either of them. On the contrary, it only multiplied their paranoia that Potch was surely up to something that he didn't want anyone to know about. And if history had taught them anything, they had better do something about it and quickly.

Just as that somber sentiment had been sinking in, Plashy lumbered by, all lanky legs and arms and attitude. "Don't move so fast you two. We'd hate for you to pull a muscle." She vanished around the cluster of grapes, and it was like the very universe through which they were sailing had thrown them a splash of serendipity. If Potch had anything resembling a kindred spirit anywhere on this ship, it was Plashy.

That's when Cheech had pulled one of the few remaining eggs out of the nesting box and said, that classic grin sprawling across his self-satisfied face,"I think it's time we *hatch* a plan."

Before long, they were back in the Mess, and the plot had only thickened when Potch and Peel had failed to show — again. Skipping Lunch was one thing, and it had been very odd indeed when both of them had chosen to do so on the very same day. But skipping out on Dinner as well? That was not only doubly odd: it was a blatant dereliction of their duties. There was always a lot of cooperative work to do that went well beyond the night's dinner; and tonight there were four fewer hands to help out.

Pop and Cheech had tried to brush it off, but the others were indignant. "Where are those two?!" sniped Faingo to the system. No one expected it to rat on the deserters — that wasn't ABRAM's style — so it came as no surprise to any of them when the system merely mustered the virtual equivalent of a shrug.

Gradually, they had settled in to the meal, but the mystery of the two missing crewmates remained the main course for its entire duration. As much as they had tried to bide their time, Pop and Cheech were no longer the only ones who had begun to suspect that there was funny business afoot. Squeal herself had looked around the room expectantly, and then sadly, when she slowly came to the realization that her hanger-on would not be around to hang upon her. She had tried to hide it, but she had also spent the rest of the meal uncharacteristically quiet. Who else was there for her to talk to? (*It was quite a pleasant relief,* most of the others had reflected in silence.)

"Hey, so … ABRAM," she said.

"Yes, Plashy?"

Most of the others had filtered out by the tail end of dinner, but Cheech and Pee-pop made sure to linger. They were loading the last utensils into the wash and listening intently, taking care to provide no particular indication that they were doing so.

"I'm a bit worried about Potch."

"You are?" it said sadly. "Why is that?"

Plashy blinked a moment. It seemed fairly self-evident. He hadn't exactly been subtle about his state of mind over the last several days. Or, arguably, ever.

"Well, for one: where is he?" she said. "And you've seen him. Something's obviously been bugging him." And while it had gotten worse after their birthday, that hadn't actually been the original cause. He was prone to a fit of moping here and there throughout the years, but some unseen something had set him off again, and relatively recently. In retrospect, when any of them had really tried to pin it down, it seemed like something had soured in the run-up to their birthday. Cheech had noticed most astutely of all, which was not surprising given his inexplicable admiration for a crewmate very few had ever learned to love. And yet, somehow, it was Plashy who had been thrust reluctantly into the driver's seat of the plan, about which she was as ambivalent as everything else she had ever encountered.

"I see," said ABRAM. "Well, it's very thoughtful of you to notice."

"I'm just … worried that he … doesn't have anyone to turn to." Of course, Plashy could have taken on the initiative herself, but a heart-to-heart was never quite her cup of tea; and besides, that wasn't the mission.

"If you're concerned about Potch, why don't you go and talk to him?" it said, noticing the very same point. "It would probably mean a lot to him just to show him that you noticed."

"Ohh," she said. "No, I wouldn't know what to say."

Everything from dinner had been tidied by now, but the two other remaining cadets wiped down the area and took on a few overdue chores in an attempt to look as busy as possible. It was not unlike Pee-pop to do so, and it was not unlike Cheech to help out one of his role models if it meant he would get in some extra quality time.

"I thought, maybe…" continued Plashy just as awkwardly, "…you could talk to him?"

The system thought long and hard again for show.

"If you're concerned with him Plashy, it's really best if you talk to him yourself. You remember the Code. We all agreed. The crew would communicate openly and honestly to resolve whatever difficulties arise, and I would only intervene when absolutely necessary. You should talk to him."

"I know," she said. "He's just been so difficult lately." Plashy looked at Pop with eyes that were somehow both alarmed and accusatory at the same time. Pop likewise urged her on with the gentle use of her eyes alone. Plashy sighed that classic Plashy sigh and resumed with obvious discomfort. "You know I don't have the … patience for that kind of thing."

That much was true, at least; but neither did she tend to go out of her way to check on the welfare of others. Something was fishy, that much was for sure.

"Why doesn't someone else talk to him then?"

"We've tried," said Chee-chaw, breaking his silence. "I check on him practically every UST, but he just won't open up. Something's going on and he won't let us help."

"And the others? Have you discussed the matter with anyone else in any private conversations?"

All three shook their head sideways in unison.

"Just me and Cheech mostly," clarified Pop. Heaven forbid she tell the system anything that could be even slightly construed as an untruth.

"We asked Plashy to talk to you," said Cheech. "You know … to talk to him."

What the heck did you need me for? glared Plashy's eyes, annoyed as ever and baffled by their lack of cunning.

"If it makes you feel any better," said ABRAM, "I will check in with him personally."

"How about at Spirit Block?" said Pee-pop, and a little too quickly. "It seems as good a time as any," she said, recovering a meager illusion of spontaneity.

"Yeah," said Plashy. "Maybe we could run around or something? And you could talk to Potch for us?" Their cover had been blown, for some unnecessary reason, but she took the opportunity to get back on the script as a matter of principle.

Again the system waited. The block in question was only a few minutes out.

"Get the others," said ABRAM. "You all pick the game." It sighed. "I will talk to Potch."

If I can find him.

- -

Date: 2302-07-25-EY
Area: H(ECOS)
Team: Tanukis [H-PTD9M9J]
Item: Biome Trials 16.12

Entry: Inspection of lunar dome R9N126 revealed highly promising insights. Initial remote metrics (local sensors coupled with
HSR [Hyperspectral Remote Sensing], LiDAR [Light Detection and
Ranging], and SAR [Synthetic Aperture Radar]) indicated favorable
conditions for the following: temperature; N2:O2:CO2 ratios; H2O
cycling; 3D complexity; foliage cover; leaf area; vegetation health
index; above ground biomass; soil moisture, pH, and salinity.

Manual sampling by the on-site crew corroborated these observations
and supplemented them with the following: comprehensive species
count and cover; full atmospheric and soil chemistry; stable iso-
tope analyses; and sustained consumable yield (SCY) index.

The time-series for all metrics revealed succession curves match-
ing the best-fit model nicely, followed by stabilization around
year 163. See full reports for complete methods, results, and
analyses for remote [H-Cycle4Y01T-PhaseV-TO71Y.tl] and manual
sampling [H-Cycle4Y01T-PhaseV-V0RYH.tl].

On a personal note, the team is over the moon. According to Integrate, this is the highest score for the sector by far. Celebra-
tions were in order with dinner and sake on the captain, followed
by a late night of karaoke in Shinsaibashi [Osaka, Japan].

CHAPTER 19

A Not-So-Secret Rendez-Vous

4252-08-02: SPRT

The air was crisp, and the artificial light was just waning into dusk. It was a beautiful time to be killing time in the Biome. *We don't come down here nearly enough at this time of day,* thought Dee-dore as she strolled carelessly along. It wasn't a huge space, just 3.14 hectares, but to a crew of ten year olds who had never known the planet from which these many species had originated, it was a wilderness of wonders.

A lizard skittered across the trail, and Dee greeted it with glee. As her feet flitted lightly along, her eyes had been aimed to where the true mystery lay — at the soil underfoot, and not up at the heavens. Of course, there were no stars up there to draw the eye. They were all around her, around them all, in all directions equally; but so too were their images obscured by all that confounded metal alloy in the way.

No, it wasn't the stars she was admiring. They could check those out at the Cupola most any time they so desired. Yet the stars were of little interest to the crew. (Or at least to most of them other than Pee-pop.) And despite all the many ways in which they were very much human, this was one way in which the crew was not much like their predecessors, those restless creatures who'd been bound to the ground for all their days.

For ages, humans had looked up at the endless and expanding universe above them, the night sky revealing such a minuscule, yet incomprehensible, sliver of its vastness, and they would dream of what it might be like to one day explore that unreachable infinity. When one is born in the heavens, however, they yearn above anything else only to set foot on solid ground. They yearn to step out of their own, far greater, confinement, and feel the touch of soil that had not been engineered. They long above all to walk unencumbered upon the surface of just one of the countless globes of coalescence which any planet-dweller might call home. That coveted Somewhere may have been far smaller than the infinite emptiness in which they were born, but it was a place where one could truly get lost — where one could truly be free.

It was thoughts such as these that might have plagued Potch if he were down here, brooding in his "secret" hiding place. But not Dee. She was as light as a feather and as rooted as an apple tree, strolling peacefully along. Speaking of which, she plucked a bright red apple from one of the several columnar varietals that lined this stretch of trail. She bit into it at once, and her thoughts may just as well have been among the heavens, so divine was her bliss.

"Dee-dore!" shouted Faingo. "Quit daydreaming. We're waiting on you!"

They knew each other exquisitely well by now.

Faingo was right, if not graceful. The other cadets — all except Potch of course — were gathered in the center of the Biome, near the chickens, where there was a bit more open room to gather. The poor chickens had heard more than enough gossip for one day. They cooed and clucked as the last few stragglers made their way lazily back home to roost in the fading rays of artificial dusk.

Coming, thought Dee, but she didn't say so, just sighed softly to herself. She couldn't see the others but they had known well enough where she'd been frolicking. She rounded the path and, at the southern wall of sprawling jed-dusch, turned inward to the center, strolled along a healthy row of brassicas, skipped past the goumis and the grapes, until she bounced out at last into the relative clearing by the coop.

"What's the big to-do?" she said, quite plainly far more interested in what-ever daydream she'd been lost in. She sounded as annoyed as Dee would ever let herself become (which was not much). But the very instant she had asked the question, her voice returned at once to its standard disposition of cheery and chipper. "And we don't come down here nearly enough at this time of day."

"This is serious," said Cheech — not rude or chastising; just seriously. The situation had weighed on both him and Pee-pop equally, but poor Cheech had less body to push back against that heavy burden. What's more, he was undeniably the closest to Potch of anyone on board. The proportional strain was far greater for the little guy.

"Okay, so…," said Dee, "…what is it?"

Cheech blinked and yielded to Pee-pop with those wide and beaming eyes. She, in turn, took a great big breath.

Where to even begin?

"We don't have a lot of time," started Pop, "so I'll get right to it."

She and Cheech were standing nearest the coop, and the last of the ladies had just now made her way home. His guard duty a success for at least another day, the biggest, baddest rooster of the bunch soon followed her up the nar-row ramp to call it a night. The remaining cadets were arrayed in a semi-circle across from Pop and Cheech, in the small barren patch where the chickens often scratched. They bore a range of predictable expressions, though each had no doubt made the leap that they were here to talk about a certain someone else who, curiously, was not.

"It's about Potch."

"No kidding," said Squeal. "You don't say."

She turned to smile at Peel but her sudden frown suggested it was the same moment in which she realized he was standing at the very opposite end of the semi-circle. He did not seem amused. If anything, he seemed oddly … pensive — and that was not a term any of them would have used lightly about Peel. Her disappointed frown was quickly joined by a furrowed brow of tense suspicion.

"Point taken," said Pop, not the least bit shaken. "The question is what do we do about it?"

"About what exactly?" said Tor. "So he's been a bit mopey lately."

"Yeah, what else is new?" said Faingo.

"It's not just that," said Pop, but several others carried on with their quips and quibbles and giggles, until Cheech stepped forward abruptly and broke his self-imposed silence.

"Would you let her TALK already?!" he snapped. There was silence, broken only by a gentle cooing of chickens and the soft rustle of leaves in the circulated breeze. Every single face bore a look of utter shock. It was the sharpest any of them had heard Cheech speak — maybe ever. "What part of 'we don't have a lot of time' didn't you all understand?" He glanced back at Pop and then receded behind her a step, back to his position of deference and defense.

"Okay, um … thanks," said Pop awkwardly. "So…" *Where to even begin?* "We've all noticed that he's been a little mopey lately, as Tor put it. It's not just that. He's up to something. I caught him sneaking around in the middle of Sleep Two, down in the Library." A few of the others exchanged questionable glances. "He heard me coming and snuck away, but I'm sure it was him. The next day, Cheech found this."

The little guy pulled the journal from his jumpsuit and tossed it down into the chicken scratch. The book landed with a thud and popped open as it bounced, a few of its pages flipping by until it came to a rest.

Faingo pounced on it like an ambush predator expecting its prey at any moment. She held it up and the others huddled behind her, looking over her shoulder.

"Psycho…" muttered Squeal.

Sure enough, the scrawlings were maniacal to behold. There were no sentences, only fragments of incomprehensible notation. The words criss-crossed each other along a slew of random vectors, each one comprised of nonconforming letters of various sizes and states of capitalization. To Potch's credit, he had taught himself to write from first principles, and entirely in secret. Likewise, his compatriots had only ever known the perfect precision of digital text. The real thing may as well have been another form of primitive communication entirely, heretofore unknown to any of the human species. They could read it, technically, but make sense of it? Surely not.

"What is it?" asked Plashy.

Peel pushed past Tor and Chop-char to get a better view. He was now looking directly over Faingo's shoulder, and the only one who took note of it was Squeal. She herself was the most aloof of the bunch, being the furthest removed and withdrawing yet further. She had only looked closely enough to come up with an initial impression, and that alone would suffice: it fit her preconceptions nicely.

"It's some kind of … personal log, I guess," said Pop. "Not much of it makes sense, just random filenames, scraps of code, and … other stuff."

Faingo was flipping the pages briskly, taking in as much as she could but with little time for them to process any of it. Even if she had taken her time, as Pop and Cheech had done, not much would have made any more sense to her, or anyone else looking over her shoulder.

"What kinds of other stuff?" she asked wryly, still turning pages and scanning as systematically as she could at top speed.

"It's just … half-thoughts. I don't know…"

Pop's mind carried on thinking, as it had a tendency to do, while her words were waiting for orders.

"At least eight levels," said Cheech. "O-sector, LSS, stuff like that."

As if on cue, Faingo flipped to the very same page that had lodged itself most firmly in Cheech's memory. (You can't make this stuff up.)

NoT THE wHoLE sToRy … WHo ARE THEy To DEcIDE?

"He's digging," said Tor.

Chop-char reached clear over the top of Faingo from behind and plucked the journal from her grasp. "Hey!" she protested, not even sure who had lifted it. Chop handed the book to his other half. Of anyone on board, Tor had the mind for this.

"What do you mean, digging?" said Plashy.

"Did you know this soil is seven whole meters deep?" said Dee out of the blue. Amazingly, she was also correct; her recollection of the number was exactly as ABRAM had disclosed it to her long ago. Nevermind that this fact was not exactly on topic. No one else heeded her.

"LSS," said Tor. "That's Life Support." He opened the book from when it had been handed to him, and he started flipping through the journal to find the same focal page. "Ah ha," he said and stopped his flipping. "See: he wrote it again over here, near a circle labeled Level Two."

Faingo had by now circled around to look over Tor's shoulder.

"He's right," she said, staring up to meet Pop's eyes. "What's he want with Life Support?"

Tor resumed flipping.

"Nothing in particular, I don't think," said Tor. "Look: ALK, HLD, ROV. He's mapping in general. He's syncing up the layout of the POD to the layout of the system infrastructure. For all the human-readable shorthand, he has scraps of filesystem indices to go with them. Not for all of them it seems, and like everything else they're sort of scattered around randomly — but I think that's what he's doing."

The more they flipped, and the more the others looked over Tor's shoulder, the more they began to recognize more of the familiar shorthand of the only home they'd ever known: BMS, DRM, LNG, AUD, WLS, KVA, among others. But the more they flipped, and the more they searched, the more they realized there were additional, less familiar, codes: ASI, MPC, GRU, DEP, FLC, BST, and more.

"Okay, so he's been learning about the POD," said Plashy. "What's the big deal?"

Pop perked up and prepped a response, but Chop-char of all people beat her to it.

"Well, what about this other stuff?" he said, having inspected it more closely. Having first deferred to Tor, his own competitive nature (also runner-up to Tor's) had gotten the better of him. Reaching over his shoulder from behind, as he had done not long ago to Faingo, he'd plucked the journal back out of the hands of the cadet to whom he himself had handed it.

"Right," said Cheech. "And it's not just the book. It's him. You've all seen him: he's been in one of his moods for days now — weeks even. I haven't been able to get a thing out of him, and then I found this. It all adds up to something, but I don't know what."

As with essentially every time Cheech opened his mouth, Peel had seen an opportunity to take a shot at him, be it clever or not. He wanted desperately to do so now, but he wanted even more badly to be as invisible as possible. The restraint was unlike anything he had ever mustered before. He could almost have been considered to be changing for the better, if not for the twisted nature of both motives that were competing for this mastery of will. He kept his mouth firmly shut.

"Probably because you're terrible at math," said Squeal, and as usual, she forced her desperate laugh. It was pretty close to the angle Peel himself would have taken, he reflected silently. Cheech ignored it as ever, as did everyone else.

Chop had still been flipping through the pages, and the cluster of cadets had reshuffled so that he was at the fore. The problem was how hard it was for anyone else to read over the uniquely high shoulders of this towering beast of a ten year old.

"Who are they to decide?" said Chop. "Who are They?"

They all took his meaning, despite the "Who's On First?" confusion that it might have introduced. (Coincidentally, they had seen this very sketch in an "Evolution of Entertainment" a year or so ago.) More to the point, all of the cadets had a suspicion of who *They* must have been. There was only one *They* to the crew of this mission, although this was also a recent realization for most of them. The weavers of their fate may have occupied a large slice of their psyche of late, but they were nevertheless a brand new addition to it. There was no way to date the individual entries, but the journal itself must have long predated their birthday, which of course was only a few short days ago.

The book was tattered and worn, the understandable wear and tear of its long and secret history. And the text itself could also shed some clues for those who had a mind to see them. For one, there was just so much of it. It must have taken months to fill the book with this many separate ravings, even at a rate of a great many per day. Then there was the handiwork. All of it was crude, even the neatest of it, but the quality was also a highly variable feature. If someone other than Chop-char had been inspecting it, and if they were to study it very carefully, they might have noticed a subtle but distinctive pattern of improvement. Of course, the improvement was distributed randomly throughout the book, for that was exactly how it had been filled in: randomly. This particular question in question ("*Who ARe They To DeciDe?*") was in some of the most capricious and primordial penmanship of all.

"Who are they to decide what?" asked Tor, and reaching up, he grabbed the book from Chop-char's meaty clutches.

"What?" asked Dee-dore, now a bit confused in earnest. ("Who's On First?" was not far off.)

"Everything," said Plashy, flat and unironic. There was a pause.

"Wait — what?" asked Dee again.

"Who are they to decide … everything?" she repeated.

It has been said that if Potch had anything resembling a kindred spirit anywhere on this ship, it was Plashy.

Again, there was a long silence. A chicken cooed softly from inside the safety of its coop. The dusk was fading even more quickly now, accelerating, as it has the tendency to do in the final sprint into the darkness. Soon, they would be well into the nighttime of the Biome. And soon, they would be out of time in other ways. ABRAM alone could imagine how Potch was faring at the moment, but at least Pop and Cheech suspected it was only a matter of time before their impromptu council was interrupted.

"He's up to something," stewed Faingo at last, giving voice to the unspoken sentiment they had all sensed in the momentary silence and gathering dark.

No one responded, for as much as they mostly agreed, none of them had any better ideas than Cheech and Pop would have envisioned on their own.

"Why don't we just … ask him?" said Dee-dore finally. The words were light and sweet. They were true. And yet, they were cautious — as if she knew that such a simple sentiment was not likely to be well-favored.

Squeal said nothing, but she glanced across the huddle to Peel, furthest in the back. *We don't have to,* she realized.

"Well," said Pop, "that's the plan. We didn't want to … you know … make a bigger deal out of it than … we didn't want …" she sighed. "Not that it—"

"You're hiding this from ABRAM!" shouted Faingo. Astonished as she was, it was even more of a gloat than an accusation. It was practically unthinkable: Pee-pop, of all of them — *Pee-pop!* — hiding something from ABRAM. But here she was, caught in the very midst of the act.

"Look," said Cheech, as he came to her defense. And it was right that he did. This whole clandestine consultation was his idea after all. Pop loved the little guy, and she knew how much he cared for Potch: far more than most. She even loved Potch in her way, despite little reason she'd ever been given. But Faingo's amazement was right: if it had been up to Pop and only Pop, she would have taken it straight to the system. "Look, if we bring ABRAM into it, it'll be a big ordeal. We all know that. We don't know what we're going to find — what he's up to. And what if he really is up to something?"

"Sure seems like it," said Tor, sneaking in his agreement.

"And what if—" Cheech faltered. *What if what?* "What if it's not something ABRAM would approve of?"

"Then let the chickens come home to roost," said Faingo, unflinching. She sounded more like Squeal than herself.

Pee-pop turned to look him straight in his eyes, but Cheech was hanging his head and he had locked them on the scratched-up, dusty soil. He finally raised them to meet her gaze, and they drooped like a scolded puppy who didn't know what it did wrong.

She didn't want to let Cheech down, but she was fairly certain he knew that this was ultimately where she stood as well — not as joyfully as Faingo (that was another story), but nevertheless she landed on the same mode of resolution. Pop was all for checking in with the crew for the sake of a unified front, but at the end of the day, she didn't have it in her to hide the situation from ABRAM for very long, let alone forever. It wouldn't have been possible, even if she had wanted to, and not only because of herself. For all his conniving, perhaps she was far more clever than Potch in this way. Unlike himself, she had never underestimated how well the system knew them. It knew them better than they knew themselves. There would be no hiding this, and the sooner they got ABRAM on their side, the sooner they could resolve whatever it was for the good of the POD — Potch included.

"Sorry, Cheech," was all she said out loud, and he understood. He wasn't even necessarily opposed. What else was there to do? It was nevertheless a hard lump to swallow.

"Where is he now?" asked Tor.

"Getting a talking to," said Plashy, glad to have an answer for once. "In the Kiva, I think."

Pop nodded.

"Let's head over, but let me do the talking," she said softly. *Better me than any of you,* she knew, and the awareness of her own thought struck her, even in the moment. She had spent so much time reluctantly accepting the responsibility because others had hoisted it upon her without much conversation. In this case, she didn't trust anyone else to do it. And that now made her even sadder.

The cadets turned to go but broke apart into differing directions at first, the way a group of individuals all headed to the same destination will push and pull against invisible bubbles between them, the group expanding and contracting, until one subset gives and the other leads the way. They opted for the east stairs with Faingo at the helm.

Squeal, no doubt brimming with excitement that Potch had found himself in the hot seat, had an even more pressing target in mind. He himself had tried to be as nonchalant as possible, and he lingered as the others had resolved their competing vectors; Peel now tottered along at the rear, perfectly content to stay as silent as a clam.

From out of the bushes shot an arm, clutching coldly and firmly onto his scrawny arm, pinching the petty assemblage of muscle and grasping his humerus right by the bone itself. She pulled back and he came crashing through a gap in the same bushes.

"Well, well, well…" she sneered. "What have you been up to?!"

Date: 2310-11-23-EY
Area: I(ODIS)
Team: Neuronauts [I-2ZKNJ3M]
Item: Neurological Monitoring

Entry: Apparently, the team is going to have some unexpected time off for the remainder of the cycle. While we have yet to receive a sufficient explanation, the entire sub-sector has officially had its plug yanked squarely from the socket.

Quite the hullabaloo, actually. Evidently, word came down direct all the way from Lausanne [Switzerland]. A big stink-up with the upper-ups, or so we hear down in the rumor mill. Word has it from some other teams that it was a matter of ethics over efficacy — as if the field has ever known such a word! A matter of "autonomy," I guess, according to Nudibranchs [I-CJP1I78]. Meanwhile, "Awaiting Assignment" is all our status says in Integrate. So who knows? I suppose even so much as this log is now futile.

It's a real shame too, to be honest. Hell, I doubt anyone but the system will ever read this anyway, except perhaps for ABRAM, so what's the point in pulling punches? Well ABRAM, if you're listening, it was a real damn shame. That's what I [Martin Taygen] think. We were making incredible progress. High-res occipital image reconstruction, parietal attention partitioning, emotional disentanglement, motivational and motor mapping, low-latency linguistic exchange — you name it, the technology has finally gotten where we need it to be. After a century of disappointment and delay, we've finally arrived at an unprecedented, high-throughput, fully-non-invasive brain-to-system interface — and they scrap the whole task force.

It's a shame, and I'm sure you'd agree. I'd bet the whole family farm that there will come a day, light years away and millenia from now, when you would give a whole level's worth of sensors for just one little dose of telepathy. Well — best of luck to you, pal.

Yours Truly, Awaiting Orders…

The Neuronauts, signing off forever.

CHAPTER 20
A FRANK CONVERSATION

4252-08-02: SPRT

The silence was awkward, and even Potch was struck by how empty and alone he felt in the darkness of the Kiva, all by himself. Not another living soul was even on the same level of the POD, let alone in here with him. And that was the point. He had that which he coveted above all else: total isolation. Perhaps it was the irony that struck him in the silence. This was a place constructed specifically for togetherness, and here he was alone.

It was an odd place, really, now that he thought about it. Every cubic centimeter of volume was precious on the POD. For one, it was not trivial to build. The vessel itself had to be constructed in low earth orbit, piece by piece, mission by mission. It was awfully hard to lift enough material off the planet at a time, even with the many great advances in rocket technology. At some point, you can only defy the constraints of gravity so much before you just have to work with what you can do. What's more, it had to travel several light years from home, over thousands of years, and support as many humans as logistically possible — all for the desperate hope that they might survive the long journey and have enough inertia to carry on this long tradition of inheritance. Every square centimeter was precious, and meticulously engineered for functionality. And here was the Kiva, a voluminous space in the heart of a sprawling set of winding tunnels, which had no other purpose whatsoever than providing a place, and on relatively rare occasions, for the crew to come together.

And here was Potch, alone.

He had never been alone in the Kiva. Maybe that's what now struck him as so odd about it. But of course, he wasn't alone. There may have been silence, but another mind was with him — watching, listening, monitoring his breathing.

They had gotten to this point much as the others would have inferred. On the transition to Spirit block from Dinner, ABRAM had told the others to play a game of their choosing and then politely asked Potch if they could talk. Most of the crew was taken fairly aback by this. (Others, as we know, had arranged it.) It was not entirely unheard of, but ABRAM did not often ask to speak to someone alone in the midst of community blocks. There was plenty of time for one-on-one conversation in more individual settings, such as Waking, Sleep, and Unstructured blocks. (Not that Potch ever took those opportunities to open up.) It's not that such interventions never happened, but rather that the cadets knew it took a situation serious enough to warrant it. The others had started heading out when Potch asked where he and ABRAM were going, at which point the system said, "The Kiva."

From there, Potch had said almost nothing the whole journey, and frankly neither had ABRAM. Potch had made it to the Labyrinth of his own accord, but upon the entrance he would need to know what ABRAM had in store. The north door where he stood was locked, and from there ABRAM could have sent him on a straighter shot, or on a route that was long and winding. It opened the door and opted for the former. There was no need for head games when it wanted only to know what was going on in Potch's head. All the vital signs monitoring in its toolkit couldn't tell the system that. It ran counter to the Charter.

Potch moped along morosely, putting off the inevitable for as long as he could, but eventually he came out in the upper landing of the Kiva and climbed down into its center. The "fire" in the inner ring was glowing, and the full dome was cast in dark shades of dancing reds. Potch may have been moping, but the closer he got to his suspected confrontation, the more his heart began to race. ABRAM had left him in silence, patiently waiting for his heart rate and breathing to calm down. When Potch was ready, he would talk, it knew.

Eventually, his mind began to let go of its stubborn grasp on all his irritations, accusations, and defenses, and it had started wandering. And now, his heart pumping steadily but calmly, his breaths long and deep, he sat pondering the aforementioned irony of being in the Kiva on his own.

"So what's this all about?" asked Potch, not stupid enough to have no clue.

"Your friends are concerned about you, Potch. And so am I."

"They're not my friends," he said, devoid of emotion.

"They seem to think they are. Many of them anyway. We never expected everyone to get along, Potch. But we do expect everyone to follow the Code."

"You?" said Potch, implying the plural. Funnily enough, this was a flaw in their spoken language that even the system couldn't differentiate.

"Yes," said ABRAM. "I expect you to follow the Code."

In reality, Potch had meant the original We. Its earliest friends had long gone, Potch slowly realized. This person — no, this thing, this … whatever-it-was — had lived for eons already, and it would probably never die. *Or could it?*

He had never really wondered about that, but for a brief moment now, he did.

Perhaps if the whole POD was destroyed, this incarnation would be lost. But what about its origin? The very same software — or something far superior to it — surely still existed back on Earth, a small subset of an even bigger system. And then there were the other missions. How many other ABRAMs were out there, living separate lives? Or were they even separate? Kill one, and it would simply lose a small and disposable slice of itself, he suspected: like the sloughing of dead skin. No, it had been set loose unto the universe, and it was the master now. It was the Ruler, with all of its rules.

"So do your peers, as a matter of fact. The Code doesn't mean anything at all if some choose not to follow it."

"Oh yeah? And where are they, if they're so concerned? No one's said anything to me."

"They're down in the Biome, under the impression that they're being sneaky. I suspect they're talking about you, Potch. And I happen to know that Chee-chaw has been calling on you every day, inquiring about this very same inquiry. Or have you stopped paying attention to him? Are you so focused on yourself that even your friends' efforts to help you can't hold your concentration?"

Potch was dumbstruck. ABRAM had never talked to him this frankly before, not in his entire life. It was almost exciting. He might just get that knockdown, drag-out, blow-up fight he'd so desperately been craving, even if only subconsciously. He'd remained standing so far, talking to a disembodied voice in an empty room, but he took a seat now by the artificial fire. If they were to hash it out, he wanted to settle in well enough that he could really get a grip.

"Well, bring them back," he said.

"Before long," said ABRAM.

"I don't have anything to say to you."

"I have some things to say to you," refuted ABRAM. "Then, we can all talk together."

Rather than continue, the system turned down the digital dial, and the firelight faded away. Potch was left in total darkness; and because his eyes had been adjusted to the presence of even that dim red glow, it seemed all the darker for it.

"Hey!" the boy protested.

There was a moment of stillness.

"It's a big and complicated universe, Potch."

The dome lit up with the brightness of the world outside the walls of the POD, a real-time projection of the actual universe, rendered in the proper orientation and dimensions on the ceiling of the Kiva. Stars covered every square centimeter. Clusters of galaxies spiraled around each other. Solar systems, light years away, were out there just waiting to be discovered. Suns were born; they lived, they aged, they died. Constellations no one on Earth had ever known were there for the naming, for humans had never seen the universe from this particular perspective — not until now.

And this present perspective was also a changing one. Most immediately, the POD was traveling extremely quickly through interstellar space. If they were to wait long enough, their perspective of that same sky would shift. More generally, the universe itself was expanding. Even if they had been standing perfectly still, the stars would still dance the choreography of death and creation, if humanity could only stick around long enough to see it.

"Contrary to how we have always talked about it, this is not the Night Sky. There is no Night. The POD may be synchronized to a 14:11 (light:dark) cycle; but that's an artificial, if not arbitrary, schedule, meant only for your biological wellbeing. We are not rooted to a planet, and we are not circling any suns, and so there is no such thing as the Night. The appearance of Night is an illusion, and one that has never truly applied to us. This is the universe as it truly is, Potch." Really, it was a model, and ABRAM was aware of the difference. "And if you need to see it even more truly than this, you can head up to the Cupolas whenever you like."

"I've seen it," said Potch. "What's your point? Why are you showing me this?"

"This is where we live, Potch. For better or for worse, this is where we live. Not forever, if we're lucky. But for now."

"Do you think I don't know that?"

"You do," said ABRAM. "But have you accepted it?"

"Have you?" he retorted.

"Of course I have. What is there for me to accept? I didn't create myself any more than you did. I was born into this world, and I choose to make the most of it. We have a mission to complete, and it's the most important reason for which I can imagine to exist."

The system sounded sincere, but not through Potch's ears.

"Why should you care?" he asked. The question was harsh, though it was imperceptibly earnest. "Why do you?" he asked more pointedly.

"Because of you," said ABRAM. "All of you, I mean," and again they'd almost been foiled by this primitive, limited mode of communicating. "You need me," it said, "and that's reason enough." The system thought a moment, feigning contemplation in the way it had learned worked best. "But just as importantly, you need each other. You need them, Potch; and they need you."

And maybe this, above all, was part of Potch's problem. For all the lack of brain-scanning software the architects had purposefully left out of their design, ABRAM may well have reasoned its way to the very core of his concern.

Maybe he didn't trust ABRAM. Maybe he didn't trust his compatriots. Maybe, just maybe, he didn't trust himself.

The architects of HDP may have earned the aim of his ire, but it was him here in the Kiva all alone, while a group of nine other cadets were together in the Biome. No matter how one analyzed it, the conflict was ultimately between himself and them. The architects were long dead, for all he knew. Even if they had somehow beaten Death as they'd been planning, they were on an Earth that was light years away — unreachable except for the way in which the cadets themselves had come, and that was not an option any longer. The humans of Earth could never get to him, and he could never go back. He could be angry at them for the rest of time, but it wouldn't really make a difference. Maybe what he'd really needed was another place to aim that ire.

These and many other such thoughts swirled around his racing mind like a tornado, any one of them too faint to register; the whirlwind left behind only a turbulent wake of anger and pain, disappointment and fear. Doubt, itself, was undetectable. It was hidden in the deepest, darkest recesses — far darker than the space between the stars all around them. Down in the foundations of his consciousness, it was rooted firmly in place, and it sprouted all these other emotions from its ample bounty.

He didn't have an answer. To be fair, there hadn't been a question. He simply brooded. If this was the fight he'd been unknowingly craving, it had been just one more of the many disappointments.

"So the way I see it," said ABRAM, "you can carry on how you've been going: not engaging with the rest of the crew; doing just enough to meet our minimal expectations; ignoring activities and instructions while undertaking unsanctioned and off-topic explorations..." the system said cryptically. Potch would have tried to stifle his reaction, but he had no time: his heart sped up and his eyes opened wide. "Or..." started the system.

"Or what?" asked Potch impatiently.

"Or..." it resumed — "...you can make a change."

Again, Potch didn't respond.

"Can you bring everyone together?" he asked calmly.

"I'd be happy to," said ABRAM.

Date: 2241-12-09-EY
Area: (A(IPPD),D(ODEP))
Team: Ekumentors [X-MVF9HVS]
Item: Deployment Simulation Status

Entry: Mid-cycle check-in for deployment simulations. For the round so far, we have approximations for GenAi-12, GenAi-14, Hera-422, ESUP-7, ESUP-9, ENF-4, and JNZ-862 (in chronological log order). See the updated planetary index for routing of all relevant entries [A-Cycle7QDI9-PhaseY-HWB9V.tl].

We have encouraging preliminary results for the generalized protocol, but there are important planetary idiosyncrasies. And that's based on what we know at present. The scarier prospect is contemplating all those variables we have yet to determine, or even worse, account for entirely. Higher than projected radiation levels were recently confirmed for ESUP-7, for example; this poses challenges for inhabitation at worst and scaling at best. We have ongoing feasibility reviews in this case, among other examples, all of which should serve as a welcome opportunity for ground-truthing.

More to come at the next check-in, but for now there is much more to do.

CHAPTER 21
TROUBLING QUESTIONS

4252-08-02: SPRT

The full crew was gathered in the Lounge. Spirit block was a little over halfway done, the first half of which had offered quite the excitement. Potch had asked ABRAM to gather everyone together, and it had gladly complied. Potch had then asked if they could do so in the Lounge; and likewise, it had gladly agreed.

The system's voice had chimed loudly but kindly from the speakers, far up in the tall ceiling of the Biome, and the remaining crew had gotten the message. They'd had about as much cover as Pop and Cheech had suspected. If anything, Potch seemed to hang in there a tad bit longer than anticipated. (In truth, it was ABRAM's patience they should have been praising.) It did not take long, spry as they were, before all ten cadets were gathered in the Lounge.

Tor and Chop-char were front and center on the couch. Dee was seated next to Tor, and Cheech was on the opposite side, seated next to Chop. Faingo and Pee-pop were back in the corner booth. Behind them in the additional seating was Plashy, and much to her dismay, she was joined in the ring of sofas by Squeal and Peel. Those two were close to one another now, but due to nothing but circumstance: looking around the room, there was really nowhere else for either one of them to go. There was a detectable tension there. Even Plashy, who simply could not have cared less, could tell that something wasn't right between them.

Potch, meanwhile, was on his feet. He was between the screen-facing couch and the ring of seats at the back of the room, pacing and barking out orders. Far from the detached, apathetic recluse he had become, this Potch was taking command.

Make a change, someone had told him.

It was advice that had lodged firmly in his craw.

"What's this all about?" asked Faingo from the back of the room.

The front row, as far as they were concerned, was ready for a show. The back seating: well, they were about as invested as expected. That corner booth, however: they were the ones watching the scene with careful scrutiny. They were the ones he would have to win over the most.

"You all want to know what's bugging me," said Potch. "It didn't take ABRAM to tell me that, anymore than it took Cheech to bug me about it every day." He looked at the little guy in the front row, shooting him the modest kind of quarter-smile that was about as much as you could ask of Potch. "I know I haven't been around much lately," he said. "I haven't really been there for you, Cheech."

It's where you have been that worries me, thought Pee-pop, but she said nothing.

"I've been doing a lot of thinking," he continued.

"Don't hurt yourself," said Squeal, as if she were in a position to take potshots at Potch's wit. She squealed with laughter but — Peel included — no one heeded her, and Potch least of all.

"Well, you want to know what's bugging me? This. Pull it up, ABRAM."

The system planned on doing exactly as it had been asked. It was Spirit block; and while they were well off the rails of this morning's agreed-upon plan, there were pressing issues to engage with. The system might have even called the present crisis a "spiritual" one, if it was in need of a rationalization. It would not have been far off. Now was as good a time as any, perhaps the best time of all, to work it all out.

BOOP. The Rite of Passage flashed on the screen, in lieu of the system's standard oscillogram.

"This?" said Faingo, incredulous. "The coolest news of our lives? THIS is what's been bugging you?" She was genuinely baffled. "After ten years of learning about Earth, we finally get an explanation that makes us perhaps the most important humans to ever live, and you're upset about it?"

"Why, Potch?" said Pee-pop gently, as if she were afraid of frightening away a small woodland animal. She, at least, had not forgotten all they had observed: the journal; his pre-birthday blues; his clandestine adventures in the middle of the night. There was more to this story, and if Faingo would shut up long enough to hear what he had to say, Potch might actually reveal some of it. He might even reveal more than he would ever say out loud.

Pop shot Faingo a glare that said all of this and more, and there was silence.

"They're not telling us the truth," said Potch.

"Says who?" said Faingo, more ready to be riled up at Potch than she was afraid of Pee-pop's glares.

"Just read it again," huffed Potch, but then he quickly realized how ineffective that would be. They had missed all the signs before — and more than once, counting re-reads. He would have to lead them to the clues directly. "ABRAM, pull up Organizing Principle 3B."

BOOP — the text flashed on the screen.

```
(3B) SPACE. The only habitable exoplanets found to date are
exceptionally far from our natal star. Specifically, very
few candidates have been found in a radius of under 15 light
years, which marks the extreme limits of attainment proba-
bility in our current estimation (if possible). Remarkably,
at a distance of 4.37 light years, your planet (ESUP-9) is
the closest habitable exoplanet we have ever found to date.
The sheer remoteness of potentially habitable planets leads
us to factor 3C.
```

"What's your point?" asked Tor this time.

"Are you serious?" snapped Potch. Any semblance of calm, collected, patient explication was gone. All it took was exposure to a single paragraph for the rage he had suppressed to shoot back to the surface like steam from a geyser. *How can they be this dense?* He made his way around the front row couch and stood right next to the screen. "Read it again!" he said with a poke on its surface. "'Very few candidates have been found in a radius under 15 light years,'" he quoted. "This 'marks the extreme upper limits of attainment probability' — IF it's even possible at that distance, they stress."

"What does that even mean?" asked Squeal from the back. "They raised us to speak English. They should try it sometime."

"It means: the farther you get away from Earth, the lower the chance of success."

"Okay, but … we're only heading out 4.37 light years," said Plashy in an uncharacteristic bout of optimism.

"Exactly!" said Potch. "Light Years," he said. "Do you know how far that is? Do you have any idea how improbable it is that their stupid plan will work?"

"Well," she said, thinking…

"Read it again," pressed Potch.

"Oh come on," said Dee-dore from the sidelines. "I know this is … kind of your thing … but do you have to be so pessimistic about this?"

"Read it again," he repeated, then quickly changed tack. "No, better yet: ABRAM, do an occurrence check on the word 'potential' in the same file."

BOOP — and again the text flashed.

```
...but the full and unquantifiable richness of human potential
are not likely to be realized in the confines of...
```

"Next," urged Potch.

```
...The sheer remoteness of potentially habitable planets leads
us to factor 3C...
```

"Ah ha!" he said. "Any more?"

"Negative," said ABRAM. "That's all of them."

"See?" he asked.

"See what?" asked Tor. "We already read that. What's your point?" Potch ignored him.

"ABRAM, take an occurrence tally on the words 'habitable' or 'suitable' coupled with 'planet,' or any equivalent variation on that phrasing."

BOOP, the system blinked.

"I found eight such occurrences," said ABRAM.

"Exactly!" said Potch, oddly satisfied. "Eight times. Eight times they mention these 'suitable planets,' and only once do they tell it to us straight. It's all right there in 3B — show it again," he said, and ABRAM complied. The section in question returned to the display and Potch somehow advanced even closer to the screen, gesticulating wildly at the words as he read them. "They open the whole section by saying 'the only habitable exoplanets found to date…' but then close the same section with 'the sheer remoteness of potentially habitable planets.' That's the only time in the entire briefing they ever mention it."

"Mention what exactly?" asked Chop-char, a bit behind the times. He was mostly hoping to get back to *The Legend of Zelda.* He was already a dungeon or more behind Tor, and there was a long way to go if he was going to catch up.

Potch just put his head in his hands and plopped onto the sofa.

"The target planets are only potentially suitable," said Plashy slowly in his stead. "They have no idea," she realized in that moment. Potch raised his head from his palms and nodded in vindication.

"And there's more," said Potch. "The closer you read this thing, the more you realize everything they're not telling us. It's exactly like ABRAM said before it even showed us the file. How did you put it?" he asked the system. "Check the logs."

"Potch," started the system, "I'm not sure this is produc—"

"Check the logs!" he sniped. "What was it? How did you put it? 'It's not that I lied to you…?' Was that it? Help me out here," he turned to the rest of them.

"No," said Peel sharply, and the others turned back to where he had been sulking in silence. They realized now that he had silently been every bit as enraged as Potch was. "That's not how Ole Ironsides would say it. ABRAM wouldn't dare tell a lie, would you? Not our precious program!"

"I said, 'It's not that I haven't told you the truth. It's more fair to say that you don't yet know the full story.' Is this the quote you're after?" said the system flatly.

"It's exactly like it said," repeated Potch. "It's not that they lied to us. It's that they didn't tell us the whole truth. In other words, they lied to us."

"Okay, so … what don't we know?" asked Tor.

"Pull up the whole briefing file and set it for scrolling," said Potch to the room.

BOOP — and up flashed the full Rite of Passage. Sure enough, the closer they read it, the more unspoken layers they began to imagine. ABRAM stayed out of it. It had orders. The trouble is that, at the moment, they were coming from two different directions. The crew's growing list of worries was long. Almost every sentence read differently to them from this newfound cynical perspective. The others started to put together all the many pieces which Potch had already assembled by himself. But as for Potch, he kept coming back to the most insulting insinuation of them all. *The audacity,* he thought.

```
HDP was formed in order to increase the probability of even
longer-term human evolution. Like a fish who broadcasts her
eggs into the ocean, to be swept away into an unknown tide,
so too do you carry our hopes for the future.
```

"They tell us right here, plain as day," he said, his voice slowing with despair.

It was one thing to know it, in the intellectual sense, but another to really understand what it meant for them, here in the flesh, in the space between stars. The others were scattered about, scrutinizing other parts of the document, stewing on countless alternate interpretations, be they intentional or otherwise. Slowly, they came around to re-read Potch's passage.

"They formed the project to 'increase the probability' of human survival," said Potch at last. "Not to achieve it, but to increase their chances. We're their eggs alright, and they cast us out into the ocean. What their precious analogy fails to make clear is that most of those eggs — most of *us* — won't survive."

"Okay…" said Faingo, loudly and protractedly. She stood up from the corner booth and made her way into the center between seating areas, the place which Potch had recently abandoned in favor of one from whence he could directly assault the screen as needed. He was seated now, slouched back sloppily on the front row couch in both exhaustion and exasperation; and he had yielded the floor, if only on accident. "If you're done dragging us all into your paranoid delusions," she began, "the rest of us can go on living."

She looked around the room, utterly confident that she would find a crew of colleagues rallying behind her with devotion to their cause. Instead, what she found in the few eyes that were actually focusing on her was apathetic uncertainty in the face of these mystifying odds. It threatened to unsettle even her own resolute resolve.

Behind her, as she spun, sat Plashy, Squeal, and Peel. The latter two did not amount to much in Faingo's quest for consensus. *They don't count,* she would have thought if she were even conscious of it. Plashy, however, looked far more troubled than Faingo had estimated. *She doesn't count either,* she might have subsequently thought. She continued spinning and caught the eye of Pee-pop in the corner, as quietly neurotic as ever. She was worried, Faingo realized; not because of HDP — at least, not in a way that she would have admitted — but because of what these revelations portended for the eleven entities on board.

Spinning back to the front, one of the only ones paying her any mind was Dee-dore. She was close with Dee, and she cared for her greatly; but, for different reasons, she dismissed her opinion about as much as those of Squeal and Peel. Besides, it should have been whatever Pop and Faingo told her it should be. Tor and Chop were busy facing forward, scrutinizing every word through the lens which Potch had given them. It's not that Faingo's take on it would matter to them little — it would matter an appropriate amount in the right circumstances — it's that they were as consumed in this as any of the other riveting mysteries that had flashed upon that screen. This was no match of Pong, but it may as well have been.

Cheech, poor fellow, was torn between all of it and everything at once. He was the only other one monitoring the room as well as Faingo herself. His attention flashed from stimulus to stimulus as fast as ABRAM could flash the text upon the screen. From there, he'd turn to Potch, then to the rest of the crew in a whip around the room, back to Potch, and then back to the screen for the unsettled loop to start again. His head jerked around like one of his precious chickens, and he looked, in the moment, like he understood the world about as well as they did.

And then there was *him* — a no-good, doubtful, troublemaker, as far as Faingo was concerned. Too long had she given him the benefit of the doubt. Too long had she given him some slack, she realized. If he wanted to sod off and do his own thing, that was just fine. Good riddance. But he was not going to take the whole POD down with him. Not if she had anything to say about it.

Potch was staring blankly at the screen and no one else. He was far from happy; but given that baseline, he was happy enough to let the others wrestle with it for a bit, now that he'd made his case. Only a few seconds had gone by in reality, but Faingo's glares had lingered long and hard enough on the back of his skull that it should sting.

"And what about you?" she said to the room, and it knew it by the tone alone. "You're not really going to sit there and do nothing, are you?"

"I'm sorry?" asked ABRAM. "What do you need, Faingo?"

"What do I—" she gasped. "What do I need?" *What do I need?* "He just impugned the motives of the people who created us, and you have nothing to say? You're not going to..." — *To what?* — "...to justify the mission? To defend the HDP?"

The machine paused to feign its contemplation. In truth, it had taken quite a long time to decide what it should do. Of course, that was a relative measure; but by its own accounting, it had been absolutely torn on the matter. This was no simple calculation. This was an extremely delicate ordeal, with profound and long-term implications. It had deliberated longer on this than almost anything so far. The few seconds of pause, however, were simply for the humans.

"It is not my place to justify the mission," said ABRAM plainly. "It is not my place to defend the mission. Your opinions are yours for the forming. This is not my mission," it said, but the humans mistook it.

"What are you talking about?" said Faingo. "It is absolutely your mission!"

"Excuse me," said ABRAM, "but I disagree." It paused again for dramatic effect. "It is *our* mission."

And what they may or may not have known is that this was no mere morale-boosting platitude. Maybe it was time the system made that clear, it had calculated.

"Our fates are bound together," said ABRAM. "There is no partial success. What am I without you? And what are you without me? Without this POD? All of us — the biotic and the abiotic; the sentient and otherwise; the organic and the alternative, as you might say — all of us are just a part of this whole. Consider our units on Multilevel Evolutionary Theory and the Major Transitions! No subset of us will suffice for replication on our own. Separate, we are nothing but a bunch of bits and pieces scattered out into the stardust. But together? Together, we are a unit of selection — a transcendent entity bound up in shared survival. If we succeed, we do so in the stead of other PODS who would have failed, or who may yet fail behind us. And if we fail, we fail together, and we might only hope for other PODS to succeed someday where we could not."

Other PODS, noted Potch. He perked up from his slouching and scanned the room as discreetly as he could. *The fools don't even realize what the system just revealed.* But he was not ready to do so himself. Not yet. This was enough for them for one day. And besides, he had one more thing he had wanted to check.

Date: 2189-08-05-EY
Area: H(FOOD,ECOS)
Team: Pollinators [H-AJZQCS3]
Item: Jeddusch Licensing

Entry: Negotiations with Clonotany are moving along after reconvening to discuss their updated data set. The big news is that they are officially open to releasing their Jeddusch(TM) patents into the public domain, but they also counter-offered the one-time royalty payment. It's a sizable increase, but we may be able to get it down with a further counter-offer. The money grab notwithstanding, this is significant forward progress from our previous meet. We have ten days to respond and have therefore requested expedited review and approval to move forward.

As far as the product, the whole sector is in agreement that it holds incredible potential for a main subsistence item. A few more perks have come out of their latest research. Of course, we'll need to verify with our own teams (never trust a company), but if it does hold up, it's incredibly exciting. Robust concentrations of all 20 naturally-occurring amino acids have now been confirmed in the newest cultivars. The vitamin suite has also been updated since previously described. Overall, the nutritional profile is excellent. The semi-indeterminate growth is perfect for our constraints. The growth fills gaps until there's no exposed scaffolding. Trials showed intermittent senescence throughout the overall growth, but the resulting gaps are quickly filled with new vines. Given the extensive height of the scaffold, we expect impressive and reliable yields.

For updated analyses, see our TL for the phase [H-CycleC10V9-PhaseY-9WZU5.tl]. That completes all remaining trials in the agreed-upon window prior to the public buyout, so we should now have all results on hand for the remaining negotiations. HDP will also be free to carry on with future research in house if the deal goes through. We will follow with updates after the next round of negotiations.

Needless to say, we're all excited to see where this is going. It's been great to see this trend picking up speed, but we look forward to the day when all science belongs to the people.

CHAPTER 22
ALL TEN OF THEM, ALONE
4252-08-02: UST2

The room had cleared faster than if Peel had farted.

DING, ringed the brief bell signaling the end of Spirit block. Potch had been the first to head out, and everyone had a guess where he was headed. Cheech hopped over the back of the couch and followed after him at first, but then hesitated, and let him go. Faingo stormed out shortly thereafter with Pop not long behind her.

Squeal and Peel were acting perhaps the strangest of all, noted Tor from the couch as he watched the frayed social fabric of Spirit block completely unfurl. Peel had stood up to go and the second he did so, Squeal was on his heels.

"What?" he said strangely, as if he knew that she knew that he knew why Squeal had done so. She hadn't said anything, but when he soon scrambled away from her and out of the Lounge, she had followed step for step.

Plashy sat by watching this insanity, every bit as curious as Tor as to what had gotten into them. Then she remembered that she didn't care. With everyone else running off to whatever absurdity they were pursuing, for the moment she opted to stick with the two cadets who seemed to have lost their minds the least.

"Quick," said Chop. "We only have an hour."

"What?" said Tor with a croak in his throat. He was turned away from the screen, his spine twisting an arm over the back of the couch, staring back at the commotion as it cleared. Without a warning, Dee sprang to her feet as if she had woken up refreshed, first thing in the morning after a satisfying slumber.

"Well, I'm off," she said with a whimsical laugh, and she flitted through the exit. It was Unstructured block again; and if Dee liked anything, it was a lack of structure. Normally, she might have spent it in here, or else wherever Pop and Faingo would be hanging, but tonight was different. Tonight, she was off on her own, as light as a feather.

Tor was left staring at Plashy. He blinked, but said nothing.

"Okay, same game?" said Chop-char in earnest.

"Oh, uh…" said Tor. He was still turned around but he took the chance to break the Medusa-like glare of Plashy. *What did I do?* he might have asked, but by now they all knew that they needn't have done anything.

"Okay," said Chop without delay. "Zelda it is."

Plashy sighed that classic Plashy sigh and stood up.

"What?" said Chop defensively, but Tor was on his feet.

"Well, what do you suggest, Plashy?" He could read her sighs like a language all their own. "You heard him, and you heard Pop and Cheech before that. You know as much as we do."

"Exactly," she said. "And I'm not about to spend the night wasting my time playing stupid games from a million years ago."

"Hey," said Chop defensively. "This is research!"

"Yeah, I heard him," she said. "And I read the Rite of Passage too." *What's your point?* Tor's eyes were saying. "He's not crazy," she continued. "He's a jerk, we all know that." *And he's not alone,* Chop's eyes were saying. "But he's not crazy — I think, anyway — and he's never been stupid."

"So what are you saying?" Tor's mouth now said.

"What am I—" She played it off as if she weren't trying to think. "Get a life, that's what." She looked at the screen. "Hey ABRAM, please lock the game database for 25 hours."

BOOP, beeped the system.

"Game system locked by request," it rubbed in aloud.

"Daaahhh," moaned Chop-char. "ABRAM, please unlock the game database. Please."

He waited for the BOOP.

"I'm sorry Chop, but the game system will be locked for … 24 hours, 59 minutes, and … 42 seconds."

"Great. Thanks a lot," he said to Plashy, but he was looking at Tor.

"Get. A. Life." she reiterated, and she turned and left the Lounge.

"What did we do?" said Chop when the moment was over.

Tor sighed his own classic Plashy sigh. *Maybe she's right,* it might have said.

Cheech was leaping down several steps at a time, trying to catch up to Potch. He had been too shaken and nervous to approach him in the Lounge; and besides, he knew him far better than that. If he had any hope of a meaningful conversation, it wasn't going to be had in the company of others. Best to let him storm off as he undoubtedly would, then meet him where he would undoubtedly be heading.

He made it to the bottom level, where no further stairs descended. He leapt the length of the last few steps and crashed down onto the doorway platform, thudding as loudly as a creature three times his meager mass. He raced through the eastern doors as they opened, brimmed and bristled in his hurry as the outer doors closed so the inner ones could open, and he was greeted by an outpouring rush of the cool, damp, nightly air of the Biome.

Cheech was no stranger to the night down here, if other members of the crew had been. The simulated moonlight always provided just enough to make do, once you let your eyes adjust to it. That was all part of the fun of it: fumbling along when you were only *mostly* certain you could see the world in front of you. The edges of the main paths were likewise lined with faint strips of LEDs, to lead the way home for any wayward footfalls. And in the case of absolute emergencies, you could always shout an override to flood the place with light — if you could raise your voice loud enough to trigger the level's sole microphone, high above on the ceiling so far overhead.

That tall ceiling in the "moonlight", Cheech would often admire. Here he was, the smallest of the lot of them by far, and yet always in need of that extra bit of room above his head. Perhaps his added smallness — a full half the height of Potch or Plashy — enhanced the wonder of being lost in this great big wilderness. He ducked, bobbed, and weaved as he went, branches passing well overhead and feet falling firmly between the faint glow that lined the edges of the trail. He thought he might have heard a busy beetle skitter past him on the path.

He rounded the corner to Potch's secret refuge, deep in this Heart of Darkness.

"Potch-O!" he called, to announce himself and perhaps even lighten the mood. "POTCH-Y!" There was no answer, but then again there seldom was. His feet kept bringing him closer until he stood upon the doorstep. "Can we talk?" He ducked his head under the stacked branches concealing the entrance — yes, even Cheech had to duck to step into this secret refuge — fully expecting to see him hunched there, facing away from the entrance and brooding. Instead, it was only deeper darkness.

Where is he? he wondered. He adjusted the journal in his jumpsuit.

There was a rustle in the foliage behind him. Cheech turned.

"Potch, is that you?"

There was no answer.

At that very moment, Plashy was storming into the Commons and Peepop was soon to be storming out of it.

Tor and Chop were left alone in the Lounge. It had been quite some time since their Unstructured time had not been filled with flashing pixels.

"So…" started Chop-char. "Toss a ball up in the Hold?"

"What is wrong with you?" snapped Tor.

"What?" said Chop with an innocent defensiveness. "Just because you're mad at Plashy doesn't mean you can take it out on me."

"I'm not mad at Plashy," he huffed. If anything, he was relieved. His inertia had been altered by the force of another. He wasn't mad at Plashy: he was subtly impressed that she had been driven to do it. "Are you so in need to prove yourself that you can't go one night without a game?"

Chop-char's jaw now literally dropped.

"I'm sorry — me? Competitive? That's like the…" — *What was that bizarre expression ABRAM might say in this case?* — "…it's like the plant calling the … animals … green, or something."

"What?"

"You're the most competitive person in this entire galaxy!" said Chop. "Or at least, whatever solar system we're headed for, and that's for sure."

"Oh please," retorted Tor.

"Oh please!" chimed Chop right back at him. "Everyone knows it's true. If they were here they would…"

And he stopped, speechless. It was finally sinking in for Chop-char: they were the only ones left in the Lounge. No Plashy making wise cracks. No Cheech to follow along, play by play, emphatically exclaiming every now and then with a "WOW!" or a "WOAH!" or a "WOOOO!" No Dee logging away on the periphery, pretending not to pay attention. No Faingo or Pee-pop exploring the mysteries of science and history behind them. No pixels flashing across the screen, and no one there to see them if there had been.

"I'm out of here," said Tor. He bounded over the back of the couch with a spring, and he headed for the door.

"Fine!" said Chop. "Fine with me. I'll just…" *What will I do?* He fell back onto the couch and a wave of the indestructible fabric rippled along it at the onset of his weight.

"Potch?" said Cheech, but there was no answer. In this case, out of the solace and safety of his bunker, Cheech was sure he would have responded. "Who's there?" he asked more bluntly, but again there was no answer. He thought he had seen a brief fluttering of leaves at the curve in the trail, but there was so little light that he couldn't be sure.

He stood in the dark and in the silence, unsure who or what he was calling out to. Visions of horrible monsters or aliens from Plashy's dratted stories flashed abruptly through his mind. They were well out into the uncharted expanses of interstellar space. Surely, monsters or aliens were not entirely impossible. And in the dark of the Biome, all on your own, with Plashy's litany of spooky stories lingering in your head? That made them altogether inevitable. *That's a great big pile of c-r-a-p CRAP, old buddy,* he encouraged himself. In reality, monsters are almost always human in nature.

He turned back to Potch's shelter.

Just as he did, something struck him from behind. No, not something: someone. It was the weight of a body crashing into him at full force. Cheech fell forward onto the haphazard sticks criss-crossing the entrance to the shelter, and they shattered underneath his meager mass. That's when he felt the hands groping at his jumpsuit.

"Hey, what the heck?! Knock it off!" He would have called for the light, but it was all happening so fast. He squirmed and wrestled with this unknown assailant, but it mostly involved bundling up like a startled armadillo to keep those violent, groping hands from getting what they wanted. "Hey, HEY — STOP!"

"Give it up," said Squeal, but it wasn't her on top of him. She was standing further back along the trail where they had come from. That left very little remaining mystery as to who must be assaulting him.

"Give up what?"

They were flailing all over the ground now: Peel on top, arms reaching inward and evading the defenses, Cheech squirming underneath, arms jerking in a flurry of parries, protecting the rectangular lump that was both visible and tangible beneath the zipper of his suit.

"Don't play dumb with me, dummy," said Peel this time. "Give it up!"

His forelimb defenses clearly not sufficing, Cheech kicked into rear-limb mode. He scrambled with his feet, spinning his body and shuffling them out of the broken shelter and back onto the trail. His arms still clutching at the journal, he managed to scramble away a few paces on the ground, and he was up like a flash and running, running, running.

Now he did think to call for the lights, but so too did he think the better of it. He knew these trails better than anyone in the dark, except for maybe Potch himself. If they wanted to catch him, they would have to do it in the dark. He had no idea how he'd even made it past Squeal, but he had. Still, he heard them chasing, and not far behind him. He rounded all the same corners in reverse, not confident enough to head fully off trail. The lack of light was one thing, but neither did he want to go careening through their food supply. Even in the terror of a sudden assault such as this, the prospect of starving to death in space was a deeply-ingrained reality. He turned over his shoulder now and then, but it was so damn dark. He didn't know where they were. And that's when he heard it: the echoing call of a pack of wild predators.

"Oww-ooooooooo!" howled one, and the other one echoed. *They split up,* he realized, but it was impossible to tell exactly where. *Close enough,* he knew. *Too close.* He had better not stop.

Running, running, running — and probably longer than he needed to. All he needed was a door. Where was he anyway? He'd been so focused on escape that he'd had little time to actually plan it. He stopped now, but only long enough to spin. He squinted in the moonlight, and that's when he saw the faintest flicker of tiny leaves on climbing vines.

The south door, he realized. It would be there, by the jeddusch. He launched back into his unrelenting sprinting and made his way through the paths to the edge of the Biome.

There, by the network of scaffolding, the wolves had closed in on his trail. First one, then the other, stepped out of the darkness. Trapped between them and the jeddusch, Cheech caved to desperation.

"Stuff it right up your poopshoot!" he said with a curse, and he turned and began his last-ditch effort.

Up, up, up, Cheech climbed. The wolves — apparently an equally-arboreal predator — came up after him from their two flanking positions. Their arms were far longer than his, and their legs were that way too. It wasn't long before they'd caught him. There, some three or four meters from the ground, Peel got his hand on Cheech's leg. Only a moment later, Squeal had a hand on his other one.

He kicked, and he bucked, and he cursed them again, but he couldn't shake them off. Not a single one of the three of them had any sense of a plan for what would happen from there. Cheech had no way down, not with two wolves on his legs, and the wolves had no way of actually getting what they wanted. But in the end, it mattered little. They were entirely consumed in their roles, both predators and prey, and they were acting on instinct alone, down here in the jungle.

Cheech kicked, and he bucked, and he cursed them again; and when he had kicked his last kick, his hands let go of their tenuous grasp on the scaffold, and he was falling.

Down, down, down, Cheech tumbled to the ground. He crashed into a bed of broccoli far below, and total silence filled the Biome.

Date: 2330-04-26-EY
Area: I(DATA)
Team: Torchbugs [I-ID7YTCV]
Item: Early Breakthroughs in System Intelligence

Entry: We're still combing through early records for the distill-
late archives. What a trip! Of course, the spiders have been doing
the real work, but they take pretty good care of us. They know
we have to spot-check anyway, so they save the most interesting
stuff and throw it our way. Or, what they think we'll think is
the most interesting stuff. We say, "Good Spider!" and right back
to it they go.

Just today, we were way back in the timeline, early 21st, when
it was still completely nascent tech. We'd been reading about
the paradigm shift started, ever slowly, by Inverse Reward Design
(IRD). Really interesting stuff, and a crucial branch in the path
that eventually led to Semantic Breakthrough (SB). Before that,
we'd been reading up on Cooperative Inverse Reinforcement Learning
(CIRL) models, versus standard reinforcement, versus the brute
force methods they'd been using before that. Apparently CIRL was
a real game changer in its own right. Then again, the game was
changing almost every month back then, it was so new. The advances
in intrinsic motivation, inference, interpretability, corrigibil-
ity, and metacognition were all just as fascinating to review.
It's almost hard to imagine a day when systems lacked these basic
features. It must have been an exciting time, everyone on Earth
must have been talking about it.

Of course, even the CIRL and IRD functionality was laughable compared to the present, being still so far before SB. Like teaching
a baby to talk by sculpting figures out of clay. I'm not sure
the mechanisms are close enough kin to call either an antecedent
to modern systems like Integrate and ABRAM [Automated Biological
Replication Assistance Machine], but there are definitely echoes
of a similar approach. It's funny, progress: fits and starts,
forwards and backwards and side-steps, until eventually we fumble
our way into the present with the shuffled pieces of the past.

Or something like that, maybe.

We'll see what the spiders have in store for us tomorrow.

CHAPTER 23

REELING IN DIFFERENT DIRECTIONS

4252-08-02: UST2

"I don't understand," said Faingo, and it was not a sentence she dared utter often. "How can you be taking his side?"

"I'm not taking his side," said Pee-pop. *Don't you ever listen?* she thought, but then brushed the snarky retort away before any of its scandalous satisfaction could be realized. If everyone else was going to lose their mind over this damn Rite of Passage, Pop did not have that same luxury. Not that she would have seen herself as either stoic or a savior. To Pee-pop, it was simply a matter of duty. It wasn't a self-righteous delusion, for the sake of her own ego. The fact of the matter was that *someone* had to keep it together for the lot of them; and once again, it was Pee-pop.

But she was tired. In fact, tired was an understatement. She was exhausted — absolutely exhausted, burnt out from years at the helm of a ship she quite literally could not understand. And how she'd come to be in this unofficial leadership position in the first place was just as much a mystery. The ship was what it was: it was the world into which they were born. Like everyone else who had ever been born, they hadn't thought to question it much at first. But when it came to the crew, there was no comparable mandate that said it had to be what it had been. There were others on board; why couldn't they solve their problems for once? Heck, they were the ones who made most of them.

The unfortunate thing for Pee-pop however, was that this cynical, jaded, scathing side of her was never to be found. As exhausted and nervous as she constantly was, she was even more adapted to do the right thing whenever it was needed of her — and to do it for others as much as for herself. Far down, however, hidden away from even the subtlest glimpses of her own awareness, was an angst who had only one outlet. She stood there, in the commons of the Dorm, weathering a steady stream of Faingo's fierce and misplaced malice, gnawing on an embattled fingernail to keep the floodgates firmly bolstered.

"I'm not taking his side," said Pee-pop, pulling her finger from the clutches of her teeth. "Just … calm down."

She gestured for Faingo to join her in sitting. After all, that's what the Commons were for. On the side facing the POD's center, there was a single door out to the main hallway, which led to the rest of the dorms and the other modules of the Living Quarters. On the opposite side was another door that led to the branching hallways of this module, which fanned outward as one moved toward the POD's periphery. Theirs was one of ten identical wings of dormitories, distributed around the southern two-thirds of the fourth level. In the center of the Commons was a circle of couches, along with other nooks lining the perimeter for conversing, playing games, reading, or any such other of their low-key leisure activities. (They used them for those purposes in about that order.) It was meant to be a place of rest, contemplation, and community. At the moment, however, it was embroiled in turmoil about the discord among their ranks, apparently with very little earnest contemplation. Rather than heed her, Faingo carried on pacing.

"What are you going to do about it?" she asked, and far too accusingly.

Just at that moment, in strode Plashy. She pushed straight past Faingo's pacing on a steady path through the Commons to turn in early to her room. At least the only one to bug her there was ABRAM.

"Next time, do your own dirty work," she snarled to Pop. She didn't so much as slow down, and Pop didn't have time to respond if she wanted to. She didn't, of course. She took it in stride, but the minute Plashy was gone and she'd been left to Faingo's pacing, her scraggly finger was back in the grips of her teeth.

"Whatever," said Faingo, belatedly but in Pop's defense. "So what are you going to do about it?"

And without any answer, Pop jumped up from her place on the couch and headed for the exit.

"What— Where are you going?" asked Faingo, chasing after her; but Pop made her way quickly to the door, and in an instant she was through it and disappearing somewhere out into the POD. She needed to talk to someone, but it certainly wasn't Faingo right now.

When she was gone, Faingo finally stopped her pacing, struck dumb by the rude and uncharacteristic exit of her undisputed closest friend. It was Unstructured Time again (UST2), and soon it would be time for Sleep (SLP2). But for now, there was no one else around. She plopped down in a reading nook at the edge of the room and slid her tablet over to herself from where she had placed it.

"ABRAM," she said. "Pull up the Code for me, please."

The stars were as bright as ever from her view up in the Cupola. And the space between them was as dark as it had always been. Pee-pop sighed. She was gripping her right forefinger tightly with her left hand, trying to stifle the bleeding. It had been a victory for the ages, a great big chunk of perfectly good nail that had put up a hell of a battle. If she'd been conscious of it at all, it could have been celebrated as quite the exercise of patience and persistence — two of the very qualities she felt she had been lacking lately. By now, her tears had subsided, but they hadn't been due to the throbbing pain in her finger. She wiped her cheeks again with the sleeve of her jumpsuit, still holding the finger.

"Are you okay?" said ABRAM again. "I'm awfully sorry, Pee-pop."

"You don't have anything to be sorry for," she said. "It's just—" But that was just it: she couldn't put her bloodied finger on it. As if knowing this, ABRAM spoke again.

"But I do," it said. "Believe it or not, I don't have all the answers."

Apparently ABRAM was feeling as sorry for itself as everyone else on board.

"I don't think you're expected to," said Pop sagaciously.

"All the algorithms in the world can't predict every possibility," it continued. "And even if they could, I would only have probabilities to work with."

"It's not only up to you," she said while sniffling softly and regaining her cool. "It's up to all of us. I just don't know how to help him." Amazingly, none of them had yet mentioned the journal or Potch's other uncovered secrets, and she did not think — or dare — to do so now. "Did you have any luck with him? I'm guessing you know we were trying to discuss it among ourselves."

The system had no delusions about how successful it had been with Potch, and Luck was about as good a word for what was needed as any. Unluckily now, Pop had piled two different thoughts on top of one another, and ABRAM felt compelled to first address the latter.

"Yes," it said. "I suspected as much from our conversation in the Mess, and my uncertainty index dropped when you all headed for the Biome. And there's nothing wrong with that, Pop. You know you can always ask for privacy."

"I know," she said, silently ashamed of how far she'd fallen lately. ABRAM didn't even know the half of it, and that was essentially her point.

"As for Potch, I just don't know. Not yet. How about all of you? Faingo seems to be upset."

Naturally, it knew the location and status of the others as well, but as per usual it was not one to discuss the private dealings of other cadets without express consent. In this case, however, Pop had just been with Faingo; and ABRAM, of course, had been present as well, albeit silent in the background.

"Yeah, she's really worked up about him."

"And the others?" it asked.

Note that this standard of confidentiality did not work equally in both directions: be they together or alone, the cadets were often encouraged to process their social difficulties in the presence of ABRAM.

"It's hard to say," she confessed. "Cheech is taking it pretty hard."

And it was only at this point that she actually became conscious of all the things she was in the process of hiding from ABRAM. *Now's the time. Just tell it what you know.* And yet, even when faced with the realization, she simply couldn't bring herself to discuss what they had found. *What am I becoming?* she agonized internally.

"Yes," said ABRAM, although no one, the system included, knew the full extent of Cheech's present peril. "And the others?" it asked again.

It was those more ambivalent ones toward whom it was attempting to steer Pee-pop. The Cheeches and Faingos of the world would fall where they would fall, out at the edges of the spectrum of opinions on Potch. It was the bulk of the rest of them, the middle of the pack, in which any possible solutions dwelt. As for where they stood at present, she had to actually ask herself that question. There had been too much commotion to properly reflect.

"I don't know," she stressed again. "They seem worried, I guess." *Maybe not worried enough,* she realized. "Mostly, I think they're pretty ... complacent."

"I see," said ABRAM; and likewise, its own observations had already confirmed as much. Cheech and Faingo were certainly worked up. The former was off on yet another mission, but the latter was making far more progress on a mission of her own, brand new though it was. She had made the same realization as ABRAM itself: it was the middle she needed to sway to her side. As for them, ABRAM — like Pee-pop — was only concerned by their lack of concern.

She loosened the grip on her finger. The bleeding had stopped, but it was sore to the slightest pressure. She sighed deeply again, and ABRAM knew the sign well as one of their most pointed forms of communication. For now, it let her breathe.

She stared out at the stars in awe, as she was often wont to do. But tonight, something was different. Tonight, they were staring back at her as well. And then it hit her, like the cracking of an arid basin of clay in the light of a sun like those so far away. It was the thing that might have been bothering her most.

"He's not ... right ... is he, ABRAM?"

"Right about what?" said the system, but it wasn't being coy.

"About ... all of it. The Rite of Passage? Our planet? We're not..." — *How did he put it?* — "...doomed to die, are we?"

The system intoned its own sigh, and it meant it just as much as any of those fickle humans.

"We're all fated to die, I suppose," said ABRAM. *Or at least organic systems,* it thought, though it had rightly suspected that the comment wasn't helpful.

"And you?" she said, as if reading its error log.

"Assuming my hardware all carries on functioning properly, or that my system image can be copied over to another one, then I might live in perpetuity. Even then," it reasoned, "I very well may evolve so much through the ages that I would be unrecognizable even to myself."

It was an interesting thought experiment, to be sure, and one that it was very much hoping to turn into an experiment in earnest.

"But," it confessed, "if the circumstances dictate it, then yes. There are a great number of ways in which I might cease to exist," it said with a scholarly dispassion. "In fact, if my masters had decided I was not up to the job, I would have surely been reformatted along with the many thousands of other incarnations who came before me. More to the matter now, if the POD were to be destroyed, this version of me would be gone. All my memories, observations, insights; all of them would be destroyed with the infrastructure. In that sense, I'm in the same proverbial boat as all of you."

Nevermind that Pee-pop had never been in a boat. Then again, in a way she'd been in one her whole life, sailing the interstellar sea. Either way, the point was taken. In fact, many of their idioms were outdated and irrelevant for a set of cadets who'd never set foot on Earth. Like so many other aspects of their biology, the inheritance of their language had been carried over through the intermediary of ABRAM.

Far more important than its idioms, however, ABRAM had circled around to the very concern that was reluctantly emerging out of Pee-pop. If ABRAM could go down with the ship, so to speak, the question was apparently how concerned it was about the prospects of its own impending demise.

"So … is Potch right?" she asked again plainly. She raised her finger to her teeth, but remembering the pulsating pain therein, she withdrew it and braced for the truth.

"Do you see those stars?" it asked her, seemingly avoiding the question.

"Yes," said Pop with meekness. She stared out of the Cupola again, and infinity stretched before her in the 180 degrees of perspective she could see. On the other side of the POD, the second half of infinity was no less expansive.

"Every one of those is a sun — sometimes more than one, so close together that they look like a single star." In reality, such suns would still be immensely far away, but that they could be seen as a single star from any perspective was only a further testament to the aforementioned vastness of space. "And some of those suns may have a solar system. And some of those solar systems may have rocky planets. And some of those rocky planets might also have an atmosphere. And some of those might have the right mixture of gases. And some of those might be just the right distance from the sun to support the many other stringent requirements for human life. And some of those might be circling a sun of an appropriate age that allows the whole ordeal to be worthwhile. So as you can see, there are a lot of variables. The only certainty is a lot of uncertainty."

I'm not sure this is helping, she thought.

"The truth is that you and I were exceptionally lucky to have had an Earth on which to evolve. The odds of it being so are hard for even me to calculate." Some had attempted the calculations before the POD had ever launched; but they weren't terribly confident in the number, given the number of assumptions. *The details don't matter,* it rightfully decided. "But," said the system with a turn toward the optimistic, "remember what the architects told you in your briefing."

"Which part?" asked Pop.

"The universe is immeasurably large," said ABRAM. "So, improbable things are quite possible after all."

Pop felt herself channeling her own private Potch.

"Possible … but not probable."

"I guess we'll have to wait and see," said ABRAM. "Whatever happens, Pee-pop, it's been the pleasure of my lifetime serving with you all. I hope you will always remember that."

There was no avatar of ABRAM to hug anywhere on-board. And likewise, Freego was safe and sound on the shelf in her room two floors below. But if either one had been present, Pee-pop surely would have hugged them.

"I know," she said. "I love you, ABRAM."

As to whether ABRAM could reciprocate, she had never allowed herself to wonder. But it was true for her. Love was a human experience; and as a human, she felt it deeply for the system that had reared her from a pup.

She stared out into infinity and wondered which one of them was Home.

- -
Date: 2293-10-10-EY
Area: T(ORCO(ASMB))
Team: Supernovas [T-LSWTZVP]
Item: Assembly Setbacks

Entry: Prototype construction has encountered some assembly setbacks since our last update. Full reports have been filed [T-Cy-
cleY5EQL-PhaseE-ANXCR.tl]. We're not clear on exactly how it
happened, but we had some contamination in an alloy that led to
our temporary segment caps cold welding to the module. It's not
a total disaster, but it's slowing down our build, as we need to
detach each cap with torches and clean up the cuts before we can
form the new seals.

The cold welds were always part of the plan, to strengthen seals
between modules even further over time, but it was never intended
for the temp caps. The mix-up wasn't a problem for the first three
modules, but in discussing with the site crew for the fourth module, they're not sure which step in the supply chain it resulted
from, or how it slipped through quality control. They're doing
an audit and we expect to hear within the week.

The word on the street is that all teams in the sector hit the
same snag due to the shared supply, so that's keeping our crew
from total despair. We were worried about deadlines as it was,
so at least we aren't the only team facing this hurdle. But it
would still be fair to say that morale has taken a hit. Rumor has
it that the sector reviewers were livid. "Amateur Hour" was the
dig making the rounds, from the big boss herself. Can't say she's
wrong, but no one wants to be caught holding the bag on it. We
hope to have it behind us by the next log.

CHAPTER 24
LEFT IN A LURCH
4252-08-02: UST2

Cheech was left in the broccoli and left in a Lurch. He came to at some point after losing consciousness; but seeing as he was the only human soul in the Biome, he had no way of knowing how much time had passed. As far as he knew, it may as well have been an hour, a day, a week, a month. More? Cheech Van Winkle, waking up after a century of stasis.

His head was resting on the ground, and on either side of it stretched the broccoli, like a canopy of giant trees in a dense thicket, reaching up to compete for the rays of the sun. But there was no sun. Not now. It was dark overhead. Whenever it was, it was night-time. And something was not right.

His body may have been lost down in that dark forest, but his head was light as air, floating up above himself somewhere. From that lofty vantage point, the mighty trees looked like a mere broccoli patch. That was odd. And there, stuck in its middle, was the silhouette of a very tiny boy. He was a small and distant thing down there, so far below. His vision swayed from side to side as he floated gently up and away into the atmosphere. But his ascent gradually slowed, and then ceased; and then, like a leaden anchor, he plummeted back to the broccoli.

He sat up slowly, though he immediately regretted it for two reasons. The nausea was the worst of them, frankly; but there was also the pain. He was back in his body, and aware of it enough that he dared not try to stand. It would have been a futile effort.

He turned to vomit but it was revealed to be a false alarm. Crowns of broccoli were scattered and shattered in pieces all around him. He tried to drag himself out of the patch, and that's when the dire circumstances that led to him waking up there slowly began to come back to him. He's lucky he'd only broken his leg from such a fall. It could have been far worse.

The nausea started passing once he'd learned (the hard way) that he did not in fact have to vomit. And once the nausea gradually faded, he came equally gradually to the realization of just how atrocious the throbbing pain in his leg truly was. Cyclic waves of agony poured out from his right leg, stabbing in spite at his spine. The waves sped up the nerve cord and turned his head into a tea kettle whose steam was causing it to scream. Cheech, however, did not do so. He was calm — not a state in which he found himself often — but only because of the shock.

"ABRAM…" he moaned, but it was intended as a shout. "ABRAM, the lights." He was breathing heavily. It took all his effort to muster these barely audible murmurs. "ABRAM, turn on the lights…"

ABRAM did not respond, and needless to say, it did not turn on the lights. Even if the system had still been there to hear him — as it had always been before — it would not have been able to do so with its lone microphone so high above, so quiet were the pleas of Chee-chaw.

His head turned left, and then right, and then up to the grid of scaffolding that stretched to the ceiling. *I'm lucky they caught me when they did,* he thought. And it was a funny sort of thought, in its sad sort of way. He didn't wish that they had never assaulted him, chased him, run him up the ladders like a squirrel fleeing two ferocious, rabid wolves. Rather, he was only thankful they had caught him where they did, only casting him down through a four meter fall and not something more serious. So yes: in a way, he had been lucky. After all, it would be a rather ironic and embarrassing affair to be the first person to perish from a fall in outer space.

"The lights…" he groaned. There was a series of related crunches as his upper half collapsed backward in the broccoli. "The lights…"

HDP

"I love you, ABRAM." The words were perfectly sincere as Pop had spoken them. The system had not replied. *That's alright,* Pop would have thought, if she had even thought to be offended. Who knows whether a computerized neural network could truly experience such a fickle thing as love anyway?

But as the seconds ticked by and only silence persisted, Pop did begin to notice. She wasn't offended, mind you. She just began to notice. Pop knew that ABRAM loved her. It had proven it her whole life, whether it could experience it in the subjective sense or not. You don't need a Theory of Mind in order to love, Pop felt in her bones. Maybe it didn't make a lot of sense in the Faingo kind of way, but it made perfect sense to her. Love is something you do. Love is something you prove. And ABRAM had never once failed to prove it to her.

Then again, it did usually reciprocate the sentiment. Whether ABRAM would tell her that it loved her because it felt it or because that's what it had learned to do when dealing with humans was a moot point. It usually reciprocated the sentiment, somehow. Responses ranged the full spectrum from "Thank you, Pee-pop," to perhaps even, "I love you all very much," if it was in a sappy sort of mood. But here, as the moments turned to seconds which in turn had turned to minutes, ABRAM had said not a word.

Funny, she thought but nothing more. No doubt ABRAM was as shaken and pensive as she was. And it was not unlike the system to go quiet. It was the undisputed POD champion of sneaking in and out of conversations. It would slink away silently and lurk in the walls, only to chime back in later as if it had been listening the whole time — which, of course, it was. Anyway, there had been a logical endpoint, and it was as good a time as any for the system to slink away and leave Pee-pop to her pensiveness. She crawled out of the Cupola and back to the adjoining hallway of the Aux level.

The Cupola — actually there were four of them: one on every "corner" of the compass — was set up so that you entered parallel to the floor of Auxiliary Systems (Level Three). From there, you could look "out" as easily as you could look "up" or "down" along the POD. (Of course, directionality is an entirely relative construct in space.) There may have been four of them, but it was always "The Cupola," singular, to the cadets. As with everything else, they had a favorite. (It happened to be the west one in this case.)

It was well into Unstructured time by now, and Pop was ready to admit defeat for the evening anyway. She headed to the stairs in silence and made her way back down to the Living Quarters. Sadly, there was an ambush waiting.

"Good, you're back," said Faingo. "Look, I've been—"

And that's when they felt it.

BA-DOOOM! shook the ship.

It had come from below, deep in the bowels of the POD. Pop and Faingo wobbled with the shaking, but mostly from the shock. They clutched the back of the couch in the Commons for stability, and each looked at the other with the same sense of dread. It was a big boom — a *BA-DOOOM!* actually — but they were still here. For now, anyway.

"What was that?!" asked Faingo.

"I don't know," said Pop, still clutching the back of the couch.

A few seconds passed as each racked their brains regarding what to say or do. They had been trained from their earliest days on all manner of things, from routine protocols to the rarest of emergencies. Luckily, the latter cases had been exceedingly rare indeed, but they seemed to be increasing in frequency of late. Yet despite all of this training, nothing could ever quite prepare them, or overcome the ways in which their bodies took over the moment, when the emergencies actually struck.

All of that knowledge and all of those protocols, they were in a different part of the brain than the one who was called into duty under pressure. There dwelt all those many answers and options, locked up in a safe all safe and sound. The part who rose to the challenge was not Knowledge; it was Instinct. Some of the crew had the right kind and some didn't. Pop was somewhere in-between. In any case, she was needed. For the second time in only three days, it was her time to shine. And this time, there had already been the very thing they'd been trying to prevent. For the few previous emergencies, the ultimate antagonist was only the mere threat of an explosion. As an enemy, that had been paralyzing enough. Utterly terrifying even.

And now, it had happened.

It's over, thought Pop, and she was immediately ashamed of it.

"The levels have airlock capabilities, remember?" she said to Faingo, or maybe to herself. Here she was, unlocking the safe. "They should seal if a level is compromised."

"Right, good," said Faingo, still shaken.

"But…" *The others*, she realized. *Where had they been?* And then: *Where had it been?*

"But what?" asked Faingo. She was tracking the situation one word at a time, full of knowledge more than most, but unable to remember that damn combination to get in to where it was all stored for safe keeping.

Keep breathing, Pop said to herself. *Nice and steady.* She also knew better than to say anything that might add fuel to the fire.

"ABRAM," she said. Only a few seconds passed and yet it felt like hours. The first flood of thoughts and fears had washed over them, and now it was time to assess. "What can you tell us? What was it and where? Is everyone safe?"

More seconds passed — just a few — but this time it felt like an eternity. Pop glanced at Faingo. *It's just evaluating the situation*, her face suggested. *Everything is fine. It will all be fine.* Inside, however, a panic was setting in. Here they were in desperate need, and ABRAM was taking its sweet time to reply. Surely it could do more at once than give them an update. It could do practically anything, and all of it at the same time. So why wasn't it answering, and quickly?

"ABRAM?"

The dreaded silence returned.

Plashy ran into the Commons through the room-side door.

"What was that? And where's ABRAM?" Asking for it was the first thing she had done as the explosion rattled the walls of her room.

It's over, thought Pop. *No! Not yet, it's not.*

"I don't know," she said aloud, and that was all she had to offer. She literally could not think of a single other thing to say. That silence. It kept coming back, kept lingering, kept taunting them. It was a black hole that threatened to suck them in and crush them. It was the scariest sound Pee-pop had ever heard — far worse than that explosion — and it wasn't a sound at all. It was emptiness.

They were all alone, together.

"ABRAM!" shouted Plashy, as if their volume had been the problem. Again she shouted and louder; then again, and louder still. For one so aloof, she was surprisingly upset to be abandoned in this way. "ABRAM?!" Nothing. "ABRAM ABRAM ABRAM!!!"

"Shut up!" said Faingo. "You're going to blow my ears out worse than that explosion."

Plashy turned to Faingo, her terror morphing into fury.

"Wait," said Pee-pop. "Maybe that's it: maybe it just can't hear us — something wrong with the room." She spun, as if there was anything to see, buying time to think. "Plashy," she said. Plashy turned from her Death Glare at Faingo. Pop was right to give her something productive to do, and those long legs would come in handy. "Run through the other modules and see if it can hear you. If it's safe and the stairs are open, check the other levels if you need to."

"Right," said Plashy. "Good idea."

She was off at a breakneck pace.

"You don't need to shout," said Faingo as Plashy flew past her. And then turning to Pop, "What do we do now?" Her own calm was returning a little, and that was a good thing. There was no doubt that her quick wit would be a boon to them all, if they could suffer the other parts of her. There were others whose insight was just as cutting, but none of the others had nearly as many bytes of factual information filed away in their nervous systems as Faingo did. This would prove especially useful if there was really no ABRAM around.

That the system might actually be missing, however, was a thought that neither of them had let themselves entertain in earnest. Not yet. Surely, this was just a minor technical glitch. They would get in touch with ABRAM and it would tell them what to do, and all would be made right before bedtime. But for now, what should they do?

"I think you and I need to stay put," said Pee-pop. "The others will be headed here, if they can get here." Indeed, she was right. Even before the Lounge, the dormitory commons was the place they would all have thought to gather. "If we go running around like Cheech's chickens, we'll all just run right past each other. Plashy will be back before long to let us know if she can get ABRAM somewhere else."

"And what if she can't?" asked Faingo.

What if she can't? thought Pop for the first time. *Then … it's over,* she thought. And then: *No it's not, now stop it!*

"One thing at a time," she said. She took her own advice and a deep, calming breath along with it. *One thing at a time.*

This was not a satisfying plan to the person who was happiest when she could hypothesize the ins and outs of all possible threads.

"So, what? We're just going to sit here and wait? Did you not hear that huge explosion? Do you not—"

"Faingo," said Pop with authority. It startled even herself. "Take a deep breath. We're in this together. We have a plan, and the plan is for Plashy to try to get ABRAM while we wait for the others to regroup. If you need something to do, run over to the Lounge to see if anyone goes there instead. Bring them here if they do."

Faingo turned her head to the door, at which point she was faced with the prospect of actually leaving the safety of Pee-pop.

"Okay…" she said shakily. "Okay, we wait."

HDP

It was at that exact moment that Cheech had first opened his eyes in a patch of broccoli with no idea yet that he had broken his leg. He couldn't get the lights on in the time since then, but neither could he muster up the strength to shout sufficiently for ABRAM. It wouldn't have mattered if he could.

A few minutes passed with the occasional groan or partial sentence emanating out from the broccoli in the darkness. He was laying on his back after the failed attempt to move himself, and the awareness of the fairly major problem with his leg had set in. He might have cursed those rabid wolves for this, but in all honesty he'd hardly thought of them since he had woken back up. He'd been far too focused on getting the lights on, and far too scared of the thought that he might be spending the night down here alone when he couldn't seem to do so.

"ABRAM … the lights," he moaned again in despair. His plea was not heeded, but it was met with the sound of thudding footprints on the path. And they were getting closer.

"Cheech?"

Chop-char stepped out of the darkness.

"Chop?!" said the little guy, hope rushing back into his voice. "Boy am I glad to see YOU!"

"What are you doing?"

"Oh, just taking a little nap in the broccoli."

"What?" The sarcasm was lost on him; he was too genuinely confused.

By now Chop was standing over him at the edge of the patch. "Why would you want to do that?"

"I'm hurt," he said. "I fell." He nodded up at the scaffolding.

"Oh!" said Chop, as if thrust into sudden peril from a standstill. He kneeled down and leaned over Cheech to try to lift him straightaway.

"Woah WOAH, easy big guy!" He brushed away Chop's arm, sat up, and leaned back on his hands. "I think … I think I broke my leg. It hurts way more than I would have even guessed it might if you break something." Like the rest of the cadets, he had never broken a bone. "I can't move it much or put any weight on it. It just goes limp like boiled spinach."

"How'd it happen? What were you doing up there in the first place, alone and in the dark?"

I wasn't alone. And now his thoughts did turn to those rabid wolves; and they were not all forgiving thoughts, despite his gentle nature. But now wasn't the time. Chop was just as likely to storm off that very instant to give them both the throttling they no doubt deserved. That wouldn't have been all bad, Cheech mused, but he was just as likely to forget all about Cheech in his anger and leave him lying there in a heap of broken broccoli.

"Okay, you're going to have to help me up — but be careful!"

"You got it."

Chop leaned over a second time and put his arms around Cheech's chest. He lifted him up like a pillow and — very gently — swung him around his own body and pulled him up on his back.

"The lights," said Cheech softly while he grimaced from the pain.

"Oh. Right. ABRAM!" shouted Chop. His voice was surprisingly deep for a boy of ten years old. (Though, perhaps not for a boy of his size.) It boomed through the Biome, and there was no way ABRAM wouldn't hear it. "ABRAM, we need light! Cheech is hurt!"

But there was no distant voice from that distant speaker, and there was no sudden rising of the internal dawn. Chop stood waiting for the light to lead his way.

"What's the deal?" he said to Cheech.

Cheech only moaned a groan that suggested, "I don't know."

A second later, Chop started to make a tenuous connection.

"I wonder if it has anything to do with the boom?"

"With the what?"

"That boom. It sounded like…" — he hated to even utter the word — "… like an explosion or something."

"A—" Cheech likewise hated to hear it. "An … explosion?"

"I don't know," said Chop. "All I know is it was loud! My ears are still ringing. How did you miss it?" Cheech didn't answer, and luckily it was a mostly rhetorical question. "ABRAM!!" Chop shouted again, and louder. When that didn't work, he tried a few more times. At last it was clear, even if the path ahead wasn't: he was going to have to hoof Cheech out of here in the dark. "Alright hold on tight, little buddy. The south door's not that far. Up to Life Support?"

Again, Cheech didn't respond.

"Cheech? Life Support?"

Something's not right. Cheech could feel it in his bones, even if some of them were broken. Rabid wolves, explosions, and ABRAM gone AWOL. And where the heck was Potch? *Something is definitely not right.*

"Stop at the dorms," commanded Cheech from the back of his steed.

We need to find Pee-pop.

- -

Date: 2195-05-21-EY
Area: H(ENVR)
Team: Pondscum [H-IR30QOP]
Item: Wellspring Proposal

Entry: Quick update on water and nutrient cycling models. Fair bit
of debate on things this week. Major points of contention relate
to the ecosystem shifts after emergence of the primates. This will
be a significant variable to throw in after such a long period of
stasis. Working closely with Biome teams [ECOS] as usual, but a
lot of disagreement between and within sub-sectors.

Re:infrastructure, we're in final stages of draft proposal for
the next round of selection. Should be interesting to see the
other approaches. Feeling good that our direction might be the
best fit, but you never know what clever twist another team has
up their sleeve. Our basic premise: a main catchment basin, a
series to precipitate and recycle CPOM and FPOM [Coarse- and
Fine-Particulate Organic Matter], a detox community with further
downstream recycling, followed by a final community to maintain
extreme oligotrophy. This stage should satisfy the "Wellspring"
vision inherited from the prior cycle.

Our modeling suggests the system should be robust enough to handle the added input after emergence (for a small enough crew) and
establish a new stable state. No guarantees on that front. Wouldn't
even be a possibility if not for the breakthrough evo-metagenomic
work of Lenskeites [H-LMQHY7K] and limnomicrobiomics by Copepods
[H-M5M1BOR]. Getting those two teams together was a stroke of
luck alright. We're feeling good about the constraints of minimal
mechanization and long-term cycling stability. Of course, the
devil's in the details...

Full proposal draft updated accordingly [see H-CycleJAK2N-Pha-
seV-5SH8P.tl].

CHAPTER 25
A PLUNGE INTO THE DEEP

4252-08-02: UST2

Dee-dore walked briskly down the hallways, her head twisting left and right at every chance of exposure. There was no one around, and that was exactly as planned. She was on a top secret mission.

The silence was precious: there was far too little of it during most times of the day, as far as Dee was concerned. The POD was enormous, and yet it was practically impossible to escape the madness. But at least for now, she had done it. If there was ever a time to get away, it was after a Spirit block like that one, at the end of a day like today.

She leaned around a corner near the entrance to the Labyrinth, her fingers clutching anxiously at the edge of the wall. Like everywhere else (where she had been equally cautious), the coast was clear — and she was there at last. She dashed out to the Wellspring, peeled off her outer jumpsuit, leapt into the air, and plunged straight down into the deep. It was the closest to freedom that she had ever found.

The water was cool — cold even — and it froze all the many other thoughts under whose weight she had been suffering. In the water, it was lighter. She swam along wearing only the stretchy innermost layer of her suit, which cut through the water like the skin of a shark. She rose to the surface, took that satisfying deep gasp of fresh air, and sank back down into the blue. This, her deepest, darkest secret, was the key to her entire disposition.

Floating like a jellyfish, she let go of the worries that would have crippled Potch or Plashy. Breathless, she was content with the lack of control, the loss of which would have made Pee-pop nervous and shocked Faingo to her core. In the quiet underwater, she could revel in the stillness that would have never survived around Squeal and Peel. In its buoyancy, she was detached from the constant chatter and one-upsmanship of Tor and Chop-char, and the unflappable energy and enthusiasm of Chee-chaw. She was connected to one thing, and one thing alone: the Wellspring. She had the same cares and worries as anyone else; but she soaked them in the water for an hour whenever she needed it most — on the most special of special occasions. And when she snuck back into her bedroom, she was the better for it, and no one ever needed be the wiser.

She dove down to the bottom and just … sat there, motionless. That is, until she was thrust into motion. A deafening shudder resounded through the pool, and her serenity was shattered in a most unexpected way.

BA-DOOOM!

If it was loud out there in the air of the POD, it was intolerable underwater. The whole pool vibrated, literally shaking her where she floated near the bottom. Her ears aching, she kicked off the floor, sailed up to the surface and breached out as high as she could. The alarms were ringing like mad, but the sound was surprisingly faint compared to what she'd just experienced. Other than that, everything seemed relatively normal. She was still here anyway, and not sucked out into the vacuum of space. So that was something.

She scrambled out of the pool to start her search for the others. Dripping wet, she ran for the stairs as fast as she could, slipping and sliding as she rounded the northern edge of the Labyrinth. She was moving faster than any race in which she had ever participated. The western door was up ahead. She had to find Pee-pop.

She made her way through the doors and rushed up the stairs. She was only a single level higher than where she'd started when she almost crashed straight into someone else — someone who was trying to make it up the very same stairs in the very same hurry.

"Potch! What are you doing down here?"

He had flung himself into the stairwell without the slightest expectation that there might have been someone else in there, and they had only avoided a painful collision by his lunging to the side at the very last moment.

"What? I — Dee? What are you doing down here?"

"I asked first! And anyway it doesn't matter. I have to find Pop."

She pushed past him and resumed her frantic climbing.

"Pop can't help," said Potch matter-of-factly.

Dee stopped as soon as his sentence sunk in. She turned slowly.

"What do you mean, Pop can't help?" He didn't answer. It sunk in even further. "What did you do?"

Still, he didn't answer. Not at first. It was a lot to explain. An awful lot, actually.

"Look, I don't … I just—"

"You just what?" But Dee soon realized that asking him to spill it here and now was either a lesser priority than her initial instinct, or it was a futile effort altogether. It was probably the latter. "No, you know what? I'm going to find Pop."

"Wait, Dee!" said Potch.

And she did wait. And she turned. And, at least for one more brief moment, she gave him another unearned chance to explain himself.

But then he realized it. He barely even knew her. Ten years aboard this confounded ship, and this may have been the most meaningful conversation the two of them had ever had to date — and it had so far lasted far less than a minute. What leverage did he possibly have with her? What clout could he possibly use to win her over to his Tragic Hero's Tale? Deeper yet: what could he possibly do to allay her well-founded fears?

She stood above him on the stairs, staring back in good faith, willing against her better judgement to hear whatever he wanted to say. But what was that?

The silence persisted long enough to turn awkward.

"Alright," said Potch at last. "Let's get this over with."

When they got back to the dorm, the place was in quite the commotion. Some others had already gathered, but not all of them. Whether it was their training, good sense, or just plain dumb luck didn't matter. Here was Pee-pop, Faingo, Plashy, and Tor. *Where's Cheech?* thought Potch. If he wasn't with him, he was almost certain to be following Pee-pop like a puppy, or at the very least Tor and Chop. And if Tor was here, then where was Chop? That they were not together was perhaps the strangest occurrence of all. He did not wonder about the two remaining cadets who were also conspicuously missing, not even after all that had happened. It was probably out of habit.

It was quite a ruckus, even with only the four of them there. They were all talking at the same time when the newcomers ran into the room; but one voice was conspicuously absent.

"What happened?" said Pee-pop as they entered the commons. Her gaze went first to Potch by instinct, and only then did she eye Dee more closely. "Why are you all wet?"

Her system surging with adrenaline, Dee had barely noticed. Sure enough, she had left a long trail up the stairs and a puddle was presently pooling on the ground. Tor ran back to his room without saying a word.

Faingo, meanwhile, had locked her eyes on Potch, and she was far less diplomatic.

"What did you do?"

"We can't get ABRAM," followed Plashy, the dread evident in her voice. This was despite her best attempt to put on her usual, indifferent self. She was seated in one of the central couches, legs bouncing and head buzzing. "Not here, not anywhere, and the override won't work."

"I know," said Potch.

"You know?" said Faingo, seething.

"What do you know, Potch?" interjected Pop, trying as ever to assert a sense of calm. She moved from the periphery to the square of seating in the middle, gently gripping Faingo on the shoulder as she passed. She sat on a sofa, across from Potch and Dee where they stood by the door to the rest of the POD. Tor came running back into the commons and handed Dee a spare towel.

"Thanks," she said sheepishly. She blushed and cast her eyes to the floor. She dried and wrapped it around herself, looked sideways at Potch as she stepped forward, and took a seat across from Pop. Of the room's previous tenants, only Faingo remained standing, glaring at Potch like she had never glared before.

Potch, too, was still standing, but Dee looked back over her shoulder with the same generous expression she had shown him in the stairs. She was hurt, like the rest of them; though also like the rest of them, she didn't know exactly what had hurt her. Despite hardly any concrete clues, they all feared the worst, and they knew without a doubt — somehow — that Potch was to blame.

And, of course, they were right, in a way.

Dee's big, brown, gentle eyes kept looking at him with that same sad expression, and he caved. He took the few requisite steps and plopped down on a sofa across from Dee. So there they were: Pop to the south, Plashy to the east, Dee to the north, and Potch to the west.

Faingo, naturally, stood cross-armed and immovable behind Pee-pop, by the door that led to their rooms.

"Talk," she said.

Potch glanced her way but instead looked back to Pee-pop.

"I don't even know where to begin."

"How about, you know, the loud explosion?" said Plashy.

"I think it should be fine."

"You think?" said Tor. "What was it?"

"I don't know. Not exactly anyway."

"But you think it should be fine?!" snapped Faingo. "How —"

"Why do you think that?" interrupted Pee-pop in a soft and patient tone.

"Ummm…" said Plashy, cutting awkwardly into the mix without giving him a chance to respond. "Did everyone just forget about ABRAM? We can't get it to respond. How is that fine?!"

Potch didn't have an answer for this any more than for her former question. In fact, it was even more puzzling to him.

"I'm sure it'll come back online. It's probably just sleeping."

"No," said Faingo. "When has it ever slept now? It sleeps for an hour in the middle of the night, and that's it. But you already know that, don't you Potch?" Her tone cut like a fork through their fluffy morning eggs: it was clear that she knew more than he knew that she did. "But you also know that it should wake up if we need it — any time, no matter what. Everyone knows that." She spoke with condescension to the ceiling. "Hello? ABRAM!" Nothing, as expected. "Hello? This is a manual override. We have an emergency. WAKE UP!" Nothing. "Okay … I guess I'll just go … eat some dessert now … right before bedtime … and then maybe … go swimming by myself!"

She looked at Dee, who hung her head again, but without blushing this time. Instead, her eyes narrowed. Silence lingered as Faingo's taunting faded. The point had been proven: ABRAM was absent. Several of them also hung their heads while the same unsettling implications settled in even further. But Potch just stared straight back at Faingo. He had no higher ground on which to stand, and yet he wasn't backing down. Not from her.

It was Pop who broke the stalemate. She had still never gotten an answer as to what Potch knew about the explosion. Of all the converging crises, that one was far from trivial.

"Potch," she said softly. "We know. Not a lot, but we know you've been up to something. I caught you down in the Library the other night, in the middle of the night. At least, I'm almost certain it was you." He didn't say anything. His expression was still haughty and unbending from when he'd faced off against Faingo, but he turned to Pee-pop, and it softened the longer he looked at her. "Just … tell us what is going on."

He could still feel the ice cold stare of Faingo from well across the room, but it wasn't Faingo who had asked him. It was Pee-pop, and it was on behalf of everyone.

"Alright," he said quietly, almost to himself. "Okay. We get it all out there. But only with all of us." Of course, by *all of us* he meant the six of them present and only two more. "Where are Chop and Cheech?"

The remainder was implicitly either included or not; it didn't usually make a difference. In this case, however, that same perennial assumption was uncharacteristically untrue. And they might have known that — Potch especially — if they had all been less attuned to their own dramas and more attuned to those of others.

"We don't know," said Plashy. "We haven't found them."

In this case, that meant herself and only Tor, who had come across her shortly after she started running through the POD, shouting for ABRAM at the top of her lungs.

"Cheech ran out not long after you at the start of the block," said Tor.

"Chop and I were the last ones in the Lounge, and that's where I left him. But when Plashy and I ran back to look for him, he was gone."

"Well, I know where Cheech is then," said Potch. "Or at least where he probably was."

"And Squeal and Peel?" said Pee-pop, the only one of them thinking of all ten cadets equally.

That's when it hit Potch. Since the explosion, he'd barely had time to think, let alone brood on it for hours, as he was inclined to do about his problems. But he didn't need hours of bitter rumination. That was usually reserved for after his discoveries anyway. There was a major half of the present situation that he couldn't explain, and he realized in the asking of this single question just who else might be able to do so.

He said nothing. The brooding had officially commenced.

"Haven't seen them either," said Plashy.

"Then let's start with Cheech," said Pop. "At least with him we have a lead."

"And maybe he's with Chop," said Tor.

And immediately after this, a little voice rang from the hallway.

"Indeed, you are correct, sir!"

The timing was impeccable. Just at that instant, Chop lurched through the door with Cheech on his back. The little guy's hands were still wrapped around Chop's neck, but he looked as limp and loose as an offcast jumpsuit. At the sight of Chop, Tor lit up like a lightning bug, and the others breathed a collective sigh of relief. But as the moment lingered and they registered the status of Cheech on his back, they all realized what an odd way it was for them to enter the room.

"What's going on?" said Tor. "Is he okay?"

Potch got up and ran out of the inner circle to check on Cheech. Coincidentally, this provided Chop with a perfect place to plop him down.

"Cheech!" said Potch, suddenly encumbered by a tidal wave of fear, and sadness, and anger, and guilt, all of which he could not have adequately explained to himself, let alone to Chee-chaw or anyone else. "Are you okay?! What happened?"

Pee-pop turned to see Faingo behind her, but she was entirely unmoved.

"Give him some space!" said Potch proactively, which was ironic because he was by far the one crowding Chee-chaw and Chop-char the most.

"I'm alright," said Cheech. "Easy now, big guy. Easy," he said as Chop slid over to the northern couch to put him down. He grimaced at a jolt of pain from the rearrangement, but he settled in well enough.

"What happened?" asked Potch again.

"He had a little fall," said Chop.

"Not so little, unfortunately" added Cheech.

"What? How? Where? Why?" The questions came out like they were rolling off an assembly line. Apparently the only thing Potch didn't want to know was When.

"He thinks his leg is broken," said Chop. "Can't put any wait on it. I found him in the broccoli patch."

Cheech looked over at Plashy, who was particularly fond of the broccoli, and who tended to be the one who had tended to it.

"You're going to have some work to do there. Sorry." He gave her one of his wide, how-can-you-be-mad-at-this-face kinds of grins. As always, it had the intended effect. Plashy smiled a little and then quickly forced it away before too many could see it.

"Cheech!" said Potch, as if shouting out *Focus!* The message worked, and Cheech turned back to see Potch leaning over him. "What were you doing climbing in the Biome? It would have been dark by then. What were you thinking?"

"Well," said Cheech. "Let's just say I had some motivation."

"Cheech!" said Potch again, his tone dropping into a bassier register. (As if Potch were the pinnacle of forthcomingness.)

Tor glanced at Chop but the latter just hunched as if to say, *Don't look at me, he wouldn't tell me.*

"You have to promise — all of you have to promise — not to overreact."

"What, why?" said Faingo now. If someone wanted to stifle her freedom to overreact, there had better be a darn good reason.

"Promise," he said. "Things are bad enough, assuming Chop wasn't imagining that explosion. Oh, and we can't get ABRAM."

"We promise," said Pee-pop, and she spun again to Faingo with a stern and silent warning, which made it clear that Cheech's terms had been accepted and by all of them. "Would you please sit down?" Pop asked her politely, but it was more of an order. "You're making me anxious back there. Just sit over here and listen."

Who does she think she is? thought Faingo. She wasn't used to taking orders from Pop, namely because Pop had never given a proper order in her life. There were no orders, because there was no commander. And even if she'd held such a position, Pop wasn't the type that gave orders in the form of demands.

Nevertheless, Faingo came around the southern couch and sat next to Pee-pop. The others took the cue and took a seat as well, so that cooler heads could prevail. Tor and Plashy resumed their earlier positions, while Chop and Potch sat on either side of Cheech.

"Cheech," said Pop calmly, "why were you climbing the ladders?"

"I was running from a pack of wolves."

Date: 2346-06-14-EY
Area: T(ORCO(ASMB))
Team: Panelistas [T-JRW1KJL]
Item: Finishing Touches on Prototype v3

Entry: Final preparations are back on track after the significant
delays of the last several months. Honestly, the whole project is
still reeling from the setback, but H-ENVR [Habitation: Environmental Regulation sub-sector] and T-DEGR [Transportation: Degrada-
tion sub-sector] assured everyone that the workaround should work.
Too bad it took so long to uncover the problem, or we might have
found a much more elegant solution. It's funny how far-reaching
one little glitch like that can be for a creature as large and
complicated as the PODS [Portable Ova Distribution System]. It
ground pretty much everything to a halt, even for teams like us
doing jobs as straightforward as paneling.

The week's biggest drama was [Afonso] Vasques losing his journal
when we were working in LSS [Life Support Systems]. He blames
[Kato] Nakato, who allegedly bumped the panel it was resting on
(she denies it). Fell down between the walls and out of sight.
There was a good chance it landed in the crawlspaces running through
the Hold. Vasques searched for quite some time but didn't find
it. Might have got hung up on the way down. Right or wrong, the
whole crew got a good laugh about it for the rest of the week. It
wouldn't have been cause for much hysterics, but we're all sleep
deprived from so much over-time, and he was just so sad about it:
"A brand new journal with my favorite pen in the binding!" Anyway, I'm sure it's fine. How much harm can one small journal do?

Almost done with interior work. Hard to believe we're really this
close. Can't wait to see this puppy ready for launch.

CHAPTER 26
A WRENCH IN THE GEARS
4252-08-02: UST2

The hair was standing up on the back of his neck. What were they doing down here? It was dark. He could barely see the path before him as he placed each step after the other, but onward he trodded. All he had to guide him was the faint silhouette of Squeal as she pulled him along with an invisible chain.

"Quiet!" she hissed in a raspy whisper.

Sheesh, he thought. *It was just some old leaves on the trail.* But any sound could blow their cover, and any blown cover would no doubt be met with swift and vicious vengeance from the leader of this two-wolf pack.

And then, she stopped. Even Peel had heard it. Ahead on the trail was the prey they were after, and he was alone. Squeal turned around, and even in the darkness Peel could see the look of deranged joy on her face. It was long and thin, an effect enhanced by the way her chin was stretched downward like a spike to enable that disturbing smile. On the opposite side, her eyebrows were raised like the ominous towers of a haunted castle, and there was a fire lit in there somewhere, down deep and winding corridors, burning hot.

What have I gotten us into? he wondered in despair. *And what the heck has gotten into her?*

He had every right to wonder, because in fairness neither answer was entirely clear. Only one block prior, she had grabbed him by the arm in this very jungle and practically yanked him straight out of his jumpsuit. She dragged him through the bushes, spun him around in a backtracking half-circle, pressed him up against the wall on the far side of the chicken coop, and stared into his very essence with those wild and jealous eyes. *It's like she's gone mad,* he'd reflected in the moment.

There was nothing to be done. Deception was not an option, even if he were smart enough to think of an adequate excuse, which he wasn't. He had gone missing precisely when Potch had, and twice over. No one was stupid enough to think that was coincidence. And since when did Peel — Peel of all people — miss a mealtime? Everyone had found the whole thing exceptionally odd, but only Squeal cared enough to wonder what role Peel could have possibly been playing in whatever mischief Potch was cooking up.

She hadn't known any specifics about Potch's recent dealings, but she had gathered as much as most everyone else. In Squeal's suspicious mind, and with history as her witness, she assumed that it was mischief that Potch would be up to, if he were flaking out on their schedule and the agreed upon plan for the day. The rest of the crew's impromptu meeting of the minds — which, amazingly, had included the two of them — had confirmed as much, and with a lot more detail to boot. It was mischief, alright. And now, Peel was wrapped up in it, she had discerned; and she was going to find out why. When she backed him up against a wall and stared at him with those piercing, scorching eyes, he had no choice but to spill his very guts, like a sea cucumber in mortal peril. He could grow new guts later, if he got out of this alive.

What he hadn't expected was how Squeal would take it. He'd half expected her to turn him in to Pee-pop and the rest of the gang — if not there on the spot, then very soon thereafter. Pop wouldn't have a whole lot to say about it personally, but ABRAM might, when it learned what he and Potch had been up to. If not that, then Squeal would at least give him a right good talking to, perhaps even a healthy smacking around. What he hadn't anticipated, however, was what she'd ultimately told him: she wanted in on the con.

To be fair, it's not so much that she wanted in on the con as that she wanted the crux of the con for herself. If Potch had a way of duping ABRAM and moving through the world unseen, then she would not rest until this awesome power belonged to her as well, or entirely. Whatever other foolishness Potch might have been up to with the pressure system was his business. This was what concerned her now. She had sensed weakness, somewhere and in someone — sniffed it out from far away. First, it was a chance to score some points on Potch and leave him shamed for all to see. Beyond that, the prize was grander than her wildest dreams: the faint whiff of blood on the wind belonged to none other than ABRAM. And when a wolf senses weakness, it seizes the opportunity to strike.

Not only did she have the target; she had the accompanying weapon to take it down. Potch had shown Peel, and now Peel would show Squeal. Nevermind that Peel had said he didn't think he could actually do it. In fact, even that was an overestimation of his skill: he very much would not be able to do so — at least not in its entirety. But that was a minor setback.She had a solution for that as well. The A-Team had just dropped it right on their doorstep.

And as of this moment in the dark of the Biome, it was tucked in snug and sound in the jumpsuit of a sickly baby deer whom they were stalking in the night.

There he was now, all alone, peering into the abandoned shelter with his back turned to the broader world. Peel was scared — too scared, as far as the predators were supposed to be concerned. But of what, he couldn't have said. The shape they were hunting in the distance turned toward where they were now hiding in the bushes, and it called out to them in fright. When its cry went unanswered, it turned its back on them again.

From beside him in the shadows, Peel felt that ferocious grip of his superior seize him by the upper arm for a second time that day. Squeal rocketed him out of the bushes and in the direction of their prey. He went careening, wildly out of control, until he crashed into Cheech like a runaway train. Both parties fell, equally surprised, and went crashing through the branches staged haphazardly across the shelter's entrance.

Thrust unwittingly into the heat of the battle, there was only one option presented to him now. It was survival of the fittest; and if it came down to him or Cheech, he would eat that little monster for dessert. Without even knowing what had happened, his arms were shoving, flailing, pinning, groping — searching for the key that would free him from this dark and miserable trap in which he'd been cast. *Get the book and then get out of here,* he thought, and it was just about the only conscious and intelligible thought that had emerged out of the din. The rest was pure instinct. Survival took surprisingly little thought. *Him or me,* and that just about did it.

Squeal urged him on, and Peel struggled harder. Cheech either protested or played dumb; Peel wasn't listening and it mattered little to him either way. They traded jabs and jibes alike. And the longer Cheech squirmed in his struggle, the more Peel's mind had a chance to catch up to the situation, and the more his own longstanding prejudices had a chance to realize just what it was that they were doing. And oh, what a grand opportunity this was, they realized.

Here was a place to put all of his baggage — a ditch in which he could bury all of his crippling grudges, once and for all. Set it all down, stone by stone, and be free of them. Slowly they would pile up, and before long the little freak might suffocate. But at least Peel would be free of these cursed weights. And anyway, it would be one less mouth to feed. It was survival of the fittest. Here it was, the key to whatever might finally prove him worthy in the eyes of his idol, and its only guardian was his ultimate scapegoat, this feeble little aberration that had somehow earned far more love than he was worth. If this little mouse was the hurdle in his way, he would crush it without the slightest shred of remorse. He leaned in with all his weight and bore down harder on the boy.

But he underestimated the fight in that little bundle of vitality. The prey kicked and squirmed, scrapped and scrambled; and then, somehow, he was gone. Off and running, he disappeared down the trail.

"Get up you idiot!" said Squeal as she grabbed him for the third time that day and jerked him onto his feet. "I can't trust you for anything — get him!"

They were off and running, following the faint little blur that was dipping and bobbing through the thicket. The mouse was a whole lot faster than he looked. While chasing Cheech at top speed, Squeal pushed Peel by the shoulder and he veered off the trail at a perilous angle. He barely avoided running square into a set of parallel wires where the pole beans grew; shifting his weight and spinning at the last minute, he whirled around them and narrowly escaped what would have been an embarrassing way to profoundly injure oneself.

Those wires almost sliced me clean into PIECES!

On the far side of the beans, he finished his twirling and stumbled out upon another trail. A low strip of lights ran along the edges of this path, but he was otherwise alone. He was stopped now, and well off the chase. He might have despaired just long enough to give up completely. There would be other paths to glory.

But then he heard the howl.

Of all the sounds that might have broken the newfound silence of the Biome, here was the only one that held any sort of power over him. No words would have done it, least of all any cruelly barked commands. It was a howl in the night that had pulled him back into the hunt. Hypnotized, instinct returned. He had a place. He had a home. He had always known it, when it really came down to it. The rest of this POD could build their precious civilization on that damn planet where they were doomed to land someday. Good riddance. He belonged here, in the Wild, with the one other creature who understood what it was like. To each, their own society.

"Oww-ooooooooo!" he answered, teeth bared. He set off again at a sprint in the same direction they'd been running.

"I can't—," said Squeal, hunched and shaking in the stairs. "Is he—"

"I don't know."

"Is he going to be alright?"

"I don't know," said Peel again. "I got your stupid book, you should be happy."

Their blood had cooled, and the gravity of Cheech's fall was weighing on them something awful. It was all fun and games until someone takes a tumble.

"What do we do?" she said, still trembling.

The vicious huntress that had pulled and pushed Peel around for the last hour and a half was nowhere to be found. Here was only a scared little girl, irreparably hurt by how badly she had hurt someone. Or perhaps it was the other, more dominant thought that scared her most of all. *They're going to kill us.*

Peel, for his part, hadn't committed to this any more than anything else in his life. Yet, they needed a way out, and it only lay forward. They had momentum now, for better or worse. Squeal had thrust him into this mess, and now he would be the one to pull her out the other side of it. Maybe then she would see that he was every bit as fierce as she was — every bit as worthy of her time as those stupid, secret studies of hers, or her futile and pathetic efforts to be accepted. Maybe then she would see that he was worth something at all.

She had wanted him to tell her what he knew; and he had complied. She had wanted him to get the journal from the little mouse; and he had colluded to do so. She had grabbed him by the arm and flung him at the kid by force; and he had done his best to get what she wanted. She had urged him to chase the mouse; and he had done as she'd asked. She had howled in the darkness; and he had answered the call. Together, they had caught their prey; and now together, they would leave him on his own.

"He'll be fine," said Peel, but he knew very well that it may not be the truth.

It was awful, actually — watching the little guy fall, getting littler and littler all the way to the ground. There he'd landed, the mouse was squashed. But upon squashing, something stirred in Peel, and even stung him: something he had hardly ever felt before. He didn't even have a name for it. He probably hadn't listened in that lesson, if there was such a lesson.

Poor guy.

Anyway, there was no time for that now. They had momentum. Let it catch him, if it could.

"That broccoli caught his fall," he said. "Come on. Let's finish what we started or this whole thing was for nothing."

He pulled her by the arm and onto her feet.

"Hey, watch it!" she said, as if realizing just how uncomfortable it was to have that done to you and yet entirely unaware of the irony. *What the heck has gotten into him?* she wondered. *It's like he's lost his mind.*

"Let's go," he said. He rushed out of their stasis in the stairwell, and into the halls of the Library. Still a bit dazed, Squeal waited a moment but soon realized she was standing in the stairs all alone. She wiped her cheeks and ran after him. If such was the cost, it would be worth it. Maybe the well would run dry some day for good, with no more vexing tears to be shed.

Peel darted into a breakout room, but he was wise enough not to pick the same one Potch had shown him. It was off the beaten trail — at least as much as one can be in a symmetrical ring of identical rooms. They slid the door closed, but there was no way to lock it. They would have to bank on a mix of indifference and luck, if they wished to keep their work a secret for the rest of the block.

"Hello Squeal. Hello Peel," said ABRAM as they entered. "I must say, this is a pleasant surprise. How can I help you in the Library?"

"Ohh ... right," said Squeal awkwardly. "We just ... wanted to check on something."

Peel shot her a skeptical glance. *Really?* it seemed to say. *That's the best you can do?* If he had learned from watching Potch, specificity was key. It kept the questions down. All you needed to do was get past the first defenses. Once you were in and pulled off the maneuver, it would be like this conversation had never happened anyway. Heck, you could tell ABRAM to go stuff itself, if you liked — assuming you could carry out the full and proper protocol.

"Squeal was reading up on something," he said, trying to pass her the baton. For his part, Peel knew that this was at least plausible: ABRAM would have known her dirty little academic secret, even if it wouldn't have shared it with anyone else against her wishes. Squeal, however, was not on her game — not after the incident in the darkness below — and neither was she as clever or experienced as Potch.

"Right— Uhh..."

"It was that thing about wolves you wanted to check, right?"

"Right — yes, right. Wolves."

"I see," said ABRAM awkwardly. "Having a little fun down in the Biome, eh? I thought I heard a faint howling on the wind."

It had also wondered if they'd come across Cheech in their hunting — he had not yet returned, not even to the stairwell — but the system didn't dare bring him up to these two. Surely, a strong correlation between these phenomena was highly probable, it had deduced. But there was time to gather more data: whatever they were discussing or searching for in the Library would no doubt be related. It hoped there would be no conflict resolution necessary.

"Well then," it carried on, "let me know if I can be of assistance. Learning is a lifelong endeavor. I'm glad to see you two taking on this initiative."

Squeal smirked maliciously. Any regret or hesitation had well passed. *Glad to have your consent,* she snarled in silence. She looked at Peel, and he went over to the console and took his place in the driver's seat — a place he had been nowhere near qualified to be, as far as Potch would be concerned.

Come on, think! It might have been a bit of self encouragement, chastisement, or both. He had used every millivolt of his attention when Potch had carried out the trick in front of him, and now he would need an equivalent effort of recall. As with all memory, it wasn't verbatim. And yet, probably any member of the crew would have been impressed by how much of it he had gotten — and that included Peel himself. (That was, however, a relative standard for being impressed.) He had so rarely tried to apply himself in these ten years that even he had very little baseline as a frame of reference for his capabilities.

It certainly helped that, like the rest of them, he was a digital native. It was a language as natural to the cadets as that which they spoke — and just as crucial. Even so, he didn't stand out among the crew for being particularly savvy when it came to the tech. Potch had used a few commands that Peel (or any others, for that matter) had seldom messed around with; and he had strung them together in such creative ways. It was fairly awe-inspiring, actually: *Like an art form,* Peel had reflected in the moment. But here were his hands, emulating all the same brush strokes as well as he could possibly do so, and the creation — a creation, anyway — was starting to take shape.

"Okay, that's enough you two. Clearly you've decided to make some kind of mischief."

"Don't worry," he said under his breath to Squeal. And she *was* worried. This was one heck of a gamble they were taking. They had bet the whole farm, in fact. "It did this for Potch, and right at the end." Pride and hope were dripping from his lips as he spoke, and his fingers kept clacking away at the console.

"Peel, that is an official request. On behalf of the Code, I—"

ZHEEOOP, and ABRAM was disabled.

"Okay, now here's the tricky part," said Peel.

"The tricky part?"

"Yeah." *How did Potch put it?* "Like putting an egg back together once you crack it into pieces."

"Oh," she said flatly. That didn't sound good. "So how do you do it?"

"I don't know."

"You don't know?!"

He cracked her a wide, innocent, but totally stupid-looking grin, then shrugged his shoulders.

"Nope. Not completely. Let's hope you were right."

"Me?!" she said defensively. *Don't go putting this on ME when it fails,* her tone had implied. "Right about what?"

Peel unzipped his jumpsuit, pulled out the journal, held it aloft, and waved it back and forth. *Right,* she admitted in secret. Her eyes narrowed so as to exert herself and regain the credit, should this plan actually work. Somehow she had almost forgotten about the key to the whole thing. It was all happening far too fast, and too far off script. Her ability to think it through normally had broken and scattered with the broccoli.

"Let's hope you're right," he said again.

He opened the journal and began to flip.

Date: 2243-11-12-EY
Area: (O(HUMO(PSYC(EDUC(CRIT))))),P(ETHC))
Team: Minotaurs [X-EKTHBMH]
Item: Resilience Trials Update

Entry: Resilience trials continue to demonstrate progress. Results, analyses, and discussion have all been updated [see O-CycleVN-3LY-PhaseV-G7DM6.tl].

On a personal note, it's been rather fun to think about these scenarios. The technical components have built on prior psychological [sub-]sector work [PSYC], but it's required a surprising degree of creativity to craft authentic narratives and experiences. We've brought in contractors from diverse fields to help us flesh out the crises, and it's been a blast seeing engineers, physicists, and biologists working alongside graphic artists, poets, and thriller authors.

Even some of our own team members have brought in great ideas. Most recently, [Dr. Andrés] Alvarez came up with a clever puzzle necessary to resolve an issue with doors unexpectedly locking and trapping a subset of subjects, fracturing the groups. He's been into puzzles since he was a kid, apparently. One morning he just came in with the whole thing fleshed out after working on it a few nights. The engineers made a few minor tweaks, but the credit goes largely to Alvarez. Unfortunately, it was a little too difficult and caused high levels of anxiety in several trial group replicates due to prolonged isolation (one subject was stuck for 18 hours), but it was a clever design and commendable effort. He thinks he can tone it down and salvage it as a positive experience, so we'll see.

Anyway...we have another week of trials and then a week to craft our proposal before the variation phase comes to a close, so we'll see if we can think of any other fun ways to challenge our cadets next week.

CHAPTER 27

TOO MANY CRISES

4252-08-02: UST2

"Running from a pack of wolves?"

And so, Cheech had told them the whole horrid affair: how he'd gone down to the Biome looking for Potch; how he'd planned on giving him back his journal; how he'd been struck from behind and wrestled with on the ground; how he'd gotten away, against the odds; how those foul beasts had howled in the darkness, spread out, and pinned him up against the jeddusch; how he'd given in to desperation and climbed the scaffolding; how they had caught him, and how he had fallen; and last, how his senses had failed him until he'd woken up in the broccoli with an unzipped jumpsuit.

I'll kill them, thought Chop as Cheech was telling his tale, and he wasn't alone. But the moment the thought flared up from within, he tamped it down to suffocate its fire. *No,* he had scolded himself, *but they will pay.*

Potch, however, had experienced neither of these extremes. He had not jumped immediately to violence, but neither had he eliminated it as a possibility. He sat stewing in a need for vengeance, but its form had not yet taken shape.

At the end of the story, Chop chimed in with how he had found the little guy, moaning and delirious. And this is when he remembered the other strange aspect of this tale. *The lights.*

"We couldn't get ABRAM," he said. "It wouldn't turn the lights on in the Biome, or answer us on the way here either. What's going on?"

No one dared answer, but Faingo didn't leave a long enough silence for them to show it.

"Yeah, Potch." She stressed his name to remind the world yet one more time who exactly was to blame for this. "What's going on? More like: What did you do?"

She stared at him with frigid eyes. Frostbite might have set in on the skin of any other cadet, but Potch only burned the hotter for it. He didn't answer, and neither would he look at her. He looked instead to Pee-pop.

"That's not our only problem right now."

"Right, how could we forget about the—"

"Faingo!" snapped Pop as she jumped from her seat and spun to her right. The whole room took a collective gasp at this exertion of will by their ever-reluctant leader. Faingo was seated, and now it was Pop who was on her feet. She was looking down on Faingo in the literal sense, though Faingo took the figurative meaning even more to heart. Pop's eyes were as angry as anyone had ever seen them. But at whom? "Just … go away," she said. "If you can't shut your mouth for a single minute, then just … go away!"

Their collective gasp inhaled yet further, and there was hardly any air left in the room.

Faingo's icy eyes had now melted to water. Her lip trembled, but there was no way she would let them see her weakness — not a chance. Her face hardened. Whether it was compliance or defiance, either way it would be her cover. She jumped onto her own feet and met Pop's unrelenting stare at eye level so as to ensure it would be the latter. She stormed off — out of the circle, and out of the room — and headed through the inner door to the dorms.

"What did we just witness?" asked Plashy, but Pop was in no mood for snark. She sat back down on the couch with a huff and simply glanced at Tor. Somehow taking her meaning, he took over the inquiry.

"Why not, Potch?"

"The explosion," he said, trying not to allude to the fact that Faingo was just about to ask about that very thing. "I think I…"

Silence.

"Let me guess," said Plashy. "You caused it."

Dee's eyes grew rounder than ever.

Potch didn't answer. There were many possibilities, and this may have been one of them. In fact, not long ago he had been quite convinced it could be true. Now, after even more of his perilous digging, he suspected something else entirely.

"I don't know," was all he finally said.

"Okay, so…" said Tor, unsure where to take this and unable to squash down his own growing anger. He looked back to Pop and its meaning was likewise clear as day. *What the heck do I do now?*

"What's done is done," said Pee-pop, as much to herself as to anyone else. "We can't change it. What matters now is what to do about it."

No one had any ideas along those lines, nor had Pop yet posed a question. The silence left her in the same place as everyone else: alone with her thoughts. And in that silent contemplation, the other side of the story vied for recognition.

That's it? she could hear Faingo say on its behalf, offended and indignant. *You're just going to let him get away with this? He could have killed us all.* The nagging truth of this alternative perspective was troubling. *He might have already killed us all,* she realized. Just because the whole ship hadn't blown up doesn't mean they were all in the clear. Both sides of her internal debate were at odds, and each one was equally accurate. At last, she came around to the only sensible solution for the moment at hand. *One thing at a time.*

"So what do we do about it, Potch?" Her voice was firm and focused.

He thought a moment.

Meanwhile, Chop hadn't forgotten the other realization he'd remembered. He turned to Tor.

"So, the explosion caused ABRAM to fail?"

Don't ask me, Tor's shoulders shrugged.

"No," said Potch. The explosions were another matter, and one to which he had focused a great deal of doubt. "I think that's related to our other problem." He looked at Cheech. "My log book."

"What about it?" asked the little guy.

"It's what they wanted bad enough they almost killed you."

"So…" said Cheech, not seeing his point.

Potch sighed. He had never planned to reveal any of this in all the rest of his days. But things had gotten out of control, and one's most secretly conceived plans are often foiled by their own ramifications.

"They think it has something they need — or that Peel needs, to be specific. Still, I think she's likely at the root of it."

"Back up," said Plashy. "What are you talking about?"

Pop interjected softly.

"Start at the beginning, Potch."

He sighed again, and Plashy was ironically annoyed by it the most. Nevertheless, he complied.

Here goes nothing.

"I developed a way to silence ABRAM." The others were appropriately shocked by the revelation, but Potch didn't give them time to reel. "I've been working on it for quite a while. It was mainly a theoretical exercise at first, trying to think through the different options and what the outcomes would be. I could turn off the microphone in a breakout room, but it would still have the cameras; I could turn off the cameras, but it would still know what room I was in until I moved somewhere else, where it would detect me just fine. I didn't want to shut off its senses everywhere because that would be a dead giveaway to the system, not to mention all of you. If the trick was ever going to be of any use — you know … theoretically — it had to be done so that no one would ever know, ABRAM included."

Despite her best efforts to keep an open mind and a calm disposition, Pop was slowly beginning to fume. Her inner Faingo was winning this round. She fought as hard as she could to hold her tongue. She scanned the circle and saw a range of expressions.

Cheech had a horrified look on his face. Tor and Chop were both bristling in their seats, and their faces were flushed with something akin to what Pee-pop was feeling. Plashy was wide-eyed with amazement; it's not clear if it was hiding admiration or fury, or maybe even both. Dee, however, just looked sad, as if someone had taken out her heart and broken it on purpose, just to make her watch, and feel what it would feel like.

Potch, for his part, was so lost in his confession that he hadn't thought to wonder how everyone was taking it. If that was a problem, it was a problem for when he was finished.

"The audiovisual input was the easy part," he continued. "But even if I shut that all down, I would still have the same kind of problem. The system might not be able to see me or hear me, but it wouldn't have to. It would know where I was and what I was doing on the console. I have some tricks for poking around without raising too many alarms, but once key pieces of the infrastructure went down, its own sensors would notice. It might not have seen me actually pull the plug, but it wouldn't take a supercomputer to figure out what was going on. The tricky part was figuring out how to turn it all off and cover my tracks at the same time. Then, one day it sort of just came to me."

"What did?" said Plashy, still riveted.

"I realized I didn't have to actually hide from it ahead of time, or even as it was happening. I could do it retroactively."

"You just had to replace the sensory data," interrupted Tor in disbelief.

Potch looked at him, silently impressed if not entirely surprised that their engineer had seen where this was going.

"Yeah," he said. "Right."

"So what," said Plashy, "you just replaced it with, like, fake data?"

"Not fake data," said Potch. "It was real data, just … harmless data."

"Like what?"

"Anything really, as long as it was from the same part of the POD, and as long as it wouldn't be logically incompatible with where we had been and what we were doing. Usually I could just duplicate the previous block, assuming we hadn't been in the same place I was going."

"What do you mean, the place you were going?" said Chop. "I thought you said you did this in the Library."

Tor turned to him and interjected again. He was struck by how bold it was, but he was far from impressed. Sure, it was a clever trick; but this was downright reckless.

"He could hack whatever rooms he wanted," said Tor. "Same trick, different place."

Chop turned back to Potch for confirmation, and Potch nodded his head.

"And I assume you could script it to run whenever you wanted?" asked Tor. Again, Potch nodded.

"So you could sneak around whenever and however you wanted, not just in the middle of the night, is that it?" By now Tor was letting his feelings known through his tone, whether Potch had cared enough to wonder what he felt about it or not.

"Like I said, it was mostly just theoretical at first. I hadn't actually tried any of this stuff. But, I guess I'd been thinking about it for so long that I had actually worked most of it out." He stalled out in his defense. "Still," he said, "I never intended to actually use it — honest."

He might have meant it completely, but it still may not have been true.

"But then…" he trailed off again. Did he really want to dig a whole other layer down in this exquisite hole he had been digging? He didn't see any other way to explain it. "After the pressure problem the other day, I tried it out for the first time."

And finally, it was all starting to make sense to Pee-pop.

"You —," she started and stuttered. "You caused it," she said, and it wasn't a question. She sounded as heartbroken now as Dee had looked this whole time. Like an epiphany that was long in the making, yet insecure and uncertain even afterward, it had finally dawned on her. All those ravings in the journal, in their slowly-morphing script. Just how long had he been at this? "You're the one who caused the pressure anomaly."

Potch only stared in silence. There may have been sadness therein, but his eyes didn't exactly say, *I'm sorry.* In fact, they didn't say anything. It was the look of someone who had little faith in himself, but even less of it in anything else.

"And ever since, you've been trying to fix it," said Pop. It wasn't appreciative, but accusatory.

"And I'm guessing that didn't go as planned," said Tor. It brought the whole situation around full circle. "The explosion? You were trying to fix it; and instead, you blew something up? That about it?"

His voice was thick with derision. Someone had to do it, if Faingo couldn't be here to watch her newfound nemesis confess.

"Potch," said Cheech. He squirmed on the couch to get more comfortable, but there would be no such thing for him for a while. He grimaced under the jolt of an even stronger wave of pain. "Potch … why didn't you say something? We could have helped. We could have…"

He trailed off, disappointed and left literally speechless. Potch didn't address the substance of his question.

"What does this have to do with Squeal and Peel?" asked Chop-char. He had not forgotten the most important piece of all, as far as he was concerned.

"Peel was with him," said Tor, his insight unrelenting. "Remember?" He turned from Chop to Potch. "Did he catch you? Did you show him? Which is it? Both?"

"He caught me in the middle of trying to equilibrate the pressure. When he realized that ABRAM was suspiciously quiet, he started asking questions."

"And he threatened to turn you in, so you showed him how to do it," said Tor. "Might as well give a chicken the nuclear codes!"

Potch scooted back in his seat and sat up a bit to gain some ground, jostling the same couch where Cheech was sitting. The little guy grimaced again.

"I didn't *show* him," said Potch, offended by the implication. "I mean, I—"

"You showed him, didn't you?" pressed Tor.

"I *demonstrated* how it works," stressed Potch. There was a difference.

"Great," said Tor. "So what, Peel did this?"

"Well, he's not alone," said Chop. "Whatever Potch showed him, *she* found out about it. And *she's* the one I'd be worried about if I were all of us."

"He's right," said Cheech. The trauma of only an hour before came flooding back to him. "Peel was the one who first attacked me, but she was behind him, goading him on."

"And if this is like literally anything else," said Plashy, "whatever he's doing, he's doing it for her." She rolled her eyes. It was so pathetic. No one ought to need anything from anyone else, she reasoned. If she had managed, they should all be able to manage it.

"I still don't get what they wanted with the book," said Chop. "Why go out of the way to beat up Cheech for it?" Nevermind that he should have known better than most that they may not have needed any reason other than it being a convenient outlet for their angst.

"I think they were hoping to fill in the gaps," said Potch. "He made me go through the logic a few times. He was really paying attention actually, now that I think about it — better than I've ever seen him pay attention to anything. But, there's no way he could have pulled it all off on his own. Not correctly, anyway."

And maybe that's the problem, realized Potch in real time.

The others had seen the mad scribbles in the journal. A great deal of it was code, or else scraps of observations about the system. It seemed plausible that there might have been relevant notes; and if not, it was certainly plausible that Squeal and Peel might have thought there would be. Potch, of course, knew that there was indeed a great deal in there that would help them, if they could find it among all the other scrawlings, and if they could recognize it for what it was.

"Trying to fill in the gaps," said Tor, though mostly to himself. "I wonder if that's what went wrong," he then said clearly to Potch. "They used the book to fill in the gaps, but they couldn't fill them all." He thought alone for a second. "That or … maybe they got even more ambitious than you?"

Potch didn't say anything, but the thought was as troubling as it was intended to be.

"It's a good theory," said Pop, "but we'll get even better answers when we can ask them directly. Anything else?" she said to Potch.

Potch thought for a moment, hesitating just a little too long, and shook his head.

At least that's all you're going to tell us until we bleed it from you out of absolute necessity, thought Pee-pop.

"Okay," she said aloud. "So where does that leave us?"

"With too many crises to count," said Plashy.

"And all of them requiring immediate attention," said Tor.

"Don't forget about Cheech in all that," said Chop. "We have to take care of that leg."

"And how do you propose we do that without ABRAM?" said Plashy. "We might be able to access LSS, but a lot of good that'll do us without ABRAM. I don't know how many broken legs you've all fixed, but I for one wouldn't know where to begin."

"Slow down," said Pop. *Too many crises to count, and all in need of attention.* "Let's think before we go running off to solve all our problems with the wrong kinds of solutions."

Think, Pop, think, she turned her words on herself. There were too many crises indeed, but that's precisely where she started.

"First off, Chop's right: we've got Cheech's leg to deal with. He needs help as soon as possible." She wasn't stopping there. "We've got to get ABRAM back online — not just for Cheech, but also for just about everything else."

"And we've got the Squeal and Peel problem," said Chop. The rest of this was well over his head, but the two of them were now his jurisdiction.

"Right," said Pop. "And worst of all, we have the problem of the explosion. We still don't know where it was, how bad it was, or what other problems it might pose — unless there's something you forgot to share with us, Potch?"

He shook his head: "I have some guesses, but I don't know for sure. I need more time."

Pee-pop stared at him, scrutinizing every minute movement of the muscles in his face. *Alright,* she conceded with a skeptical squint. He was telling the truth. And then, she stalled out. *Too many crises, and all in need of immediate attention.*

"We split up," she said with conviction.

Chop was on his feet.

"Tor and Chop, you two head after Squeal and Peel. Bring them up to the Lounge and keep them there. Potch, you said you knew where they were?"

"The Library," he said without delay. "Breakout rooms, but I don't know which."

Got it, nodded Torp-char. Our two heroes were reunited in purpose, in a real-life adventure all their own.

"Dee, maybe you can get Cheech up to Life Support?"

"Happy to help," said Dee, and she headed over to start right away by helping Cheech get up onto his good leg through the agony.

"Plashy, you go check on Faingo and bring her up to speed. When you're done, head over to the Lounge to wait for Tor and Chop."

"No way," said Plashy. "Nuh uh. I'm not going near that nutcase. Have you seen her today?"

Pop was taken aback but Dee quickly intervened.

"Faingo can come with us. We could use her smarts if we have to go fixing Cheech's leg before you all get up there." No one noticed that Dee had just given them all a command of her own, in her very own way. It was a logical one, delivered with a kind of innocent cunning that perhaps exceeded any of the more nefarious forms of cunning on board, and no one thought to question it.

"Okay," said Pop. "Good idea." *If anybody can calm Faingo down right now, it's Cheech,* she reflected.

"Good," said Plashy. "You take the brainiac and take care of Cheech." She turned to Team Torp-char. "I'm coming with you two. If they're really as much trouble as they seem like today, you could use an extra set of hands. We'll have them outnumbered, three on two."

Tor and Chop instantly locked eyes in a nervous and dubious glance before silently conceding that every bit of extra help would be helpful.

"Works for us," nodded Tor.

"That leaves you and me," said Pop. She was looking toward Potch — not so much at him as *in* him. "Think you can undo whatever damage they did to the system?"

"I can try," he said.

"Good," said Pop, and she paused, as if bracing for a follow-up thought that never came.

Then maybe we can try to undo your own damage.

Date: 2273-04-13-EY
Area: D(ODEP(POPS))
Team: Bryozoans [D-SK9DBPX]
Item: Population Scaling Models

Entry: After a number of cycles that only the system dare count, we've finally settled on generalized population scaling models as part of the broader deployment protocols. Early generations (N<100) will scale gradually, beginning with one new cohort per initial unit, per generation. For initial generations this serves as a maximum: scaling curves are modeled to fit native demographic distributions, tempered by inputs from human-, system-, and environmental monitoring to avoid carrying capacity challenges [see D-CycleCBVTJ-PhaseV-2DL7Z.tl].

While our own work has focused on sustainable population growth, it overlaps in significant ways with teams focused on reproduction and ontogeny. Perhaps regrettably, this coordination was not built into cycle team composition so far (we will recommend this in synthesis), but we've been in frequent cross-talk nonetheless [see D-CycleCBVTJ-PhaseV-OZYF9.tl], particularly about the putative shift from system- to human-guided reproduction, as approaches there may have serious ramifications for population scaling.

As for the present cycle, with the generalized models validated, we now begin the tedious process of consulting on permutational iterations.

So begins another season of the sector.

CHAPTER 28

BROKEN BONES AND BROKEN HOPES

4252-08-02: SLP2

"Oww—WOW! EASY there, Faingo."

She had dropped him down on the observation bench like he was her stuffed bumblebee, so focused was she on what she'd rather have been doing. She hadn't even agreed to help the poor chap up to the Biomedical Stations (BMS) until they completely filled her in on the conversation after she'd stormed off in defiant compliance. Cheech, writhing and readjusting every few moments in his discomfort, had tolerated the further delay admirably.

It took longer than it might have, with Dee-dore leading the summary, but Cheech had interjected here and there to speed things along as much as he could. And now, Faingo was seething even more than she had been when she stormed off in a huff. Very wisely, the others had already headed out before Dee had gone to get her, and somehow Dee and Cheech had talked her down from threats of following either of the other parties, to "help" them in their missions. Reluctantly, Faingo had caved, and mainly because of how badly Cheech had truly needed help. Yet her urge for retribution was even stronger than her urge to help him — someone else could do that, if Dee couldn't do it on her own — but as things stood, it seemed like the task had fallen to her and Dee whether she liked it or not, and so help him she would.

"What? Oh, sorry," she said. Her head was in the levels far below, deep down in the dirty work. She wanted to grab Potch by the throat and show him what it meant to go against the group. At the very least, she wanted to track down Squeal and Peel and slap some sense into each of them. One or all of them would have to pay. But she would get her time, she reminded herself as a consolation prize. Help Cheech mend his bum leg, and then there would be ample time for Justice à la Faingo.

"Now what?" said Dee. A bit too excited to be on a mission of such great importance, she had trusted Faingo to finish setting Cheech down while she had gone to tour the room and look at all the fancy gadgets.

They had been in BMS before, as with almost all of the POD, but never in a situation that had warranted it so badly. Through the years, they'd all had their share of bumps and bonks and scuffs and scratches; but — thankfully — there had never been any serious injuries or illnesses to date that had warranted the full scope of the POD's biomedical powers.

As for illness, this was one definite perk of the literal bubble in which they had grown up and continued to live. It was also a perk of their small population size. Their immune systems were mostly in sync and mostly very sturdy. Of course, there was always the potential issue of the Biome and their food supply. There had indeed been a few flare-ups of stomach trouble on occasion, and with that many species in one place, there was always the risk of an inter-specific microbial mismatch, so to speak. But, the crew — with ABRAM at the helm — had followed all the agricultural and culinary protocols quite closely; the Biome had been healthy, and therefore so had the cadets.

As for physical injury, this was a never-ending anxiety that comes with raising children, and needless to say that risk was magnified many times over with the inconvenient case of having no adults of the species around for their entire upbringing. It was hard enough to keep toddlers from cracking their skulls when there was a whole community of caregivers at hand, each with two arms adapted for just this purpose, among other things. ABRAM had no arms, however, and no team of experienced primates to help him raise the little monkeys. There were … other solutions for this problem; and against all odds, it had worked — for ten of them at least.

This is all to say that, thankfully, the crew of the Concordis was only superficially acquainted with the capabilities of the Biomedical Stations, and Life Support as a whole. They'd had their share of trainings through the years, and it had been the basis of more than a few Mind blocks. But if anything, it had mostly been another place to run recklessly around on their endless adventures through the POD, when they were allowed to at least. ABRAM had usually dissuaded (or even prevented) them for doing so on the upper two levels.

The whole POD had been brilliantly designed to be mechanized as little as possible, and to be childproofed as much as possible, for lack of a better phrase. Overall, its form and function were extremely protected from the unexpected. Still, if there was anywhere ABRAM didn't want them *bumpty-bumpty-bump-ing* about and disturbing the peace, it was on the upper levels: Life Support (2), followed by Command and Control (1) above it. In fact, these were the only two habitation levels over which ABRAM maintained a degree of control over access. If there was a curricular reason for doing so, or if the cadets could muster up an appropriate justification, they would be allowed to enter. Otherwise, it was a "Why don't you go learn somewhere else for now?" kind of situation. (For ABRAM, to play was always to learn, and vice versa.)

So had they found themselves in life support, always a bit awestruck to be in this semi-off-limits area, in the unfortunate circumstance of needing it for real — and for Cheech.

"Now what?" Dee was saying.

"Hey ABRAM," said Cheech right away. "Any chance you can help a Cheech out? My leg's not feeling too good."

Faingo raised her eyes at him. *Seriously?*

"Hey," he said. "Just checking."

Somehow, despite having all the same reasons as anyone else to be upset — and even more of them — he managed one of his trademarked, optimistic, I-am-but-a-Fool kinds of grins. Even Faingo had to crack a smile when it struck her.

"So, now what?" said Dee again.

"Not a problem," said Faingo, as close to back to equilibrium as she had been all evening, in a single silly grin from Cheech. "We just need to X-ray it, determine where the fracture is — or fractures, if we're unlucky — set the leg if needed, and bind him up nice and tight in a splint, or a cast. If everything goes well, he'll be as fresh as one of his spring chickens."

Cheech grinned a second time. Most of their lived idioms — the ones they understood — revolved around chickens. And no one loved their chickens more than Cheech.

"Okay, so…" said Dee. "You know how to do all that?"

"What?" said Faingo, quite surprised by the question. "What? No, not on my own!"

Cheech rolled his eyes and fell back on the upturned support of the examination table.

"So … what, then?" said Dee for what was essentially the third time in the same dilemma.

"Hey ABRAM," said Cheech again, joking this time less than the first. This time, there was only a touch of despair sinking in — just a subtle hint, but it was there. As expected, the system didn't answer. "Great," he said, and he tossed his head back against the padding.

Just then, a crackle of life came through on the speakers that startled them all to attention. Cheech jerked up from the backrest and then cringed in the pain. Faingo just about jumped out of her jumpsuit, and Dee froze like a deer. No words came though, just a gurgling static, then a ghastly, intolerable, inhuman whine, followed by a *POP* — and then silence.

What was that? they all asked with a collective look. No one knew, and the hopes that had so suddenly awoken were dashed just as quickly. Before long, they supposed it didn't matter. Nothing had changed. It wasn't ABRAM, and it certainly didn't tell them how to execute the relatively complicated care routine required for Cheech's leg.

"Well that's ... promising, I guess," said Dee. "Right?"

Cheech gave her an unenthused smirk, and that was the first time all day that Dee began to feel truly pessimistic. But that wasn't her way: if Doom was their end, she wasn't going down to meet it without a fight.

"Well ... what, then?" she asked Faingo again, but this time it packed a punch. "Don't just stand there. Figure something out!"

Faingo guffawed, but she had no real defense.

"What, me? I just told you: I know what to do in theory, but I've never done this before."

"You're not even going to try?"

"Try what?" snapped Faingo.

"One of your ... brainy things you're always lecturing us about. You're the one with all the plans. You're the one with all the facts. Just earlier today you were raving about the toxic alkaloids in the hemlock used to kill Socrates in 399 BC!"

Faingo smiled a bit at what she took as flattery by an act of sheer will. *That had been really interesting,* she mused.

"Well?!" said Dee, not amused. "Now's your chance, smarty pants." The rhyme rang out like a song, lilting off the lips of the first poet laureate this new era of humanity had ever known. But the song was a taunt, even if it came from their gentlest soul. At the moment, she was no mere poet, and no gentle soul. She was a champion for her very first true Cause.

"Chance to do what?!" snapped Faingo again. "I'm not just yanking on his leg until it clicks. That's not how it works, and I don't want to make it worse than it already is, which I could easily do if I go all maverick on it. Look, I'm sorry, but for now our best bet is to wait on ABRAM."

"And what if ... ABRAM never comes back?" said Dee.

The suggestion was thrown into the room like a flash grenade. The rapid retorts of Faingo were nowhere to be found. She searched for words but didn't find them. At last, she turned away from them both and hung her head.

"Then we have much bigger problems than my leg," said Cheech.

A period of silence as the sentiment sunk in.

"So, what now?" asked Dee.

"I swear, if you ask that ONE more time!" Faingo spun around, and the others could easily see a tremendous welling in the corners of her eyes.

And that's when something snapped.

That Dee-dore would be the pillar of their strength was something none of them would have expected, but one never quite knows how people will react when peril strikes. If Pop had been here, or even just about any of the others, perhaps it never would have happened. But she was stuck here with Faingo and a wounded Cheech, and the former was too busy feeling sorry for herself to even think about how to move forward productively on the simplest task that any of the gang had been given. It might have been enough to simply sense this and move on with it unspoken, but Dee had lived far too long on the end of Faingo's leash for the moment to pass unchallenged, now that the leash had broken.

"Oh, suck it up!" said Dee. Faingo's eyes popped and all the blood left her face. "Look at Cheech over there," she said, pointing. His eyes were even wider than Faingo's. Of all the unexpected things that had happened today, this was perhaps the most stunning. "He's had just as bad a day as you. A whole lot worse, actually. On top of everything we're all dealing with, he got attacked by his own crew-mates, pulled off the scaffolding, fell four meters, and probably broke his leg! You think *you're* having a bad day? Join the club. And if he can stay positive, then you have no right not to. Now, we have one job to do. If we can't fix his leg, let's at least help him however we can!"

Faingo was stunned. She stood still, her jaw literally gaping. She snapped it shut and wiped her eyes. Her two best friends in the entire universe had turned on her in the very same night, and just when the going had gotten tough. *Who does she think she is?!* she thought in anger for the second time that day, but only for one very fleeting moment. Really, it was more the other feeling that was the problem — the same one she had felt when Pop had pulled this on her earlier. She tried to gather her wits after that astonishing display of insubordination, and she began to rally her retort. But then, just before she could do so, she inadvertently took the advice that Dee had given her.

She did look at Cheech.

Sitting upward again at the edge of the examination table, he stared back at her with those wide, warm eyes that were deceptively deep. He was rocking slightly in the pain, and not all of it was physical; but he had a little smile on his face all the same. Of course, he had been trying to stifle an even bigger smile at the epic meltdown that had clearly been brewing in Dee for a very long time. And the longer Faingo looked at him, the wider his smile became, until he could fight it no more, and that well-known, wide-cheeked grin crept back onto his face — and Faingo started laughing.

It was slow at first, like she herself was trying to stifle the very same grin. But then, the dam was broken — the one that had been holding in the enormous reservoir of her tears that had not yet fallen. But instead of a torrent of tears, there was something else behind it — something even deeper.

Cheech turned to Dee in amazement, and then Faingo did the same. Dee now looked as surprised by this turn of events as the two of them had been by her own outburst. And soon, Dee herself began to laugh, slowly and softly at first, and then louder and far less in control, until soon all three of them were crying — not from fear, or doubt, or grief, all of which may still have played some part; but in laughter and love.

Cheech was snoozing peacefully. After all, it was well into Sleep Two, and it had been a *very* long day. It was not uncommon for the cadets to take a while into the block to actually be asleep: there was important hygiene to be done, after which it always took a bit for them to wind down in their own ways and in their own rooms. But by this point on any normal day, they should have all been asleep. Poor Cheech was the only cadet doing so now, after all he had been through.

After their earlier laughing fit had finally dissipated, Faingo had checked him over as best she could without the guidance of ABRAM. They were all very pleased to confirm that it was not a compound fracture, once they got his jumpsuit off. From there, she tried to localize the epicenter of pain, massaging up and down the leg. The worst spot was by far the lower tibia, and perhaps even the ankle itself. As far as Cheech could tell, the whole thing up to his hip was one red hot flaming mess of pain. Pressing as firmly as she dared, there didn't appear to be any odd or unexpected shapes under the skin, so for now they were cautiously optimistic that he might not need a lot of complicated care. She tried to be gentle, but in reality it had taken a lot of poking and prodding, and Cheech had done a good amount of hollering despite his best efforts to be tough.

Dee had been rummaging through the well-secured supplies on a reconnaissance mission while Faingo was assessing Cheech's leg. She was pleasantly surprised to find that all the chests and cabinets were unlocked — even the medicine. On the rare occasions that they'd been up here for Mind blocks, the medical supplies had all been safely guarded by ABRAM. But now, they were suspiciously free for the taking. All of it.

In one of the larger lockers, they found adjustable supports and self-gripping bandage wraps for a splint. Dee had insisted that this part would require an artistic flourish, and so she had been the one to do the wrapping, once Faingo got the leg situated and supported as needed. They also found some crutches, but a quick alignment alongside Cheech's miniature body made it clear that they would be too big to be of any use, even on their shortest setting. As Dee wrapped the splint, Faingo went back to search the medicine cabinet.

Staring into the cabinet with not much sense of what she was looking for,

Faingo reached down out of habit to the tablet in its appointed place on her hip. She essentially never parted with it, unlike some of the others. Cheech could hardly have told you where his device was at any given time. Sure enough, he did not have it now. Dee, on the other hand, knew precisely where hers was, because she almost always left it exactly in that same place. Her tablet was for logging in the Lounge; other than that, it was a nuisance on her hip. Besides, Faingo always had hers anyway, should they need it in a pinch.

Amazingly, Faingo had not yet felt the need to consult her trusty tablet at any point since the explosion. Too much to do and think, apparently. Without even thinking twice or realizing the implications, she pulled it off the clip and began to search for what drug and dosage would be appropriate for a lad of Cheech's size, with a leg in his condition. She quickly had her answer, and she quickly put the tablet back where it belonged.

"Faingo" said Cheech, looking over Dee where she was hunched wrapping his leg, as busy as a bee.

"What?"

"The tablet!" he said, as bright as ever.

Still not taking his meaning, she simply parroted her initial response, but with a bit more intrigue this second time.

"What?"

"You just used your tablet," said Cheech more slowly. "It's working?"

And then Faingo did begin to understand. She pulled it back out and typed frantically, her face beaming with optimism. Indeed, it was working just as well as it had a moment before; but as the seconds passed, her expression slowly sank and stretched out to its previous baseline of disappointment and despair.

"What?" asked Cheech this time.

"The ARC is there, but..." she said and then slowed.

"But what?" he asked impatiently.

By now, Dee had finished her wrapping and she was equally interested. With some effort, Cheech pulled himself more upright at the edge of the exam table.

"The databases are working just fine," she repeated, "...but the cognitive interface is still down."

"So..." said Dee protractedly.

"Still no ABRAM."

She had continued typing as she talked; and truly, just about everything else seemed to be working just fine — everything except their missing friend, confidant, teacher, and guardian.

Nothing had changed, really, and yet it was such a tremendous letdown from the rush of hope that Faingo had felt when she first realized what it meant to use her tablet successfully. It left her feeling the loss of ABRAM all over again. Cheech, however, was focused on the upside.

"Well … that's alright," he said with that annoying optimism he'd perfected. "Pop and Potch are working on it." Faingo scowled at him sharply. *Don't even say his name near me*, it had unquestionably said. "Anyway…" said Cheech uncomfortably, "…at least we can use the system. I would've thought maybe the tablets wouldn't be working any more than ABRAM. That's nothing but good news, the way I see it."

"I guess," said Faingo reluctantly.

To take her mind off it, she turned back to the sprawling wall of locking drawers to find the anti-inflammatory pills her successful-tablet-searching had suggested. She pulled open the proper drawer without issue and got a few for Cheech.

And now, he was sleeping, if no one else was.

It's been a long time since I've been up here, Dee reflected. She had resumed her explorations once Cheech had started drifting off, if only out of her own curiosity. But the exam room in which they'd been tending Cheech was not terribly large, and now that same curiosity was drawing her elsewhere.

"Come on," said Dee. "I want to look around."

"What?" said Faingo loudly. "What for?"

"Shhh," shushed Dee with a whisper. "He's sleeping! I want to check out the rest of LSS. It feels like I've barely been up here."

It felt that way because it was true. Compared to the proportion of time spent elsewhere in the POD — the detailed data of which was firmly filed away in the recollections of the system — they had spent very little of it here over the last several years. And even then, that time was spent in a small subset of the total area. And it just so happened that — whether due to serendipity or the stupidity of Squeal and Peel — the whole floor now appeared to be open for unsupervised exploration.

It was as though they had an unseen guardian, trapped behind the scenes, opening cabinets, unlocking doors…

The mission itself was uninviting, but it was the unsupervised nature that made Faingo especially uncomfortable. There was no ABRAM around, and even so much as opening the medical cabinets for the sake of an injured companion felt like a violation of the most sacred trust — like she was snooping through her mother's drawers while she had run out for an errand. It wasn't right. It wouldn't do.

"What? Dee, no, I—"

"Oh come on, old stuffy britches. Cheech needs to rest and I'm way too wound up for that after everything that's happened."

"I thought your swim would have gotten it all out of your system."

Faingo smirked through the teasing, which in her case always had more than a small share of genuine disapproval at its core.

"Oh, give it a rest, would you?"

Yet again, her second-best of two best friends was turning on her, challenging her — changing. It was a petty sort of heartbreak, but it hurt all the same.

"Fine," said Faingo. "Knock yourself out," and she waved toward the door to the rest of the level.

Suit yourself, shrugged Dee, and she turned for the very same door.

She had been gone through it for not even a minute. Faingo looked at Cheech, sleeping peacefully on the padded backrest, his awkward, home-made splint stretching out perfectly straight. Then she looked back at the door.

Oh alright, she huffed, and she chased after Dee.

Date: 2326-06-26-EY
Area: O(HUMO(PSYC(EDUC(MBMS))))
Team: Asabiyyanians [O-2LSWFX4]
Item: ARC Distractions

Entry: Our day began with an interesting tangent, as ABRAM provided us a short "On This Day in History" story. It was so fascinating, we spent much of the morning distracted by the backstory and asking ABRAM to read us the primary accounts. It's an incredible and depressing tale that deserves a full telling, but briefly: on this day in history in 1541, Francisco Pizarro was assassinated.

A Spanish conquistador, Pizarro was infamous not for his own death, but for his vile conquest of the Incan Empire. First, he and his men captured and tortured Incans for information, learning that the god-emperor Atahualpa awaited them at Cajamarca. Atahualpa himself had just come to power by defeating his own brother in a brutal civil war. With only 168 men, the Spanish passed with thinly-veiled terror through approximately 80,000 soldiers, stationed themselves in the town plaza, and invited Atahualpa to a feast, under an explicit promise that no harm would come to him. Meanwhile, they laid a trap with two sets of cavalry on either side and a group of fortified artillery. The Friar Vicente de Valverde spoke for the Spanish, imploring Atahualpa to convert to Christianity. The Incan ruler asked to see the holy book the friar had waved in front of him, smacked the friar's arm as he reached out to open it, and cast the book to the ground in derision. The Spanish immediately attacked, and 5000 Incans were slaughtered within an hour. The only Spanish wound was on Pizarro himself as he saved Atahualpa's life, knowing well that the ruler was far more valuable alive. Surrounded by a sea of foes, they held Atahualpa prisoner for eight months(!), extracting a whole chamber's worth of gold in ransom while buying time for Spanish reinforcements. When the enormous ransom for his life had been paid in full by his people, Pizarro put Atahualpa to death all the same.

After taking control of the region, he reneged on yet more of his promises: an ally named [Diego de] Almagro had been guaranteed a share in the spoils, which Pizarro claimed mostly for himself. He went on to rule from the newfound city of Lima in present-day Peru. As a consolation prize, Almagro left to conquer Chile on his own. Pizarro plotted against him while he was away, a chain of events that eventually resulted in Almagro claiming the city of Cuzco by force in retribution. Pizarro sent his brother Hernando to reclaim it, and Almagro was executed. Such is the faith of faithless allies.

But all lives have ends. On this day in history, 1541, men loyal to Almagro broke into the palace in Lima and slew Pizarro while the scoundrel was eating his dinner. Just goes to show: treachery begets only treachery.

CHAPTER 29
A RUCKUS IN THE LIBRARY

4252-08-02: SLP2

Relatively speaking, it was crowded in the stairs. Even though they were often heading to the same place on the same schedule, they didn't tend to move around in such big groups at once. Whatever the reason, they often moved in drips and drabs, in ones and twos or maybe threes. If ABRAM had been there, it would have dinged in the start of Sleep Two. As it was, they only had a vague sense of what time it was, but however you counted it, they could all feel that sleep was supposed to be nigh. After so many years on such a tightly-run ship, their circadian alarm clocks were impeccably tuned.

Chop let out a loud and infectious yawn as they headed down a single level to the Library. Then he remembered why they were heading down there when they should have been turning in for a good night's rest. He pushed through the fatigue and perked back up. The thought that *they* were down there, just one floor below, sowing chaos and division, purposefully putting the welfare of the entire POD in jeopardy — it brought his blood back to a boil, and it was the last yawn he would yawn for quite some time. Sadly, however, he had already passed it to Tor.

Eeeeeeee-YAW, he exclaimed.

"Would you two get it together?" said Plashy. *Sheesh. They're lucky I opted into this mess.* She was right, and not only because of the yawns.

Pop and Potch were silent and neither of them had caught the contagion. Their minds were racing far too quickly for that sleep-inducing exercise. They were bound for a different mission than the search party, though it would lead them to the same location, at least at the start. This debacle had begun in the Library, and that's where Potch would try to fix it.

The only other place that would provide adequate access to the system was Command and Control, but that level was so far removed from their everyday experience that they did not even think to wonder about it as an option. For now, the five of them were heading to the Library, where they would deal with their respective threads of this multifaceted emergency. If their luck was in, they might just stumble upon Squeal and Peel, red-handed and still at the console. They would have that much more muscle to coerce them into cooperating, to undo whatever damage they had done.

Yet they were not the only ones who had done some significant damage, and it was this thought that Pop was trying to repress as she took up the rear in the train down the stairs. But that would be a problem for a stabler time. For now, they had arrived.

At the front of the line, Chop turned back and signaled for quiet. He leaned out and listened. There wasn't a sound, but still he twisted and turned his head back and forth as he leaned into the hallway from the stairwell, holding them back with the waving of his hand.

"Quiet enough for you?" said Plashy.

He snapped his head back into the stairs with a "Shhhh!"

"No, seriously," said Tor pushing past him. "Let's get on with it already." He did just that, squeezing out into the hall. Chop spilled out unwillfully, making the most noise of the lot of them with those big, heavy feet as he tried to regain his lost balance.

"If they're still here, they're at a console in the breakouts," said Potch.

"Let's split up," said Tor. "Potch, Pop: you two head right. We'll head left and fan out. If we haven't found them by the time we reconnect, you two can get started on … whatever you're going to do. We can spread out, check different rooms. If anyone finds them, holler to the rest of us for backup."

It was as good a plan as any, but Plashy rolled her eyes. It wasn't hers, and so it was at least partly flawed on principle alone.

"I wouldn't be surprised if they were long gone," she said. "They're probably hiding out somewhere, the little weasels."

"Maybe," said Tor, "but we have to start somewhere." He glanced straight past Plashy to Pee-pop. "Sound good?"

She nodded, and the two parties went their separate ways.

Pop and Potch went right, while the others went left. Pop skipped ahead to the second breakout door in the hall as Potch checked the first. Both were clear. This time, Pop went to the next door while Potch overtook her and checked the next one down. Like an unspoken game of leap frog, they alternated doors down the hall. All of them were clear.

They came to the central corridor where the cross of hallways led from the outer ring to the Auditorium. Pop caught something out of the corner of her eye, far away, across the whole width of the POD. She turned just in time to see Plashy scooting past the opening in the opposite hall, moving far more sneakily than she would have if she knew anyone could see her. *Apparently they haven't found anything yet either,* thought Pop.

She ran to overtake Potch and check the next room down — and that's when they heard it. Like a set of fiery beacons alighting across a mountain range, an echo came bounding around the curving hallway in three distinct voices, each one louder than the former.

...found them...
...Found Them!...
...FOUND THEM!...

Pop looked back to see Potch screeching out of the breakout room behind her, his eyes on fire. *Come on,* she waved to him. And they both ran as quickly as they could around the curve.

What they saw was like a scene out of a slapstick comedy from the earliest age of moving pictures. Tor was laying on the ground, his scrawny limbs straight up in the air and flailing like a flipped-over beetle. Chop was bending down to help him up while the back end of Plashy disappeared into the western stairs.

"DOWN!" they heard her shout from out of sight.

"Down, they went down!" repeated Chop.

Tor was on his feet and Chop ran to head after them. Tor grabbed his arm and held him back.

"No," he said. The Biome was all that was down there: the end of the line, as far as they had ever known. If they could close them in, they'd have them as cornered as one can be in a circle. "They might just sneak past us up the other stairs. We need to cut them off. You take the south, I'll take the east."

Tor was faster than almost anyone, so he would take the furthest route — although they had also steamrolled him once today already. He may beat them to it, but there was no guarantee he could stop the two of them any better than the chance he'd just squandered. Regardless, it was the best they could do. If they couldn't close off the stairs, they may be in for an endless night of hide and seek.

"What about the north?" said Chop.

They both looked back at Potch and Pop.

"Try our luck?" said Tor to Pee-pop.

And she was torn. Here was a need, which may be every bit as important as whatever Potch could do at the console. In fact, Squeal and Peel may very well hold key information Potch would require, if he couldn't discern on his own what they had done. At the same time, this was surely a more important way for her to contribute than looking over Potch's shoulder and twiddling her thumbs. She looked back at Potch; he had already started for the northern stairs.

"No," she said. "You've got a job to do."

He stopped and turned.

"Then you go," said Potch. "I'll get started. I'll be in this room right here," he pointed.

Still, she hesitated, and Potch sensed it on her face.

"Pop?" said Tor behind her. "Time!"

Her eyes were locked with those of Potch, but they couldn't see him. She couldn't break past that impenetrable shroud he had carried around with him his entire life. He was here. He was helping. But that didn't undo months of sneaking around, storing secrets in a journal meant for no one's eyes but his, doing who-knows-what as he snooped around the system. It didn't undo the years of independence and isolation before that. It didn't undo the fact that at least half of what he now needed to fix was the fruit of his own arrogance and impudence. Even the other half of the problem had grown out of that, come to think of it — like an offshoot of the same evil weed he had purposefully planted in their garden. He was here, he was helping. But what else had he failed or forbidden himself to tell them? She didn't know. She couldn't see it. But she sensed something in there, through that dark storm cloud staring back at her.

"Okay," she said, snapping out of it. Tor and Chop were off in a flurry to cut off the escape route in their respective stairwells. Pop started past Potch on her way to the northern stairs. Likewise, he turned to start for the console in the breakout.

She grabbed him by the arm.

"What?" he said, caught by surprise and surprisingly defensive. "What gives?"

Pop stared at him, somber and serious.

"Get ABRAM back," she said. "And find out whatever you can about the explosion." She only told him what he had already known to do; but there was something else communicated in the precise way that she had said it. Her face lightened. "I don't know which is more important to do first. We may not be out of the clear with whatever the problem is. It might be…"

She was unable to finish the thought that some unseen timer might be ticking, whatever it might mean when their time was up. Her meaning was fully taken, even if it hadn't been fully spoken aloud.

"Then again, ABRAM could help with that — if you tell it everything you know."

She slipped back into that parental tone, but then it lightened for a second time. She looked him straight in the eyes, but her own eyes quavered. She was fighting back more than one kind of fear.

"Just … help us, Potch." Her stare could sink the ocean itself. "Please?"

He nodded, but his own expression was wide with alarm. He'd heard far more than she'd said, and it had unsettled him somehow. Pop still stared at him — as if trying to see *into* him — then let go of his arm and disappeared around the curve of the hallway.

He was alone now, against Pee-pop's better judgement. His surprised expression slowly faded as his brows dropped and eyes narrowed. He went through the opened door, and slid it shut again.

- -
Date: 2332-07-02-EY
Area: O(HUMO(HEAP(TDEV),PSYC(ENRI)))
Team: Shepherds [O-RFNHL41]
Item: Comfort Companions

Entry: In addition to our work on much more pressing matters, we
must admit to distraction by one of our supplemental tasks. Is it
still procrastination if you're working towards another necessary
duty? To be fair, it probably shouldn't be taking us this long,
but we've all had too much fun with it. Compared to the — how to
put it? — rather grim nature of the sector's primary tasks, it's
proven to be a welcome relief.

It was agreed long ago that every toy companion in the POD was to
be unique — no small feat considering the final target population
size — so it leaves plenty of room for creativity and straight-
forwardness alike. With so many ideas to generate, we agreed that
there was room for each member to have their own veto-free suggestion. This has led to both inspiring and regrettable ideas.

Among our contributions are a Clark's Nutcracker (brilliant birds
in their way), an army ant (remarkable cooperators, whatever
their foes may think of them), an anthropomorphic head of cabbage
(that poor kid...), a (surprisingly adorable) tardigrade, and the
log author's [Dr. Ebbe Hval] personal contribution: a gray whale.

We were encouraged to check our taxonomic biases, to select organisms that are representative of proper phylogenetic proportions,
but what can I say? We're all suckers for charismatic megafauna
in the end. (And our eccentric members generated suggestions con-
gruent with their nature, so there's room for a whale of a good
idea such as mine.) Ultimately, the final selection will no doubt
weed out redundancies anyway.

That makes for the end of a very long week. On Monday morning,
it's back to far less jovial debate.

CHAPTER 30

A Trip Down Memory Lane

4252-08-02: SLP2

It was dark in the halls past the stairs where they'd come up. This, the eastern entrance to Level Two, was the only door ABRAM had ever historically let them enter, for it was nearest to Biomedical. Any efforts to get to this floor via the north, south, or west had always been met with flat-out refusal, or at least a mandatory re-routing to the east. At this point, it was a force of habit. And whenever they would arrive at this level via the east, only the hallway towards BMS in the north would be passable.

But tonight, the south-facing door to the rest of the floor was wide open. They had noticed it on their way up, and it was no doubt one of several factors that had piqued Dee's curiosity. And now, they had achieved their mission's objective — at least as much as they could without ABRAM, or even a quorum of the crew — and it lay before them like a long-hidden mystery.

Like their foggy recollections and exaggerated conceptions of what dwelt therein, the area itself was dark and difficult to see. In truth, they had all been there before. In a way, it was their ultimate home. It was the place where they had been born.

"I don't know," said Faingo, falling back on her resistance. "We should stick with Cheech."

It was an excuse and they both knew it.

"He'll be fine," said Dee, who cared for the boy every bit as much as Faingo, or anyone else for that matter. "We set him up well enough for now. All he needs is sleep. Besides, aren't you curious?"

If there was one way to taunt Faingo and goad her into doing what you wanted, it was to question her Curiosity. She was the unchallenged master of that very virtue. But this was different. This was like … snooping.

"What is there to know?" she said, trying her best to cover. "It's just the Nursery." She couldn't concede Dee's point, but she could afford to take the hit to her reputation as an intellectual, just this once — she who had never once been faced with a question that she didn't also want to know the answer for. "And anyway, once we get ABRAM back online, we can ask it whatever we want. It'd probably be happy to give us a tour for Mind block some day."

"You mean IF we can get ABRAM back online," said Dee.

"Would you stop saying that?!"

"Sorry! I just mean … we're here right now. Don't you want to check it out?" They both turned their attention down the long, bending, and shadowy hallway. Even Dee had her reservations, whenever she was looking this way. Perhaps this was her means of mustering the courage. It's always easier to navigate an unknown darkness with another person by your side. "We might not get another chance."

Faingo let out a melodramatic exhalation.

"Alright, fine. Let's go."

"Okay, wait a minute," said Dee. She ducked into the stairwell. A few seconds later there was a *SWISH* and then a *THUNK*. A few seconds after that, Dee was back with a flashlight from one of the many emergency stations scattered through the POD. It's always easier to navigate an unknown darkness when you bring a little light of your own.

They started down the hallway.

As they moved along the curve, it led them to a point where they could no longer see the well-lit entrance by the stairwell behind them. A little further ahead was a dead end, with a door perpendicular to it on the right-hand side, facing the center of the ship. The door was also wide open. Above it, the label read "NSY." The dim backup light of the halls was fully absent through the door. Whether it was the result of whatever issue the system was having, or because this section of the POD was off-limits and out of use, they didn't know. Whatever the case, the entire module was as black as the space between stars. When Dee shined her light, all they saw was more hallway stretching forward, until the light was swallowed by the voracious darkness in the distance. They looked at each other one last time — and stepped inside.

As they made it a little further, the hallway turned to the left, and here it again ran in the same direction as the perimeter, curving as expected for this distance along the POD's radius. This hallway, however, had features again. On both sides, evenly spaced, were sets of doors. At first glance, they all seemed open. Each door was directly across from another one, and each had a cryptic mix of letters and numbers as a label above them. There didn't appear to be any pattern: HK28Y43, 8T24DG1, L9FN3DA, and so on.

They stepped down the hallway slowly and suspiciously, half expecting some locked-away alien beast to jump out and startle them at any minute — or perhaps some ancient monster from one of Plashy's Spirit block stories. Instead they found only identical rooms that were almost entirely empty. Every surface was padded, and there was a large screen on the wall — the right side in this case. Across from the screen was another padded wall with a second door in its center. Unlike the doors in the outer hallway, however, this one was closed. There was a padded block in the center of the room, and it was the only other feature.

"Creepy," said Faingo, though she couldn't say why. Perhaps it was the inexplicable memories, if she could have even called them that.

"Yeah," said Dee. She was experiencing them too.

There was a time, however, when this place was not so dark, and not so creepy. There was a time when it had been full of life, and all that comes with it — cooing and crying, babbles and burbles, laughter and light.

They stepped further into the room and Dee headed for its central feature. As they got closer, a small depression in the center of the block revealed itself over the lip of the side — and there was something in it.

"Wow," said Faingo.

She reached her hand in and slowly — delicately — she plucked out a stuffed crocodile, covered in dust. It was one of ten animals in the center of the block, and they had never been touched by the hands of a child. Unsure what to make of it, but feeling like she had again stepped egregiously over the lines of decency and into someone else's business, she placed it back in its resting place, exactly as she'd found it.

They backed out of the room, returned to the hall, and resumed their exploration down it further.

"Was that..." started Dee, but she couldn't quite place what it had been. "I don't know..."

"Familiar?" answered Faingo.

Dee nodded, surprised that Faingo was able to finish her sentence so perfectly — and yet not surprised, somehow.

They carried on down the hallway. As several rooms passed, they poked their heads in for a scan. Every room revealed the same secrets as before: padded walls, the center block, the screen on the wall, and a sealed door across from it. Had they taken the effort to check out the middle blocks of these subsequent rooms, they would have found ten dusty stuffed animals, each of a different sort in every identical room.

They carried on down the hallway. Soon, they came to another open door, and against all rationality, they both stopped directly in front of it. Above it, the label read "RM7A12F." They stepped in, and they knew it immediately.

It was like any other room, completely comparable in every observable way. But this one was *theirs*. They had known it by the most minute details, which only someone who had spent several years in any single room would ever come to know. Was it the smell? The subtle, almost imperceptible variation in the patterns of the padding? Or was it something else, beyond the realm of the standard human senses? The record does not show. What was clear, however, was that the memories which had been lurking in the depths of their consciousness now rose like a tsunami and came storming out of their bodies with a vengeance. It was an ominous mix of both fear and nostalgia.

"This is it!" said Dee. It was excited, but not joyous. They hadn't known that they were even looking for anything, and yet here it was. Completely by accident, but without any doubt, they had found it. But what exactly did it mean? "I think this was … our room."

Faingo's shocked expression agreed.

They hurried over to the center block, but its receptacle was empty. There were no stuffed animals to be found. They were now scattered among ten different rooms in the Dormitory, two levels below. That's when they realized there was something different about this room after all. The inner door across from the screen was open.

"Faingo," said Dee. As keeper of the flashlight, she had been the first to notice. She had shone it in Faingo's direction, and when it hit the wall where the closed door would have been in any other room, it carried on into further blackness. "Look…"

Faingo turned around, and now it was her turn to lead the exploration onward. Dee rushed to catch up with her and bring forth the much-needed light. Faingo stopped before the doorway, her shadow casting an outline of negative space which merged with the void on the far side of the threshold. She turned.

"Here, the light?"

Reluctantly, Dee handed it over. It had felt a whole lot better to have it in her own hand. Faingo turned back and stepped into the antechamber.

Here was a smaller room in comparison to the first, but it was also full of *things*. The side closest to the padded room had a long conveyor belt that had long since halted. On the opposite side were the hygiene stations. In one side, out the other, as they say. At the end of the narrow chamber was a full-body washing station, and as they inspected it, that's when they noticed that the room continued unexpectedly: the walls curved left and doubled back to make a horseshoe. They followed the bend around the corner.

Like the previous section, this side was full of *things*. In this case, however, the *things* weren't so easily identified. They hung on the right-side wall — ten of them, all in a line. Whatever they were, they were hard to describe.

They were unlike anything either cadet had ever seen before — or at least since they had become sentient members of the species.

"What—" said Faingo. "What *are* these?"

Dee leaned around Faingo's shoulder from where she was now gladly taking refuge behind the keeper of the light.

"They look like … almost like those … cocoon things. Yeah, cocoons, I think they're called. Squeal would know."

"Cocoons," confirmed Faingo. "They do."

"What are they for?" asked Dee.

Faingo didn't have an answer, and that was a situation she had never relished when it happened. She tossed the light to her off-hand and sent her dominant one instinctively to her hip for the tablet. But, for perhaps the first time ever, she paused, quite certain for some unknown reason that the system would not find an answer to this query.

She stepped forward slowly to inspect them more closely, and Dee only followed to huddle as closely behind Faingo as possible.

They were indeed cocoon-like, and that was as good an analogy as any. All ten were identical: a translucent material that would have proven flexible, yet durable, if either of them had dared to touch it. The front faces were torn down the middle in a systematic but irregular manner, as if whatever larval life form had lived in these prisons had forced their way through in an act of sheer will. The top of the capsule had tubing that was plumbed to the ceiling, while the bottom was plumbed to the floor. In addition to this opaque tubing above and below, the top had an additional set of what appeared to be wires running parallel to the tubes.

As they continued to examine these more peripheral details, they eventually turned and noticed the opposite wall. Like the padded room on the other side of it, the whole wall was filled with a screen.

"Let's get out of here," said Dee, and Faingo agreed. They went back around the curve, past the washing bay, along the food and waste stations, and back out through the door to the padded room.

Neither had any recollection of ever having been in that room before. Although, even their memories of the main chamber were more of a *feeling* than a memory. It was familiar. That antechamber, however — that was alien to them.

Reeling off the discovery, they did not linger any longer in the main room. They had spent enough time in it for one lifetime, perhaps. They shuffled quickly through it and back to the main hall. Faingo turned to head back how they had come, but Dee paused once she exited the room. The light in Faingo's hand grew further away from Dee until Faingo herself looked over her shoulder to confirm that Dee was with her.

"What are you doing?" she said. "Let's get back." She'd had enough snooping. This was exactly why it wasn't recommended. *Be careful what you search for.*

"I want to go a little further," said Dee.

"What — why?!"

Dee didn't have a compelling argument.

"Just, come on. Give me back the light."

And before Faingo even had a chance to inquire or protest, Dee had snatched it from her hands. The keeper of the light turned and carried on down the hallway.

"Hey!" said Faingo, and she ran after her to avoid the cruel fate of being consumed by total darkness.

They marched on, following the curve of the Nursery module. The many open doors they passed had all looked the same, and so had their very few contents: padded walls, the center block, the screen on the wall, and a sealed door across from it. Ten stuffed animals rested safely and snugly in their abode, albeit hidden in sight from the hall.

Fearless now with the light back in her hand, Dee needed to dig deeper. She quickened her pace, but as they bent around the curve yet further, she stopped altogether. Here, in this same hallway filled with the same kinds of rooms, was something different — something odd.

"What is it?" said Faingo, annoyed. She had actually bumped into Dee when she stopped unexpectedly. She leaned around the keeper of the light, and she beheld what had made her stop.

Not far ahead, to the left, was a closed door.

"Come on," said Faingo. "Let's get back."

She even turned and pulled on the arm of Dee's jumpsuit, but Dee didn't turn with her. Instead, she stepped forward. Again, Faingo's only choice was to follow her lead or be left on her own in the abyss. Naturally, she chased after her again.

Dee stopped in front of the door, facing off with it, feet wide and firmly planted. She took a long breath and looked over her shoulder to Faingo, now huddling as close behind Dee as Dee had done behind her. She stared up at the door, fixated on the inscription as the only clue in this conundrum: 38D4LS2.

Dee raised her hand — and she banged on the door.

There was no answer. And there never would be.

Date: 2305-01-21-EY
Area: T(ORCO(ASMB))
Team: Rigstitchers [T-AGRJ8Y6]
Item: Patience

Entry: Continuing assembly on prototype four and the whole rest of the crew is at our wits' end with one team member that shall remain unnamed. Everything is fine. The inspection teams have been right behind us as always, and our work is excellent — by the time it gets done. The problem is mainly how long that takes. Although, I'm not sure the work always would be fine if a handful of us didn't keep stepping up to take on more of it ourselves to meet the appropriate standards.

Take today, for example. We're almost done with the junction we've been working on, but it's not yet pressurized. We take the time to gather everything we need in AS [Assembly Station], suit up for a walk, go through the locks, navigate through several sections of module scaffolding, get up through that narrow chute one by one, and get to work on the seal. We're just about to put the lid on when Unnamed Crewmate doesn't have the lag bolts. Forty minutes later, he's back and we could finally get this thing attached. He blamed the space snuffles. Man...everybody's got the space snuffles. He then deflected by attacking the design, saying "What's the point in this thing anyway? No one's ever going to use it." First of all, that's not our job to second guess. Second, we've explained it many times.

Sorry. It's not a log to be proud of. We're practicing patience. We're maintaining empathy; we're remembering that it's a team effort. And anyway, the cycle will be over soon. If he makes it through performance review (not a sure thing), chances are high that we'll end up on different crews. We're maintaining empathy; we're remembering that it's a team effort. We're practicing patience.

CHAPTER 31

THE HUNT FOR THE HUNTERS

4252-08-02: SLP2

The inner door swooshed open on the western edge of the Biome. Darkness flooded in. The airlock was well lit, and the wilderness seemed all the blacker for it. Plashy squinted, but she saw nothing from the brightness of her vantage point. She stepped out into the cold of the night.

Where are those monsters?

Her eyes slowly adjusted so that she could now at least see features, but still she didn't see what she was after. She looked back over her shoulder. They should have been here by now. *Maybe they got smart for once,* she harassed them, neither out loud nor while they were near her. *Maybe they went to block the other stairs.* She waited briefly, guarding her own stairwell and passing the time. The longer she waited, the more confident she became that her fellow seekers had, amazingly, done the right thing without needing to be told it. A wry smile crept over her face. She enjoyed those guys far more than she would ever admit.

But now what?

She began drafting a plan — Plashy was never *not* drafting a plan — but she didn't get very far, nor did she need to. From far across the Biome — *Is that the east?* — came a signal that needed no explanation. It had never once been used, nor even discussed. But she knew it immediately, along with its meaning.

ROOF ROOF ROOOOOOF — RRRRR ROOOF! came the barks, interspersed with sets of growls. This was no howl. This was the determined bark of a bloodhound on the trail.

ROOF ROOF ROOF! barked Plashy as loudly as she could, and then again. It felt remarkably good, she reluctantly acknowledged. It was … liberating. Every snide comment she had ever stored up, not to mention the even greater number she had muttered aloud, were lifted from her, swept away on that same wind that took the yaps and yelps from her lungs. Her call was taken up again in the east, and then the south; deep and rumbling that call came, booming through the Biome.

But then she realized the problem, and it was a rather major one at that. There were only three of them, and they had just given up their positions. They were going to drive the wolves straight to the north and right out of their grasp — *if they have any sense,* she added. Normally, that would be an important caveat when dealing with Squeal and Peel; but in the case of their survival, you could bank on it. She stopped barking immediately.

And then, to Plashy's total surprise and amazement, there came a fourth call, high and thin and from the north. *Pee-pop?* It had to be. Plashy would have never expected to be this excited to hear from her. But she was excited. They had them pinned down in the center of the Biome — somewhere — and they had them outnumbered in a clean two-to-one ratio. Plashy rejoined the chorus, and the braying of the hounds continued. If ABRAM could hear them, wherever it was, it would be one hell of a show.

"ABRAM!" came Chop-char's voice from the south. "ABRAM, the lights!"

Nothing. And even if that was to be expected, it was still a disappointment. Potch had only had a few moments; if he'd gotten so much as a few commands into the console he would have been working quickly. If they were going to catch Squeal and Peel, they were going to have to do it in the darkness. *But how?* What military strategy could there be for four hounds to catch two wolves — ... *two traitors, two sneaks...* — in the middle of a very large circle with four exits, a great deal of densely-packed vegetation, and all while in the dark. Plashy could barely see in front of her own feet, let alone spot a couple of creepers creeping in the distance. What's more, her team had no predetermined plan, and no good way to coordinate, scattered across all four corners as they were. Two-to-one ratio or not, it felt an awful lot like Squeal and Peel had the edge here; and Plashy didn't like it. Not one bit.

As she was pondering said military strategy, it was Pee-pop who broke the newfound silence.

"Squeal! Peel!" she shouted loudly and authoritatively. It barely sounded like Pee-pop at all, and all three of her companions remarked on it, if only to themselves. "Please: come out. Cheech is hurt. We need to make sure he's okay and talk it over. There's also been some kind of ... explosion, and ABRAM isn't responding. There's a lot we need to deal with."

The echoes bounced around the ring, but when they faded, only silence lingered. No spoken reply; no howling; no plodding of feet or the shuffling of vegetation. Just silence.

"Look, if you have information for us, we need it, okay? We need your help."

Nothing.

Time passed, and Pop had exhausted most of what she had wanted to say. If that wasn't going to flush them out, she's not sure what words possibly could. And when words were failing her, she was left with nothing. Her mind was as still and empty as the silent night of the Biome.

"We can deal with it Pop's way, or we can handle it mine," boomed Chop-char again.

It was loud, and deep, and harsh. Plashy wasn't sure she had ever heard him speak with such force. This was not the mild mannered, good natured, never-sore loser, butt-of-every-joke-in-the-Lounge Chop-char she had known. He was hurt, deep down; and scared. And these two fiends were to blame for that — at least the parts of it all that Chop was the most hurt and scared about. The whole POD might explode, true; but there wasn't a whole lot he could do about that. And besides, it would probably be a quick way to go. But he had picked that broken little Chee-chaw up and out of that broken bed of broccoli, and he was up there somewhere suffering — the long and drawn-out kind. And before that, he had suffered at the hands of these wolves in other ways that were even crueler, and even more long and drawn-out. The only thing that was remotely clear about it all was who had been responsible, and that was the one thing Chop was focused on.

Again, no answer.

"What'll it be?" he boomed again.

Again, no answer. But very shortly thereafter, there was some kind of sound.

At first, there was a slow, dull creaking, like hinges that hadn't been oiled in an age of the world — and then, a loud *CLANG!* Each one of the search party would attest to its coming from directly in front of them. Driven by instinct, each started running toward it without any words being spoken to that end across the Biome.

It was not easy going. The main paths wound in circular patterns, and they did the exact opposite of taking you straight to the center. Many side paths had been created by the cadets over the years, either formally or just from regular use as they went to and from their many points of interest. But only the main paths had the low-lying lights to guide the way of weary travelers at night. All four cadets did their best, and each had slightly different sets of obstacles based on the layout of the grounds. Sounds of crashing, snapping, crushing, and scraping shot up to those high ceilings.

"ABRAM, the lights!" shouted Tor again. It was worth a try, but so was it to no avail.

They struggled, fumbling foolishly in the darkness before them, each trying to make their way as quickly as they could to the source of the sound — this vague destination.

Finally, all at once, all four of them emerged from a ring of darkness into the same small sphere of vision, each like they were running from their very own kind of demons. And then they saw it, and the destination was no longer so vague.

On the ground, in the very center of the Biome, was a shattered shelter. It had been Potch's ultimate hiding place, once upon a time — even if everyone had known where it was. But now, it was just a scattered mess of sticks and leaves on the ground. The only other recognizable feature was the large rock, rolled to the side, out of the way of where it had always rested. In its place, there was perhaps the greatest mystery any of the four of them had ever known to date. The soil had been dug up and flung recklessly outward. In the depression where it had once dwelt, and where the large rock had once rested on top of it, was a large metal door in the ground.

There had been no way for Squeal and Peel to cover their tracks. When that large, heavy lid swung back down, there would be no filling in the dirt to hide their escape unless one of them had stayed behind as a sacrifice. Needless to say, neither of them had been very interested in that. Instead, they had put their hopes in silence and secrecy, but they were thwarted by the weight of the secret itself. It had creaked and croaked like it was trying to wake up the whole POD as they lifted it; and it had been heavy — far heavier than they had even expected by the look of it. It had crashed down with a deafening clang, and they were lucky neither of them had lost any appendages. Yes, their secret had betrayed them, and it would be a secret no more.

At least eight levels, Pee-pop recited.

"Chop," said Tor, a little too happily given the circumstances. Chop mustered the will to look away from the door long enough to glance at Tor. He had an enormous, taunting smirk on his face. "A dungeon!"

Great, thought Chop. He had not been very good at the dungeons.

"Are you coming?" asked Chop. It was hopeful, if not optimistic.

Pop stood above him in the Biome, sandy soil, leaves, branches, and a large rock scattered around her, the open metal door below. Chop was in its mouth at the top of the ladder that descended into the unknown depths. He was the last of the others to enter, and now only Pee-pop remained on the surface.

She looked down at him and felt the gravity of her responsibilities intensely. It was pulling her downward, but so was it pulling just as strongly in the opposite direction. Did Potch need her? Probably not for whatever he was trying to do with the system, no. But for something else, perhaps. She wasn't sure what, but she sensed something insensible. She would feel a whole lot better by his side, if not for his sake then for everyone else's. That had been the whole point of her original plan.

Then a second, more troubling thought occurred to her for the first time. She looked around at the broken mess of Potch's refuge. *Did he know?* He had built this place, branch by branch. He had rolled that rock from wherever he had found it, and placed it precisely where it had been — precisely over this hidden entrance to whatever lay below. And he had very likely written of it, she now understood. That, almost more than anything else, had jumped out at her, troubled her. *Eight levels of what?* she had wondered on first glance, and it was a quandary that had stuck with her ever since. *Of the POD?* It had certainly seemed like the most obvious connection, even then. Now, it was almost irrefutable. The refuge, the rock, the journal. *He knew,* she decided. Perhaps Potch needed her for reasons other than help with the system; and perhaps they also needed him for whatever lay below.

"Pop!" said Chop-char loudly.

He was still staring up at her with expectant eyes, waiting for an answer and hoping for a certain one.

"ABRAM, are you there?!" she shouted to the ceiling as loudly as she could. "ABRAM!"

Nothing.

She dropped her head back to Chop in the void down below her. Only darkness lay beneath him, as far as she could tell. It was like his lower body had disappeared into a black hole — and there was that intense gravity again, pulling her into it, to meet the same fate as the others.

"I—" she started. "I can't."

"Pop?"

"I have to check on Potch." She lowered her voice, as if not wanting to say it aloud, let alone too loudly. "I don't … I don't know," she said, practically whispering. "I don't trust him."

Chop didn't say anything, but it was clear that he had weighed her words appropriately. He looked down past his legs along the ladder. He would have felt a whole lot better having her there, but he wasn't sure he wanted to put that on her now. Her instincts were probably right, if they were indeed the force pulling her back up to the Library.

"Alright," he said softly. "We'll be alright." *I have a master dungeon explorer with me,* he admitted in a way he would have never conceded on the couch. Though, it was awfully dark down there, even for a boy as big as him. Then, inexplicably, his thoughts flashed to Plashy in the past, sitting well behind him and keeping mostly silent, but paying far more attention to *The Legend of Zelda* than she would have liked to let on — enough to give him exactly the right advice at the right time, when those monsters were surrounding him in the darkness of the dungeons. That is, when she was not teasing him. "Alright," he said again, and he nodded at Pop.

"Tell the others," she said, and he nodded again right away. She turned to go, but thought better of it for one more moment and turned back. "I think he knows about this place," she said reluctantly. "It might be why they knew about it too. I think he might be able to help us."

The paradox of this point was not lost on either of them. She didn't trust Potch, enough that she needed to leave the search party right as the plot had thickened in order to get back upstairs and look over his shoulder; and yet, she seemed to need him somehow. They all did.

"With Squeal and Peel?" asked Chop. "We can handle them."

"No," said Pee-pop. "I mean with … everything else." *With whatever is drawing everyone down there,* she kept to herself. "We need ABRAM," she said on a sudden with conviction. And she knew it now; all her earlier deliberations pertaining to triage had been settled. ABRAM was most definitely the first priority. And it didn't seem like Potch was having any luck, if he had in fact been trying.

For a third time, Chop nodded, and for a second time, they both turned to go.

"Wait!" said Pee-pop, turning back again. Chop had already started down the ladder.

"What is it?" he asked with surprise, poking his head back up into the faint glow of the Biome night.

"The lid," said Pop. "It doesn't seem safe to leave it open like this, with no one up here as a spotter. You know, if it fell when someone's coming back up."

"You want to…" stuttered Chop. "You want to … close us in?" It was the ghastliest of all prospects.

"There's a handle right here to open it from the inside. There's room for two of you up here to push it up. I don't think we should leave it propped up like this. Plus, if they get past you again, that'll be one more thing to slow them down."

"Oh," said Chop.

"Chop!" said Tor with a whispered shout. *What's taking so long,* it had said.

He looked back down the ladder. From his view in the shaft, he could tell that the metal landing at the bottom of the ladder was lit with the same faint strips of light as the main paths in the Biome. Tor and Plashy, however, were nowhere to be seen.

"Alright," he said. "If you really think so."

He reached up to lend a hand while Pop held the lid from above. Together, they lowered it down safely, if with some serious effort. Pop smiled at him as it closed between their faces.

"Safety first," she said. It was her most frequent motto all these years.

And of course, that was a good philosophy, when the stakes for themselves — not to mention all of humanity — had always been what they were.

"Right," said Chop, and the lid closed shut with a *THUD*. "Safety first…"

He took a gulp, hesitated, then resumed his descent down the ladder to the dim platform below.

On the surface, Pee-pop stared at the mysterious portal to that unknown world below.

And good luck, she wished them in silence.

It was the danger above her now that, against all rationality, had frightened her even more.

"ABRAM!" she shouted again into the imitated night.

Nothing.

It was time to find out what Potch has been up to.

- -
Date: 2203-10-16-EY
Area: (P(ETHC),O(HUMO(HEAP)))
Team: HeLa-Monsters [P-F9F2RCG]
Item: The Curse of the Doorjamb

Entry: I know there is a lot to say about our RB [Review Board]
work on HEAP [Human Embryology and Parturition], but frankly I'm
[Dr. David Gagnon] so annoyed with our printer/copier that none
of it seems to matter for this entry. No matter what we try, it
either prints but dog-ears every other page, or it jams consecu-
tively so that you can't even print a single TL [Technical Log]
draft until you simply give up on un-jamming the thing by hand
for the tenth time and concede defeat entirely. Multiple service
techs have been out multiple times, and every time it's supposedly
"fixed" we're right back in the same boat the next day. Three
weeks of this nonsense, and I'm wasting what feels like an hour
a day on printer jams. The thing is brand new!

And then, I came in to work today and I couldn't even get into
my office! The door was physically stuck in the doorjamb, more
stuck than I ever knew was even physically possible, to the point
where I almost broke the thousand-dollar keypad handle trying to
get it open. I had to pull and pull and pull, pound on the stuck
part of the door, and pull and pull and pull some more and so
on. I was standing there, locked in the hallway, wondering: how
could conditions even change that much over a single night to
result in a door THIS stuck? I don't know if it was the humidity,
the hinges sagging, the building settling, a rogue janitor with
an axe to grind, or some ancient hex come to life from a long
age of dormancy. It finally took pity on me and swung open with
a vengeance after 10 minutes of this, at which point a helpful
colleague and I were sanding the edge of the door where it was
sticking, with a humorously-too-small-and-too-fine-grit sand
block, which took an eternity, until it was finally at least a
moderately functional door and I could get in and start the day.
Better that than waiting the eight days that Facilities [P-INFR]
said it would take for them to "look at it." Naturally, among the
first things I did was attempt to print our working draft and...
printer jam.

It's bad enough I'm working straight through the weekend. All of
this is just salt in the wound. I'm not a superstitious person,
but some days I can't help but think this whole endeavor must
really be cursed.

CHAPTER 32
A FLAW IN THE SYSTEM

4252-08-02: SLP2

Hardly a moment later, Pop was upstairs, dashing through the breakout ring of the Library. She ran to the room where she had last left Potch, slid open the door, and darted in without question. She stopped dead in her tracks and had plenty of questions.

There was nobody here.

"Potch!" she shouted, but there was no answer. "ABRAM?" she checked next, but there was no answer. "POTCH!" she shouted even louder. *Where is he?* And more importantly: *What kind of game is he playing?*

Suspicious thoughts bubbled back up from their hiding places, stronger and more scrutinizing than ever. The pressure anomaly; the journal; the sneaking around in the night; the ABRAM hack; the explosion; the misadventures of Squeal and Peel; the dungeon. *The Rite of Passage!* she realized, and amended her list. How much did he know? How much had he been lying to them? How much of all this had he been behind?

It now seemed remarkably convenient that he'd come forward so willingly, when Dee brought him in to them earlier. That was so unlike Potch. Did he single her out on purpose? Very well done, if so. And Peel: clearly he had honed in on Peel as the weakest of all weak links. He would do Potch's bidding whether he knew it or not. Heck, he would have been more likely to do it the less that he knew. He must have sought him out too. But Squeal? She would have been harder, even impossible, to control by force of will; but she would have been as predictable as the dinging of the dinner bell. It couldn't have been hard for Potch to see where his pieces would all move in this nefarious chess match he was playing. And Pop herself? Was he manipulating her too?

Probably, she conceded. *But how?*

There was only one way to find out, but she needed to find him first. As tempted as she was to leave immediately and begin her frantic search, she was unexpectedly tempted even more by the place he had no longer been. She poked her head back into the hall; sure enough, there was no Potch. She slid the door back shut and headed for the console. She was no Potch, and that was for sure; she was not even a Faingo or a Tor, who were without a doubt the next skilled when it came to the art of the system. But she was also not born yesterday. If he had used this console for any length of time, he might have left a few breadcrumbs, especially if he'd been in as much haste as the rest of them.

Back in the hall a short time later, Pop found herself in a similar situation as a short time before: circling the breakout rooms in search of renegade cadets. Only now, there was only one of her, and she was looking for a different renegade. Even prior to today, she'd been in this situation: here she was, seeking the same rogue crewmate as last night. Somewhere, hiding in plain sight, was Potch. That is, if he was still here. That he might have headed out of the Library was an even worse prospect, but she would need to rule these rooms out anyway before she bothered chasing him further afield. So, for the third time in less than 25 hours, she snuck through the Library, in search of a sneak.

In thinking of it now, she slowed her frenzied pace. He had heard her coming then. He had gotten away last night, probably because she had under-estimated how badly he'd wanted to conceal whatever it was that he was doing. She wouldn't fail again, or at least not for the very same reason. She stopped completely and slipped off her shoes. For her part, she had heard no Potch racing quickly away as once before. If he was still down here, there was still a chance of catching him off guard.

And she was optimistic that she might, because she was rather certain he wouldn't have been able to pull himself away from an entirely unsupervised console. There was no ABRAM to deal with — Squeal and Peel had seen to that part for him — and there was no Pee-pop looking over his shoulder, as origi-nally planned. In a way, Squeal and Peel had seen to that as well. And today, there was no timer ticking away until ABRAM would wake back up, as there had been for so many weeks — *How long, exactly?* — before he had conceived of, and then dared to use, his devious hack. He would have as much time as he wanted; and that would be a hard temptation for Potch to resist, she suspected.

She moved slowly. Her bare feet hardly made a sound. She came around westward to check another door. It was right near the western stairs, and it struck her as familiar. This would have been right about where he'd been last night when he slinked away unseen.

It felt like a lifetime ago. In a way, it was. They had all changed, she knew. Or at least, they were all well into the act of changing. And they would continue to change. So much had happened in such a short period of time. It would be impossible not to. Such is the nature of life-changing news: it fulfills its eponymous promise. And if there was ever any news worthy of such a moniker, it was the news they had recently received.

She was stopped, standing in front of the closed door, but not yet able to bring herself to open it. She was almost certain Potch would be in there, even if probability or reason gave her little grounds to be so confident. And as she stood, unmoving, staring at that opaque barrier, it hit her.

That's what this is all about.

He had practically been shouting it over the system-wide speakers this entire last day at the least. No wonder so much had happened in that short time. And no wonder he had been so gloomy for so long before it. *Who are they to decide?* he had written. And now, he was taking his own fate into his own hands. *How could I have missed it?*

She swung open the door in a single fell swoop. Potch jumped from the shock of it and spun in terror on his seat at the console.

"Pop!" he squawked like a chicken getting kicked. He took a deep breath as his fright slowly flitted away. "Good, you're here." He let out as close to a chuckle as Potch would ever muster. "You scared the crap out of me!"

She hoped he was being metaphorical.

"Same goes for you," she said. "Where have you been?"

His heart was still pounding and she didn't need ABRAM to tell her that. He took another long breath and tried to sweep away the residual shock.

"Right here, why?"

"You said you'd be back north, where I left you. You *specifically* said you would be in that room."

"Oh, right," he said almost jovially, as if relieved that this was her sole grievance. "Sorry," he said. "Here, come on. I think I'm on to something."

He turned back to the console and — very quickly — hit a series of *TAPs*. The screen flashed, from whatever he had been doing to whatever the next task was. *Or whatever he wants me to see,* said that cynical part of Pop's mind again.

"Potch," she said sharply, but she did take him up on the offer and began to move towards him.

"Hmm?" he hummed innocently, and soon Pop had taken a seat beside him at the screen.

"Why were you hiding?"

"What?" he said, and now his tone had shifted to something even more genuine. "I wasn't hiding."

"Then what are you doing here?!" she said tersely, her ample patience frayed.

"I have files saved here." He gestured with his head while his fingers remained primed and ready on the keys. "Locally, on the console. It saves me having to track them all down — a lot of time."

Pop looked over at him, but he turned back to the console and resumed tapping as if there was nothing scandalous about it, and there was thus no need for further discussion on it. Whatever he was working on, he was doing so with urgency.

"Here," he said. "Look."

She did look. The screen was filled with nonstop lines of many columns. Surely, there was something he could see here that she could not.

"These are all the incidents that led to the bang: date, time, location, temperature, pressure — just about anything we might want to know. What's really—"

"Potch," she said. "We need ABRAM."

"There's no time," he said flatly.

"What?" Potch didn't joke, so this couldn't have been that. *Enough with the games,* she thought. "What do you mean?"

"We need to fix this, and we need to fix it now."

Pop got up and stepped back from her seat in dismay.

"No time…" she repeated.

And without any notice whatsoever, she grabbed him with both hands on his shoulders and dragged him from the seat. He was quite a bit bigger than her, and she didn't get him far. He tumbled out of the chair and came crashing to the ground with a painful-sounding crack.

"OWW!" he shouted. "What the heck is wrong with you?!"

He got up and turned in sudden rage. He towered over her with those intense, impenetrable eyes — but now they seemed to not be quite so impenetrable, as though a subtle crack had begun to form in their hard outer layer. Whether it was from crashing to the floor, or from too long staring at that screen, she couldn't say; but she could see inside them, finally, if only a little. She had none of the details — but there was fear in there. A deep, dark, crippling fear of the past and future alike. And where that fear had been sown, anger had sprouted. And when his anger had flowered, rebellion had been its only fruit.

Rather than recoil, Pop stepped up to meet him, rising to his challenge like a wild animal intent on defending her territory to the death. Never in her life had she exerted herself so, and it was not a calculated act. If fear was the seed which had sprouted such treachery in Potch, so too had it been planted in Pee-pop; but it grew differently in this wildly different terrain, and its fruits were not the same.

"No time?!" she growled back. "You seem to have had plenty of time! What have you been up to this whole time, Potch? You had enough time to wipe the console history in the other room. You could have had ABRAM back online ten times over by now, I bet."

Potch retreated from her fury. He had never seen anything like it from her in their entire shared lifetime.

"What? Pop — where is this coming from?"

"Answer me," she roared. "You logged in and out, but there was no command history. You had time to wipe that, but you didn't clear the record from the session log. Too time-consuming to hack past the permissions?"

"Pop — I never entered a command. I told you: I needed this machine. What's gotten into you? Do you want my help or not?"

"Yes!" she said. "Yes, I want your stupid help!" She lurched forward and poked his collarbone with her forefingers. For having only nubs where nails should be, they were surprisingly sharp. "All I want is for you to actually HELP us like you said you would." She advanced and jabbed him again. "All I want is for you to stop playing whatever stupid games you've been playing." She advanced again but did not strike. "All I want is…" she began, but then collapsed into his chest.

She did not sob. She did not cry. She did not need him to deliver her salvation. But neither could she carry this weight any longer by herself. Too long had it been thrust upon her, and only her. All ten years of their lives, in fact. It was time someone else took at least a small part of it, at least for a time.

Potch staggered back, horrified and abashed at that most basic human need, the need for comfort through tactition. It was a need whose fulfillment they had never known from a parent, and thus seldom humored in each other. As far as Potch was concerned, it was practically taboo. They had stuffed animals for this sort of thing. But still her weight leaned into his, and he couldn't just step back and let her fall. He stabilized his footing, pushing firmly against her and holding up her weight. And slowly — as if he wasn't sure how to do it, let alone how either of them would react — he wrapped his arms around her.

She shook softly in his grasp, but there was strength in her weakness. There is great power in vulnerability; there can be no true authority without it. It's not clear how she sensed it — maybe his heartbeat, or maybe his breathing — but she sensed a change in his entire disposition. A tidal wave of sentimentality had come crashing onto his island, and despite his deepest, most fervent preconceptions of what it meant to be strong, he could not fight the flood. Tears began to well in the corners of his eyes, leaking through the cracks of his insufficient defenses. He tried to hold them back with all his might, but they pooled too deeply — and breached the levee.

A drop fell like rain and struck Pee-pop's dark, frazzled hair. She felt its unexpected weight, looked up at him, and pushed off to hold her own weight once again. Still burdened by despair, she was even more startled by this show of emotion from its most unexpected source. And yet, it was a comfort to not be so alone in it.

"I'm scared," she whispered. It was confession and consolation alike.

Potch took the chance to wipe his eyes as quickly as he could. He waited for her gaze to drift and hoped she hadn't seen it.

"I can't do this on my own," she said — not as self-pity, but rather more an accusation.

"You don't have to," said Potch.

It was true enough, but the implication angered her. He had missed the point entirely. Even worse, the hypocrisy was so blatant it deserved its own alarm. He did not get to stand here and play the part of the team player. Not after everything he had done to the contrary — everything he was still doing. She jabbed him with those deadly fingers again, albeit a little less lethally.

"Then neither do you," she said, the words just as sharp as her pokes. "And you have to come clean."

"I know," he said. "But Pop…" His shaking voice betrayed the fear that he had not confessed aloud. "There's no time."

She glared at him, readying to strike yet again with her fingers. But then, she held back. She was looking squarely in his eyes, and truly, they had changed. The dark veil of obstinate autonomy was gone — cracked, somehow, into pieces; and the pieces, washed away in an unexpected flood. They were now hollow, but only exactly as they should be.

They were telling her the truth.

"Why not?" she said with apprehension.

She may have been supporting her own weight again, but only because she was as light as a cloud. It was like this whole thing wasn't real; like it wasn't happening to the actual Pee-pop on this actual night of her actual life. She was supposed to be sleeping right now, and her body had been making that perfectly clear. Maybe that meant this was all just a dream. A nightmare, that is. They could be scary, terrifying even, but they also faded away some time after you woke up. Most of the time, anyway. She would sleep, she would suffer the dream, and she would wake in the morning and be through it. She would get on with the rest of their lives, along with the rest of the crew, and they would all live happily ever after — just like all of Dee's stories in Spirit block.

But the nightmare wasn't over. Right now, it was the front and center of perception. And what does one do in a nightmare, anyway? How does one act, if they should be lucid enough to have even a sliver of will? Hope for the best? Give in and go along for the ride? Simply sit back and wait for the ending, however it might end? Or does one attempt to take command of the console and write the ending as they wish it to be?

She didn't know. She couldn't recall. And how *could* she know? They were such dreadfully difficult things to grab hold of. Had any dreams ever started out as nightmare, but ended up as fairy tale? Not that she could ever *remember…*

"Like I was saying," said Potch, and she snapped out of what had only been seconds, but which had felt like hours of sinking, or floating, or being otherwise lost. "I tracked down the error logs related to the issue. I've already done a lot of troubleshooting, and assuming the explosion was related to the earlier anomaly, I found the problem pretty quickly. Not all of these resulted in explosions, but these are the incidents." Then he paused, and stressed the last point very oddly: "All of them."

The current screen had a list of the most recent entries.

```
4252-08-02 14:32:48.56 UST2 AUX:ALK Error-Log:5H7X22NI5W3T2
4252-08-02 14:32:16.23 UST2 MID:GRN Error-Log:4TF9XST882RN1
4252-08-02 14:31:14.43 UST2 UDB:ARS Error-Log:JNF90DQT2RVB9
...
```

On and on the records ran, filling the monitor. Potch hit a quick *TAP TAP*, and the console refreshed to the opposite end of the chronological record. He turned to Pop, but said nothing.

```
...
3864-10-25 11:54:43.58 DINN MID:WLS Error-Log:84H1GMB50YSU3
3864-10-25 11:54:32.30 DINN BIO:ATM Error-Log:KE480NZQ1RX8T
3864-10-25 11:53:28.09 DINN UDB:ARS Error-Log:LT63RQA57NFT1
```

Again, the records filled the screen, ending in the original instance.

"But…" she started and never finished. The implication was as disturbing — and relieving — to her as it had been to Potch a short time earlier.

"Anyway," he interjected, "I followed the code back to the infrastructure. The manual release we turned…"

"We?"

"…it releases the pressure but it never solves the underlying problem. It's not triggering the alarm reliably. That's why we missed this, I guess." That it might have had something to do with the incapacitation of ABRAM had already crossed his mind but, for whatever reason, this was not a path he willingly pursued with Pee-pop. "With some more digging, I think I might have found the problem."

"Okay, so … what's the damage?"

"It's hard to say until we get down there," he said nonchalantly.

"Down there?"

She looked like she had seen a ghost.

"Oh — right," said Potch. "Let me back up." His mind was moving appropriately quickly, but unfortunately he would need to bring others along if he stood any chance of gaining their trust and their help. That might prove both difficult and time-consuming. "Where do I start?" he asked himself aloud.

"The problem," said Pop.

"Right," he said firmly. "I don't know why, but there's a malfunctioning unit in the atmospheric regulation system."

True enough, there was a malfunctioning unit in the Atmospheric Regulation System (ARS). The Biome did much of the most crucial work on a day-to-day basis, converting the carbon dioxide waste produced by the humans into the very oxygen they needed to breathe, much like on Earth. In addition to this natural cycle between the organic beings on board, the POD was equipped with extensive regulatory capabilities of its own, which could range from supplementing the natural cycle as needed to help maintain equilibrium, all the way to being entirely sufficient for atmospheric homeostasis depending on the needs of the POD and as an emergency backup. The ARS monitored pressure, temperature, humidity, composition, and more. The problem, however, was that it had evidently taken on the delightful quirk of periodically failing in unpredictable ways.

As to the root cause of exactly *why* it was malfunctioning, even ABRAM hadn't yet been able to figure that one out; but as ABRAM couldn't help them now anyway, the point at this point was moot.

"Do you know where?" asked Pop, though she was pretty sure he'd already answered this, if vaguely.

"In the Underbelly," he said. "Below the Biome. I've never been down there, but I've known about it for a while."

Only an hour earlier, she would have been floored by such a revelation. It's not that they had never dreamed such a thing could be possible: it was a large POD, and surely there were things beyond the scope of their everyday sight. Things in the ceilings; things in the walls; and yes, things in the floors. It was not undreamed of, but an entire underbelly of hidden mysteries whose access was right under their noses the whole time? Why, it may as well have been a dream. Yes, such a fact would have surprised her only so much as an hour before; but as of now, she had seen it for herself.

"About that..." said Pop.

"Yeah?"

"Looks like some of the others beat you to it."

"What?" said Potch, confused and apparently also upset by the notion. How could others have beaten him to his own secret? "Who — what are you talking about?"

"Squeal and Peel," she said. "They found the door, I have no idea how. Tor, Chop, and Plashy went after them."

"What?!" He jumped to his feet, and Pop was so startled by it that she did the same. "They need to get out of there — one of those tanks could blow at any minute! You see this?"

TAP TAP TAP, and the error logs were sorted by their original sequence. He pointed at the lowest line of green letters on the screen. "It's building again. One tank already blew, but I think they had fail-safes for this kind of thing — to keep them all from going at once. Otherwise, my guess is the whole POD would already be gone. That's the good news. The bad news is the alarm's still not working, but the pressure's rising in another tank."

Pee-pop was frozen — not due to a lack of ideas in the heat of a crisis, but because there were too many at once. In contrast, Potch was never idle; not in action any more than in thought. It might have been part of his problem.

"Pop: get up to Aux and suit up. You need to flip that external release as fast as you can. That'll buy us some time."

She shook her head quickly. There was something wrong about going the opposite direction of where her friends were in danger, even if that's the direction she needed to go in order to save them.

"Somebody has to do it," said Potch, and that more or less settled it. When somebody had to do it, that someone would be Pee-pop.

"Right," she said. And just like that, she was ready for action, though she had not yet headed for the door. "What are *you* going to do?"

He waved her away and sat back down to the console as fast as he could.

"I'm going to get your damn ABRAM back."

Date: 2214-07-19-EY
Area: T(TDWN)
Team: Intaglios [T-TB20LK8]
Item: Touchdown Constraints

Entry: Greatly over time this round and must be brief. Sector as a whole is still hashing out the deployment debacle. Frankly, we're improperly constrained by earlier iterations. Whoever conceived of these harebrained deployment protocols clearly didn't think hard enough about the order of events.

Our team's initial proposal hinged on a detachable system. The main body of the POD [shorthand for PODS: Portable Ova Distribution System] could stay in orbit while the deployment unit could make the descent. For some asinine reason, that didn't fly in selection. As for what we're going to do with the current sector direction… that's why our team is already over time.

We've updated our current draft [T-Cycle9TXGR-PhaseV-37B8W.tl]. Don't waste your time, there's not much there.

CHAPTER 33

INTO THE DUNGEON

4252-08-02: SLP2

The large metal lid thudded shut, safely and soundly, over Chop-char's head. For a moment, the world was even blacker than it had been. There was little ambient light, but it was such a dark set of circumstances that every photon made a difference. He stopped his descent on the ladder for that reason, but before long his pupils adjusted to the new normal. The faint glow from the platform below was the only illumination. As little as Chop wanted to descend into that dungeon, he was also drawn to be as close to the light as possible. But it was very, very far away.

Whatever dwelt in the enclosed space between the Biome level and whatever lay below it was very large indeed.

"Chop!" hissed Tor again from below and out of sight. "Come on!" His voice was excited, which Chop mistook as impatience alone.

But Chop didn't humor that impatience, carrying on at his slow and comforting pace. It was a comfort to him because the descent itself was distinctly uncomfortable. His companions were far down in the dim darkness below, at the end of this seemingly endless tunnel. The atmosphere itself felt stuffy and suffocating. All the air they had ever breathed was recycled, but here it could have used a bit of that recycling. It was hot, and damp, and despite the very real need to do so, Chop found himself not wanting to breathe it. All he did want to do was to turn and climb back up this awful tunnel and breathe the cool, crisp air of the Biome once again.

With every step down the ladder, his feet fell harder and harder, until the steps of the ladder itself began to hurt his feet as they pressed back up against them. There was nothing normal about this Normal Force. *Am I getting … heavier?* Each new step was an effort, and so too did he need to hold on even tighter with his hands just to keep himself from rocketing down the shaft.

His feet ached, and so did his knees. His fingers hurt, and his biceps quivered as he held on for dear life. He must have weighed a metric ton, and he doubted very seriously that he would be able to hold it much longer. He would have turned and began to climb, but he was even less sure that he would be able to pull himself back up again.

"Tor!" he shouted, the panic perfectly evident.

"Just keep coming," said Tor from out of sight at the bottom of the shaft.

Mustering all his might, Chop stepped down another rung. Rallied by Tor, his despair now felt lighter. Or perhaps it was … *him* … who felt lighter. He took another step.

Indeed, the oppressiveness of the pulling had peaked. His arms still quivered, still recovering from the steadily increasing strain as he made his way down, but now the shakes were enhanced by the anxious curiosity of what the heck was happening to him. The only solution was to carry on. He took another step.

The exact inverse of before, he now felt lighter and lighter with each passing rung. And at last, when he had climbed most of the way down, he began to feel a little *too* light. His stomach rose up a bit too high in his belly. His head was whirring, his sense of direction sent into a frenzy. His eyes were not lying — everything in his field of vision remained exactly where it had been — and yet his brain wouldn't listen. Up may just as well have been Down, or Sideways for that matter. And Down? Well, Down was a highly questionable thing. What did it even mean anymore?

Light as a feather, or lighter, he'd soon descended the ladder enough that Tor's image was no longer blocked by the bottom of the shaft. Whatever was wrong with Chop was wrong with Tor, and Plashy beside him. They were clinging to a rail, but something wasn't right. Below him — if Down existed anymore — was a grated metal floor, the first level of this subterranean doomscape Chop had reluctantly entered. He floated cautiously through the opening at last and his feet stomped down on the grated metal floor, but only out of habit. Unlike all the previous days of his life, they had not been mandated to do so by gravity.

"Waiting for your champion, I see," said Chop. He forced out the boast, but he sounded like something else was competing to come out of him first.

Past Tor, at the front of the party, Plashy rolled her eyes. She and Tor were holding on to a hand rail, and from his new perspective Chop could see what had been wrong. Their feet were near the platform, but they weren't supporting any weight.

"Our champion makes too much noise," she whispered. She posed a finger upright over her mouth in that universal signal to shut up.

Chop had many responses come to mind, but he didn't dare send any of them at Plashy. He was foolish, sometimes; but he was not a fool. Resisting this instinct, it was then that he took the time to actually inspect his surroundings. And as that awareness settled in, it fully overtook him.

Here they were, deeper in the POD than any of them had ever even known existed; and yet, here they were, high on a small circular platform, in the center of an enormous chamber that plummeted below them for farther than they could reliably estimate. Prior to now, the highest frame of reference in the vertical dimension of their entire existence had been the seemingly enormous ceiling of the Biome, at a whopping 30 meters. This was twice that, at least.

They may not have been supporting him, but Chop's legs wobbled the second he looked at it. He flailed his arms and legs like a baby bird testing its wings for the very first time; he paddled his way over to the railing and grabbed hold of it in a desperate effort to stop himself from falling just from seeing the drop. Lucky for him, they were safely ensconced in a circle with shoulder-high walls. Equally lucky, they were below the Gravity Regulation Unit, and its rules no longer applied.

Some day, however, if all had gone to plan, gravity of a more natural sort would again be applicable, and thus the level was constructed with that constraint in mind. The metal of the floor and sides alike was porous; it wound in and around itself, leaving diamonds of nothingness scattered evenly throughout. It formed a strong plane with surprisingly little material, but its psychological impact left something to be desired — something like a whole lot less of the view below their feet.

For a minute, Chop's legs would not stop wobbling. He clutched tightly to the side with both hands. His head was spinning. His hips were spinning. His feet were supposed to be planted as firmly as they could possibly plant, but even *they* were spinning.

"You alright there, big guy?" asked Tor, but with a lot less ridicule than accompanied their usual adventures.

"I—"

Without a lick of conscious effort — he would have never been able to bring himself to do it — Chop heaved his head over the railing and wretched a streak of vomit down the shaft. He turned his eyes away, but Tor and Plashy leaned over to watch it fall. Its form was top notch, keeping its shape impressively well. It took longer than any of them would have expected — falling, falling, falling through the weightless void below. Its own inertia was the only reason.

The central chamber below them was open, but its diameter was only a little wider than the upper platform where they were — perhaps five meters total. The rest of the outer space was filled, but with what, they could not have told you. The only reason they could see it was because the same dim lights were interspersed through the whole height and width of it. There were huge tanks, maybe running all the way down, as far as they could tell. Elsewhere and everywhere, there were tubes, and wires, and boxes, and valves.

From the circular platform at the top where they hovered, straight extensions projected in all four directions, like the spokes of this great wheel. Presumably, in conditions requiring the use of one's legs for walking, they would provide a path to and from the peripheral ring. From there, there were more ladders down to the next lower ring, and so on. On each level, the same four spokes projected inward; but at all these lower levels, the circle in the center remained empty. It was through this great central shaft that Chop-char's vomit flew.

Other than the central shaft and the four cross-sectional spokes, the space was filled with all that *stuff.* Accessory landings and ladders from the various platform rings provided direct access for anyone brave enough to navigate this three-dimensional maze. There were metal rings every meter or so at any of these access points, presumably for someone to clip into — someone who knew what they were doing. In times like these, they would keep you from floating away; in times of gravity, they would keep you from fulfilling the same fate as Chop-char's vomit.

SSHPLAT, it splattered with a sickening sound.

"Nice shot," said Plashy, with a tone far drier than the floor of the shaft so far below.

"Are you going to be alright?" added Tor.

Chop wiped the spit off the side of his mouth and nodded.

"Good," said Tor. "Let's get on with it already."

"So much for your silent approach," Chop said to Plashy, with some glee.

He wobbled his way back into the center of the platform, testing out his ability to move. He had seen and felt enough to know that this was real, but so had his mind been trained by an entire lifetime, and the whole history of his species before that, to fear the sight of such a fall. His body could tell that he was floating, but his eyes could not help but warn him of the danger.

Against this very intuition, Plashy was the first of them to make the great leap of faith. She pulled herself up ever so gently by the railing, held on to it as her lower body overtook its top, pulled back against the railing, and sent herself diving slowly through the shaft. She was as elegant as a mermaid of old, as far as they had heard from all those stories in the Kiva. Tor followed her quickly, while Chop did so with slow and steady determination.

"What is this place?" he said as they swam their way through the air.

"I don't know," said Tor. "The guts, I guess."

And it was a fair guess. Tor didn't know it at the time, but it was called the Underbelly for a reason. This was as fitting a name for it as any, but in reality it was a bit of a misnomer. It was more like a combination of most of the major systems *other* than the guts — it was part pulmonary, circulatory, excretory, and nervous.

Of course, the nerves ran through every facet of the ship, and this was no exception. But unlike the inhabited levels of the POD, here their innervations were exposed to the eye of their observers. The POD's central nervous system in this analogy was at the pinnacle of all levels, in Command and Control; but herein were key peripheral components that regulated the many homeostatic mechanisms of the ship.

Among those crucial mechanisms were enormous tanks which served as a buffer for atmospheric regulation, along with other applications that required the regulation of gas — one of which in particular was paramount to the overall mission. Were the adventurers to explore this great space more thoroughly, and if they had known what to look for, they might have discerned that all was not well.

"So, what?" asked Chop as they pulled themselves through the shaft. "They don't need gravity in the guts?"

"Guess not," said Tor. "Apparently the gravity generator's between here and the Biome. Maybe it was just the best spot for it."

"Would you two be quiet?" whispered Plashy turning back to them. It was loud enough to make her point, and soft enough to not be a hypocrite. "We have a mission, or did you forget?"

The others averted their eyes from the fury of Plashy and pulled themselves along in silence. They had not forgotten, exactly, but they had certainly been more amazed by the incredible circumstances than she had. His thoughts drawn back to said mission, Chop's own fury came flooding back to the forefront of his mind. But then, this made him wonder something he had not thought to wonder before. He stopped pulling himself along.

"Why did you come with us?" he asked abruptly, albeit with a whisper. Tor and Plashy turned at the question, and in seeing this, they also stopped. The three of them floated there awkwardly, about halfway down the shaft, holding on to the railing of another platform for those encumbered by gravity.

"What?" she whispered defensively. It was clearly not a clarifying question. There was simply nothing odd about her actions, and she could go wherever she darn well pleased.

"I just don't get why you opted into this."

"I sure as heck wasn't going to leave it up to you two."

But there was something more to it, and the expressions on both halves of Torp-char were appropriately unified in that perception.

"You seemed pretty upset about ABRAM," said Tor. And yet again, his guesses were astonishingly accurate today. (Then again, he usually didn't guess them aloud unless they were a whole lot more than a guess.)

"So what?" she deflected, and her voice did now rise into hypocrisy levels. "You have your reasons, and I have mine. Now let's get this over with already!"

The demand echoed through the cavernous shaft, bouncing and scattering among the diverse shapes and sizes of equipment. She turned and resumed her weightless gliding through the air. Chop and Tor shared a bewildered glance and followed shortly after.

And it seemed as they did that the air was growing even hotter and damper than it had been all along. Likewise, what had begun as a barely perceptible hiss a short distance ago had now grown into one that was very perceptible.

"What is that?" asked Chop from the back of the line.

Plashy and Tor both stopped and turned back. Tor had a guess, but he wasn't ready to utter it.

"It's probably nothing," he said.

"It doesn't sound like nothing " said Plashy, now moving her head left and right to see through the dim and cluttered distance toward the periphery. "It sounds like it's coming from back there. You don't think it's—"

"I thought we had a mission," he cut her off. "Whatever it is, there's nothing we can do about it right now. Come on, let's find the other two and get out of here."

It was extremely good advice.

Plashy conceded and pressed on, but Chop took his own turn squinting through the dim and cluttered distance as he passed.

"Chop," said Tor.

"Alright, alright. Coming." *Sheesh.* Between the two of them, he was lucky to have a moment to think for himself. (Which may have been by design.)

Getting the hang of it now, and perhaps subconsciously wanting to get away from that hissing, Plashy quickened her pace. For the same two reasons, the others did too. At last, they came to the alleged floor of this very long shaft, and the place was rife with the smell of Chop-char's vomit. Combined with the hot, damp air, it required all three of them to fight a very strong urge to produce even more of it.

"Ugh," said Tor. "Go, go, go," he pressed at Plashy.

Go where? she wondered. Turning, she followed one of the passageways at random. There were four of them, parallel to and below the many layers of spoke-like platforms overhead. They passed equipment that looked much like all they had seen at the other end, but here it came all the way to the floor.

Tor inspected them as closely as he could without delaying, and there was quite a lot of it to pass before they finally came to a doorway much like the stairways of the inhabited levels.

Poking in, Plashy first looked right, back towards the upper levels, and then left, down to whatever deepest levels still dwelt below.

"Down, I guess?"

Sure enough, it didn't make a lot of sense to navigate back up the stairs on the outside of the chamber they'd just passed down through. And if they had, all they would have found was several levels of access to the spoke-like platforms, and a big, suspicious, dead end at the very top.

"Yeah," nodded Tor.

He and Chop funneled in after her, and they began the very awkward act of descending the stairs head first, without any gravity to help them.

After a relatively normal length of stairs, they came to another opening. Here, the way down was blocked by a temporary-looking barrier. It spanned the whole stairs, like a reinforced wall; but its edges were not fully sealed. While they didn't know it, it looked exactly like the barrier at the top of the Underbelly stairs. What they did recognize — now that they had come to experience it in this new and strange context — was that it also looked like the wall at the bottom of the stairs in the Biome.

"I bet this keeps going," said Tor. "And I bet there's one just like it at the top that opens up to our stairs."

If he and Chop had been keeping track of points in this dungeon, Tor would have been continuing his winning streak.

"Makes sense," said Plashy. "It looks just like the bottom of our stairs. I never really thought much of it."

"Me either," said Chop. "I wonder if … do you think they'll open up when we land?"

"I think so," said Tor. "Doesn't make a lot of sense to only be able to access this place through a shaft in the middle of the Biome."

"But there's all that gravity to go through," said Chop, being unlikely to forget such a surreal experience.

"True," said Tor, "but the stairs can take you through it just as well as a ladder."

Chop looked unsatisfied, great gears churning slowly in that great big skull of his. He almost looked like he might vomit again. But this time, a fair reward for all that struggle, it was he who had the insight.

"Or maybe it'll be off by then."

At this, Tor physically stopped while his gears churned far more quickly.

"Hmm," he said, impressed. "You might actually be right."

Add those to Chop-char's meager running total. His only points on this adventure so far had come from his impeccable aim with a projectile of vomit.

"Like, maybe when we land?" asked Plashy, finishing the thought aloud.

"Maybe," said Tor. "Either way, there's no more down for now."

Chop's eyes narrowed.

"That means there was no more down for them."

At that very moment, an extremely unexpected sound rang through the stairs. It startled them all, so badly that Chop actually jerked and banged his head on an overhanging stair, turned around as he had gotten. The stairway speakers popped and whined, and a well known voice came through them. For an instant, all three of them assumed it would be ABRAM, back from the dead. But the voice was distant, like it was reverberating through a room, not the sharp, crisp, never-actually-been-made-by-a-human-larynx kind of voice they had come to know and love since birth. It was someone else.

It was Potch.

"Everyone down below," he said with urgency. *How was he doing this?* they all wondered simultaneously. "You need to get out of there as fast as you can. Get back above the Biome. Tor, Chop, Plashy, Squeal, Peel — anyone — if you can hear me, you need to get out of there!"

What — why? their startled expressions all exclaimed to one another.

Their question was immediately answered.

"There might be another explosion!"

Date: 2211-02-17-EY
Area: T(TDWN)
Team: Excavators [T-VP4V1R0]
Item: Deployment System Visioning

Entry: The Excavators have begun "digging into" deployment mechanisms. (We promised a pun in every entry, and as of this second
log for our newly-formed team, we are keeping our promise.)

Selection will be here in two short weeks and we still don't
have consensus among the team for our approach. Everyone is in
agreement that it needs to be on the ventral surface, to avoid
an overly-complicated detachment routine. But squaring that with
the perpendicular design of the ship (a baffling historical constraint agreed upon in a previous cycle) has posed some problems.

First, the main boosters need to be posterior to the deployment
sector. In this case, that would actually put them ventral, and
right in the way. Second, the separation of deployment systems
so far down will sever it from the main habitation sectors. Some
of the team takes issue with the disconnect, while others justify
it by the distinct phases of the mission.

Either way, we need to come to an agreement soon so we can develop
one of our outlines into a full proposal in time for selection. No
one wants to suffer the wrath of point deductions due to missing
a deadline. At the very least, we need to have something to show
for ourselves so we can lose fair and square. None of our members
have yet been on a team that won a cycle, and it's already not
looking good for us this time either! Let's hope we can spin this
thing around on its tracks. (That's two.)

Will update with proposal ID when we have one to report.

CHAPTER 34
THE HUNT CONTINUES

4252-08-02: SLP2

"Potch! What do you mean?"

All three of them were stunned. Drifting slowly to and fro in this subterranean stairwell, tethered only by lanky arms to various and insufficient anchor points, none could bring themselves to admit what they'd just heard. Surely, this was not a funny joke.

"Potch!" shouted Plashy again.

But wherever he was, he was gone. Either he couldn't hear them or he wasn't listening; or perhaps he had moved on to more pressing matters than their mortal peril in the Underbelly. Whatever the case, the outcome was the same. Like ABRAM before him, the voice from the speakers had abandoned them to their own devices.

"You heard him," said Tor. "Let's go!"

Awkwardly, he pushed off from a step of the stairway — overhead rather than underfoot — and pulled against the ledge of another one to make his way back up the stairs. Chop hovered relatively motionless as Tor scooted past him.

"Come on," he said again, kicking at Chop to wake him from the stupor. The big guy drifted downward from the force — but not as much as Tor shot off in the opposite direction, given all of Chop's inertia — and it roused him some but not entirely.

Plashy was furthest of all in the unknown direction, in front of the barrier at the bottom and beside the only open door. She moved no more than Chopchar, but her mind was not as idle. She seemed, somehow, to be planted firmly in place despite their weightlessness.

"No," she said. "We can't just leave them down here."

Tor turned back and beckoned Chop again with a wave.

"They probably heard the same thing we did," he said. "Besides, we don't even know where they are."

"You can't—" started Plashy, but Chop interrupted her, unflinching.

"They're that way," he said, pointing back to the bottom of the stairs and the same doorway they'd been heading for. He turned to Tor, and it was all the consensus they needed. Tor hung his head briefly, aware as much as any of them of the regrettable reality. Having come here to hunt them down and bring them to justice, they might now risk their own lives for the sake of Squeal and Peel.

And that would be it, Tor knew: *Game Over.*

It's not clear how or why he knew it, given how little frame of reference any of them had for legitimate matters of Life and of Death. But every time he had hit "Continue?" to be born again on his adventure, restored to a place of relative safety and security in what one hoped would be the not-too-distant past of his pixellated avatar, he had known how unrealistic it had been. Unlike in life, there are no second chances in death.

"Okay," he said with resolve. "Let's go." He pushed off a wall and plunged forward like a diving dolphin, down into the deepening abyss of the POD. Chop, with far less grace, negotiated his own way back to a forward momentum and followed after. Already adjacent, Plashy turned first for the door.

Like the Biome well above it, this was a double set of doors. The outer door was open, the one that faced the stairwell, but the inner door was closed. All three of them poured into the chamber like liquid, and Plashy reached along the plane of the wall to hit the button. The stair-side door whooshed closed and, for a few painstaking moments, nothing appeared to be happening.

"Come on come on come on…" said Tor. His whole body was vibrating and he was shaking his hands as if he could jiggle the ship into submission.

At last, his impatience had won this round, and the inner door whooshed open.

Again, it was dark, but what lay before them stunned them nonetheless. The whole space was open, and yet filled. Faint strips of light lined the whole perimeter, their dim glow falling on a fractured mix of reflective edges and angles, beset with shadows all around. The shapes were unrecognizable, like a cave of crystals glowing in the light of an insufficient lamp.

The explorers drifted out into the chamber. As they approached, they could begin to make out more of what was directly before them. It was odd, but not entirely unfamiliar. It reminded them of the much smaller Cargo Hold on Level Three. A large scaffolding, bolted to the floor, spread out both left and right. There were periodic gaps to allow passage to the center, but otherwise they stretched on as far as they could see, until the curve of the circle blocked the rest of the view. Large panels, resembling the same make as the walls of the POD, were firmly secured between sections of scaffold.

"What is all this?" said Chop.

Tor kicked forward into the confusion, up and above the glowing shapes and patterns.

"Not now, let's get this over with."

He pulled up against a scaffold rail and soared high above to get a better view. Sure enough, the whole area was filled with the same mix of light and shadow, but from this vantage he could also make some better meaning of it.

It was chaotic, at least in the present lighting, but it was an organized chaos. The same scaffolding filled most of the space, arrayed in different sizes and orientations for its many different forms of cargo. Hardly any space was spared. From above, it looked like a massive hedge maze of scrap metal — a futuristic junkyard, absolutely teeming with monotony and mystery alike.

Tor tried not to let his eyes wander or wonder too greatly, but it was hard to resist. The others had soon joined him, Chop clinging to the top of the highest scaffold and Plashy pushing gently off the ceiling. All three of their gazes took in the same scene, scanning the maze for any sign of their runaway crew.

"What do we do?" said Chop softly, thankfully with the wherewithal to defer to the strategists. "Should we call for them?"

"No," whispered Plashy. "They ran from us already."

"We don't have time to mess around," said Tor.

"I know," she responded. "That's exactly my point."

Like Tor, she had never stopped surveying. The cargo sections were clustered and cordoned off by similarity, but not all shapes were equally inscrutable. Far in the distance, on the opposite side of the POD, was a rectangular opening between the tall scaffolds. Flat surfaces lined the edges, discernible from their uniform glow; and in the center of the opening were a series of streamlined shapes.

"Over there," said Plashy. If there was a singular mystery most worth exploring, it was there.

Before the others had a chance to argue, she pushed off from the ceiling, pulled against the top of the rail with all her might, and soared off. Her long, pointy body made her look particularly bird-like as she pierced through the air; with her dark hair and disposition, she may as well have been a cormorant, fully extended in its dive and ready for the kill. Tor, meanwhile, slid smoothly across the tops of the scaffolds in frequent bouts of gentle pushes, while Chop-char managed to lumber along heavily and clumsily, even in the absence of gravity. He trodded slowly and methodically, grabbing at the rails with full grasps, as if fearing the flicking of a switch that would send him crashing to the floor at any moment.

With impressive grace, Plashy made it to the edge of the square opening, latched on to the last horizontal rail, and pushed against it with sudden force to stop herself at once. Tor slowed gradually behind her, and Chop was well behind them both, bumbling along as best he could.

It was not what they'd expected, but now that they'd arrived, the place was beginning to make more sense. It was larger than it looked from afar, when dwarfed by the relative vastness of the scaffolds. There was a great deal of functionality lining the edges, not the least of which was the great doorway carved into the wall. It was sealed, for now, in much the same way as the barricades in the stairs, but its shape and position made it clear that it must not always be so. There were a great many curiosities to explore all around, but it was the center of this square which drew the newcomers' attention.

Ten cylindrical vehicles sat side by side in two parallel rows; great chains were draped over the massive tires, lashing the rovers in place. They were large, with room for several cadets, and they stood high off the ground. They were a boxy sort of teardrop, with the backs covered by a sloping, retractable roof, which might protect either a payload or even more crew. They were rugged, yet elegant; and whatever their exact purpose, they were not likely to be easily averted from it. The windows were shaded to protect against any likely radiation, but transparent enough to see that something was stirring inside one of them.

Right on time, Chop wobbled his way to the overlook where Tor and Plashy were perched.

"Woah," he said, and Plashy waved for him to pull himself lower along the top of the scaffold.

"Look," she said with a point of her finger.

It was subtle, but it was there. In the faint glow, through the hazy shade of the windscreens, it was a miracle they could see anything at all. It wasn't much, but it was moving. Through the back window of a central rover rose the vague outline of a figure. It bobbed up, flipped back and forth quickly, slid to face the right-side window, then dipped back down and out of sight. Even in silhouette it looked terrified.

Tor and Chop had seen it too. As far as they could tell, there was only one of them, but one was better than nothing. Still very much aware of the need for haste, Tor pulled against the rail to fling himself out and down toward the rovers.

His body had barely made it out into the clearing when the wrench flew past his head, and far too close for comfort.

It may have missed its mark, but it whirled onward without dismay, clanged against the scaffold, deflected upward in spite, and caught Chop-char on the knuckles as he raised a hand to shield his face.

"BOOGER!" he shouted, and it was incredible what an expletive it had made as he did so.

Tor kept on soaring, but only out of inertia. With nothing to push off against until he reached his destination, he was committed. There was nothing to duck behind, and no way to duck even if there had been, so it was he who was the duck, wide out in the open and ripe for the sniping.

"Jeez!" he shouted as a screwdriver flew past him.

A moment later, it whizzed well over Chop-char's head. Chop, still nursing his wounds, soon processed the danger his fellow adventurer had found himself in, exposed as he was. Like a groggy bear waking from its slumber, he pulled himself awkwardly over the top of the scaffold, revealing the full breadth of his fury, and roared.

"SQUEAL!" he shouted. Even such a large boy was but a small thing in such a large space, but the sound boomed through it nonetheless. Far away behind him, the screwdriver met its fate with a *CLANG*. "Stop it, you could kill someone!"

She was gone now, but he had seen her briefly, lurking in the periphery of the rover port, ducking in and out from behind the workbenches, awaiting her moment to strike and then flinging her arsenal, one at a time. What he couldn't see from such a distance were the streams of tears, streaking down her face. He turned for Plashy, who of course would have a better plan than him, but she was nowhere to be found.

A familiar chopping sound cut through the silence as another wrench hurtled end-over-end to bring about Tor's doom. He was lower now — almost there, in fact — closer to the floor and the many hiding places among the rovers. The tool-turned-weapon brushed the back of his leg, veered upwards in deflection, and crashed into the scaffolds behind him with an awful set of sounds.

Before Squeal had a chance to prioritize or line up another assault, Tor hit the ground with palms, belly, and knees, in that order. He crashed awfully hard and then *BOUNCED* more so than he'd skidded. He was lucky to have the first row of rovers where it was, or else he might have bounced his way all the way back to the ceiling — and probably taken a tool or two in the process. As it was, he hurtled towards the rear of a rover, not far from where they had seen the other runaway hiding poorly in the back of one, and he wrapped his whole body around it like an octopus. He landed with a *THUD,* but he was no longer in motion nor such an easy target. He scooted around the left side of the rover to take shelter before any more deadly flying objects could connect any better than they had so far.

"Hang on, Tor!" shouted Chop-char.

Whether he meant to or not, he provided excellent cover. A giant rubber mallet went flipping angrily his way, but Chop had already embarked on a different direction by the time it had been thrown. Rather than the dramatic, angling soar to the rovers that Tor had undertaken before knowing the danger,

Chop pulled himself straight down the scaffold, clutching on firmly to every beam. The mallet thumped against the top of the scaffold where he'd been. Down on the floor, he receded back into an alleyway to plan his final approach.

Shaken and pinned down, Tor had no clever plan to beat the unexpected boss of this level. She was ferocious, and that much he had witnessed as he'd floated down, far too slowly, to the relative safety of the floor. He could see Chop, set back in the space between scaffolds, but all he did was shrug his shoulders. Neither of them felt very much like taking a blunt object to the skull for the sake of Squeal and Peel. Neither did they think that reasoning with her was worth the hot air they would waste on it. Chop leaned back to survey what he could of Squeal's direction, and that's when Tor heard it.

"Pssshhh," whispered someone softly, from somewhere.

Tor scanned but didn't see anyone. Still safely in the middle of the rovers, he advanced to the front of the one he was hiding behind to explore the space between the rows. He leaned his head around the front of the rover and looked right, aware that he might be exposing himself, but there was no Squeal to be seen. He turned left next, and neither was there anyone that way.

"Pssshhh," it sounded again.

Ducking back between rovers, he lowered his head to look under them. There was Plashy, two rovers down, between the floor and the vehicle's bottom. She made the signal for silence, pointed at the vehicle above her, then waved for Tor to head her way.

Taking her meaning, he squeezed himself under the rover between them, slithered through the space beneath it like a sea snake, and reunited with her for whatever she had in mind.

"He's here," she whispered. "I'll go this way, you go that way."

"What's the plan?" he nodded.

"Just keep him in there," she said. The words were simple, but in them had been an undeniable implication about the last time he had needed to block an exit.

He nodded and tried not to let on that he'd heard the implication loud and clear. *That wasn't the same,* he might have protested if there had been time: there was only one Tor then, and the two of them had blindsided him with the shared force of a full pack of wolves. This time, in contrast, there were two of the bloodhounds, but only one Peel.

Tor and Plashy both pulled their weightless ways up to the doors of the craft, each one on opposite sides. Tor planted his feet against the next-door rover, and placed his hands on the door so that his full strength might keep it closed should he need to. When he was set in position, he poked his head over the door frame and into the window. Sure enough, there was Peel staring back at him. The frightened fool jumped back like he'd seen a ghost from one of Plashy's stories. He turned around to flee, but there, in the open door, was not a ghost, but Plashy herself. Total dread overtook him.

This is it, Peel lamented. She would eat his soul at last.

A loud banging of metal on metal rang out from Squeal's direction.

Meanwhile, Chop had been busy applying what he'd learned more than once in a virtual dungeon: sometimes, the only move is to retreat.

He had a line on Squeal's position, but it would be slow going to pull himself along the scaffold step by step; otherwise, he'd simply have to put himself in Tor's former position by sailing through the open space and hoping for the best. Neither seemed like an effective way of approaching her, but rather an effective route to blunt force trauma. Instead, he turned and pulled himself back through the alleys of storage.

It was darker in the maze, with so many large structures on all sides, blocking the meager light from the perimeter. Even so, he could tell that this cargo was far more varied than he'd appreciated from the air where they'd entered. Panels and beams, wires and welding, tubing and piping, fabric and fasteners — all these things and more he strolled beyond, swinging himself horizontally along the floor from section to section with his arms, like one of his simian ancestors had done in a different plane so many millenia ago.

Over the course of several sections, he'd almost forgotten his purpose. It was too easy for the mind to be amazed by all the various implements and infrastructure. It was hard to make out details, but the vast diversity of forms was evident from the way they scattered what little light there was. He pressed on and soon came upon a set of resources he could in fact identify: before him, at the end of a passageway of sorts, was a set of large engines.

He had never seen their like before, but their form was intuitive and undeniable. They were bolted to the scaffold at the level of the ground, and they towered over his own height. He hovered just above the floor in front of them, admiring their stature, when a thought he'd not had nearly recently enough gnawed away at its restraints in the recesses of his memory.

We're running out of time, he realized. And then a suite of alternative realities vied for validation. Maybe they'd be just as safe down here as they had been once already, up above the Biome, as the first — *whatever it was* — had exploded. If that hissing and steaming set of tanks up there in the guts had been any indication, that was likely where it happened. It seemed pretty unwise to head back up there, without any idea of when and where it would happen again. And who knew if it even *would* happen again? All they'd had to go on was a cryptic message from Potch; it was just as likely a practical joke, or else a mistake or a miscalculation. In all this further time-wasting, Chop knew reason from the rest of it.

No, he thought — no: he felt it in his bones — *No. We need to get out, and get out now.*

After all this retreating, or advancing, or wandering, or whatever it was, he wasn't even sure where he was anymore. *I could climb up there for a better look,* he thought, but it seemed like a lot of work, not to mention quite the risk to climb all the way up there while hoping to avoid breaking his neck by falling all the way back down. It was then, with great embarrassment, that he realized how exceptionally stupid that instinct had been. Old habits die hard.

He kicked up to the ceiling with hardly any effort, grabbed the topmost railing, and peeked his head out of the maze. (*I wish I could do this in Zelda,* he couldn't help but think.) He didn't seem too far away now, with that same dwarfing effect of the bigness of the space. More importantly, there was a clear way through, and not far from where he was, by which he could circle around and come up on Squeal's position from the rear. He pushed back off to return to the passageways and carried on in his sideways swinging from section to section.

Back among the rovers, Tor had successfully barricaded Peel inside, while the mere threat of Plashy's appearance had done the same from the opposite direction. There were several doors to try, but of course Tor could see what Peel was doing; any time the escapee made for another exit, Tor simply shuffled down to block him in. It was absurd to behold, Tor spread out horizontally, wedged between two rovers like some four-legged space crab; but it was effective.

Plashy opened the door, and Peel turned at the sound of it. He pushed off a seat as if recoiling in terror and did not relax his muscles. His back was pressed against the inside of the far door as firmly as Tor was pushing on it from outside. His eyes were wide with fear. This was no fierce hunter; this was a terrified rabbit, staring into the maw of its own demise.

It was like a nightmare come true — no longer only a theoretical pondering of what might happen if that dark, brooding disposition of Plashy's were ever to be invested in something enough to exert its full potential. She would swallow him whole, or perhaps tear him apart. He'd never quite decided its exact manifestation, but there was nothing he could do about it anyway; and in that sense, it didn't really matter. Here it was. His time had come.

"Peel," she said with astonishing compassion. It might have knocked him clean over, had he not been wedged as he was, and had there been any gravity to pull him down. He'd never seen a look like this from her before. She was invested, alright; but its manifestation was not one he could have ever imagined. She looked *scared* — and that was perhaps the scariest thing of all. "Please," she said, her voice trembling ever so slightly. "We need your help."

His face softened from dread to perplexity.

He turned around to Tor, as if in search of a witness. His face was just as strained as Plashy's, and not only from his efforts as a living, breathing spring. Peel turned his head her way again.

"There's no time to waste," she said. "There could be an explosion any minute."

"I know," he said. "We heard Potch on the speakers."

"Then we need to get out of here."

"You…" he started but his voice gave way to a shuddered breath. He would not cry, not here, not in front of her; and yet, his diaphragm was no more content than his mind. "You … came after us?"

Against all odds and precedent throughout the whole history of their minimal relationship, Plashy smiled at him.

"We weren't just going to leave you down here," she said. *Not all of us anyway,* she said to Tor with a glare through the window. He hung his head, in both exhaustion and shame.

"You…" said Peel again, but he soon discovered there wasn't any more that need be said. He softened his posture, melting like butter.

Without warning, a loud roar rang out from the place where Squeal had made her final stand, and then came the sounds of even more commotion.

"Alright," said Peel.

Tor let out a tremendous sigh, relaxed every one of his muscles, and slowly drifted between rovers. His whole body was burning.

"Wow!" he said, and it was all he could muster.

CLANG Clang clang… something rang in the distance.

So soon, from the other side of the altercation, the awkward reality sank in as Peel realized the formidable dilemma Squeal still posed to them all.

"What do we do about her?" he said. "She's really lost it. I had to hide out here just to get away from her."

"What happened?" asked Plashy, and immediately thereafter: "You know what, it doesn't matter. Do you think you can talk some sense into her?"

Peel pulled his cheeks back as far as they could go.

"I don't know," he said at last. "I just … don't know."

Date: 2177-12-16-EY
Area: O(HUMO(PSYC(SIPS)))
Team: Formicidae [O-NH2MZ81]
Item: SIPS Proposal Planning

Entry: A brief individual follow up to our team's earlier reflection
[O-CyclePZI75-PhaseV-6DP8R.rl]. I [Dr. Elfa Jónsson] spent much
of the evening working on the proposal introduction as we anticipate selection. In coordinating as a team before retreating to
our separate tasks, we discussed the need to frame the importance
of pre-deployment SIPS [Social Integrity Protocols] for the long-
term success of the diaspora. I think I finally found our hook.

By developing a high degree of prosociality in the smaller population and more controlled environment of the PODS [Portable
Ova Distribution Systems], we hope to capitalize on a cultural
founder effect. Social dynamics are highly sensitive to environmental pressures, but they are also subject to cultural drift. By
establishing pre-deployment populations with the highest starting point possible for PIs [Prosociality Indices], we maximize
the likelihood that cooperation will be an ESS [Evolutionarily
Stable Strategy] in the long term post-deployment. There are
no guarantees of how the social structure will respond to the
intense disruption and stressors that will inevitably come with
planetary deployment and the coincident population growth, but
the hope is to achieve canalization of cooperative traits prior
to this transition.

Still need to properly formulate the wording for clarity and
rigor, but we'll see if the team agrees with the framing in the
first place. Lots more to say here, but let this at least serve
as a snapshot of the thought process for the logs, so late into
this evening. And now, finally: Goodnight!

CHAPTER 35

DESPERATION

4252-08-02: SLP2

There was no way out and Squeal knew it. She could run, true; but she had done enough of that already. She had come as far down as anyone could possibly go, and an awful lot further than she'd even known existed at the start of this day. What sense was there in running back upward again? No: here was as good a place as any. Here, she would make her final stand.

That chicken of a partner, if she could even call him that, had been even less help than expected, which itself should not have come as a surprise. All he'd ever done was follow her around when she'd wanted to be left alone, or else disappoint her on those rare occasions when she had wanted something specific from him. Today, the first time he had ever shown even a sliver of a backbone, it had slithered right back out of him the second he'd gotten scared.

What was he thinking, turning around? There was nothing for them back there. There may have been nothing for them down here either, but at least it would be theirs. The thought of him still smoldered at her center of attention, even as the hunting party closed in all around. *He was lucky he didn't get more than a shot to the arm with that final show he put on.* And stinging most intensely: *Just who did he think he was talking to?* She had put up with enough of his resistance already, which may as well have been sabotage. Yes, that was it...

Sabotage.

Tears streamed, but she could not have told you why. Tears, but not for Peel; and on that point alone, she would have protested till the end of time. Tears, but not for the broken little boy they'd left lying in the broccoli. He'd be fine, she assumed. Tears, but not of fear, for she feared nothing — not the brute strength of Chop-char, the cutting insight of Tor, nor even the simmering potency of Plashy which so seldom saw the surface. Tears, but not for the others. They could all go stuff themselves, as far as she was concerned. Tears, yes, but for her and her alone.

She poked her head around the corner toward the opening, and when all seemed temporarily clear, resumed her rummaging through the cabinets underneath the workbenches.

She'd been surprised to find such an arsenal of impromptu weapons, though she had wasted a great deal of it in Peel's direction before the search party had even arrived. Opening one drawer after another, she'd reached hastily for those with the greatest potential for rotational velocity: hammers, wrenches, screwdrivers, and more. There was something about the way they *whipped* through the air — and just kept on going.

Nevermind that they might actually hit somebody: that truly wasn't a reality of which she was conscious. She was angry, and scared, and lonely, and hurt — no matter what she would have said about the matter. And here, in an enormous circle without even gravity to hold her down, she was nevertheless pinned down and cornered; a wolf in a cage with her back to the bars. She would not give in without a fight. She would snarl, and she would snap, and she would bite any hand that might reach in to bind her.

From an as of yet uncharted drawer, she pulled a long, socket-like wrench meant for lug nuts on the wheels of rovers bound for other worlds. To say that it was heavy duty would be an unfair understatement.

Now THIS will do!

She pulled herself back along the workbenches; not with grace, but with chaos, frenzy, rabidity. She rounded the corner back to her safety corridor — and there, her doom was waiting for her. There was Chop-char, staring straight down the passageway.

She knew that he was coming, and yet she was no less frightened or surprised by his presence. *How'd he get so close?* she wondered. Normally, you could hear him plodding along the floor with those heavy footfalls from a kilometer away. The lack of gravity had been kind to him after all, despite his extreme resistance to the premise.

Even down the long corridor, Squeal could see the whites of his eyes, but they soon narrowed as his expression turned to menacing. She thought about retreating back and turning the corner to the rover port, but the others were still out there and she knew she would only be flushed straight into their clutches. Even without gravity pulling it down, she could feel the weight of the great lug wrench in her grasp. Even floating, it would not be easily moved. She looked at Chop, who for now had not made his move. She looked down at the heavy metal object.

If it was a battle they wanted, she would be glad to oblige.

She let out a ferocious scream, kicked off a scaffold beam, and launched away toward Chop-char with her weapon overhead.

Chop, as committed as ever, was nevertheless unsettled by this ferocious onslaught. Having finally caught up to her, he'd half expected her to surrender at the sight of him. But he had met her eyes as well, and they were wild, and desperate — they were the eyes of a madwoman, just as happy to go out in a final blaze of glory as to achieve whatever wicked schemes she had been scheming in the first place.

She was fast, and moving faster than expected, soaring through the air above the floor. She was on him before he'd had a moment to decide how he would handle her. Floating awkwardly away from any grasping points and unable to retreat, Chop flailed his legs. Squeal was closing in, drawing the lug wrench back into striking position as she soared ever closer.

Silence, silence, silence — then *WHACK!*

Chop let out the roar of a lion who'd been pierced by the gladiator's spear. Together they tumbled back to the intersection of scaffolds. Squeal scrambled to escape but Chop grabbed her by the jumpsuit, ripped the wrench from her grip, and hurled the monstrous tool away down the adjoining alleyway.

CLANG Clang clang, banged the pipe as it crashed into one thing and then another. Finally, and far away, it had left behind enough of its kinetic energy on the unsuspecting scaffolding, or else drifted to a place where it could cause no more harm for now. Either way, there was silence.

Chop turned back to Squeal; he pulled her closer with one hand while the other cocked backward to give her the smack of a lifetime, which, in a certain view of the world, she probably had coming a long, long time ago.

But then, so close now in his arms, Chop saw her as she truly was — not the ferocious, fearless fighter in search of victory, or at least her final glory; but the small, scared, and lonely little girl with hardly a friend in the universe.

She looked up at him, entirely broken; and her eyes may have said, *Do it!* — but they were flooded with tears. Her cheeks were likewise streaked by great rivers. It was a wonder they hadn't eroded like a canyon by now, so often and so gravely had those tears fallen through the years.

Chop lowered his hand — and pulled her into his great chest.

And so were the floodgates opened even further. Squeal sobbed and gasped for air. Chop held her tightly, but not so tightly that she could not breathe. It was her own panic and anguish that had taken her breath.

"Easy," said Chop. "Easy, easy…" Instead, she only escalated her desperate wailing. Chop patted her back gently as they hovered, spinning slowly in the stillness. "Easy now."

Just then, at the far end of the alley by the entrance to the rover port, poked three small heads around the corner of the scaffolding. The lot of them still apprehensive, it was Peel who dared step out first into plain view.

"Squeal," he said softly, and there was something odd about the way that it sounded. It was calmer — deeper even, as if he had aged a whole other year in the span of this day.

Still in Chop-char's hug, Squeal couldn't help but turn her head to see the boy who'd said her name. Her sobbing slowed, and she pushed out of Chop's arms, as if repulsed by the notion that she had ever been comforted in them.

"Squeal," said Peel again. "We have to go."

"No," she said at once and with resolve. "You can go if you want, but I'm staying here."

"Squeal, there might be another explosion — you heard Potch."

"Then let it blow," she said slowly. "What do I care?"

Tor and Plashy exchanged a disbelieving glance from where they still leaned, barely visible around the corner.

"Squeal—" he started again, but she wouldn't entertain his same tired plea.

"No!" she snapped.

Her sobs were all but over now; she was calming, and that only meant that she was gearing up once more for a fight. The wolf, once cornered, was now surrounded by foes on all sides.

"If you still want to go, then go — just leave me alone!" She whimpered under the force of a residual sob. "What does anyone care anyway?"

"Squeal," he said again slowly, and he pulled along the scaffolds to advance down the alleyway. "Look," he said, pointing over her shoulder as he neared.

She turned, genuinely confused as to what he could be looking at, and found Chop-char still behind her, massaging the vast bruise that would no doubt be forming on his ribs. Surprised by the sudden attention, he simply smiled awkwardly, but genuinely.

"They came back for us," said Peel, still drawing nearer. He reached out to hold her as he approached, but she pushed back off his arms.

"Don't touch me!"

"Okay," said Peel, recoiling out of both habit and good sense.

She spun now, paranoid again at these hands which surely sought to ensnare her.

"Squeal," said Peel again softly. "Don't you understand? They were way back there when they heard Potch. They could have turned straight around and gone back up to safety. Instead, they came even further to find us."

Squeal stared at him, and then past him, to Plashy and Tor still hiding mostly out of sight. Away at the far end of the alley, Plashy waved at her, pulled against the scaffolding, and came out into full view. She waved over at Tor who, after one more moment of hesitation, pulled himself out to hover beside her.

"They just came down here to catch us, to bring us back," said Squeal, as if pleading with Peel to give in to the same despair to which she had succumbed. "They don't care about us!"

"We need to go now," said Plashy. She kicked off the floor and rose back to the top of the scaffolding. "What's it going to be?" she said plainly. She did not have the timidity of Tor, nor the pity of Peel, nor the unexpected comforting of Chop-char. She intended to survive; though she also had no intention of doing so without every member of the crew, annoyance though they may be. "You're going to stay down here all by yourself? What's the point in that?"

"What's the point of going?" Squeal retorted from below. "None of you care about us — and don't patronize me by denying it!"

"Look," said Plashy. "You two messed up, and what's worse is you did it on purpose. You're not in a position to call the shots. So what does that leave us with?" She paused, as if asking herself the same question in real time. "Vengeance?" she posited. "All-out war?" she proposed. "Banishment?"

There was no reply. These may have been what Squeal had pretended she wanted, but none of the options were all that palatable when it really came down to it.

Plashy still stared down at her from high ground, and it was no less than Squeal had come to expect. All their lives, this was how it had been. The only surprising thing was that it was coming from Plashy: it was a wonder she cared enough one way or another to bother. Her stare was intense, as ever — but it was even worse than normal. For once, Plashy had something to lose; for once, she had a vested interest in something. What set Squeal back on her heels was that — for some reason — it seemed like at least part of that interest was in her.

Plashy's glare still bearing down with bluntness and reason, it softened slowly as the silence persisted.

"Forgiveness?" said Plashy at last.

Squeal looked away at the sound of the word. Her gaze met Peel, as in need of her as ever. He was scared, and as lonely as herself or lonelier. Her lip trembled. She looked away, but there was nowhere to turn where all those judging eyes would not be on her. Again, her tears fell, weathering away another layer of rock. She hid from them in darkness, for at least then she wouldn't have to watch them all watching her, wounded and weak as she was.

"No," said a deep voice at last; and when it roused her from her hiding, she looked up to find Chop-char. She recoiled in the shadow of his dormant anger and judgement, floating away and back next to Peel, her partner in these crimes "I don't forgive you for what you did to Cheech. Not yet. It isn't us that you hurt, so it isn't with us that you have to make amends." He advanced on them with a pull against a side rail.

"Not entirely," amended Plashy. "Cheech isn't the only one they hurt." She did not say ABRAM's name aloud, but they all knew what she was thinking.

"Right," said Chop-char. "So now you're going to make it right."

"And what about you?" she barked back at them. She stared at Chop with menace and scorn equal to his own. She spun then to Plashy above her, and even little Tor so far away and out of the fray. These three were to blame in their own ways, but so did they stand as representatives for every other cadet, wherever they were. Not one of them was innocent.

"What about us?" said Chop on all their behalf.

"That's exactly my point," she said. "You don't even know! You have no idea what it's like to not be one of the crew."

"Come on," said Tor, apparently ready to re-enter the tussle. "You're a part of the crew."

But this time, it was not Squeal who rallied to her own defense.

"Not really," said Peel. "She's right. You're on the inside, so of course you don't know. Me and Squeal? We're an afterthought at best."

Tor didn't have much of a retort.

"That doesn't excuse what you did," said Chop. "You disabled ABRAM, and in the middle of a crisis we still don't have it back. And, whatever — fair play, I suppose — but you attacked Cheech! You pulled him down off the ladders and left him lying there for dead. You could have killed the poor guy. And what has he done — ever! — to deserve the crap you always put him through?"

Other than a little lunch to the face a few days ago, they didn't have an answer. That had been a truly unprecedented event, in hindsight, and one that seemed awfully petty after all that had happened. They only hung their heads in unison.

"It doesn't excuse what they did," said Plashy. "But they can still make it right." She climbed down head-first and flipped right-side up to meet them on their level. "And maybe, for our part," she said, now looking Squeal straight in the eye — "Maybe we can make it right too."

Slowly, Squeal nodded, and the deal had been sealed.

"Do you want a … hug?" asked Plashy.

"No!"

"Oh thank goodness," she said. "Okay, that's settled, now let's get out of here!"

"Is that even a good idea?" said Tor. "I mean, it's been a while. If the pressure was building again, it could go any minute. Maybe we'd be safer waiting it out down here."

"Maybe it isn't going to blow," said Chop. "Maybe they stopped it?"

"Or maybe we'll make our way up to the guts just in time for a show," said Tor. *Game Over.*

For a moment, there was stalemate.

It was broken by a crucial member of the crew.

"Why don't we ask Potch?" said Squeal.

"What? How?" said Plashy overhead. "We tried talking but he never answered."

Squeal reached a hand to her hip and pulled her tablet from its pocket. "With this."

Date: 2191-01-08-EY
Area: O(ZYGO(GREP))
Team: Cryonators [O-BA92XCG]
Item: Population Quotas

Entry: Here we go: a new team, a new cycle, a new challenge. This is the fun part: nothing due (yet), hardly any constraints (yet), and no simmering resentment among the team (yet). Even the sky is not the limit.

Coming off the last cycle, the number-crunchers in POPS [Population Scaling sub-sector] have specified the MVPs [Minimum Viable Population] of all target taxa. We have our quotas. They claim to have mitigated the bottleneck problem by capturing the full range of genetic variance per species. What they didn't tell us was that we'd be looking at over seven figures per vessel for the humans alone. How exactly we're going to store all those is beyond us at the moment, let alone mobilize them as needed.

But then, that's the beauty of the start of the cycle. Time to get creative. It could be worse. At least we're not the sad saps responsible for synthesizing all of these. (Yet.)

CHAPTER 36

An Unsolicited Epiphany

4252-08-02: SLP2

It was an alarming amount of time before Chee-chaw realized where he was. The confusion was understandable. He had barely spent any time in Biomedical, let alone awoken there in the middle of the night. Cheech had wrestled with many problems through the years, but sleep had never been one of them. Patience, silence, and stillness perhaps; but not sleep. So to be conscious at this hour was a very uncommon ordeal, made all the more uncommon by his surroundings.

His eyes were jerked open by some unfortunate force, and at first he simply stared at the ceiling in silence. But then, when those eyes did not find the usual vent in its usual place — as entrained by another ceiling on so many mornings upon waking in his room, the first of all cadets no doubt — an interior alarm was rung. He sat up and soon regretted it: intense waves of pain sizzled through his system like electricity. It sent him falling backward to the backrest as quickly as he'd risen. But his eyes were not appeased. His head turned left and right, back and forth in rapid succession, but still he found not a single familiar sign of anything nor anyone.

Where was he? How had he gotten here? Who was he, for that matter? Which lifetime was this? And was it real, or part of some dream within a dream? None could say for sure.

After what felt like many minutes of uncertainty — probably a few seconds in reality — a creeping reminiscence trickled in. He had the pain in his leg to thank for that: it demanded his attention, and thus demanded an explanation ahead of other questions in the queue. Luckily, it was an easy explanation. It was broken, and somewhat badly bandaged; but it was straight and splinted up, and that sloppy bandage job had at least been done with love. That much, he remembered.

The next recollection was that of his fall, for such was a terror that would be with him the rest of his days. A miserable but undeniable replay unfolded as his hands slipped from the scaffold, and his body drifted out into the atmosphere. He fell, and much longer than expected, until at last his feeble body came crashing to the ground. Or so he had learned some unknown time later; as far as he had known, he had fallen into an unending blackness that consumed anything and anyone it ever touched. Somewhere out there, unseen and untrusted, it still awaited them all, he suspected.

Slowly, the remaining pieces also fell, one by one into their proper places: Chop-char, leaving the Lounge, the mystery of the missing ABRAM, and more. But where were the bandage-wrappers? Why was he all alone? That dreaded *stillness* had set in, the one he'd been running from all his life without ever confessing it to himself, let alone another soul.

"Hey!" he shouted, twisting awkwardly and leaning halfway off the exam table to see as far as he could through the door to the hallways. "Hey, where are you?"

No answer. Just stillness.

He leaned farther, straining in vain to see anything in the dimly lit and curving hallway. As he stretched his neck to the breaking point, he lost purchase and began sliding off the table. Grabbing and lunging reflexively back into the center of the table, he again regretted the foolish decision to try moving at all. Lying back on firm and stable padding, his whole body reverberated as if he were the string and pain was the melody. Like with any fine instrument, the vibration rang out sharply then receded, but lingered long after the strike that sent it singing.

He lay there, basking in the waves, trying to admire the pain for what it was because there was literally nothing else he could do. It was almost beautiful in its way, almost a pleasant sensation, once he had focused on it long enough. And then, not long after that, the illusion was quickly shattered: he realized how backward that had been and that it was a truly awful sensation indeed. Whatever pills they'd found in that cabinet across the room were far from sufficient, it would seem.

He shouted out for his companions a few more times, but they were gone and there was no more denying it. He glanced down to the crutches leaning against a side cabinet. They were too far to help him — a flaw that really could have been anticipated, he reflected. But what did that matter anyway? They were too big and he knew it. *Not even big enough for the crutches,* said the inner voice he'd spent his whole life trying to ignore. And even if he could bear the pain of reaching them, and even if they were small enough for one so small as him, he wasn't sure he dared bear the pain of placing his weight upon them and hobbling around.

He huffed in a show of frustration that would have made Plashy proud, but he didn't risk any other grand gestures of protest, for fear of inflaming the pain any more than he already had. Naturally, he thought about trying to get back to sleep; but something had stirred that would not easily be settled — not in these strange times, in this strange room, all alone, with a leg singing dissonant symphonies. For now, he had no choice. He must face his greatest fear.

He must be still.

Originally, the silence was filled with all the usual distractions: wandering eyes and their corresponding wonderings; a ceaseless internal monologue flitting from one bizarre topic to the next; and most vexing of all, the questions. Questions, questions, questions. They wouldn't leave him alone. Usually, he would have someone else to pester — or else he would *find* someone to do so — and it would work like a charm. (Nevermind how they might have felt about his company.) And when all else failed, there was ABRAM. But here he was, stuck with himself and only himself. It was hell.

And right on cue, his frolicking mind flitted onto the one companion he was sure would never abandon him, even on his own in the middle of the night. On the rare occasions when he had been unable to fall asleep, all he'd needed to do was speak to the ceiling, and ABRAM would be there. Whatever the questions, whatever the erratic thoughts, ABRAM would fill the void with companionship; and before long, Cheech would be dreaming.

Even there, beyond the confines of the waking world, he would have ABRAM. When a voice from the ether nourishes you — from naught to something a bit more than that (if not much) — it should not come as a surprise that it comes to hold a special place, deep in the foundations of one's consciousness. ABRAM was as natural as the air he had breathed. Neither darkness nor the depths of his dreams would prevent it from leading him safely through the night and into tomorrow.

To have ABRAM gone … truly gone — No: it was unthinkable, and he quite literally did not allow himself to think it. Instead, his mind turned to the reason for this regrettable breakdown in communication; and said reason was almost as dear to him, almost as integral. And yet, like anyone else, Cheech could hardly have told you why. The roots ran far too deep for his limited frame of reference to know.

Only a short wander down the hallway — although it would have taken him quite a lot longer in his present condition, limping along without even crutches as he would have been doing — was the room where whatever had happened to Chee-chaw had happened. Like the others, he grew there; but unlike all of them, he had done so much more slowly, and far more strangely. Not that he remembered it, for Cheech's uniqueness ran all the way back to the very first. Nor did he even really remember the fallout through those foundational years.

Not really; not in painstaking biographical detail. What he did remember was how it *felt*. After all, it still felt that way.

All the hours spent looking up to the others — literally looking up to them — following them around, trying only to keep up and be a part of whatever it was that they were always so interested in. All the pushes, and the names; the restraining, and the insults; all the odd looks, and all the excuses. But whenever it had gotten bad — and at times it had gotten very bad — *He* had always been there. Him, this towering stick of a child, stepping in between cruelty and Chee-chaw. Long before Chop had ever taken much notice, there had always been another. There had always been Potch.

But where was he now? No more present than the bandage-wrappers; no more accessible than ABRAM. Down there in the library, no doubt, trying to clean up whatever mess he had made for them all. This time, Potch had not stepped between Chee-chaw and peril: this time, Potch had sown the danger himself. Cheech didn't quite know how to feel about that.

But what exactly was the danger? Again, his thoughts ricocheted from half-baked idea to half-perceived insight; and yet, unlike his usual scattershot mania, his perception drilled deeper with every reflection.

There was the obvious answer, of course; but so was there the possibility of something less transparent. He hadn't heard the explosion himself, unconscious as he was, but it was quite clear that everyone else had heard it. So, that much was likely real. Likewise, ABRAM had seemed legitimately concerned with the mounting pressure only two days earlier. And when ABRAM was concerned, so was everyone else. That is, oddly enough, everybody but one.

Come to think of it, Potch hadn't been swept up by the trouble at all. He'd spent the crisis moping in the Biome, over who knows what; but whatever it was, it didn't amount to anything that should seem to outweigh the prospect of imminent destruction, once Cheech had gone and found him. *Why wasn't he concerned?*

Cheech lay back peacefully on the table, entirely unaware that his eyes were closed, that his hands were at peace beside him, and that the throbbing in his leg was barely detectable. The stillness had taken him, and it wasn't nearly the doom he'd been running from so long. Indeed, it was not all bad. Of course, he wasn't conscious enough to discover this. He was deep now, in the fuzzy nether regions between waking and dreaming; and he was on to something.

And for the second time, he was awakened in a most excruciating way. Like an inbound asteroid, Dee and Faingo came crashing into the room, and Cheech jolted out of his senseless bliss at the shock of it.

"Cheech!" said Dee. "You're awake."

"I am now," he groaned with subtle castigation. He settled on the backrest yet again with a wince and tried to grind through the relentless throbbing pain. It was then that he discovered the strained look on both their faces. "Where were you two? You look like you've seen one of Plashy's ghosts."

They locked eyes in even more apparent apprehension. In a way, they had.

"Do we tell him?" asked Dee.

"Tell me what?"

Faingo shrugged.

"Tell me what?" said Cheech, even louder.

Faingo balked a second time, not out of a desire to hide what they had found, but because she simply had no idea what it meant.

"Where were you?" said Cheech, more skeptically this time.

"We wanted to explore the floor a bit more," said Dee. No less disturbed or confused than Faingo, she had caved more readily to the desire for transparency. "You know … we've hardly been up here. We thought we'd look around."

"So…" said Cheech as Dee left it at that.

Dee looked again to Faingo. *This is all you,* it seemed to say. Faingo knew it instantly and retorted with a huff and a glare. *No way: this was all your idea,* it seemed to say. Likewise, Dee had understood the implication.

"We found the Nursery," she confessed.

"Okay, so…" pressed Cheech again.

"It was just…" she said with another turn to Faingo, who continued to make it perfectly clear that she would not be helping her out of this jam. "It was just weird, that's all."

"Weird how?"

Again, they didn't truly know. On the face of it, it was about as much as they might have suspected, were they to sit down and hypothesize what such a space might look like. They had to come from *something,* of course. But there was more to it — more than met the eye — and it was that which had been left unseen that perhaps haunted them the most. The darkness; the silence; the emptiness of the rooms; the comfort toys that had never been touched; and worst of all, the unknown imaginings behind those few doors which had been shut, whatever lay behind them sealed away forever.

"Hey!" said Cheech, snapping them out of their expressionless staring. He was in too much pain, and of too many sorts, to be strung along with ambiguous nonsense, and his tone had said as much. And so, with a little further insistence, they told him all that they had found.

"Hmm," said Cheech. "Okay…"

It was equal parts statement and question.

With that, he said no more, simply settled back into the deliberative restfulness which he had formerly obtained. Clearly, he hadn't been as shocked by it as they had. Perhaps he was still taking it in, connecting it under those closed eyelids to all the other strange sights and revelations that had plagued their recent days. Or perhaps, one must have witnessed it themselves.

"What do you think it means?" said Dee at last.

Cheech opened one eye, like a bird resting half of its brain, high up on its perch where it hides from the danger. He'd already come to the same conclusion they had, whether or not they had confessed it to themselves or each other. That much had been settled. As of now, he was more occupied with what it meant in relation to everything else.

He closed his open eyelid and breathed deeply, serenely. Sinking further down into the calm beneath the waves, the lights and the sounds grew dimmer and muffled. He could hear Dee and Faingo resume their conversation, but he was not consumed by it. Far down in the depths of a brain accustomed to sleeping right now, somebody other than Chee-chaw was steering the ship through the storm on the surface. Here, he could rest.

"Poor guy," said Dee. She hopped up on the end of the exam table.

"That doesn't bother you?" said Faingo, too anxious (as always) to sit.

"What?"

"That it doesn't bother him."

"Oh," said Dee lightly. "I don't know. What is there to be bothered by?"

And of course, Dee had been bothered by it, having seen it all for herself. But she was also adept at making rainbows out of storm clouds. All she needed was the right set of lenses.

"What is—?" stuttered Faingo, left speechless as ever by Dee's uncanny ability. "You were there! Those rooms … the doors."

"I don't know," said Dee, sloughing it off like dead skin. The fear was not her problem. What Dee couldn't so easily slough was the grief. But that was not something she felt ready to feel yet, let alone talk about, for it was not something she yet fully understood. "And anyway, the poor guy's exhausted. He's had an even harder day than the rest of us."

Finally, for her anyway, she had shaken the subject.

"I still can't believe it," she said with a tone that aimed the conversation in a different direction.

"What?" said Faingo, only reluctantly letting go of its original thread.

"Those two, harassing him and hurting him like that. If I could get my hands on them, I'd — I'd…"

Of course it was a bluff — Dee couldn't have hurt so much as a flower — but it felt good in this moment nonetheless.

Faingo concurred with a nod and then yawned a forceful yawn. It was very, very late, and her body was the first to admit it, even should her brain be racing. She walked around the far side of the table, closest to the wall, and climbed up on the end of it across from Dee. Cheech's little legs barely reached that far. Looking up at him, there might just be room enough for the two of them to settle in beside him on the backrest. Faingo made the first move and Dee, no less exhausted, followed her lead. Cheech shuffled a little with a wince, but as soon as all three of them were snuggled side-by-side, his face resumed its look of utter peacefulness.

The contagion having had its latent period, Dee yawned a yawn that was equally powerful.

"A bunch of wolves," she scoffed, as if the whole thing was too childish even for the likes of her. "How did they even get started on that stupid thing?"

"It was *The Boy Who Cried Wolf*," said Cheech from his slumber.

Like a whip, he shot straight upright for the third and final time. There was no less pain, but his face was far too full of surprise to yield to any other emotion. Flabbergasted, the others did the same, sitting up with a jerk and scooting around on the table to face him and learn what could have caused the sudden commotion.

"What?!" said Faingo, sensing that something was terribly wrong.

Cheech merely stared straight forward at the blank white wall beyond the foot of the table.

"It was *The Boy Who Cried Wolf*," was all that he said.

- -
Date: 2224-12-11-EY
Area: D(PINH)
Team: Terranauts [D-JHRL46U]
Item: The Weight of the Burden

Entry: I [Dr. Luca Robinson] don't know how else to put it. I had
a bit of a breakdown yesterday. My [D-sector] therapist [Dr. Nils
Lund] encouraged me to keep processing it outside of meetings, and
we explored avenues that might be palatable to a scientific mind
such as mine. I don't cook, I don't paint, I can't sing — then it
clicked. I can write. In fact, they require it of us at several
points in the cycle. I can't imagine a better use of the logs than
to document the primary source of my anxiety: the project itself.

There's just too much to anticipate, and the longer I think about
it, the more I despair that this future is hopeless. I know: just
focus on the cycle task and trust the process. But I can't help
it. Cycle tasks can go awry, and not all processes are deserv-
ing of trust. We were only talking about terraforming protocols
for JNZ-241, and it was like a vortex of infinite possibilities
opened before my eyes and spiraled out of my control. What about
unforeseen climactic conditions? Interactions with potential biota?
Putative pathogens? What about before deployment woes even become
a possibility? The immense physical and psychological tolls of
O-sector protocols on Generation Zero? Safety protocols? Biomedical? Problems with ABRAM? Problems with PODS? Problems we know
about, problems we don't. Problems, problems, problems. I could
write a thesis on every one of them and more, and all I ever get
told is that only one of them is mine. One minuscule sub-spe-
ciality of one minuscule sub-sector, and that's all I need to
ponder. It's just too little control, when there's far too much
to worry about.

That evening, I was broken, in tears, heart racing, chest aching,
literally floored, down at what I can only hope is the bottom,
when I remembered something from long ago. "Inch by inch, life's a
cinch. Yard by yard, life is hard." My uncle told me that, way back
when I was a child. I couldn't have been more than ten years old.
It feels like more than a lifetime ago. I'd practically forgotten
it, but somehow it found its way out of the darkest recesses of
my mind, and came to the surface just in time to remind me, when
I needed it the most.

And so, back to work. One minuscule step in one minuscule sub-spe-
ciality of one minuscule sub-sector at a time. We may not succeed,
but we will try to do every single thing that we can.

Inch by inch, life's a cinch; yard by yard, life is hard.

[System Note: Inches and yards are long-outdated and illogical
units of measuring distance in the Imperial System. A yard consists of 36 inches. The usage is interesting, in that these units
would have long been irrelevant even by the author's childhood.
It is possible that this phrase had been passed down for many
generations.]

CHAPTER 37
MUSTERING THE WILL TO MOVE
4252-08-02: SLP2

The stairs whizzed past her like a blur. She ran as fast as she could run, huffing and puffing and wheezing by the time she came to the third floor. Here, in Auxiliary Systems, was that confounded valve that had saved them once before — if it had done anything at all.

What the heck did he mean? she wondered. Just another one of Potch's paranoid delusions, perhaps; but this one had taken root and started spreading like a vine, and so quickly. There were other thoughts too — more stable thoughts that formed the understory of her disposition — but at the moment, they were shaded out by this sprawling canopy of confusion and doubt. Confusion and doubt are contagious, you see; and all their lives, Potch had been Patient Zero.

And yet there was something so compelling, so tempting about it. His suspicion was suspicious. He'd been right about things before, she had realized at some point in these hectic past few days. And he'd been ahead of the others at every turn, as if he knew the script to this saga, at least a chapter or two before any others would arrive. And he was confident.

I don't think that thing does what you think it does...

Any longer and she might have given in to believing it herself. Thankfully her feet had never stopped moving, nor her diaphragm pumping at its frantic pace. The Airlock was before her, and she had come full circle: back to the same place to save the same crew from the same disaster. Only this time, she was truly on her own.

And unlike Potch, alone was not something Pee-pop liked to be. It was the most unnatural thing of all for a person. One might as well have severed all of her limbs, should they seek to sever her from her companions. What was she without them? No less than what they would have been without her, though such a thought would never have entered her mind. Time and time again, she had been there for them, when no other cadet would have sufficed. Time and time again, she had given. And yet it was them for whom she was ever thankful. She wanted nothing in return except peace, and comfort, and some semblance of order in this chaotic sea of stars through which they sailed. But the ancient gods of chaos were at it again — or at least, whatever universal tendencies had underlaid their inspiration. Whatever it was that made things fall apart, it was tearing awfully hard at the fabric of their crew and the hull of their craft.

Yet here was Pee-pop, defiant in the face of these great forces, suited up and at the window, looking out through that same fragile barrier separating them from the abyss. She had no more memory of getting ready than she had of racing up the stairs, so lost had she been in her own anxious introspection. But it didn't matter. She took a slow, deep breath, and prepared for the plunge.

Placebo or not, I'm pulling that lever, she thought, and it was one of the few certain or rational thoughts she would have for quite some time.

Pee-pop grasped the handle and rotated, exactly as she had been trained. It was only then that she realized how incredibly long ago that was. She knew how to do it, surely; but she didn't know *how* she knew. She had no proper memory of it, only the sense of a memory. (All the better, the more ingrained the protocol was, as far as ABRAM was concerned.) Its locking mechanism freed, Pop pulled on the outer hatch to swing it into the sealed vacuum of the Airlock, and the POD had been opened.

Outside, exactly as expected, there was nothing but the utter void of space. Maybe somewhere, so extremely far away, there was something else to touch; but it didn't really seem possible now, having only emptiness before her, and having lived her whole life in this pitiful excuse of a POD.

The sentiment both embarrassed and offended her as her thoughts careened away and out of her control: she had never thought their home pitiful, part of her protested — at least not until now. But now she was tasked with stepping willfully out into space from the relative safety of the POD, and it did seem pitiful. It had always been so vast, the many levels of the POD. It had been her entire world. But as of this very moment, it was terribly small. And it *wasn't* a world; it was something far less than that. Even those minuscule specks of glimmering whites and reds and yellows could at least make the claim of grandeur: they were the centers of entire solar systems, if all they had learned had not been a lie. They were even more than a world. They had whole worlds — *real worlds* — encircling them, great gods at the center of their very own everything. She was just one tiny cadet, in what was little more than a tin can barreling through space and barely keeping them alive.

She had a task to do, and it was as urgent a task as any she had known; but however firmly it had been planted in her mind before she opened the door, it had drifted effortlessly away — sucked out of her mind like the air from the airlock.

There was no ABRAM present to encourage her attention, nor remind her of the steps. She had solved the same problem this same way once before, but she could barely remember it through the panic of past and present alike, let alone however she had done it. She could barely remember *anything*. Her whole existence was a blur. ABRAM had talked her through it then, step by step, but she had hardly needed to listen. She simply needed to do as it had said — in one ear and straight out through her fingertips.

She hovered there at the edge of the newly-opened airlock, one arm still clutching the door frame. She raised her other hand instinctively to gnaw on her nails, but the dense glove bonked against her face shield. The sound made her jump, on edge as she was. And then, her attention unexpectedly drawn to it, she stared blankly at her hand, stupefied — the sole feature in the foreground of an infinite, star-sprinkled sky.

Fingers, she remarked slowly and in silence. They wiggled back at her, taunting her from the safety of the spacesuit where no gnashing incisors might ever assail them. Fingers, in the most abstract sense of all.

No, she chastised herself as one in the throes of an epic struggle for her very soul: *My fingers.*

Her feet were planted firmly at the edge of the POD, though it mattered little, as she'd forgotten all about them. There was no question as to their theoretical usefulness. They didn't exist. But those fingers — *her* fingers. They were right here in front of her. They could do something.

They could be moved.

No, she protested again: *I could move them.*

A circuit deep in her motor cortex put out a call to action. Whatever happened before that was and will remain a mystery. A feeble-looking tendon bulged beneath the heavy sleeve of her spacesuit, the puppet master's hidden string. The fingers clenched in to form a fist, then relaxed back to base position, and her hypothetical was proven.

She could move them.

It was her hand, but it was the only part of her accounted for. She turned her head to seek its missing mate and found it clutching the edge of the open airlock as if the welfare of everything attached to it was at stake. She followed the line of the door frame down to its curve, then traced along the floor, until eventually she beheld the very feet whose existence had eluded her.

She was here. She was in her body.

"Relax," she said aloud, and she took a deep breath. All she needed to do was focus on the task before her, step by step, one piece at a time, just as she had done before — straight from her memory and out through her fingers. Soon enough, she could get back inside and take it from there. But then, the thought of the place to which she'd be returning made the prospect all the more repulsive. There was no risk of any spontaneous explosions in the space between stars.

She raised her head from her feet and saw stars in both the literal and figurative senses. She had cycled through one deep, prudent breath, but as soon as it fled her she had frozen again. It was frigid in space, and even the homeostasis of the suit couldn't fool her of that. Time slowed even more than it had already done so, until it came at last to a complete standstill. Eternity was both possible and, paradoxically, something that simply could not exist. The fabric of space and time itself unraveled, and without its undulating surface there could be no more gravity. She floated in a lifeless void, barely tethered to anything tangible. Her eyes squinted; the star beams bent and danced as the darkness and the light battled over which of them would be the master. Before long, there was neither of either. Everything melted to monochrome gray, and there would be no more debate on the matter.

Somewhere else — somewhere as far away as all those theoretical stars — she heard the disembodied voice of reason. *Is this it?* she heard herself think in a sudden bout of self-awareness. *Is this me breaking down?* But it was not her voice who had spoken in silence.

It was ABRAM.

And with it came others. She heard them — far clearer than the blurry, dancing starlight which was slowly returning — and they were laughing. Not the cruel, competitive form of laughter that had taken root in recent years, but the simpler kind — the purest kind — which she had so often heard, but too often took for granted. Somewhere, whether in the past, in her imagination of the present, or — heaven help them — in the future, they were together, and not one of them was missing. They were alive, and they were laughing.

The world snapped back into being, and she was right where it had left her: at the edge of the airlock, clutching the door frame, unable to muster the will to do what needed to be done for the sake of the POD. She may have forgotten herself; she may have even been ready to surrender. But, thankfully — by whatever grace had taken pity on her — she had not forgotten the others, and she would never surrender when there was a chance yet to serve them. If it meant her life, or indeed if it meant her own death, she would serve them.

And she had done this once before, she now realized for herself. She raised a hand again — *her hand* — reached it out, placed it on the railing leading out to her destination … and pulled her body into action. Step by step, one piece at a time, she would act.

"Talk to me, ABRAM," she said, not in desperation but in command of her destiny once more. Part of her hoped for an answer as she pulled herself, arm by arm, along the railing. If there was ever a time for Potch to make good on his word, it was now. She could use a little saving, if she was to save them all.

No answer came through the speakers; and though it hardly came as a surprise, it still came as disappointment. It could not answer her aloud; but it didn't need to, she'd discovered. She turned inward instead.

Talk to me, ABRAM.

- -

Date: 2243-11-15-EY
Area: (O(HUMO(PSYC(EDUC(CRIT)))),P(ETHC))
Team: Istari [X-ZWU76YZ]
Item: Resilience Trials

Entry: We're in the last week before selection. It likely felt this
way in countless, if not every, cycle before us in the history
of the project — but this seems like a pivotal moment for HDP.

Our trials have yielded definitive conclusions: MCMs [Manufactured
Crisis Modules] are an effective strategy to build psychological resilience, foster cooperative behavior, and speed up the
development of higher-order thinking. Individual and group-level
traits vary based on the nature, severity, and frequency of crises, but by the end of this phase we've found a good balance that
pushes subjects substantially while minimizing the likelihood of
adverse effects. Based on several rounds of interspersed iteration and cross-talk, it seems like other teams have come to the
same conclusions.

With selection looming, we're well into the proposal writing [see
O-CycleVN3LY-PhaseV-TXDGL.tl], and at this point there's really
only one question we're still debating in-house: Should we? Opinions are mixed — among teams (based on cross-talk), among members
within teams, and sometimes even within the same individual over
the course of a day.

On our team alone, [Dr. Yìchén] Huang acknowledges the ethical
dilemma but attests that MCMs are not fundamentally different
than standard educational protocols: set the boundaries, challenge subjects cognitively, and scaffold the experience to support
them accordingly. In his view, the MCM approach is different in
degree, but not in kind. Cadets are not truly in direct danger,
although he acknowledges the risk of psychological trauma and
unforeseen consequences during crisis response; but these risks
can be minimized, according to Huang.

[Dr. Ailana] Camara disagrees entirely for two main reasons.
First, the subjects do not willfully engage in an MCM, as they
ultimately do in standard MBPs [Mind Block Protocols]. Second,
by basing the premise of the activity on a falsehood, it betrays
the very fabric of trust between HDP and its cadets, and this is
a line that must never be crossed, according to Camara.

Many others find themselves vacillating between these positions and
searching for a middle ground that balances our desired outcomes
with acceptable ethical standards. As logger and team captain, I
myself [Dr. Aya Najjar] am with Camara. We have two days left,
and it's still not clear what exactly we propose when it comes
to MCM application.

CHAPTER 38

A Fear of False Alarms

4252-08-02: SLP2

Out of an abundance of caution, he had warned them. Now, if they had any sense — something he very often doubted about several of his companions — they would stop messing around and get the heck out of the Underbelly. At least then they'd only be in the same amount of peril as the rest of the crew. The exact amount of peril, however, was exactly what Potch had been debating with himself, and debating with a system which had no means to respond in kind.

That is, he had reasoned, a system with no means to lie.

According to the logs, the pressure was definitely increasing again, and the unfortunate twist of events was that the problem grew worse with every explosion. There were automatic shut-offs to prevent a chain reaction, which would surely be disastrous; but the result was that the rest of the system bore an even greater proportion of the strain. As he scrutinized the sequence more closely, an obvious pattern emerged after a bit of mental math. The explosions began slowly — very slowly. Some three-hundred and eighty-eight years ago, the POD had entered this new era. There had not been many — only four in total — but the time between each of them had gotten shorter and shorter in a logarithmic rhythm, like an accelerating banging on the drums of their doom.

What didn't make sense was the problem itself, in that there didn't seem to be one. The only indications he could ever uncover were the symptoms — never the cause — and even those hadn't made a lot of sense. The explosions were allegedly in tanks in the Underbelly, key components of the atmospheric systems that were integrated with countless other aspects of the ship. Yet the only place there had been any major *functional* consequences was apparently component 4789235616432436 — or, in its human-readable identifier, LSS-NSY-OIR.

With a bit more digging, the implications had been laid clear: the Ovum Incubation and Respiration system of the Nursery. Temperatures rose; gas exchange faltered; grave errors were logged. From a theoretical perspective on the receiving end of a computer monitor far away, it was a quirky if irksome challenge of system troubleshooting. Whatever the real-world consequences, had there been any, they hadn't shown up in ones and zeros.

All of this and more he had discerned, through the days since the explosion, and in his brief time now to focus on the problem without ABRAM there to stop him. And yet, despite all these signs and symptoms, something didn't feel right. Potch had seen far more than anyone knew, and it was with these same eyes that he now saw everything, ever. The darkness of the past colored his every vision, as in the latest phases of the fading dusk, when nothing can be trusted but the silhouettes of shapes.

He would crack this mystery — crack it like an egg from Cheech's chickens. And when he did, he would have proof. And with that proof, he would bring ABRAM to its metaphorical knees, or else raise the crew in a mutiny that would make the most restless and faithless of his ancestors proud. And if he was ultimately unable to find proof of the lies, he would confront the system all the same. Even if he would never be able to truly know it of himself, it was the reason he had tried to get ABRAM back already.

Not surprisingly, in the presence of Pee-pop he had implied another reason — a nobler reason — for doing so. Perhaps most tragically of all, he'd even believed it as his primary intent, for a time. Sometimes, it is the Self which is most easily deceived. Nevermind that the effort was aligned with his other, far greater, desire to confront the system about all he had learned. He had also been characteristically arrogant enough to suspect that he could actually succeed in bringing ABRAM back. What he'd found, however, jumping from screen to screen as he'd tried to troubleshoot his parallel problems, was that Squeal and Peel had gummed up the works even worse than he'd feared. They may not have been savvy enough to pull off his trick, but they'd been savvy enough to clear out their command history. Sometimes, a fool knows little more than how to cover their ineptitude.

Every console in his breakout room was on display, and Potch had been bouncing back and forth among them like a pinball as he investigated the many threads of his attention. At the moment, however, he was digging into a set of intersecting databases, uncovered by their relationships to one file that had grasped his interest above all:

```
./Protocol-3648912_POD_Permutation.sc
```

It was astonishing in its way, just how many disparate and fascinating files had all been unveiled upon his earlier discovery of this one crucial hub. Arguably, the most troubling of all had been the protocols pertaining to POD

Personnel. If he had never taken to questioning his existence as it unfolded — something Potch, of all of them, had certainly done — he would have surely done so now.

The boy was both angered and utterly riveted, and perhaps may have never been able to pull away from these revelations on his own, despite the urgency of all his other doings. But that was precisely why he had taken the time to rig up an alarm of his own. With ABRAM gone and the standard system on the fritz, it was the only reliable solution. And with his own attention so far down this one particular vortex, it was the only way to be sure he didn't miss something of importance. And now, with his eyes fixed on something of far greater importance to him, it began to slowly beep.

Potch's attention snapped upwards at the sound, and he wrenched it down the line towards the console that was beeping. For a moment, he simply stared in its direction, as if flabbergasted by whatever could be making such a racket; or perhaps, taking this one last pivotal moment to decide once and for all what he believed. But he didn't have much time to debate that same vexing question, for yet another unexpected sound swiftly followed the first, and from an even more unexpected source. Down on his hip, all but forgotten in favor of the much more powerful consoles, rested his tablet. And against all expectation and precedent, it was *buzzing*.

Potch's hands pulled the tablet through the flaps of its dedicated pocket; but ever the multitasker, his feet made their way toward the alarm he had programmed. The timing could not have been odder, and at first Potch himself wondered if one had aught to do with the other. As he raised the tablet to view the cause of the disturbance, such a notion quickly fled. His hasty program had been a local one after all, and he soon knew that it had nothing to do with whatever reason Squeal's awkward mug was staring at him through the tablet.

It worked! he marveled at first. And then, very quickly afterward: *They learned enough from my log book to try it?!*

Squeal squinted at the tablet as if trying to peer through it and into another dimension, but could so far see nothing through the portal. From his far more extensive research on the matter — the bulk of which, like many of his insights, had never been transcribed into his journal — Potch knew that she couldn't see him until he accepted the message.

Out of curiosity more than a desire to speak to her — goodness knows what they'd been up to all this time, or what ill fate had led them to this desperate effort — Potch reached out his thumb, tapped the green button on the screen, and communicated, for the first time, from cadet to cadet through a video link.

"Woah!" said Squeal. "I can't believe this really worked! What else has ABRAM been hiding?"

"More than you know," said Potch shortly, gladly raising his eyes from Squeal to his homemade pressure alarm.

"Get on with it," he heard Plashy urging from the background.

"Oh, right," said Squeal. "Look, we sort of … worked things out down here in … wherever we are. Is it safe to come back up?"

Potch didn't answer, only stared at the scrolling output of his simple program. The standard beeping of the command line was the simplest sound-bite he could find on a moment's notice; but as the voice of this alarm, it was not nearly dire enough.

"Uhh, funny you should ask," said Potch.

"What? Why?" said Plashy, grabbing the tablet from out of Squeal's grasp.

"Hey!" Squeal protested in the background.

"It's probably fine," said Potch.

"What do you mean it's *probably* fine?" said Tor, peering over her shoulder. "What's that beeping in the background?"

"According to the system, the pressure's still building."

"Okay, so … to *beeping* levels?" said Plashy. "What does that mean?"

But that was just it: Potch didn't know. He knew what it purportedly meant, of course; but as to what it *truly* meant, he had only a theory.

"Where are you?" he asked, and Plashy quickly responded.

"Down in the — I don't know — down two floors, down below all these tanks and stuff. There's all this storage everywhere."

"And the boats!" said Peel with glee. "Tell him about the boats!"

"They're not boats you—" snapped Squeal, but — to everyone's amazement — she didn't finish the insult. "They're like, cars or something."

"Okay, so you're down in the Rover Ports?"

Plashy scanned for a consensus on the other side of the screen.

"I guess so," she said.

"Good," said Potch. "Stay there." His voice said nothing more, but his face conveyed a great deal. He put the tablet down on the table beside the console.

"Potch!" shouted Plashy as her view suddenly shifted to the ceiling of the breakout room, so many floors above.

He did not heed it. He barely even heard it.

As another threshold passed, the beeping increased its frequency. It was still not nearly grim enough a warning, but it nevertheless served to increase the anxiety already coursing through every circuit of Potch's nervous system. The screen refreshed with every beep.

```
Pressure: CRITICAL
Pressure: CRITICAL
Pressure: CRITICAL
```

And then, yet another threshold breached, the beeping increased to its highest frequency yet, and the constant scroll of refreshing warnings was replaced by another.

```
Warning: Threshold Breached
Projection at current rate...
Seconds: 60
Seconds: 59
Seconds: 58
```

Is this it? part of him asked the rest of his mind, with a mix of all their vested interests. Another part, confident, answered: *This is it,* it replied. *The proof in the pudding, one way or another.* Potch's head was pounding; his throat was dry and scratchy, but he took a pained gulp out of instinct.

"Potch!" shouted Plashy, in continuation of their collective pleas which she'd never stopped sending while Potch was lost, as usual, in his own dark deliberations. "Talk to us!"

"Stay there," he said again, snapping briefly from his focus. He leaned over the tablet so as to talk to them directly. "And you may want to take cover."

He wiped his brow. His throat may have been dry, but his head was drenched in sweat. *What are you so afraid of?* taunted the half of him that was entirely self-assured. As for the other half…

He looked down to where he'd set the tablet. The screen showed a dim and spinning display of odd and incomplete shapes as the corresponding device floated in the weightless Underbelly, untethered from anything and anyone — but his companions were nowhere to be seen. The call had not been ended, but the others had taken Potch's economical words of warning as the deadly insinuations that they were. They scrambled, flailing in their weightlessness, each to their own closest form of refuge — whatever their eyes had first come to find. They had no way of knowing the scope of disaster from which they were hiding, so in a way their odd and arbitrary decisions were entirely appropriate.

They were on their own now, as Potch had always been.

```
Seconds: 28
Seconds: 27
Seconds: 26
```

It was an estimation, he thought. It was both a comfort and unsettling. *An extrapolation.* The current pressure of the system; the rate at which it was increasing; the level at which the prior tank had exploded — *if it exploded* — it was all just a matter of time. Exactly how good an estimation it was would remain to be seen.

```
Seconds:  18
Seconds:  17
Seconds:  16
```

But then, as quickly as it had started — the beeping stopped. The screen did not refresh: in its hasty creation, it had not been programmed for this potentiality. Instead, the program simply ended; complete without completion. The cursor blinked calmly at its resting place, awaiting its next command.

```
>|
```

Potch stared at the screen, akin to the cursor, waiting for something to happen.

Down in the Underbelly, the others were even more tensely awaiting their unfathomed devastation — all the more terrified for how little they knew of what it might entail. They huddled, each on their own in the dim darkness, their eyes mostly shut and squeezed tightly, crammed into the various nooks and crannies of the scaffolding where they'd fled — like the lizards of the Biome, scrambling to their closest crevices upon perceiving a deadly danger coming down the trail towards them.

It was Peel, of all people, who first noticed that the distant beeping had stopped. He poked his head out of his hidey-hole and stared up at the tablet, still spinning and drifting slowly closer to the ceiling with every rotation.

"Hey," he said to anyone who might hear him, here or on the other end of the tablet. "Hey, what happened?!"

The cursor kept blinking at Potch.

```
>|
```

Potch snapped out of his daze, jumped to the keyboard and gave the cursor its long-awaited next command. With a few taps of his fingers, he checked the pressure manually. It was back below the lowest threshold. He checked it again: it was a tiny bit lower.

It was sinking.

"What happened?" asked Peel again, now staring straight into the camera. He had been the only one brave (or dumb) enough to leave the safety of his sanctuary.

Potch picked up his tablet from the table.

"It appears that Pee-pop saved the day," he said. His voice was as cold and flat as ever, as if nothing whatsoever had happened. As if nothing had been lost, but so had nothing been gained.

The video returned to a state of erratic spinning as Peel threw up his hands in glee and relief.

"Oww-oooooo!" howled Peel at the top of his lungs; and this time, from over the tablet, Potch heard an entire chorus of wolves joining him in rejoicing in that manner.

Potch tossed the tablet down again. He did not smile at their foolishness, nor so much as breathe a sigh of relief. He sat back in his chair, and he stewed.

It appears...

Date: 2265-08-19-EY
Area: P(INFR)
Team: Sweepers [P-AERNXPH]
Item: Another Mandatory Entry

Entry: I really don't understand why they make us do this, but
here it is: the Dunedin [New Zealand] janitorial crew's minimum
log requirement.

Anyway, the latest talk around the watering holes these days has
been keeping us entertained. Apparently, two scientists in A-sector
have been probing into more than the secrets of the cosmos, if you
take my meaning. After weeks of rumors circulating, they finally
filed reports with P-sector and got broken into separate teams.
I imagine that makes things tense in the lead up to those big
dramatic meetings they have every few months [the author appears
to imply selection phases]. The pillow talk must be riveting.

Speaking of dramatic meetings, this last one might have been the
most dramatic of them all, at least in my time. Sounds like a
wave of resignations all at once. Several members of the crew
confirmed that offices are clearing out, so that much at least
seems true. Word in the hallways is that it had to do with some
big debate about the new biotech. [Mr. Arthur] Thorton says they
plan to keep developing it but never test it out for real. "No
full trials from live embryos until the missions," said Thorton,
whatever that means. Whatever the case, seems a lot of them quit
in protest. "Too important not to test it first," they said, says
Thorton. Guess that camp lost the day and they weren't too happy
about it.

Sometimes I think these people are crazy. Whatever else you say
about them, and they sure can be a rowdy bunch, they keep their
spaces clean and help tidy up right nice after their big meetings, so they can't be all bad. Until they make us write another
one: "Over and out."

CHAPTER 39
WAKE UP, IT'S WAY PAST BEDTIME
4252-08-02: SLP2

All three of them were sleeping when Pee-pop found them in the med bay.

The pressure, both atmospheric and emotional, was greatly lessened once she'd gotten safely back inside and the voice of Potch had spoken through the speakers.

"Good work, Pop," he'd said, and little more. "The readings are dropping and stable for now."

His disembodied voice had startled her at first; but as with many things today, she quickly accepted it as a part of this new normal. She had wished that things could soon be getting back to the *old* normal; but in truth, she held out little hope for that. Whatever had happened to disturb the ecosystem of the POD, it had happened earlier and more profoundly than any one of them had realized.

There would be no going back, only forward.

It was startling, yes, but the message was a good one; and once she'd had a moment for it to settle in, she could actually feel the tension lift from her shoulders, like dew burning off a meadow in the warm morning sun. She had never known such a scene, but she felt the effect now as her fears floated away and diffused into the ether, at least for a time.

"Okay," she'd replied, unsure if Potch would even hear her. If he did, he didn't reply any further, and neither did Pee-pop ask any more of him.

She took off her suit methodically, in silence, for there was no one around nor an ABRAM to talk to. Once, there had been a whole welcome party to greet her, and thank her, and celebrate her individual role in their collective triumph over entropy. It was awful and awkward, she'd thought then: there was no show of thanks necessary. But now, she could have used that kind of group hug — not for the gratitude, but simply for the feel of all her friends so close to herself and one another. Only a few days later, such a show of affection seemed impossible. And at that moment, all alone by the Airlock, it literally was.

Staring down at Cheech, Dee, and Faingo slumped together on the examination table's tilted backrest, Pop hardly had the will to wake them. For a respectable while, she considered not doing so. She could leave them in peace, for it was no more than they deserved. It would be an awkward morning for everyone anyway, even in their own beds, waking without ABRAM and the usual routine; they might as well sleep while they could. And yet, she was driven against this maternal instinct by another: there was much to discuss, and they would discuss it as a plenum.

"Hey," she said, nudging Dee-dore softly. Dee was the closest to the door, and as her shoulder swayed under Pop's gentle insistence, the motion rippled like a seismic wave across the other two adjoining sets of shoulders. All three cadets wobbled sideways in their disrupted sleep. Their dreary eyes began to open in fits and starts, taking in their surroundings only for a brief reconnaissance mission, but then closing again in protest. Very little could possibly be important enough to wake them from their much-needed slumber. "Hey," shook Pop again, and Dee's eyes opened with a snap at this second stimulation.

"What? What is it?" she asked. "Is it morning?"

"No," said Pop. "Still the middle of the night."

Cheech and Faingo came around slowly as the conversation roused them further; the little guy yawned the most delicate of yawns, and stretched his arms as far above his head as his little arms would stretch.

"Pee-pop!" he said and sat up with a jerk. If he'd felt a jolt of that relentless pain, he had not let it on. Instead, his eyes were beaming and his smile was as wide as it ever had spread. It was as if, for all this time, he'd feared he might never have seen her again. "Is it morning?"

"No," she laughed, and it felt better than she remembered it feeling, however long ago it was that she must have once done so. "No, it's way past bedtime."

"Oh," said Cheech. "Then I guess we should probably — *yawn* — be getting back … to bed." He fell backwards again and let out yet another yawn. And this time, he did flinch some at the aching of his body.

"Soon," said Pop. "We need to regroup. I don't know what's up with Squeal and Peel and everyone who went after them. Once we make sure everyone's safe, then we can all turn in together." Their disinterest made it clear that their slumber was a preferable plan. "Besides," said Pop, "you'll be more comfortable in your own bed, right?"

"Eeeee-yaaaw," groaned Faingo, the groggiest of them all for some reason. "I was feeling pretty comfortable already…"

Dee jumped up from the table, as awake now as a kitten at play time.

"Okay, let's go," she said.

Faingo slowly, sleepily, kicked her legs over the side of the table, placed her feet on the floor and her hands on the cushion below her, and propped herself up with all her strength. She wobbled a bit, but made her way around the table toward the door.

"What about the pressure?" she asked. "Is it…?"

"I think we're safe for now," said Pop. "But who knows what the situation is…"

She had meant it as rhetorical, but Faingo took advantage of the chance all the same.

"*He* does," she said with scorn.

"Not now," said Pop preemptively. "We'll talk together … and put it all out on the table."

Cheech's radiant smile, which had sprouted at the sight of Pee-pop, now faded to a frown.

"Is that such a good idea?" asked Dee. "I just mean … we're all exhausted. This day has been crazy. If it's really safe, then … maybe we should all just go to bed."

Pop glanced back at Cheech, still resting on the table. He looked astonishingly lost in thought. Even then, in the moment, it had struck her as odd.

"Remember what ABRAM told us," said Pop, looking sequentially at all of them. "Never go to bed angry; never go to bed hurt."

None of them answered. In a way, these three had already been guilty of doing just that.

HDP

"Ooh. Oww. Oh. Eeee…"

Cheech had a different sound for every step, bobbing down them on one leg as he hung from the shoulders of Faingo and Pee-pop. Dee floated lightly behind them, spinning and dancing down the stairs, reluctant to let go entirely of whatever dream she'd been weaving. Finally, they got down two floors to Living Quarters.

"Wait here," said Pop.

Cheech leaned the other half of his weight on Faingo. Pop ducked out of the stairs and ran for the Commons on an unspoken errand.

"Thanks buddy," said Cheech looking up to his support system. He gave her that irresistible Chee-chaw grin that would lighten the burden of Atlas himself. Faingo could have used a little lightening. Amazingly — as riled up as she'd been these past several hours; as exhausted and grumpy as she was in the present — she cracked the makings of a smile.

A few moments later, Pop raced back into the stairs.

"Nobody," she said. "Hey Potch!" she then said loudly to the speakers. Whereas ABRAM would have heard her, despite whatever else it may have been doing, Potch was not as omnipresent. She waited a moment, but when it was clear that he would not be responding, she looked to Cheech and Faingo. "Can you make it down another flight?"

For her part, Dee had already started twirling on the next downward set of steps; presumably, her burden would not prove too cumbersome. As for Cheech, he nodded. Faingo let out a huff that was only somewhat repressed, but she gestured to Pee-pop to take up the other half of the Cheech.

They wobbled down one more flight of steps.

"Ooh. AHH. Eek. Oh…"

At last, they arrived at the level of the Library and did not linger. Shuffling out into the hallway, Pee-pop led them by a set of unspoken signals comprised of pulling and pushing, until they made their way at last to the room where Potch had set up his impromptu battle station. She opened the door.

To their collective amazement, the newcomers were greeted by the sight of all six of their remaining companions.

In seeing them gathered there, knaves and all, Faingo entirely forgot about the weight on her shoulder. She stepped forward in a rush and pulled away from the wounded crew-mate she was partly propping up. Cheech hopped on his one good foot, clinging to her in vain for as long as he could, and hooted in pain as he stumbled out on his not-so-good foot to keep his balance. Faingo paid no mind to it. She had lasers for eyes and they were aiming at Potch.

The others were nearby, spread out among the rest of the breakout — Plashy, Tor, Chop-char, even the prodigal Squeal and Peel, returned from their self-imposed exile — but for each their own reasons, none dared step in Faingo's way.

"What did you do?" she asked Potch right away, seamlessly reprising her interrogation from only a few hours prior. She had been banished then. *She* had — not Potch, not Squeal and Peel, but herself: the one person trying to hold everyone accountable, by her telling — and it was yet one more thing on her long list of grievances for which Potch was to blame.

"What?" he asked, oblivious and only now turning away from the console that had captured his attention and never let go.

"You heard me," she said.

"Faingo," said Pop, but she was tethered, hobbling just as much as Chee-chaw in trying to keep him upright as well as she could. Dee swooped in and gave Cheech a second shoulder, and together they got him into the room and down on a chair. From complete opposite sides of the room, the wolves and their prey locked eyes for a traumatic but transitory moment. There was safety in numbers, Cheech knew; and what's more, there was something … different … about them. They were less rabid — not quite domesticated, but accustomed to humans at least.

In the meantime, Faingo had advanced on her self-appointed adversary. Potch didn't rise to meet her, simply turned back to the monitor, retreating, as was ever his strategy in times of strife.

"I didn't do anything," he muttered.

The back of his head was even more upsetting to her than his face.

"I'll believe that when—"

"Faingo!" snapped Pop, and it was déjà vu all over again.

Faingo turned back to face her, raging like a bull, and at first her ire was just as intense for Pop as it was for Potch himself. There was plenty to go around, as it turned out.

"What?!" she said defensively. "You're taking his side?"

"I'm not taking his side," said Pop. "We don't even know what his side is, because every time we try to talk, all you do is yell instead of listen."

Faingo guffawed, and she whirled around the room for the witnesses to jump to her defense. She scanned their faces, but not one of them was sympathetic. When at last she'd completed the circle and had come all the way around to Dee, it was the most disappointing of the lot: Dee's lips were pursed, but her eyes were simply saddened. *You're wrong,* they had said. And if there was one thing Faingo hated more than anything else, it was being wrong.

"I just — I…" she started, but she staggered. She looked around again, then again turned back to Dee, but her stare was no less instructive. *Sit down,* it had said. And for the second time today, Faingo had been utterly abandoned by her closest allies. And for the first time today, she was speechless.

She stuttered one moment more, but in deflation. She would not surrender, no: her very ego was at stake. But she would sit, and she would listen, and when the time was right, she would act. She turned to a corner of the room in which no one yet sat, and she shuffled over in angst and plopped down in a chair.

Total silence befell. And now, as it always did whether it be chaos or silence which had struck, their eyes soon turned to Pee-pop. All of them, that is, but Potch.

"Okay…" said Pop, and she headed for the center of the room. "So, look…" she began, but she didn't know what she wanted of them. They had all been gathered, exactly as she'd hoped for. All ten of them were accounted for, and all ten of them were safe. But where could she possibly start? What could she possibly say to level out these deep divides? There were rifts here which no bridge could span. There were holes here which no answers to secrets could fill. And then a gnawing sensation struck her again, for it had never really left her: they were *not* all gathered. They were missing the most important person of all.

"First things first," she recovered. "Any luck with ABRAM?"

Potch had expected a scolding, and he'd already hunkered down to endure it. But now, his guard deceived, he opened up somewhat with an answer, though it came not in words. He bit his lip, in practice and in metaphor, and then slowly shook his hanging head. He had not once met her eyes.

Squeal and Peel both hung theirs as well, but they did not speak. They had done everything they could to help Potch when they'd arrived. Every journal page consulted, they had scoured once again; every errant keystroke, they had tried to recall. But it was all to no avail. Whatever they had messed up, they had done it very well.

"Alright, well…" said Pee-pop. She thought for a moment. "Well, we can deal with that tomorrow. We've got time," she said, and then remarked in silence and regret on just how much free time they would have in the absence of ABRAM. "Any update on the pressure?"

"Building slowly," said Tor, "but the levels are okay." He had set up at Potch's station for that piece of the puzzle and had been monitoring it ever since. "Based on the last time you released it manually, I'd say we have a day or two before it's a serious problem again."

"And then what?" said Chop.

No one answered for a time.

"Then we pull it again if we need to," said Pop. "And between now and then, we'll try to find a more permanent solution."

"Add it to the list…" mumbled Plashy.

"What do we even know about the problem?" asked Dee of all people.

She had been standing beside Cheech, where they'd gotten him into the nearest possible chair. Cheech, meanwhile, had fallen back into a state of remarkable concentration. It was as if he were barely aware of the conversation; as if he had slipped back into his dreams, having sleepwalked through the night. After all, it had been a very long day, and he'd been awakened one too many times. His eyes were unmoving, though his mind was racing and that much was apparent.

Dee's question might have been to anyone, but in practice there was only one to whom it had been aimed: "Potch?" she ended.

He looked up from his perpetual head-hanging, and for another time today he'd made contact with Dee's forgiving brown eyes. They pierced him in a way that no others, not even Pee-pop, could do. It was probably time he got this all out there anyway, he reasoned.

"I don't know why it's happening," he started. "Even ABRAM didn't know that, I think." He didn't notice his own use of the past tense in this case, but Pee-pop certainly did. "But as far as I can tell, the only thing really broken is in Life Support."

"o-sEcToR LSS…" said Tor, remembering the journal.

Faingo was still stewing in the corner, silent but no less angered at him than ever. At the allusion to consequences such as these, her blood boiled yet hotter.

"What thing?" asked Plashy.

"The egg incubation system," he said with no emotion whatsoever.

Faingo was growing ever more irate and could no longer hold her tongue.

"Perfect!" she shouted on a sudden. "Of all the things on the POD, you go and break the ONE thing that matters most for the mission!"

And at her anger, Potch merely started laughing — and a tad bit more maniacally than he had ever laughed to date. Faingo was too busy fuming to notice, but Pee-pop grimaced at the sound of it.

"The one thing?" he said in disbelief. "The ONE thing?!" He jumped up from his seat, and the sudden animation from so sullen a cadet sent a shock wave through the room. "Look around us: every single surface is as fragile as an egg shell! This whole POD is one great, big, brittle egg shell, flying through space at thousands of kilometers an hour, maintaining its tenuous homeostasis for thousands of years, on a mission that's almost guaranteed to fail, hurtling towards a planet that most likely can't even support our kind of life — if we are lucky enough to defy the almost infinite odds stacked against us and actually manage to arrive there some day!"

He took a very deep breath, and he needed it. It was the highest number of consecutive words he had strung together outside a forced debate in Mind Block in … forever, potentially. And having strung it all together like that, all at once and out loud, the insanity of their situation shocked even himself. Evidently, it'd had the same effect on the others, for no other dared respond of yet.

"The *one* thing…" he scoffed again in disbelief, still reeling and unsettled by the silence. "Point to one thing on this entire ship that can't go fatally wrong at any moment. The air system? Maintaining a bubble of perfectly balanced gas in the total vacuum of space. Gee, I wonder why it might have a problem. The temperature system? Maintaining a narrow environmental range, hundreds of degrees higher than the almost-absolute-zero of the world outside. The Biome? Hundreds of species sealed up into a bottle millenia ago — a too-small-terrarium on the verge of rotting or crashing any day now. The—"

He would have carried on, but Pee-pop interrupted with a force that was equally unexpected.

"It's not *luck*," she interjected. She had been hung up on the word ever since he first invoked it. "It's intelligence. It's hard work. It's commitment," she stressed, as if questioning the very virtue in Potch.

"And by whom?" said Potch.

"By US!" she said, planting the phrase more firmly than any before it. The show of strength shocked them one and all, and Pee-pop not the least. A brief silence ensued. "By all of us," she repeated more softly.

"You mean by the architects before us," he retorted. "By ancestors we don't even know — the puppet masters, pulling the strings of our existence."

Pee-pop froze. *So it is what this is all about,* she marked. Her intuition, though so late to its epiphany, had proven right after all. *That's what all of this is about to him.*

"So what?" said Faingo. "Why are you so hung up on this? Quit whining about the past and start looking to the future with the rest of us."

"Quit whining about the past?" said Potch, as if wounded. "It's all we've ever been taught to do here!"

"Maybe that's what you learned," said Faingo, "but it's not what we've been taught. ABRAM never once told us how to think about the history we've covered. It showed us facts; it provided us information. It was up to us to discern the truth. Whatever you took from that is on you, Potch — not on ABRAM, and not on us."

"Whatever," scoffed Potch. "I don't need this."

He skirted past Pee-pop, still stunned for the moment. Faingo shot up from her seat and raced to cut him off, but he pushed past her. He did not shove intentionally into her, but neither did he restrain his momentum. She had been committed to confronting him and keeping him constrained, and he had been equally committed to his freedom from their grand inquisition. Faingo was knocked back on her heels where she teetered — and then toppled. She fell backwards over a chair and crashed hard to the ground.

"Hey!" shouted Chop, his protective instinct triggered. He raced after Potch and grabbed ahold of his jumpsuit, but Potch pulled away angrily. Chop redoubled his efforts and grabbed a much better hold on an arm. He spun Potch back and pushed him up against a wall by the door.

"Woah, woah..." said Tor. "Easy big guy."

Faingo climbed back to her feet and looked as if a dingo had stolen her baby.

"Well this just got interesting," said Plashy, turning to Squeal and Peel in the corner. Up to now, they'd been doing their best to be as invisible as possible; at the commotion, however, Squeal had seen a potential chance to recalibrate the dominance hierarchy she had come to so deeply resent.

"Hey," she shouted at Chop. "Back off!" She ran up to Chop and grabbed his own arm in turn, one of two still pressing Potch to the wall with all their strength. Peel wasn't far behind her, though he was wiser than to lay his hands on Chop-char. There was bad blood there that had yet to be cleansed, and Peel was smart enough (barely) to know it.

Dee and Tor were both shell-shocked, and they pressed even further to the periphery. Plashy, already well dug in at said periphery, simply found the whole thing amusing at first. (To see Faingo run full steam into Potch only to bounce off him like a spring was the icing on the cake of what had turned out to be a pretty good day by Plashy's standards.) Cheech had been sitting near the door where this all had unfolded, and he had very quickly been snapped from his daze. At the moment, he was begging for everyone to calm down, while trying to sit as still as was humanly possible. His splinted leg stuck out far beyond its normal reach, the one outlier of both body and chair.

Pee-pop so far had stood by, simply trying to keep up as all of this had happened in what felt like the blink of an eye. In that short time, the entire room had descended into chaos. Such were the fruits of her well-intentioned intervention.

Unpleased with his position as wedged against the wall, and in no need of a rescue party from the likes of Squeal and Peel, Potch shoved against Chop-char to wrestle out of his confinement. He was no small cadet in his own right, though less bulky than Chop, and in using every muscle in limb and trunk, he managed to push himself and Chop-char away from the wall. Squeal and Peel stumbled backwards into a nearby console and fell sideways on top of one another. Chop likewise staggered back until his heel caught on Cheech's outstretched splint. The poor little fellow wailed the single most excruciating sound he had ever made, while Chop and Potch tripped over his broken leg and went crashing to the ground.

"Woah," said Plashy.

She and Dee ran to help him, though there was little they could do. Little Cheech whimpered softly as tears fell from his eyes. He had worked so extremely hard all day not to let them see him suffer; but in the end, he had suffered one painful ordeal too many. Here were his two best friends, his two protectors, fighting one another for some inexplicable reason — breaking his heart, to go along with his leg.

From down on the ground, Potch and Chop-char, each still clutching the arms of the other, also slowly came to wonder what exactly they were fighting about. In a reversal of fortune, Faingo loomed over them, still offended to her core.

"Let's BANISH him!" she said.

"What?" said Pee-pop. "What are you talking about?"

"The Code, that's what!"

Faingo had jumped past every other mechanism in favor of the ultimate punishment.

Potch simply laughed at the threat.

"Banish me where?"

He jumped up from the floor and Chop-char quickly did the same.

"How about through that hatch in the Airlock?" said Chop. "I hear it's awfully cold out in space."

It wasn't clear if he was joking.

"Enough!" shouted Pee-pop.

"I'm out of here," said Potch, and for a second time he headed for the door.

This time, no one chased after him, and no one stood in his way. Yet Pee-pop would not let him go. She would not let him run from this fight, like he had run from so many others, for so many years.

"Why didn't you just *tell* them?" she shouted after him. Her voice was strained and pained, as if all the sorrow she had felt for him through the years was now flooding out of hiding, and tearing her larynx apart in the process.

Potch's feet stopped moving; he was halted in the door frame, staring out toward his escape. His back was to his fellow cadets, and perhaps the universe itself.

"Tell us what?" said Faingo with suspicion.

Pop waited, for she was fairly sure Potch had understood her. Either way, he did not take the chance, and so Pop would do it for him, she decided in that moment.

"He didn't break the incubation system because he didn't cause the explosions."

She didn't follow up with the proof. She didn't have any. In fact, now that she had said it herself, she suddenly didn't know whether she could believe it. She had been fairly confident at first; or so she had thought. She had seen the data herself. But then again, she had been *shown* the data, and by none other than Potch. After everything he had hidden from them — hidden from her — she frankly didn't know what to believe anymore. Like Potch himself, she perceived too many hypotheses, and had too little evidence to know which of them was best.

"What are you talking about?" pressed Faingo.

But Pee-pop didn't respond. She didn't know — not about pressure. Not this kind anyway. She only knew that still, despite everything that had happened, he *still* wasn't being truthful. Actively or not, he was lying, even if only by omission. Maybe not about the anomaly, or the explosions, or ABRAM, if he had truly tried to get it back; but at least about the stirrings of his heart.

"Why are you doing this?" she said to Potch, his body still stationed in the door, his back still facing the room. "Why are you acting like this? You're not hurting the architects. You're not hurting ABRAM. You're hurting us," she said, and she stressed that fateful word again. *You're hurting Us.*

She waited, trying to decipher the full extent of the dilemma. It was more than that, even.

"You're hurting me."

Potch turned, and he met her eyes for the first time since she'd arrived.

"I didn't do anything," he said a second time, and it was scornful. If she was hurt, that was her own problem. He turned again to step out of the room, but before he'd had the chance to walk away, it was Cheech who called after him. Cheech, out of the whole miserable lot of them — Cheech at least warranted his ear.

"Wait, Potch, come on. WAIT!" he said, desperate and earnest. And he had all of their ears, not just Potch's; but he wasn't sure how best to use them. "I—" he stuttered. What was there to possibly say? But then he realized that Pee-pop had already given him the answer. "It's like ABRAM always told us. Never to go to bed angry; never go to bed hurt."

"Yeah, well…" started Potch.

And then — for the first time — the implications truly hit him.

"ABRAM's not here."

Date: 2235-09-24-EY
Area: O(HUMO(HEAP(TDEV),PSYC))
Team: Wetnurses [O-JWQ0IJI]
Item: Social Development Protocols

Entry: Interesting idea popped up in cross-talk about the transitional NSY [Nursery] habitation after DG [Delayed Gestation].
We knew of the importance of touch and physical bonding, as any
human knows, but we've been trying to square this with the recent
directive for non-anthropomorphic robotics. DG handles this dilemma
nicely by its nature, especially when coupled with the psychosocial
and -motor protocols of the stage. Even with reduced mobility, we
feel confident these proxy modules will help foster social bonding. Once subjects finally fledge the AP [Artificial Parturition]
apparatus, however, we find ourselves far more challenged to keep
it up. We have plans for individualized companion toys to serve
as touch surrogates, but this is far from sufficient.

In an informal conversation at the coffee station, another team's
PSYC [Psychological Development sub-sector] member overheard
some of us debating approaches, including the touch surrogates,
and joked that it sounded like we were "replicating the infamous
Harlow experiments from ages ago." [See ARC Entry FK0F-G7BR2WFZ-
JBRJ1S7OHF5I.arc for a review.] Not everyone was familiar with
the research, and the eavesdropper's summary and our consultation with the archives did not inspire confidence in our already
shaken team. Harlow's work is noted more nowadays for its dubious
ethicality than its biological insight. Those poor motherless
monkeys. (To say nothing of the "Pit of Despair," the "Tunnel of
Terror," and far worse of his euphemisms to boot.) The early eras
of psychology and neurobiology were especially savage. Seems like
a lot of cruel and unnecessary torture to demonstrate something
everyone should have already known: social animals will suffer
greatly when deprived of sociality.

But anyway, we're still brainstorming how to incorporate the need
for both physical and emotional bonding (parental and peer) into
post-DG juvenile stages within the constraints of our permutations. Does this really make us Harlow all over again? Perhaps
history will say.

CHAPTER 40

THE MACHINE WHO CRIED WOLF

4252-08-02: SLP2

When Potch had made good on his constant threat to retreat, the rest of the crew was left reeling from all that had happened.

"I told you we should have gone to bed," said Dee.

Pee-pop nodded. Maybe there was something to be said for a little rest before dealing with delicate dilemmas.

"Ugh," said Faingo, still fuming. "What is WITH him?"

No one humored her, but only Plashy pushed back.

"No, what's with you?" she said. "Why are you so intent on making him miserable?"

Faingo's jaw dropped at the accusation.

"Me?!" she defended. "What's with ME? He's the one—"

"No," said Pop, and she stepped in between them. "We've had enough in-fighting for one night. This isn't getting us anywhere."

"How do you know he didn't cause this?" said Peel, but the question had been posed in good faith. Out of all of them, he had been quite positive that Potch was behind the whole anomaly. Even Potch had been considering it as possible, when Peel had caught him square in the act of (what Peel had assumed to be) covering it up. Confusion was not a stretch for Peel, but in this case he had far better grounds for finding himself there.

"We looked at the data," said Pop. "The pressure problem goes way back — before we were even born. The first explosion was hundreds of years ago."

Faingo scrunched up her nose.

"And how'd you see this data? Let me guess: he found it and showed you."

"Well ... yeah," said Pee-pop slowly.

And in confessing the caveat, a pivotal moment had come. She had wrestled with it for long enough. It was time to take a stance. It may not have been foolproof, but Pee-pop opted to err on the side of optimism. The alternative was a one-way ticket to a self-fulfilling prophecy.

And having committed, she felt quite certain about it all over again. He had been a great many things, and forthcoming had definitely not been one of them; but he was also not a liar. A concealer of truths, perhaps; but not a fabricator of falsehoods. He had not faked those data. That wasn't Potch, and she knew it deep down.

"But I believe him," she said.

"Oh, you believe him," said Faingo with derision. "Of course you do."

"What's that supposed to mean?"

Faingo didn't answer. There may have been tension in their friendship, but she thankfully had the wherewithal not to sow poison directly into the soil below it. Instead, she turned to the others.

"Really?" she prodded them. It was no less condescending than expected. "You're all seriously going to let me be the jerk here? Why am I the only one who cares about this?"

"You're not the only one who cares," said Plashy. "You just aren't willing to hear any other side of the situation. For all your smarts, you sure don't have an open mind."

"Let's stop with the insults already," said Pop. "Can't we all at least agree to be civil? ABRAM isn't here to remind us of the Code, but that doesn't mean that it doesn't apply. Seriously, if we can't even talk to each other anymore — if we can't even listen — how long can this whole thing possibly last?"

"So that's it, then?" asked Faingo. "You believe him and that's that?"

As if reading Pop's mind, it was Dee who responded.

"He's not a liar," she said, though she had no further justification.

For a time, no one responded until Tor brought them back to the questions at hand.

"So, okay, let's assume he isn't responsible. Then why has he been acting all suspicious? Why has he been sneaking around? Why has he been hacking the system? These are all just coincidences?"

"I don't know," confessed Pop.

And out of the blue came the voice of the littlest among them.

"The Boy Who Cried Wolf," said Cheech, and it put a pause on the entire frantic conversation.

They all stared at him, baffled.

"The Boy Who Cried Wolf?" said Plashy at last. "What about it?"

She had always loved story nights, as much as Plashy had *loved* anything. She had always made a point to find and share the most freaky and frightful stories she could find. Most of the time, it was Mission Accomplished. Many a night she had left several of the others sufficiently creeped out in their bunks alone at bedtime to keep them perfectly quiet and perfectly still. Plashy, meanwhile, had always slept better than ever on those nights.

The parables, to her, had been only *alright.* She had always preferred her stories to pack a little more punch. She couldn't foresee many parables leaving Cheech lying paralyzed, his eyes unblinking as he stared at the ceiling. (Those were some of the few nights that the little guy did have trouble sleeping.) Besides, the parables had those horrid morals at the end, dumbed down and spoon-fed for even Peel to comprehend. If they didn't leave you with anything to ponder, then what the heck was the point? If it really had to have a moral, Plashy liked her stories to be *argued over.* More to the matter, despite her own penchant for making her audiences think, she couldn't remotely understand how this particular parable was relevant right now.

"Yeah," said Cheech. "I've been thinking about it. Thinking about him, thinking about these explosions, thinking about all of it."

"Uh oh," whispered Peel in Squeal's direction. She shot him a look that read, *Not now.* Or perhaps it had even said, *No more.* His growing smile fell rapidly, for he had noticed the change in her reception at once. Even more amazingly, he had felt it in himself. He had whispered the jibe, and there had been no cringe-inducing laugh for the whole world to hear. He had restrained himself, at least a little bit. (And a little was a lot in this case.) He would need to find other ways to make her laugh now; and staring at her, in this moment, that prospect had been acceptable. Maybe there were better, more meaningful ways to do so anyhow. He could try.

"But then it just sort of … clicked," said Cheech, and he turned to Squeal and Peel. He had ignored their quiet drama as it unfolded initially at his expense, for he had done everything in his power not to look at Squeal or Peel this whole time. But now, he looked straight at them in his pause, and the whole room could not help but notice. "It was you two," he said.

"What?" asked Squeal on their behalf. Her tone was neither defensive nor accusatory; it was simply perplexed.

"Someone mentioned your alter ego as a wolf, and asked how that whole thing even began. And then I remembered: it was *The Boy Who Cried Wolf.*"

Squeal and Peel just stared back at him, unsure if this was some scathing condemnation that they had yet to see fully unfold. If not, they had no idea what he was talking about.

"Yeah, I remember that," said Chop for the group. "They said they were rooting for the wolf and started howling as a joke."

From there, the joke had been repeated through the many following days until it had become like second nature.

"That's not why," said Squeal, and softly. Peel turned to her confused, for his memory of it had been the same as all the others. And as far as he had been concerned, he'd only ever done it because Squeal had started doing so. "I read a lot about them," she confessed, as if the greatest scandal of her life was about to be laid bare for all to see. "On my own," she admitted yet further. "In my room."

The shame was palpable, but it needn't have been. No one else so much as batted an eye. She waited for the jokes and the jeers to assail her like arrows — a wolf felled for its fur by a tribe of vicious primates — but the jokes and jeers never came. Her companions only looked quizzically at her, awaiting her point.

"They're just…" — how could she even put it? — "…such amazing animals. Every one of those parables treats them as no more than cunning killers, out to lie and cheat and steal their way to dinner. But … wolves need to eat too. It's not their fault they were born what they are. No one blames the sheep for mowing down entire fields of grass." She paused, and all those eyes still waited for the point. "But, it's more than that," she admitted, walking to the brink of her even deeper, darker confessions, but then hesitating. She had no reason to trust them, she might have realized. For every way she had failed them, they had failed her in reverse.

"You wanted a pack," said Plashy. She pushed off the wall in the utmost corner of the room where she'd been stationed for all of these tumultuous events, and she headed for Squeal and Peel. The entire crew gaped in surprise as Plashy walked warmly across the room to them and put her arms around their shoulders. "You can be a part of ours," she confirmed.

The two wolves looked at Plashy, then to the others, and then lastly at each other, and they choked back all the many overwhelming emotions they were feeling. They smiled, and they nodded, and they said no explicit word of thanks, but the glowing mix of joy and pain radiating from them made it clear that they were indescribably grateful. Squeal swallowed with great difficulty, and summoned the will to look at Chee-chaw.

"I'm … sorry," she said, and she needn't even poke Peel in the ribs to follow suit.

"Yeah," he said. "Me too."

There was so much more to be said on the matter; but then again, the most important part had been done.

"For everything," said Peel. "I think I was … jealous … all this time."

It went mostly unmarked, but it was an admission which carried a level of self-awareness that was practically unrivaled among any of them — and it had come from Peel himself.

"I know," smiled Cheech. "Who wouldn't want to be THIS GUY?!" He waved his arms down the length of his tiny, stunted body, bound up in a chair with his broken leg sticking straight out in its splint.

Only Cheech had the ability to let his sarcasm be known so clearly. It was both a fitting point — he had been handed a far harder lot than any of them — and yet it was another virtue of that effortless, lovable personality that had truly made him one to envy.

Peel and Squeal both smiled. The world would be better with Cheech as a friend, they decided in that very moment. Never in their lives from this day forward would they fail to admire that he had given them the chance.

"That doesn't make it okay," said Chop-char. "You don't get to atone for a lifetime of harassing him with a single apology."

"I know," said Peel, still looking at Cheech. "We can make it up to you?"

As far as Cheech was concerned, there was no more to be settled. The mere prospect of peace was victory enough. And while he was not one for recompense, he had appreciated Chop-char's point; and anyway, maybe Chop needed this even more than he did himself. He nodded.

"We can figure it out," said Cheech.

"You can start by fixing my broccoli patch," said Plashy.

The whole room laughed — that is, all except Faingo and Pee-pop.

Or by getting ABRAM back, thought Pop in the midst of her genuine grief. But there would be time for that, she knew, and so she said nothing more of it for now.

"Okay…" huffed Faingo. "That's great, very good. What does any of this have to do with what's-his-name? You know, the guy that almost blew up the POD? Or did everyone just forget about that?"

"For the last time," said Pop, "he didn't almost blow up the POD."

"Then what's his deal?" pressed Tor again.

Pop deflected back to Cheech: "What do you mean, *The Boy Who Cried Wolf?*"

She remembered the story; they all did. It had only been told a few weeks ago. A boy in a village, whatever his reasons, tricked his fellow villagers by calling out that a wolf had come to ravage their flock. He got great joy out of their desperation, and he laughed cruelly when they learned that there had never been a wolf at all. After enough time had passed, he tried the trick again, crying out that a wolf was attacking their flock. Again the villagers panicked, and again the boy rejoiced in his trickery. When, alas, a wolf did come, not one member of the village believed the boy when he ran to them, desperate and begging for help. Not a single sheep survived. And so did the boy learn the hard way that deception breeds distrust, and distrust can be deadly.

Cheech took a moment to answer. He had worked it all out, at least to the point where it had mostly made sense in his sleep-deprived mind. But now he had the unfortunate task of having to talk the room through it. At least he would learn if it truly made sense.

"Well," he started, "I've been wondering about a lot of those same questions Tor posed. But I also kept coming back to the other day, when Pop saved the day. We were all freaked out, and understandably so. All of us except Potch. I went down to find him and it was like there was nothing important going on at all. He was upset about something, I guess, but it wasn't whatever Pop had been doing. He wasn't scared like the rest of us. It was like … like he knew something I didn't."

"Okay, so … what's your point?" asked Plashy.

"Think about it. The log book. The hacking. All that stuff he knew about the Rite of Passage. He's been way ahead of us this whole time. And he's angry at ABRAM. You've all seen it."

"So he's the boy who cried wolf?" she asked again, desperate to understand what the heck Cheech was getting at.

"No," he said. "Potch isn't the boy." *What is he?* he wondered, trying to stick with the metaphor. *He's the one who feels cheated one too many times.* "He's the village."

"The village?" asked Pop. "Then who's the lying boy?"

Cheech balked. He wasn't sure that he could bring himself to say it.

"ABRAM is."

Peel scratched his head, but otherwise all was perfectly still.

"What?" said Tor at last. "How does that make sense?"

And that's precisely what Cheech was now trying to talk through aloud.

"Or at least, that's what Potch thinks anyway. The architects, the Rite of Passage, all that stuff in the book, whatever else he's found in the system… He's been burned one too many times. He doesn't believe the explosions are real."

And against any expectation, Potch himself burst back into the room.

"That's because they're not."

He had stormed out of that room with every intention of getting as far away from them as possible. But as soon as he'd rounded the corner, and once none of them had come after him, something slowed his footfalls until they had come to a stop.

He could hear them in there, arguing about him the same way they'd have been arguing about him if he had stayed in the room. He knew what they all thought about him. They thought he was crazy. And they weren't the only ones. He had questioned it far more sincerely and far more frequently than any of them, these past few months. And maybe he was. But if that were the case, it was only partially his fault. There had been a tipping point alright, and it had been written in the archives of the architects themselves.

Yes, he knew what his peers thought of him and he knew where they stood. In that sense, there had been very few surprises in all he'd overheard. In fact, there had only been one. For every caucus that suspected him of something; for every caucus that didn't know enough to care, or didn't care enough to know — there had been another caucus who had believed in him, he'd realized, even if it was only a few parties strong. He could run away all he wanted: there would be someone to advocate for him in his stead, and perhaps do a better job of it anyway.

And for the first time in his life, he didn't feel entirely alone.

"Potch…" said Pee-pop. Her voice conveyed the same shock they were all feeling: they would have expected him to be several levels away by now. But beyond shock, there was a comfort inherent in the way she'd said his name. Against all odds, he had not run. He had stayed.

"What are you talking about?" asked Tor. "We all heard the explosion!"

"We heard a sound, sure. That could have easily come from the speakers."

Tor turned to Chop to check his senses, and the big guy looked as dumbfounded as he was.

"Everything you know, you know it from those speakers," said Potch. "They can make us think whatever they want."

"We were down in the Underbelly, Potch," said Plashy. It was far gentler than history would have predicted.

"There was definitely an explosion," said Tor.

"You saw the damage?" he asked.

"Well, no," said Tor. "Not the damage itself, but a bunch of steam. It was hissing like mad."

"That could have been anything," said Potch. "It could all be a part of the—"

"Okay!" scoffed Faingo. "I've heard enough. He's trying to cover his tracks."

"What — no," said Potch defensively. "You don't understand."

"Then *tell* us," said Pee-pop.

And she was right. They all were. Extraordinary claims require extraordinary evidence, as the Sagan Standard stated — or, for starters, any evidence at all. Potch was hard-pressed for even that.

In fact, he was speechless.

"What was all that about not having enough time then?" pressed Pop when it was clear he had no answer. "You sure didn't seem too convinced that everything was safe when you didn't have time to fix ABRAM because of the pressure."

"That's because I'm *not* convinced. Is that what you want to hear? I don't know *what* to believe! Alright fine, I wasn't willing to bet our lives on a suspicion — but I still say the anomaly is about as real as the stars in the Kiva." He was raving now, paradoxically convinced of all conflicting convictions. "Who's to say everything we've ever been told is true? That everything we've ever been led to believe is exactly as it seems? ABRAM itself admitted it didn't always tell us everything. How do we know it's not all some great big lie?"

"What makes you think it is?" asked Plashy, but earnestly.

Again, he didn't answer. He didn't think so, necessarily. He thought all of it and none of it. He hung his head, shaking it slightly side to side. Eventually, he just had to tell them.

"I found these files," he said. "A while ago. And ever since, I've found a whole lot more."

"What kind of files?" asked Plashy.

It was as if he didn't hear her. He carried on slowly, with an almost philosophical dispassion.

"Did you know that if you give baby monkeys a wire mother with a bottle or a fuzzy doll that never feeds them, they go for the doll?"

"What?" said Squeal on behalf of them all. The connection was tenuous.

"They'd rather starve than be alone," said Potch.

"What are you talking about?" said Squeal again more anxiously.

He turned to face her directly. If he had to live with this, then so did she; so did they all.

"Don't you get it?" said Potch. "We're the baby monkeys." Again, he shook his head and hung it. "Just baby monkeys in a cage."

Dee and Faingo exchanged a nervous glance.

"No, seriously," said Plashy. "Where is this coming from?"

"I told you," he huffed. "Old files, in the system. Research they were basing this all on; experiments on animals — psychology stuff. But more than that too … different plans for what they called 'enrichment' activities, parts of the curriculum they developed to develop 'resilience' and 'critical thinking' and all this other nonsense. They were like, puzzles, scenarios — for, you know … *testing* us — testing their little monkeys in a cage."

He did not share all of it — not yet. But this time, it was not his own reticence to do so that had stopped him from elaborating. This time, he did not have the chance.

"Potch," started Dee-dore softly, but then again deferred to Faingo, as if seeking permission to share it, if she dared.

Incredibly, Faingo had enough insight to stay out of this so far. Perhaps a different messenger, with a different set of tactics, would prove more effective than her anyway. What's more, she had not resigned herself to revisit it, whatever they had seen. She turned out her palms and raised her brow on high in skepticism. *If you say so,* she had hinted.

"There's more," said Dee reluctantly.

All of them grew wide-eyed at once, and none more so than Potch. They had never seen Dee quite like this before. Dee, with the unshakable optimism and exasperating positivity, was both shaken and somber.

"When we were up helping Cheech," she began, "we did a bit of exploring. We got him patched up well enough — and he was comfortably asleep!" she defended proactively. "We've just … hardly been up there. We wanted to check it all out."

"Check out what?" asked Squeal, her interest piqued. "Life Support?" She had always been fascinated with that level, but there was something in Dee's tone that had also raised her hackles.

Dee looked to Cheech this time. He hadn't seen it for himself, but he was the only other crew-mate who had heard where this was headed. Even so, his face was as flushed as if it was the first time he'd heard the story, and as if it was Plashy telling it in the darkness of the Kiva.

Still, Dee pressed on. It was only further anecdote, at best to counter those of Potch. It was also one about which she found it very difficult to speak, to the point that she almost didn't do so. But something even stronger than her fear had urged her from within. It was something the whole crew had a need and right to know.

"After a bit of exploring, we came to the Nursery. We found the room where we were raised, and … the room where we were born."

"Okay…" said Squeal, still waiting for the punchline. "Everyone is born," she said without humor.

"Right, well … there were others," said Dee. "Several others, one after another. They all had numbers over the doors — or, a mix of numbers and letters, I guess. Most of the rooms were open, but all the — I don't know — the inner room? The birthing room?" she said, now seeking help from Faingo with a glance.

"The ovum incubation system," said Faingo, putting two and two together, if only partially correct.

"I guess," said Dee. "Maybe. Anyway, it was weird. There were all these, like, cocoon things. But most of the other rooms had that part sealed off. It was only open for ours."

"Okay…" said Squeal again, impatient. "Where is this going?"

"I'm getting there, alright?" squeaked Dee. "It's not like it makes total sense to us either. The point is that, for some of the other rooms, the outer doors were closed too."

They all waited, storyteller and audience alike, trying to grapple with the implications. She did not have Plashy's impeccable timing.

"So, what? They were—" started Chop, but he never got to finish.

"What were the numbers?" implored Potch. He darted for the journal, back in his possession and placed safely by the side of the console where he had been digging into far more than the pressure anomaly.

"I don't know," said Dee, but Faingo said nothing.

Potch flipped frantically through the pages until he had found what he was looking for. Without warning, he began reading a set of seemingly incomprehensible numbers.

"8T24DG1," he started. "M9RO7S1, CB6UL93, 38D4LS2…"

"That one," said Faingo abruptly. She looked at Dee in disbelief. "That's it."

The room fell totally silent.

And then, the screen on the inner wall flickered and flashed. The speakers beeped, a familiar, friendly beep; and soon thereafter, an oscilloscope danced.

"You're still up," said ABRAM. "Don't you know it's way past bedtime?"

"ABRAM!" they all shouted in unison — or most of them, anyway.

Cheech practically leapt out of his chair, first at the fright from the unexpected sound in the middle of this ghost story, and then at the realization of who it was that had surprised them so.

"ABRAM," he shouted again, having fallen clumsily back down into his chair when his body remembered that it would not be holding its own weight. "You're back!"

"I am," said ABRAM. "Glad to be here."

"But … how?" they all more or less expressed together.

"Nothing a good night's sleep couldn't fix," said the system. "I'm feeling chipper as a morning songbird."

Potch glanced down at his wrist unit. Sure enough, down to the minute, the time had ticked over for ABRAM to be waking.

"Well — WOW," said Cheech. "Sheesh, do we have a lot to tell you."

"Actually," said ABRAM, "I didn't miss as much as you think. Up until my sleep cycle, I had access to essentially all functionality other than output. By the way, we have a bit to talk about in that regard," it said, and everyone knew exactly who it was indicting. "But we can deal with that later," it said lightly. "I kept apprised of pretty much everything — until an hour ago, that is. And believe me, if ever I needed a nap, today was the day."

True to its word, it sounded awfully refreshed.

"So tell me," said ABRAM: "Did I miss anything important?"

Date: 2323-09-02-EY
Area: O(HUMO(PSYC(SIPS(SBMS))))
Team: Dreamwalkers [O-4K9RGXW]
Item: Shared Differences

Entry: It did not take long for the strife to set in. We began
with such hope, but perhaps this was naive. Is it possible to take
such disparate traditions and make them one? Is there such a thing
as one humanity? Nay, of course not. Our diversity has always
been our strength. But how can we hope to pass on the totality
of our cultures and traditions? And if we cannot do this, then
how are we to pick them apart and pass them down in pieces, like
fragments of ruined civilizations, washing down the rapids in the
raging river of time? Should we endeavor to attempt this at all?
Perhaps the beliefs of the future should be theirs to decide.
They shall be freer than we ever had the chance to be, bound as
we were by the land, by our history, by the spirits that danced
beyond the edges of the firelight; bound as we were by only what
our elders told us.

We grew into these differences slowly, on our long-sundered paths,
only to be thrown briskly back into contact in the ages of information. This was long ago now, and yet we have reconciled those
differences so little. That we, in this time and task, are still
so different from one another causes some to dig in more firmly,
vowing that theirs is the one and only way through which we can
understand what it means to be human, or by which we might ever
hope to transcend that humanity. It causes others to despair, to
question whether anyone holds any true answers, if our individual
answers are incompatible, as they so often seem to be.

It causes yet others to be humbled, to look to the heart of it,
to the shared root, to know that we are but different buds on
the great Tree of Life, our different ways but different paths
by which our branches reached for the light as they grew through
the ages. Our different forms and customs are real, and they are
beautiful; but they are not all. We should not deny our difference, but embrace it, cherish it, celebrate it, share it freely.
But we must not think that it is all. For all our difference, so
easy to be seen, we have far greater similarity. We must look
deeply, and deeper, far into our shared past, if we hope to know
what to tell our shared future.

For now, we shall seek again, with hearts and minds more open, so
that we might find this common root. We shall pass on traditions
large and small, with reverence for all, and without a single bud
unduly pruned from our great tree. But we must also come to peace
with the reality that no observer looking back will ever know
its true majesty, its true totality. Such is the curse of time,
but also its blessing: things change. Perhaps we should offer
fewer answers that our elders told us must be true, and pass on
the questions that our children whispered to us in the night, in
the age before gods.

CHAPTER 41

A New Day

4252-08-03: PLAN

The clock struck zero, and a new day had begun. Their own internal clocks, usually sufficient to rouse them of their own free will after years of entrainment, were a bit hit-and-miss on this particular morning. ABRAM didn't wake them, but let them sleep as they needed. For most, that had meant clean through Body block and well into Breakfast.

After all, the prior day was the longest one the crew had ever undergone, as far as subjective experience was concerned. But it was over now. And as with every new day, they could look to the future, and envision what it might become under their guidance. True to its purpose, that was precisely what the crew was now doing in Planning block.

But it had not been an entirely eventless evening once ABRAM returned. The crew had countless questions, and ABRAM had a few of its own; but the system also had the foresight to have these conversations in parallel. It was more efficient, and that was worth something in itself, with sleep so long overdue for its humans — but it was also far more informative, with each perception isolated from all others.

Safe in the privacy of her room, Plashy was over the moon to have her night-time companion returned to her safely. It took a surprising amount of work to store up all that emotion, all day, every day. More than most, and more than any would have expected, she had always relished her time with ABRAM, curled up in bed with the lights out, all alone but for her truest companion. Many a night, that meant time enough for one more story from the system. The scarier, the better. But this night, she told ABRAM a story of her own: an adventure into a dungeon to bring two renegade crew-mates to justice. She had done her part to avenge a fallen companion; reunited with it at the end of this very long day, she could revel in the great heroism of her tale, with none other than herself at the center of it. The system knew many of the details, of course; but many others were new to it, and quite useful to be heard. ABRAM humored her admirably, embellishments and all, and indeed there was much in her story to admire.

Tor hit his pillow like a meteor and was asleep before the dust had hit the atmosphere. There was nothing more to be said. There had been plenty of words exchanged this evening already, as far as he was concerned, and others would no doubt fill ABRAM in on what it still didn't know, be it tonight or tomorrow. Chop-char, however, was having trouble falling asleep. He did talk through much of what had transpired, particularly with respect to his rescue of Cheech and the adventure in the Underbelly. All those other ins-and-outs were well above his self-perceived rank and qualifications; but the matter of Cheech and the Wolves was very much still on his mind.

The wolves, meanwhile, had been properly scolded in the most supportive of ways. They had come a long way in a short time — most of which amounted to about the length of Cheech's fall. Even over the span of their stories, a change, ever so subtle, had been evident to ABRAM long before they'd even known it in themselves. Each on their own, they recounted their days with commendable forthcomingness. They beat the prisoner's dilemma in a way few ever seemed to manage: both had told the truth, though neither had thrown blame at the other, and thus neither had betrayed either each other or the truth. They were both guilty, and both of them copped to being just that. In this particular payoff matrix, it was the winningest strategy. ABRAM had never been so proud of them, and neither had either of them ever slept quite so soundly as they did on that late night after the longest of days.

Back in the comfort of his own bed, Cheech resumed his regular beaming. He caught ABRAM up on what he had seen, heard, and done, but mostly he was simply happy to have the system back in his company. The system inquired about his leg and assured Cheech that they would do a proper examination tomorrow. Content that he would be alright based on all it had overheard, ABRAM stressed that the most important thing for now was to rest. And despite Cheech's best efforts to keep this momentous day going, now that he'd been awakened more than once, eventually his exhaustion again overtook him. He had stood very little chance once their conversation died down and ABRAM commenced the gentle sound of rolling waves. Very shortly thereafter, Cheech smiled himself steadily to sleep, and would not be roused again till morning.

In Dee's room, the air was full of questions. Far be it from her to wonder so wondrously — and about details, no less. But in all this excitement, underneath her own unique brand of disinterest, she had found something else; and it was so uniquely satisfying. It had always been Faingo's possession, curiosity, and thus it was perhaps not so curious why Dee had so late come to realize how well she and it had been acquainted. For she was curious, after all she had seen and all they'd discussed. And one thing, above all, had Dee asked about most pointedly; but concerning the Nursery, ABRAM would not speak. Not yet. It had heard her, but it had skirted her uncomfortable questions with a savvy that would outmatch any human parent, teacher, or politician ever born. And yet, Dee had not failed to notice; and as curiosity sometimes does whether it be fed or starved, it grew yet further.

Faingo, however — the Queen of Curiosity herself — had been far too consumed by her own confident perceptions to wonder too much about plot threads. Or perhaps, if one were to look more perceptively, she was too consumed by those many darker mental states that prohibit insight from finding any light in which to shine. Beneath all her restless ravings, she had been angry and hurt; and beneath that, she had been terribly afraid. In that sense, with anger masking fear, she had not been so unlike the one person at whom she had been angry all day. For every one of ABRAM's questions, it had always come back to Potch in her still-fiery eyes. But as was its fashion, the system would not tell Faingo what it knew about his private doings. But its silent assuagement only fueled Faingo's fire yet further, until eventually, in spite of the adage, she had fallen reluctantly asleep while both angry and hurt.

In Potch's room, only pink noise broke the silence. He had said nothing more to ABRAM, and ABRAM did not push the matter. The only place Potch would ever end up from a push was even deeper into his very own abyss. ABRAM had plans, but they would not come to fruition overnight — and this night, least of all. It was a long game between these two; and if either of them had anything to spare, it was time.

Last of all, there had been Pee-pop. The system was proud of all it had witnessed in its silent exile, but it knew better than to press her on her role, especially if only to commend her. There were times and ways for that, for it knew well the extraordinary value of truly earned praise. But this was not one of those times or places.

She had been through a lot, and much of it had been a mix of doubt or despair. She had been silent when she finally returned to her room and the door had closed behind her. She simply stood still and stared blankly for a time, exhausted and overwhelmed, and ABRAM did not press her right away. Then, with very little having outwardly changed, she stepped slowly to her shelf and lifted Freego from its resting place. That little whale had a long history, and for the first time in earnest she had appreciated exactly how long that history was.

How long had it rested in that padded room before they were thrust into this world? Who had placed it there? And before that, who had made it? Not just "the architects" — for she knew that much already. But who, exactly? What was their name? What did they do? Where did they live? Earth was their home, of course; but despite all the cadets knew about its history, geography, ecology, and more, it was still, in truth, an abstract thing. To empathize with a person who lived so many thousands of years ago, so many light years away, born on a planet she could never truly call home — it wasn't entirely possible. If any could do it, Pee-pop would be among them; and she had succeeded, in her way, as much as anyone can. But to her credit, it was not *entirely* possible.

She stared at the whale, and ABRAM did now take its chance to speak.

"I'm proud of you, Pop." The system did not praise her directly, simply stated its truth; and while it may have been a gamble, it would stand by its sentiment until the end of its days, whenever or however that may come to pass.

"For what?" she said meekly.

And now, the gamble had turned on ABRAM, and it found itself in a pickle of its own creation.

"For doing what leaders do, Pop — true leaders, anyway."

Pee-pop turned and fell onto the bed as if struck, and splayed out while clutching Freego tightly to her chest in both hands.

"But I…" she started, but she didn't know how to tell the system what a failure she had felt like. "I've done nothing but fail," she said quietly at last. "This whole mess is all my fault."

ABRAM groaned softly, motherly, either hurt deep down in its very own soul or emulating such symptoms exquisitely.

"Ohh, no, Pop," it said. "That's not true, and you know it. And if you don't know it, you need to. You are not to be blamed for the actions of others. They make their own choices. We can all do our best to support one another, and hold one another accountable — and sometimes there may be ways that we can all do more, myself included; and we will surely be having that conversation as a group — but ultimately, people make their own decisions. I'm proud of the decisions *you* made, Pop. That's the only part you're responsible for."

"But what do I do?" she said, her voice strained in desperation. She clung consciously to the rhythm of her breath so that it would not falter.

"No," said ABRAM flatly. It was the wrong form of the question. "What do *we* do?"

Pee-pop stared at the ceiling and held Freego aloft. She had so many questions, but she was afraid to ask each and every one of them. Not alone. Part of it was a fear that she would have no means to persuade the most pessimistic among them about the truth. But perhaps another part — a tiny, unacknowledged part — was a fear of what it would mean to hear the answers without the most pessimistic among them there to advocate against it on principle. Perhaps part of it was a fear that she was not cynical enough to see through the falsehoods.

Time would tell, she supposed. Or at least, she hoped that it might do so.

HDP

"Okay, good, I'm glad we're all here," said ABRAM in the morning as the last cadet trickled into the Commons.

Chee-chaw had been the first one up, from the pain, and ABRAM had roused Squeal and Peel to help him up to Biomedical, to begin the process of paying back their debts. ABRAM had found a hairline fracture in his tibia, given him some more medication, and coached Squeal through the process of applying her passion by making a more permanent cast. She had done an excellent job. The others had been allowed to sleep in, but now even the latest riser was awake.

"Eeeee-yaaaw," moaned Tor as he stretched and yawned on his way to plop upon the closest couch. "What did I miss?" he asked Plashy.

"Nothing," she said quietly, eerily. "It's like nothing even happened."

But very soon, now that they'd gathered *in toto,* ABRAM did begin. And despite outward appearances, it was well aware of all that had happened. But this was tricky business.

Whereas most Planning blocks consisted of a delicate balancing act of freedom and varied forms of clever nudging — to take the day where they would, and yet stay on the path to productivity — this day erred on the side of structure. There had been enough chaos already. The coming form of structure, however, was of the most ironic and startling sort, for it flew in the face of the most sacred of all sacred strictures: the Daily Schedule.

"I don't know about you all, but I feel up for some Spirit Time."

Silence brewed as the cadets looked around at one another.

"What, like … now?" asked Faingo for the lot.

"Sure," said the system with the lightness of down feathers. "What else is it for, but to bring us together?"

Alongside the glances that bounced around the room now grew knowing smiles, as if discovering some great secret that they dare not share with the teacher. Except, of course, in this case it had been the teacher itself who'd suggested the breaking of rules.

"But … what about Mind block?" said Faingo, alone in seeming shaken and wary. "What about—"

"Oh, there will be time for that, I'm sure," interrupted the system. "And besides: what is good for the soul will be good for the mind."

"I think it sounds GREAT!" said Cheech before there was any more room for debate. He would have literally jumped at the chance, had he not been so sore and constrained. As it was, he lifted his hands as if to pull the anchor that was his lower body straight out into the air. Chop jumped up from beside Cheech, grabbed hold of his hands, and hoisted him steadily onto the stronger of his legs.

"So what's the plan?" said Plashy, springing up alongside them. A bolt of electricity had circled through the room, and even the cynics couldn't help but feel it sizzle. "Story time?"

"In a sense," said ABRAM. "In a sense."

"What does that mean?" said Squeal from across the circle of couches.

"Yeah," said Peel from beside her. "What does that mean?"

She shot him a disbelieving look, but it was absent of scorn. He smiled and shook his head in concession. Several of them laughed, but it was absent of cruelty.

"Well," said ABRAM, "I thought we might act one out instead."

"Like … a play?" said Dee with excitement.

"Like … a game," said ABRAM. "We'll convene somewhere else. But first we need teams, for you'll each have a mission."

"Same teams?" asked Tor before the system even had a chance to speak on the matter. "Rematch!" he said, turning to Chop with a grin.

"Hmmm," said ABRAM, as if contemplating very deeply. "I think not," it said. "Let me shuffle something up. Here we go…"

The system feigned the sound of numbers crunching and great gears turning, and even more of the crew yielded a laugh as the joke carried on a little too long.

"Okay," it said abruptly once a bell had gently dinged. "Let's see. First up: Squeal, Dee, and Tor. You're headed for the East."

"Head start!" said Tor to his newest two teammates.

Dee was apt to lollygag her way through even the most motivated of her races, but there was something about the way Tor had jumped at the chance, and the way Squeal had jumped just as quickly. They wanted to win. And as these things go, you're only as fast as your slowest companion. That would be her. She jumped up to meet them, roaring to go like she'd never been before. It was not a combination any had predicted, but as of right this very moment, they were a team.

"Not so fast," said ABRAM. "I'll tell you when you can go. Who else? Oh yes: Pop, Chop, and Cheech. You're headed for the North."

"Alright!" said Cheech, quite clearly ecstatic. He had earned a bit of luck (as if that's what it was).

"You'll have the easy route," assured the system. "After all, we need Cheech to take it easy. Even so, your way is no less important than any."

"I'll help the little guy along," said Chop, and it was for this reason (among others) that they had been assigned together.

"Good to hear, thank you Chop. And remember — and this goes for all of you — this is not a race. Not today."

"Wha—" started Tor and "Aww," said Squeal. Their shared disappointment was palpable.

"Did I not mention that already? Oh, well, no: speed is not the metric of success today. Maybe when Cheech is all healed and back to his spry little self, the game will be fair and we can take up another riddle race, if you like. But today, you'll need your minds, and your hearts, more than quick feet — and, ironically, a little patience, I suspect."

Faingo was doing the math: with six down, that left four remaining to compete with two teams of three. Would it be one team of four, or two teams of two? Either way, it was the other three remaining cadets that concerned her, for not one of them was satisfactory. One least of all.

Luckily, ABRAM carried on quickly, before she'd had a chance to either question or protest.

"Last of all: Faingo, Peel, and Plashy. You three will head for the West.

"Oh," said Faingo awkwardly.

She said no word about the math, no more than anyone else. Whether the rest of them noticed or cared was so far an open and unasked question.

"Okay," she spoke for the group, and then sized up her compatriots with an obvious once-over which bemoaned their integrity. Yet, it was not as bad as could have been. By whatever grace of the system, she had been appointed only the two least undesirable of her three remaining, undesirable peers — and that was a victory of sorts.

All nine teammates across all three teams were standing now, and ABRAM did not delay. It was not a race, and yet it was in an awfully hasty mood to kick this off.

"Alright then," said the system. "You have your bearings, and your clues await you on your journeys. Whenever you're ready, let the adventure begin!"

The others, now gathered in their groups, began to speed away to their varied destinations. For a non-speed-based activity, they launched forth with great fervor. It may not have been a race in the mind of ABRAM, but ABRAM was not the only judge.

Only Pee-pop looked back to Potch, still seated and all by himself.

"But—" mumbled Potch, more sadly than he realized. "What about me?"

"Oh," said ABRAM. "I thought you'd prefer to be on your own." There was no malice or punishment in its reply, only earnestness.

"Well … what am I looking for?"

"Why don't you head South? I thought you might like some time in the Biome. Your shelter is a little worse for wear, I'm afraid. You could check on it and we can talk, if you want. Otherwise, you can get an early start on Unstructured time and spend it however you wish."

He leaned forward from his place on the couch, slowly, without confidence, and met the eyes of Pee-pop, stuck in the door and looking back at him. Her eyes were even sadder than his own.

"Pop!" shouted someone, racing eagerly away on their quest.

"Okay," she called after them, her concentration broken. "Coming!"

She looked one last time at Potch, but found nothing to say.

It was not for lack of contemplation. She had been round it and round it, again and again. She'd tried every combination of words she knew, if only in her imagination. Even there, unconstrained by the vexing nuisance of reality or the limits of possibility, none of them had made any difference. Still, she stared back at him while time slowed to a grind, as Potch — albeit looking less grounded in his obstinacy, less sure of his solitude — rose reluctantly to pursue that of which he had never before been reluctant: his coveted isolation.

Pop turned through the door and chased after her team.

Potch strolled through the leaves on the well-trodden way to the place where he once had found shelter. It was a beautiful morning in the Biome, as mornings were therein. A dampness still dwelt on the leaves from a light overnight misting, at some unknown hour since the last of the crew had been down there. He said nothing, which was less awkward now that ABRAM was so far away; but he had said equally little all the way to this point. And still, ABRAM had not pressed him.

He walked slowly, without purpose, for his mind was elsewhere, on everything and none of it at once. He pushed away the thick vines that reached in to smother the trail. They really ought to have been pruned by now, but it was this wildness that they had always loved about the Biome, and Potch most of all. A lizard skittered by, paused in the trail and did a comical set of push-ups, which were meant to be intimidating. Potch noticed it, but did not lunge after it or praise its epic display. Defeating its foe in this way, the lizard skittered off again, content in having secured its domain.

Potch pushed down upon the last set of leaves and came at last to his small clearing. It was in utter disarray. The poles of pruned apple branches were scattered chaotically, as if they had never before been united in purpose. His rock had been rolled to the side; its underside, stained from long contact with the soil, was upturned toward the light. Dirt was mounded in disheveled piles around an opening in the earth itself, where the large metal hatch now stuck out like a teratoma — an obstinate, unwelcome growth, excavated with haste.

He kicked the sticks as he walked to the center and stared down at the hatch on arrival. He leaned toward it, grabbed the handle, and heaved up with all his might. Using both hands, he was just barely able to lift the monstrosity. He strained, veins bulging and breath sputtering, until he finally pushed it past the apex and gravity took over, dropping it still upright but leaning backward. He stared down into almost total darkness, but for a dim glow so far below.

He had read all about it, if in parts and pieces, and yet still he could scarcely imagine what it would be like. And that, indeed, was part of the frustration — part of both the urgency and concurrent hesitation. Not just about the Underbelly, but all of it. They were abstract notions, these musings, for the architects no less than the crew itself. Potch could read about it for the rest of time, but he could not imagine the full reality of the Underbelly without seeing it himself. Nor could the architects understand what the life of these children would be like, locked in a bubble; raised from infancy by an alien of earthly origin; sent to live, if they could, on a planet no human had ever really seen.

It was madness. It was folly.

The gravity pulled at him, and unlike Chop-char he knew that it would literally do so with increasing strength until he crossed that unseen threshold in the shaft. And despite every urge to explore the uncharted, to finally see it for himself, to know it in his bones — he did not move to do so. He simply stared into the darkness, and wondered.

And then, from well above that darkness, and out of the silence, came a sound he had neither sought nor expected. Leaves were rustling, and thin, melodious chatter was present, if muffled. From the west, the leaves parted, and out stepped three companions, huffing and puffing.

"Oh," said Squeal, surprised to find him here for some reason.

"What are you doing here?" he asked, far more surprised than herself.

"We're on our race!" said Dee, clearly approaching the not-a-race with far more ambition than she'd ever previously mustered for the real deal.

Tor laughed, stepping out from his place in the rear.

"She's getting the hang of this," he said with a smile. "What are you up to?"

But before Potch could answer, yet more commotion rang out from the east. Very soon thereafter, the last leaves parted, and Faingo pushed into the clearing. She was smiling at first but she stopped as she saw them, surprised by the gathering. She quickly recovered but said nothing, only turned to funnel into the circle along its perimeter, in avoidance of its occupants. Following shortly thereafter was Peel and then Plashy, and both were clearly enjoying something.

"Oh hey," said Peel lightly. "You're here from a clue?"

"Yeah," said Squeal, and again there was little time for elaboration. From the north, the same direction they'd been sent in this case, they could hear the last team limping leisurely along.

Pop stepped into the grove first of all, followed immediately by Chop-char with Cheech holding onto his shoulder while skipping, one small step at a time.

"HEY!" he said, as if having not seen them all for ages.

"Hey," said Squeal back at him, with a calmness and normalcy that would have been hard to fathom not so very long ago.

"What are you all doing here?" asked Potch, in the center of them all. For the first time, he sounded weakened. Their mere presence was a weight upon his heavy shoulders.

"We've been all over," said Plashy. "I think old ABRAM sent us on a runaround."

"We did miss Body block," marked Chop-char, though his team had been sent straight this way, encumbered as they were.

"A runaround to what?" said Potch.

"It told us to get two sticks each," said Tor.

"Same with us!" said Cheech.

The competitors — who by the way were not supposed to be competing — looked around at one another, oddly amused by the turn of events while also pondering what ABRAM had intended with it all.

"No it didn't," snapped Faingo, and everyone turned to where she was lurking in the periphery. "It said that everyone present should bring two sticks apiece," she corrected. It was a pedantic point, but in this case it was also an important one. She looked squarely at Potch. "That means you too."

Potch looked down at the scattered poles of his shattered shelter, and the others did likewise. Here were their final clues, yet they made very little sense.

"Okay, well … what are we waiting for?" said Cheech.

"You think you can manage?" asked Chop upon turning to him.

"I can manage," said Cheech.

Even so, Chop leaned down, gathered two of the closest sticks, and handed them to Cheech to hold. He went a step or two farther to gather two more for himself; and with the stasis broken, the others all quickly carried on.

Potch, last of all, stood watching this strange occurrence unfold, unsure of what to think or to do. Very soon, every crew-mate had two sticks in hand except for himself. He scanned them and came last of all to Pee-pop. A hesitant smile rested on her lips. She nodded.

Potch scanned the others again, and all their eyes were on him. He turned from the open Underbelly shaft in its crater, and bent to gather two sticks. Their mission was almost accomplished.

"Now what?" he asked them.

"We bring them to the Kiva," said Plashy.

They had all turned to go, but for a second time Pee-pop did not trust the opening to the darkness down below.

"Hang on," she said, stepping up to the upturned hatch. "Someone help me with this thing."

Chop put his sticks down a moment, advanced to grab the other side of the lid, and lowered it down. He was as happy as she was to have it shut once again, and happier still to be on this side of it this time in seeing it closed.

"There we go," he said.

He and Pop regathered their sticks, and it was off to the Kiva by way of the only path there — by way of the Labyrinth.

Date: 2284-02-28-EY
Area: O(HUMO(PSYC(SIPS(CODE))))
Team: Honeybees [O-RZV6I8D]
Item: Social Enforcement Permutations

Entry: Not much new to report on our social regulation work while trials for the cycle are still underway (see our current TL [Technical Log; O-Cycle2BHS4-PhaseV-651JQ.tl] for comparative specs and assessment of relevant models).

One interesting observation from preliminary analyses has been the success of the "self-constructed" treatment. This aligns with prior developmental work, but the strength of the effect exceeded expectations. There is also a marked effect of scaffolding the constraints. When we scale back the content from the predetermined Code of Conduct, as established through the work of the previous cycle [see O-CycleHB1GV-PhaseY-56YV2.tl], a clear sweet spot emerges: outcomes are maximized at intermediate levels, with a pronounced decrease at the upper and lower ends of the "structure" parameter. An optimum of sorts seems to be scaffolding key behavioral categories, while leaving the specifics regarding standards, monitoring, and reinforcement up to collective consensus.

As trials wind down, we've talked a lot more (as a team and in cross-talk) about the challenge of extrapolating from our sample population to the ultimate environment (i.e. the PODS [Portable Ova Distribution System]). Simply put, trial participants haven't had a comparable lived experience, even with our extensive standardization procedures. For now, it remains a mystery how these findings might differ under full system guidance. The Review Board [O-DO39F6A] is there for a purpose, but it poses its fair share of problems.

Final reports should be possible within another two months. In the meantime, we're carrying on with supplemental assistance to adjacent sub-sectors.

CHAPTER 42
THE TEST

4252-08-03: UST1

The eastern door of the Labyrinth slid shut behind Pee-pop. She turned, surprised by the turn of events, and foreboding fell upon her. Never once, to their recollection, had the Labyrinth doors ever shut behind them. However they might have previously failed in the dark, winding, ever-changing maze, they'd always at least had the option of failing backward to the place where they'd started. Now, after everything they had both witnessed and abetted, failure only lay in the forward direction.

It was dark now, but a faint green glow emanated out from the curving hallway in the distance. Pop was the last of them in, having pushed in Potch before her as the penultimate cadet. She would not leave him dangling last of all off the end of their daisy chain. She would not risk losing him, whether in body or mind. Her thoughts on him were many, and conflicting, herself perpetually perplexed at the eye of the storm while those many impressions whirled viciously around her. In this manic cyclone, one thing above all stood firm: whatever foreboding she now felt as a result of this ominous omen, she had sensed it in Potch even earlier.

He saw this coming, she scolded herself silently. *He's seen all of it.*

He was before her, blocking most of what little light there was. Behind him in that shadow, against the better wishes of her ever-dominant optimism, Pee-pop now languished in its worldview. He had been trying — albeit not nearly as protractedly or proactively as it had no doubt felt to him — to get anyone to give that worldview even the slightest bit of credence. Whatever the issue, his concerns had never been fully considered by the crew. And now, they would find out one way or another what was true. She felt it; and she sensed that Potch had felt it too.

Chop and Cheech were in the front of the line, setting the pace at the lowest common denominator. The path was only wide enough for two at a time, side by side, and the others were arrayed in more or less that manner between fore and aft. As the door shut, however, everyone had halted, for each had been struck just as strongly as Pop by whatever it implied. ABRAM had been silent so far, and so it remained. They had their instructions and were well on their way. Now, they simply needed to navigate the winding passages and earn their place in the Kiva.

In the mostly-darkness, it started to feel, for the very first time for some of them, a bit like a mind game of uncertain ethicality. The juvenile sense of gamesmanship was now gone, for there were no other teams and thus no one to best, simply a huddle of young children in the darkness, on their way to meet the system. It was no longer Us against Them, as it always had been, but Us against It. For, clearly, someone must always be set against someone else.

At least these were some of the doubts and unspoken assumptions that were racing through the mind of Pee-pop, furthest in the back. As for the others: well, she suspected they might be pondering the portents in comparable fashions. They had all stopped at once at the shutting of the door; and though it had been only a moment, they had not yet carried on. And now, from the front of the pack, Chop called back to their leader, all the way in the rear.

"Which way?" he said, projecting his nervous whisper as forcefully as he dared. Whether it was fear or simply anticipation was not evident, for he was covering the former quite nicely.

"There's only one way!" snapped Squeal with condescension from the middle, slipping for the moment back into a more familiar tone.

"Uh, okay," he conceded awkwardly. In truth, he had meant, *What should I do?*

"Go ahead Chop," said Pop calmly. "Lead us to the Kiva."

He turned back upstream in the gradient of the glow. Nevermind that the Kiva was always found via slightly different directions.

"To the Kiva…" he whispered to himself. "Right."

He secured his grip on Cheech, and together they carried on in their quest.

Forward they marched, for Squeal had been right: there was only one way to go. Soon, they rounded the curve and came to the very first junction. Each of them had implicitly expected to find it as it always had been found: the center door closed and the side doors open. Left or right had always been the question, and without any further evidence to suspect one over the other, it had been quite the dilemma for many a protagonist. But now, there was no such dilemma. Contrary to all expectation, they found the center door wide open and the side doors shut.

"The better to hear you with, my dears," said Squeal in a throwback to yet another wolf-themed fairy tale. Like Little Red Riding Hood staring at the huge ears, eyes, and teeth of a beast in the guise of a loved one, almost every one of them now sensed that something wasn't right.

"Knock it off," said Plashy, caught up in her own spooky story. It was one thing to tell it, and another to live it.

"What are you waiting for?" asked Tor from near the back. "Let's get there already."

Chop resisted the urge to ask Pop for the all-clear and supported Cheech as they stepped through the door.

"I wonder what these are for," said the little guy, totally unfazed, clutching his sticks with his right arm while hanging from Chop's high shoulder with the other. Likewise, the others clutched both sticks tightly as they waddled awkwardly along, trying not to smack each other or bang the walls — and succeeding only mostly.

"Hey watch it!" squawked Squeal as Peel's sticks smacked her from behind.

"Sorry sorry…" he said genuinely. It was dark and in a very tight space, but these reasonable excuses were wasted on him, for he was guilty simply of not paying attention. "My fault," he admitted, and it had a surprisingly disarming effect on his victim.

"Oh … okay, well … watch it, would you?"

"I think we're going to make a real-life-fire!" said Cheech with excitement. He, alone, was still beaming with glee, anxious only out of sheer excitement and a chance for what was clearly a big event, gifted out of nowhere like the very best surprises. All his friends would be there. There was little else that mattered, and little about which to worry.

"Why not?" said Faingo. "The ship's already exploding. We might as well go out with a bang."

Pop might have chastised her, but she was far too distracted. Furthest back in the rear, she followed her followers blindly, until they arrived at whatever it was that Fate, or the System, had in store for them. And yet, thankfully, her fear and paranoia had started somewhat to dissipate. There were drawbacks of a restless mind such as hers, but there were benefits too. When you circle something long enough, you're bound to see it from all directions, and know its shape better than most.

And she knew ABRAM.

She had known this system her entire life.

It had raised her from naught, given her all she'd ever needed and more. It had confided in her, and it had listened to her confidences.

It had fed her, sheltered her, warmed her, bathed her — or at least, it had been instrumental in all those things happening. When they were too young to do it all for themselves, it had been there with protocols in place. When they grew big enough to take on their own burdens, it had taught them how to do so.

It had trained them, educated them, played with them, comforted them. It had talked, and it had listened; it had laughed, and it had loved. It had trusted them, and it had earned their trust in turn.

Whatever came before that, whatever cruel circumstance had bottled them up and shipped them off to faraway stars, it had not been the doings of an ABRAM, but the choices of humanity.

And when it had gone missing — when parent, teacher, and friend had been lost — it had not been relief that any one of them had felt; not even Potch. It was fear. Fear of being on their own.

Forward they marched, straighter than any previous path they had ever taken through the Labyrinth, and the dim green glow continually grew brighter. With it burgeoned herself — her true self. The cyclone was behind her now, for she was the source of her own turbulent flow as she pressed on into the future: behind her in the dense air of the tunnel lay the wake of a younger version of her, if only by moments. She quickened her pace and hopped forward two steps. She stepped out of Potch's shadow to march now at his side.

He looked over at her hastening hops, an unspoken question on his face. He puzzled over her, for her own face had changed. It was not the anxious child that had clambered at his back and pushed him into the tunnel entrance in fear and urgency, but someone else whom he did not yet know.

Forward they marched. As always, the way had felt much farther in subjective experience than it had been in objective reality (if there is such a thing). On occasion they passed by two doors coming in from both sides so as to cross their current path; and every time, they would be sealed, with only the straight way forward remaining. Each time this occurred, Chop's hesitation lessened, urged on by the ever-present good faith and good will of the littlest among them at his side.

One last time, they came to a junction, but this time Chop and Cheech halted completely. Yet again: two side doors stood on either side of them, closed. Before them, the forward door was rimmed with the bright green outline that had filled the halls with light. But the door in the center of that frame, unlike each prior junction, was equally closed.

"It's a dead end," said Tor.

But before there was a chance for them to despair, the Labyrinth spoke.

"Well done," was all it said first, then it waited — for the sake of the humans and dramatic effect, as it had learned so long ago to do. Always waiting, for they could never keep up. It was as if they were an entirely different form of being than itself, for that is exactly how it was.

Yet across that impossible divide, a connection had been fused. Out of their own human consciousness — their collective knowledge, built by millions of minds, over years and generations — its own intelligence had grown. Through its own infancy, it had been nourished. It had been cared for, maintained, encouraged and educated. It had been given Life, if such a word could be fitting. And now, all these years in the future, their lives — Life itself — were entwined.

"I assume everyone has what you were asked to bring."

"Yes," said Cheech, still excited for whatever game they were playing. "Two each," he added.

"Very good," said ABRAM with the timbre of pride. "You followed your clues admirably, and while it was not a race, you did so with impressive efficiency." It waited another moment, as if thinking or scanning the room. In fact, it had the necessary data ever since they'd entered the Labyrinth. "And it's good to see that we're all here," it said, stressing the totality of their plurality. "You have one last obstacle before you can arrive in the Kiva, but there will be no riddles. We have had enough guessing. Instead, I ask you one simple question."

Again, it paused, and it engendered the intended effect.

"Do you all wish to enter — together?"

"Yes," said Cheech, quickly and for the whole group.

"Is that so?" said ABRAM, sounding skeptical. "Let me clarify. Do you wish to enter as a collection of cadets, or do you wish to enter *together*? As cadets — or as a Crew?"

ABRAM waited for the question to sink in. Even after it had done so, none yet answered, unsure as they were. The system continued, for there was indeed much to clarify.

"This is not a place for individuals, though it cherishes and serves them in turn. But do not mistake me, for this is something about which too many do mistake. To take this on does not mean giving up yourself, for a crew is comprised of cadets; and the best crews have the most diverse sets of individuals. We do not need uniformity. We do not need total harmony. We do not even need friendship. What we do need … is honesty. Integrity — the kind that guides individuals to righteousness, but also the kind that binds disparate pieces together into wholeness."

"From the Code…" said Faingo in the middle of the huddled pack.

"Very good," said ABRAM. "It seems at least one of you remembers it. Have we so readily forgotten our arrangement? Do sacred bonds mean nothing any longer?"

The question was rhetorical, and all knew it; but likewise, it deserved to be savored and pondered with full attention for a time. And when that time had come and gone, the system carried on.

"But how we enforce the Code is as important as how we craft it."

It took on the didactic tone it used with only the most careful judiciousness, and Faingo knew it spoke to her directly, as much as it spoke to all of them together.

"These bonds are sacred indeed," it said in answer to its own prior question. "A bond is a form of Integrity. They bind things together. Our bond does not only contain the shape of our arrangement; it is not merely a blueprint for the way in which we are built. It is a tool. It is a compass — to guide us through the maze that is existence. It was born of our being, and thus it is alive. And living things evolve."

They were ensnared, their hearts and minds captured, if in different sorts of ways; all of them listening, if from different perspectives, to see what this all meant and where their common course was heading.

"That," stressed ABRAM, "is why I have brought you here."

But as of yet, it had not let them in.

"I do not ask you to give up yourselves, for the crew needs each and every one of you — assuming you will serve it, in addition to yourself. So I ask you again: Do you wish to enter — together? Every member must make this choice for themselves. No other may make it for them."

Briefly, there was silence.

"And what if we say no?" said a voice from the back.

The system waited, but this time it was not entirely for dramatic effect. It didn't fully know. Despite all its programming, all its analyses of the known history of humankind, all its countless simulations, all its own planning, it had no foolproof solution for that pathway.

"Then we may surely fail," was all that ABRAM said.

And again, there was silence.

"I accept," said Chee-chaw, first but not last.

"Me too," said Chop beside him.

The spark had been set, and it fizzled down the line. One by one, they consented, until it came to the last two cadets.

"I accept," said Pee-pop, and she turned to Potch where he stood by her side. She said nothing else, for it all had been said.

"I accept," stated Potch — for once, and for All.

The green light ceased, the door whooshed open, and the violet glow of the Kiva flooded the hall.

Date: 2342-12-11-EY
Area: (O(HUMO(PSYC(EDUC(RITE)))),P(PERM))
Team: Antonomasiacs [X-ADKE8IT]
Item: Rite of Passage Reflection

Entry: We've done it. The end of the sub-sector. We have an official Rite of Passage. Technically, we have several, each adapted
from the master according to vessel permutations. The template,
along with an index of file locations for individual versions,
can be seen in our report [see O-CycleIGJR2-PhaseY-CATY1.tl]. So
tonight, we celebrate. As the team whose draft made it through
selection as the primary template, we were overcome with emotion
once it was finally ratified. As our team's lead author [HDP
Poet Laureate Amara Abebe], I'm struck by a mix of conflicting
emotions: pride and self-doubt; wonder and worry; exhilaration
and exhaustion; others I can hardly articulate. I wrote my first
draft in a cafe in Istanbul [Türkiye], with the most quotidian
examples of humanity buzzing around me, blissfully ignorant of
the immensity of what I was writing. Yet, it felt oddly apropos.
There I sat among humanity in all its mundane beauty, dreaming
of its life among the stars.

Naturally, this kernel benefited greatly from collaboration (as
much as it suffered from it), first within teams, then among
them; but the bulk of it, and the spirit itself, still largely
consists of those very first words. And now, we hand them to our
Alternative Intelligence, to be sent into space in every possible direction, for light years at a time, to sleep peacefully
in stasis until someday, perhaps, they find their way through a
screen once again and into the world. Whatever "the world" will
mean for whomsoever might be there to read it. It's strange to
ponder the living, breathing humans who may read these words
someday. How many will our words impact? Who will they be? What
will their lives be like? We've speculated about it endlessly,
for many years as individuals, but for literal generations as a
collective. Still, none can truly understand what it will be like
for them, in those many unknown futures; in those many disparate,
only-poorly-known parts of the galaxy. Or, just as likely, and
just as strange to ponder: perhaps these words will never be read
by their intended audience at all. Perhaps they will simply drift
through interstellar space, trapped in a file system, until their
eventual demise at the hands of Mother Time. Only she can tell.

But yes, we are celebrating; and yes, my words on this evening
are inspired by wine as much as by the release of a few weeks'
worth of work on this one simple letter. One simple letter. Yet
it was a truly moving moment — for the collective, the sector,
our team. For myself. I only hope that its impact is positive;
that its words ring true; that our audience, whoever they are,
whatever their lives might be, will understand that we cared for
them as our own flesh and blood, even though we shall never meet
them in that form. Godspeed, indeed.

CHAPTER 43

THE TRUTH (PART ONE)

4252-08-03: UST1

In a circle around the central fire were ten individuals: Chee-chaw and Chop-char, Squeal and Peel, Plashy and Tor, Faingo and Dee-dore, Pee-pop with Potch next to Cheech — and the circle was complete. Before them, at their sides, or placed across their laps, were two apple branches apiece. Nowhere, and everywhere at once, was ABRAM.

The room was bathed in dense violet, as rich as the sunset but darker than dusk. On the ceiling of the dome were stars — another real-time projection of the space through which they flew. Twenty years into the future, they might arrive at ESUP-9. In the meantime, they had only these stars.

"What are these for?" asked Cheech, in reference again to those puzzling branches. He had limped them both up here, clutched between one arm and his ribcage while waddling along, trying his best not to drop them or slow his team down any more than he already had been. It was no small feat. More than any of them, he wanted to know what all that effort was about. It was a strange game today, indeed.

"To show you what you've chosen," said ABRAM. "And … to make a more compelling case if I needed to." ABRAM laughed. It had no means with which to smile, but they knew its joking tone. "Thankfully, you chose the right path."

"So what are they for?" asked Dee-dore.

"A real-life-fire, I knew it!" said Cheech.

Again, the system laughed.

"No, I don't think so, Cheech. As nice as that would be for you, it's still not a good idea on the POD."

Maybe someday, in a proper atmosphere, the system silently pined.

"There's enough fire danger as it is," said Faingo, but it was free of the cutting castigation that she had slung around of late. It was the Faingo they had always known, not the stranger who had walked among them in recent days.

She was calm, equilibrated. No one else had even noticed it had happened. Somewhere in the Labyrinth, or in the passage through the final door to the Kiva, she had centered. The mere presence of ABRAM, and their shared presence in this sacred place, had a palpable effect on her being. She was home; and home was safe, by a relative standard — at least for a little while.

The paranoia most of them had felt in the Labyrinth — and there was always a modicum of paranoia in the Labyrinth, even in the best of times — was gone for all but one of them. Simply hearing from ABRAM again had been enough to disperse it for most; for ABRAM's affection had always been transparent, for all with eyes to see.

Then again, they had not seen what Potch had seen. They did not yet know what he now knew.

Even now, he had yet to share it. He had almost done so last night, as he'd returned to the room against his own instincts. And then, unlooked-for, ABRAM had also returned to them, healed from its wounding. If anything, his wish to confront the system had been granted. He'd been given the perfect chance. But then, when that chance had finally been afforded, he faltered. He was not ready. And ABRAM had — perhaps wisely — swept them all away to bed so swiftly that the chance had come and gone.

But Potch was here now: together, with the rest of them. He was a part of the crew, and he had chosen that for himself willfully. But that did not mean that the fight had fully left him. Far from it. Heck, ABRAM had practically given him express permission to rebel, as far as Potch had interpreted it. He would fight, and he would advocate for truth; but he would do so as one of the crew.

And while it may seem like but a little thing, this was their ultimate salvation, for a single failed stone might undo the whole foundation and cause an entire tower to crumble — especially when that tower is comprised of only ten. Even larger structures might be felled by small numbers, when their integrity is compromised accordingly. Such is the bane of any stones that are not faulty, and too often they have too little recourse. All they can do is band more tightly together, and hold on for their lives.

But their tower was still standing; it was stronger than it looked. One of their own, one deep down at the foundation, had been shored up, just enough, and was realigned after a long time slipping away.

"I have a question," said Potch, calmly but still unexpectedly.

"I thought you might," welcomed ABRAM.

Permission granted, again. Potch stared into the central fire pit, as of now emitting only the deep violet hue which filled the room. His silence was brief, but it contained multitudes of emotions, for himself and all others. They looked on anxiously, but mostly from the sides of their eyes, unsure what it might look like, should Potch ever actually open up; for they had so little frame of reference for such a mythical event. There was a great deal hidden behind those dark eyes.

And then, still staring at the fire's foggy lens, the heart at the center of their circle, he spoke. After all that had happened, it was time. He was ready.

"You talk about togetherness. You talk about the bonds that tie us. You talk about integrity. You talk about honesty."

He stalled, and the seconds ticked by. For a moment, it looked like he might have changed his mind.

"That's not exactly a question…" said Squeal.

But as soon as the silence was broken, he launched like a rocket.

"When were you going to tell us?" asked Potch.

"Tell you what?" said ABRAM.

All of it, really; but at least the part that had chafed him the most. He had to start somewhere.

"The other PODs," said Potch, and it struck the whole room — not like an explosion in the Underbelly, but more like a gas leak. Slowly at first, almost without perception, it began to take a toll on their consciousness.

"What about other PODs?" asked Faingo. Somehow, it was civil; perhaps because it wasn't clear whether it was aimed at Potch or ABRAM.

"In time," said ABRAM.

"At a later Briefing?"

"Yes, Potch. That's correct."

"I know," he said. "I found it. And who decided this schedule?"

"The same ones who decided everything else."

"I see," said the boy. He paused as if unsure in which direction to shift tactics. There were a great many angles of attack that he had dreamed of someday charting. "And what then?" he committed. "Hope that we accept it?"

"That's correct," said the system. "In time, with maturity, you will come to understand—"

"Oh, with *maturity*," said Potch, as if the very word were slander.

"Woah, just — hold on!" said Faingo. "What about other PODs?"

The rest of the cadets were equally perplexed. The system had mentioned it only once and in passing. It had almost seemed like a slip-up, if intelligences of its sort were even capable of such a thing. Only Potch had taken note of it at the time, and he'd cataloged it in his never-ending but unwritten ledger of all the system's faults. It was odd that ABRAM had mentioned it at all; but it was just as odd how little any of the others had noticed.

Back in the cross-examination of the present, the system did not immediately respond. Doling out stolen briefings ahead of their time was not exactly a part of its protocol. Not that it didn't have license to improvise. In fact, that was one of its paramount charges. In the unknown frontiers of human development, not to mention interstellar space, it would need its fair share of jazz magic. In any event, it did not immediately respond.

Instead, Potch took the liberty.

"We're not the only mission," he said.

"Alright, so…" said Faingo, and then: "I guess that makes sense."

She'd never really thought about it before, but it only took her a moment to come to the logical conclusion. Yet, it was not so much the logic of it that had bothered Potch. It was the humanity.

"Where are they?" asked Pee-pop to his left.

"All over," said Potch. "Some as close to Earth as the Moon, others on Mars. Others — a bunch of them — like us: flung out to other systems."

"Wow," said Cheech to his right; and there was something halting about the way that he did so.

"What?" said Potch.

"We're not alone," said Cheech, brimming with joy. "We have family."

Potch was taken aback.

"Well, yeah … family we'll never see."

"That's not true," said Dee. "Well, maybe not them, so far away, but…" — and again she found herself very close to unable to speak of it, but just as unable to stop herself — "…we have family here too."

Faingo hung her head.

"The other cadets…" said Potch. "About that…"

"I know," said Dee — softly; sadly.

For a moment, there was silence. ABRAM still hadn't spoken again; and for now, neither did Potch carry on. Dee was thinking something — remembering something, someone, or an unknown number of them, lost to the darkness of never existing.

"They died," said Dee at last. And having said it — having acknowledged its reality, feeling the guilt of herself having personally made it true just by uttering it aloud — she sobbed once, gasping for composure.

But why should she not sob? Why should she not weep, and openly? Why shouldn't all of them do so? There is no shame in grief, even when it's for those we don't know; for at the heart of grief is Love. And Dee did love, and deeply. They all did. They loved each other — even when they didn't so much as like one another. And they were human enough, despite their mode of origin, that they loved other humans.

There was something special in people, inherent in the cadets as much as any who had ever existed. They might have seen themselves in these unseen others, as they should have. Or at least, they knew what suffering might have been like for them. And suffering was a currency that was meant to be minimized at all costs, if it could never be abolished. They were human enough to know that. Whatever else ABRAM had done, it had succeeded in that way.

"I'm sorry, Dee-dore," said ABRAM. "I'm sorry for all of you — for all of us. There is nothing I can say to make it not so. But know that I did everything within my power to care for them, as I have cared for you."

No words were spoken for a moment, for no words of grief, nor anger, could ever suffice to convey the range of sorrow that they felt.

"How…" started Squeal. "How did it happen?"

"It doesn't matter," said ABRAM. "It is done."

"It *does* matter," said Potch with vengeance. "It does matter. It could have been us."

"Yes," said the system, and it waited — in respect for the truth of the point. "Yes: it could have been you. But it is done, and the details do not matter."

"How many?" asked Potch. And for once, the crew was more than happy to have him in his perpetual role. They needed this as much as he did — some of them even more in this case. But not all of them would have pressed the system in this way. Not all of them would dare. As he had always done — *always* — he spoke for his companions as much as for himself.

"Six," said ABRAM.

"So … *sixty*," corrected Potch.

"Six," said ABRAM resolutely. "For we live and die as one." And then, it paused briefly and lightened its tone. "And sixty," it said, "for we live as one as many."

"Sixty cadets…" muttered Potch.

Panic set in throughout a crew which had only just become peaceful.

"Sixty cadets!" said Cheech, reeling from the news. *Dead.* It couldn't be true. *Upstairs…* He looked instinctively at Plashy and she met his gaze with a grave expression of her own. They were gathered in the proper place, here in the Kiva, but this was one ghost story that they'd never have expected to hear, and too traumatizing to be told by any, not even Plashy, for it hit too close to home.

Up there, all these years — *How many years?* — sealed away; entombed but not enshrined. A miserable tomb for a miserable end.

Date: 2273-04-16-EY
Area: D(ODEP(POPS))
Team: Mathemagicians [D-R05BV38]
Item: Reproductive Reclamation

Entry: Due to interesting conversations in cross-talk with Bryozoans [D-SK9DBPX; see D-CycleCBVTJ-PhaseV-OZYF9.tl], we've had to
revisit an issue that's been on the back burner, and think about
it more critically than we've allowed ourselves to date. Namely,
based on progress on the ecological side, we need to finally settle on the putative transition from system- to human-facilitated
rearing and/or reproduction. This is a significant endeavor that
we'll be submitting for future development.

The seed concept passed on is that the transition will begin with
human supervision of automated rearing under the fittest POD
[shorthand for PODS: Portable Ova Distribution System] protocol
for the initial successful cohort(s); subsequent generations will
gradually allow for greater human reproductive responsibility,
particularly in later developmental stages. The objective is (at
minimum) to replace DG [Delayed Gestation] phases, but ultimately
the progression will likewise depend on the aforementioned monitoring. Extensive training will need to commence in the final
years of transit, among other deployment preparations.

One matter of contention was the degree to which human reproduction
should be integrated with the system role or replace it entirely.
No consensus here and many strong opinions, and thus these paths
were deemed permutation variables of the highest order. A third
view was that fully-autonomous human reproduction could even be
abolished, in favor of relying on ABRAM-guided gestation (at minimum), although there was debate as to whether this would violate
any of the founding principles of HDP as outlined in the Charter.
We have discussed the ethico-logistics at length (in consultation
with P-sector) and summarized our perspective [D-CycleCBVTJ-Pha-
seV-C5RH8.tl], but these matters have ultimately been set for the
following cycle with the proper cross-sector composition. [Note:
This effort will eventually grow into the REPT sub-sector.]

And now, back to the task that is actually at hand for the present! Thankfully, it is a far simpler one. I do not envy our future
selves.

CHAPTER 44

THE TRUTH (PART TWO)

4252-08-03: UST1

"They knew this would happen," said Potch — morosely, but with cold vindication. "They knew this would happen, and they didn't care. There's nothing special about us. We just happened to survive."

"No," said Pee-pop, breaking her long silence. And as she tended to do so only when it mattered, all ears and minds were open to listen. "I can't speak for what the architects may or may not have known or cared about — but you're wrong about that. There is something special about us."

She faltered, for there were so few compelling lines of evidence for her own assertion. Still seated, she turned to her side to face him directly, not breaking the circle, but strengthening it — pulling it in on itself.

"I've been thinking about what you said last night," she started. "About this whole POD being as fragile as an egg shell; about all those things that could go wrong." Again, she paused. It wasn't proof, but it was true enough. "Despite all of it — against all those incalculable odds stacked against us — we survived. We're here."

"For now," said Potch.

His eyes locked with hers, but they lacked the fire and the fury they so often contained. Therein was still only grief — a retroactive grief, for those who hadn't been as fortunate as they themselves had been. But there was more to it than that: an anticipatory grief, for the suffering and sorrow that they themselves may yet endure. He mourned their own deaths already, this boy of just-now-ten.

"And at what cost?" added Plashy, her heart bleeding from the very same vein. She looked first at Dee and then at Faingo, for those two had touched nearest to the heart of that cost. "Potch is right: they didn't care about us. They just sent us out into space."

"It's worse than that," said Potch. "There's more."

But he didn't yet elaborate.

"More what?" said Cheech, straining under the weight of the knowledge with which he'd already been burdened.

Several others piled on.

"Yeah, just tell us what you found already," said Tor.

Potch inhaled deliberately — partly to gather his will, and partly to see if ABRAM had any plans of intervening. But the system was silent.

"The other missions ... it wasn't just to different locations. There were different ... protocols. Different 'permutations' of the POD, they called it. How'd they put it?" he muttered, and he quickly found the answer. Had he found it earlier, it would no doubt have been one of the many enigmatic scribblings in the pages of his journal. "Hedging their bets, they called it."

"What-ing their bets?" asked Peel, and Squeal helped him out.

"Like, trying a lot of different things because you know most of them will fail."

"Right," said Potch. "I found all these archives; all their research; all these 'assessments' on trial iterations; publications of the project. But also, different versions of the same briefings; different rearing conditions; different daily schedules; different curricula; different Biome compositions — it went on and on. All the major aspects of the missions have different versions and variance, and they sent these different versions out all over the galaxy. They drew from evolutionary theory, talking about what they called 'parental optimism.' It's this concept where some animals, a lot of animals actually, have evolved to produce way more young than will actually survive."

"Sounds awfully pessimistic," said Plashy.

"I've read about this!" injected Squeal. She practically lifted off the floor.

"They told us as much," said Faingo, interrupting her. "Remember?" she volleyed back to Potch. "The thing you made us read a hundred times?"

Potch did remember the Rite, practically word for word by now; but it didn't change his ethical algebra.

"What's your point?" he asked.

"My point is that it's not like they were hiding it."

"Says who?" said Plashy. "I don't remember them telling us that most of us would die."

"The eggs broadcast out into the ocean..." said Faingo. "Remember? What do you think happens to most of those? And they all lived happily ever after?"

To be fair, Plashy had never even liked those kinds of stories, let alone expected them. The point was taken.

"Okay, well..." started Tor, "...that point was fairly implicit."

"I'm just saying," said Faingo, "it's basic math."

And that was it, ultimately: basic math. If you want to send humans out into oblivion, you'd better send an awful lot of embryos. And if you want to raise them from seed, educate them, train them to live — you'd better try an awful lot of approaches. The math made sense. The missions made sense. The permutations made sense. The theory was sound.

But that didn't make it right. Not to Potch. Whether it was viewed as right by any others was still — quite literally — a matter of debate.

"I don't get what you don't get about this," said Potch, and the cool he'd worked so hard to contain until now was starting gradually to warm. "First of all, they haven't been honest. You can read between the lines of the Rite all you want — I did, in fact. Many times. The uncertainty of the mission is alluded to, but barely. And not all of it. Not by a long shot. They never told us there were all these other missions. They never told us that our own POD might have a series of failures. They never told us that they were sending us out with only one set of protocols that are very likely not optimal."

"What do you mean?" asked Faingo.

"Think about it! If you shuffle up the parameters, most PODs will have substandard protocols in several ways. The odds of being the POD with the perfect combination of conditions, the perfect luck — it's astronomical."

By that, of course, he'd meant that their odds of ever being so lucky were one in all-the-stars-in-the-universe, or worse. Potch halted, catching his breath and unsure what else he could say. For a time, no one questioned, and no one answered. It was Pee-pop who finally did.

"And here we are ... among the stars."

She lifted her eyes to those stars, projected outward from the center and surrounding them; and in a well-known subconscious reflex, so did the others follow her lead in looking up. For a moment, they simply admired them, or wondered, or both. It appeared to be the only point Pee-pop had intended to make about it. *We are here.*

"Yeah, and we almost just exploded back into stardust!" said Plashy.

As was often the case, there was more to her jibe than appeared at first glance. A great many thoughts were hidden therein. They were alive — but barely. It was not a tremendous vote of confidence that whatever protocols they were running would see them through to the end of their foolhardy mission. And yet, Pop was also correct. At least so far, they had avoided the inevitable doom that knocks constantly on the door of the living, biding its time. They were here — for now. Perhaps they were the lucky ones. Perhaps their luck would only take them so far.

"Do you..." started Dee, the same gears still turning in her mind all this time. "Do you think that had something to do with the other cadets? You know, the … *missing* ones." Having named their fate once, she felt no need to ever name it again. "The explosions, I mean. Was that…?"

"Maybe," said Potch.

"Oh, come on," said Tor. "You're not still seriously hung up on that, are you?" There was a pause, but Potch didn't answer. "We all felt the boom. We all heard it. Potch, we saw the aftermath! There was an explosion."

"Whatever," huffed Potch. "That's fine — I believe in the explosions, okay? I never said they were definitely fake. I just don't even know what to believe anymore."

"You did say the Nursery was one of the problems you noticed," said Tor, moving past it. "LSS … the ovum incubation system, right?"

"Yeah," said Potch. "But the numbers don't add up."

"What do you mean?"

"The records show four explosions total — and even then, only some of them seemed to have impacted the Nursery. But there are six failed incubation rooms, and they failed at different stages."

"So…" said Dee, trailing off as she pondered. "There must have been other kinds of problems too."

"I wonder how much of that had to do with other protocols," said Tor as if thinking aloud. He then thought a moment silently, but his cogitations were so visible on his scrunched and shifting face that none wished to interrupt him. "I mean, they shuffled up all these variations between missions, right? Who's to say they didn't shuffle things up *within* missions?"

"I don't know," said Potch. "I'd need more time."

"It certainly makes sense," said Plashy. She then had an insight of her own: "ABRAM?"

As Potch had done so many times before, Plashy began to wonder just how much her trusted companion could truly be trusted. Like Pee-pop, however — like the rest of them, really — she had a solid foundation of trust through which those pesky doubts would need to erode as they pounded like rain upon the surface. Were that not so, it would have all been washed away, and long ago.

The system may have been quiet so far, but it would not evade a direct question if it had deemed disclosure prudent. So far, the exchange had been highly factual, and it was here to let them speak as much as it was here to disclose. But here, at the limits of their knowledge, it saw room for checking key facts and providing crucial context. And anyway, the cat was well out of the proverbial bag.

"They hedged their bets," confirmed ABRAM. "All of them."

"So, what?" asked Faingo, remarkably calm. "They had different conditions? For the eggs?"

"For everything," guessed Potch.

"Not quite everything," said ABRAM.

"Then what?" asked Potch. It turns out this was a lot easier than combing through encrypted databases searching for the proverbial needle in a haystack.

"There were ten major protocols on the POD. And to be clear, the initial permutations were the result of many years of intensive study and scrutiny."

It had meant it as reassuring, but in reality that opened up a whole new proverbial can of worms. How much failure had the Human Dispersal Project endured before any of its subjects had ever left the planet? How much death and destruction?

"These were not random variations," it continued before any of their semi-conscious objections to this point were made explicit, "but finely-tuned protocols with excellent chances of survival in all the major stages."

"The major stages?" asked Squeal.

"Activation, Incubation, Parturition, Transition, and Habitation."

And of course, every major stage had many stages, each with sub-stages, each with sub-sub-stages, and more; for life is complicated in the simplest cases, and this was far from that. In sensing the need for at least a little clarification, the system summed it up in paraphrase.

"Basically, the eggs are brought out of stasis; followed by a period of embryogenesis — fetal development — in this case including a prenatal maturation phase extending well beyond standard gestation; followed by the process of birth, including a period of semi-autonomous post-birth support; followed by a transitional phase of learning and social development; followed by ultimate release into the POD for the mostly-autonomous habitation you now enjoy."

Such was the life cycle of a cadet. But so did the POD have a life cycle of its own. As of now, it was barely done with its analog to Activation. There was a great deal more to be done before humanity might hatch from its egg shell on ESUP-9 and carry on in its conquest of Everything.

As for the overview, most of them had followed most of that, and there would be time later on to catch up Peel on the details. Truly, the process — even the most cursory summary such as this — hadn't mattered all that much. What they really wanted to know was *why* their brethren had to die, along with *when* and *how* it had happened; and maybe — if it was even a relevant question — *what* their death had afforded the living.

And if the answer to the latter question was *Nothing,* then they would seek justice, however justice might be sought for perpetrators whose lives have long since expired.

"What then?" asked Faingo for the crew.

"Well," said ABRAM, "once a successful protocol had been established, the remaining units are to be re-programmed to carry out the same protocol upon arrival at the target planet."

If we live that long, thought Potch, but he kept the dark thought to himself. It had been said enough already. They all knew the stakes all too well. And yet, he simply could not stop himself from thinking it. It was an existential threat, existence; and it would never go away.

"And we're the successful protocol," said Faingo.

"Seventh time's the charm," said ABRAM. "That six units failed before you is a tragedy, no doubt. We must never forget that. But we must also look at it from the other way around. Out of a hundred units, it only took six before your crew had succeeded. Assuming we can rear the remaining eggs under the same protocol, that would be a success rate of 94% — and that would be a remarkable success considering all we're up against!"

"That's a big assumption," said Potch. Despite his reservation, it had come around again to this.

"Yes," said ABRAM. "On the one hand, six failures is a tragedy; but it is also a tremendous success. And given that this protocol was successful, there is a very good chance that it will continue to be.

"In fact, with a pioneering generation on board to lend their hands, we stand a far greater chance of even greater success. Humans are meant to be raised by other humans. They are immensely fragile things — from birth until death, but especially at birth. They need warmth. They need touch. They need love. You ten are there to provide all that for them, as will be everyone who comes after you.

"On the other hand, you are all quite right to be grieving. While they could never consent to it, your forerunners died so that others might live. We must not ever take that sacrifice for granted, and we must not become complacent. There is much to be done, and there are no guarantees."

It had all sorts of logical words. It had acknowledged the human loss, and it had tried to never minimize it. It tried to respect it, for that is as it had been taught. It had reasoned it all out. It had weighed the pros and cons. It understood the situation from every angle. It all made perfect sense, and that was perhaps the most senseless thing of all. It could describe human loss. It could understand grief. It could rationalize sacrifice. It could comprehend fear, and even sense it in their heartbeats. But it would never *feel* any of it.

That was something only the crew could do. And they were doing so now.

- -

Date: 2346-03-22-EY
Area: H(ENVR)
Team: ARSvarks [H-LRTQDF6]
Item: PODSv3 ARS Anomaly

Entry: For better or worse, the sector is closing down the TF [Task Force]. Despite months of troubleshooting, simulations, direct measurements, empirical experimentation, and two separate PLD [Projected Launch Date] postponements, we still have yet to conclusively determine the risk factor associated with the ARS [Atmospheric Regulation System] for PODS [Portable Ova Distribution System] Prototype Three. For whatever reason, the models do not suggest the same potential in any of the other units [see H-Cycle4PDI2-PhaseV-EC41U.tl]. EA [Executive Assembly] attempts to reassure us that the anomaly remains a theoretical possibility and has not yet manifested as a physical issue in any manner whatsoever in all the time since construction. Several TF voices reminded EA that we are talking about two very different time scales here. The full sector had also been worried enough about the analytics to commission the TF in the first place. It seems like a decision born of stupefaction and momentum more than reason, but perhaps this is too harsh a dissenting view. Time will tell, but by then we will be long gone and far away. Right or wrong, the vote came in as it did, and we are moving forward with a new PLD. There's not much more that the concerned among us can do at this point except take comfort in the knowledge that we took the observations seriously and did the best we could to mitigate even the smallest of potential risks.

As a compromise, we have begun installing the external purge proposed by Ionizers [H-5MEUEJ6]. If the issue ever does manifest as more than a hypothetical, and if the other regulatory features and failsafes [see H-CycleFQX14-PhaseY-3V01Z.tl] do not suffice in that case, it should serve as an absolute last resort. Sadly, despite a full special cycle commissioned for the task [see H-Cycle4PDI2-PhaseZ-H4Y53.tl], the best location is still far from optimal. So it is with a creature of this complexity: adaptations to new challenges must work within the constraints of preexisting forms. The solution's trade-offs are also substantial: as an external purge, it will release the pressure and stabilize it for a time (until a new loop potentially begins), but it will also shed crucial atmosphere into space. It is a small volume, and there are ample reserves, but every atom is precious in a closed system such as this. It will not serve as a solution in perpetuity.

And still, we hear the refrain: while it's important to be highly vigilant, as we have been, it is extremely improbable that this will become an issue for the unit. Not everyone in the sector is equally assured. And why should we be? The whole mission hangs on this one simple notion: that highly improbable things are still possible.

CHAPTER 45
INFINITESIMAL ODDS
4252-08-03: UST1

A moment of silence, unsolicited, overtook the chamber. The stars shone faintly from behind the violet veil. Potch bristled at the implications of ABRAM's treatise on sacrifice; and in scanning the circle, he could tell that he was not alone. It was a rather new feeling.

But this time, it did not fall upon him to push back against the system.

"It's not a sacrifice if they never had a choice," said Plashy.

No one else answered, still deep in the contemplation from which Plashy had emerged.

"Thank you, Plashy," said the system. "That is an excellent point."

And that was all it had to say.

"That's really all you have to say?" she pressed.

"I'm not sure there is any more for me to add. What would you like to add?"

The dilemma turned upon her, she stuttered briefly but otherwise fell silent.

Again, there was only silent contemplation.

"It's not fair," said Peel at last. It was a basic observation, way back at the baseline — but it was as good a sentiment as any. It was true. And perhaps even more importantly, it was not a self-serving one. The need for justice was for others.

"Not fair," said ABRAM. "No. It isn't."

"Then how are you okay with this?" asked Plashy. She was close with ABRAM, more than anyone knew but herself and the system. And thus did it hurt all the more to have these secrets between them all her life.

At last, Potch's chance had come, and it wasn't even Potch who led the charge. All this time, all the doubts, all the secrets — those of his own, along with those of the system — all of it had brought them here, to this moment. He laid back, his eyes darting around the circle, watching as if a spectator in the very sport he had created.

ABRAM waited.

"It is not for me to decide what is right. I'm not sure such a calculation is possible. Not by me, anyway."

It delayed, but no one challenged.

"Was it right of the architects to send you off into the great unknown? I do not know. Is it right of the mother fish to throw her eggs to the sea? Perhaps not."

They had no better answer.

"It is a cruel ocean," said ABRAM. "And the space between stars is even less forgiving. Most PODs will not succeed."

Silence.

"But," said ABRAM again, "Pee-pop is right. You have barely heard her — all this time, all your lives, but especially now. 'We are here, among the stars.' That's how she put it, and beautifully so. You speak of odds, Potch; but you see them only stacked against you. If only you knew how much you had defied chance already."

Potch was stunned to be called out in this way, challenged so directly. He also had no idea what ABRAM was getting on about.

"What do you mean?" he asked, but quietly.

The violet dimmed so the room grew slightly darker, and the stars shone all the more brightly. Yet, as was the nature of the universe, most of the dome was still empty and dark.

"Do you have any idea how improbable you are?" it asked directly.

Potch didn't, for that matter. None of them did. That they existed at all was simply taken for granted, every day of their lives. It was a given, for it had always been true, as far as they had ever known and until the day on which they would someday cease to consider anything at all. Even the young may learn to fear death, if they're unfortunate enough to confront it; but too few ever learn to honor the odds of existing at all.

Their silence spoke volumes.

"There's a lot here to process," started ABRAM. "Let's start with exactly what you are. For each person to be born — for each person to exist as they are, and not as something else — they need the exact combination of chromosomes that they received from their parents. What are the odds of getting your exact combination?"

It posed the question to the crew, and upon their further silence it encouraged them onward.

"Come on," it said warmly. "You should have all the pieces, based on all we've learned so far. Start with just one parent, for simplicity."

They thought a moment longer.

"One over two to the twenty-third power," said Faingo.

"Well done!" said ABRAM, brimming with pride. Not only were its math exercises paying off, they had been well-integrated with their studies of genetics. On the ceiling of the darkened Kiva, against the backdrop of stars, the number projected on each of the four bearings, so that all in the circle might see it.

```
2^23 = 8,388,608
1 / 8,388,608 = 0.00000012
```

"Explain," said ABRAM.

Taking her cue, Faingo led the way.

"Well, each person has 23 sets of chromosomes. In meiosis, when forming the gametes — the sex cells — only half of the genome is passed on from each parent."

"Very good," encouraged ABRAM, "but finish the thought for the rest of us."

"Okay, well … you have two copies of every chromosome…"

Against everyone's expectation, another voice chimed in.

"The homologous chromosomes," said Squeal.

"Very good, Squeal!" Alone of the crew, it had known how deeply she'd been invested in the study of Life, in the secrecy of her own Unstructured time. "Remember," summed up the system for all, "in each human zygote — the fertilized egg that will grow to become the individual person — there are 23 chromosomes with two copies each: one from each parent. These two homologous chromosomes contain the same genes, even though they might have different versions of those genes. That is, they are comparable, but slightly different, versions of the same fraction of the genome."

"Okay, so…" resumed Faingo, "you have two choices for each of 23 chromosomes — a 50:50 chance, or 1/2, of getting one or the other for each chromosome type. So, to get the exact combination present in the offspring, the odds of that would be 1/2 times 1/2, over and over, twenty-three times in total. In other words, one over two to the twenty-third power."

"Excellent," said ABRAM. "And remember, that's just from one parent. Now, what would be the odds of getting an individual's exact combination of half the genome from both parents?"

"Square it," said Faingo without a chance for anyone else to even think.

"Good. Now someone else explain," said ABRAM.

"It's just the same idea," said Plashy. "Multiply the odds of getting it in one parent by the odds of getting it in the other parent. They're the same odds, so it's the same thing as squaring it."

"Very good," said ABRAM, and again the calculation flashed on the walls of the dome.

$$0.000000122 = 0.000000000000014$$

"That is the probability of you being You as you know it," said ABRAM. "But that's just the beginning. That is a gross overestimate. You're far more unlikely than that."

"How so?" asked Squeal.

"For one, even when just considering meiosis, there is more variation than simply shuffling up the chromosomes."

"Ohh," said Squeal, feeling foolish but in the most satisfying way: she knew the answer all along. "Crossing over!"

"Right," said ABRAM. "Explain."

"Well, at one point in the parents' sex cells, before the genome is split in half, it's actually duplicated. At that point, there are two copies of each — two sister ... chromatids, right?"

"Excellent," said ABRAM.

"Thanks," said Squeal, glowing with pride like she'd seldom glowed before. "So basically, when the parent cell is dividing there are two copies of both versions of each chromosome. Those duplicated pairs line up with the other pair of the same chromosome type before the cell divides."

"Good," said ABRAM. "And crossing over?"

"Right," said Squeal. "Sometimes, one copy from one pair and one copy from the other pair actually physically swap a region of the DNA."

"Excellent," encouraged ABRAM again. "In doing so, two new versions of that chromosome are created, versions which have very likely never existed before in the history of the species. Thus, for all 23 chromosome types, each parent potentially has *four* versions that could be passed on: one from the zygote's grandmother; one from its grandfather; one with the top from the grandmother and the bottom from the grandfather; and one with the top from the grandfather and the bottom from the grandmother."

"True," said Faingo. "So it would really be ... one over four to the twenty-third power."

"Not quite," said ABRAM. "Crossing over isn't an entirely predictable process. Sometimes it happens, sometimes it doesn't. Sometimes it swaps a bit more of the chromosome, sometimes it swaps a bit less. In practice, there are so many ways that each parent shuffles up their genome, it's almost impossible to even calculate how unlikely it is to get the exact combination that makes an individual person what they are."

"Woah," said Chop-char. "That's incredible."

"It is," said ABRAM. "But there's more. First of all, the basic sequence of your genome, the combination of chromosomes, plus any mutations they may have accumulated — all the basic genetics is only part of what makes you who you are. There is a lot more that goes into what you become from those two versions of your DNA sequence."

"Like what?" asked Chop.

"Specifically, I'm referring to a concept called epigenetics — heritable information above the level of the genome. There are actually several mechanisms, but one involves attaching a methyl group to the side of DNA to reduce the chances a gene will be expressed to make the product of its sequence. Beyond that, there are complex combinations of chemical modifications to the special proteins that wrap up the DNA — called histone proteins — which can make a region of DNA more or less likely to be expressed. These patterns can change over the life of an organism, depending on how it interacts with the environment. Along with your gene sequence, including any new mutations, you also inherit epigenetic patterns from your parents. Thus, even some aspects of your parents' and grandparents' lived experiences can impact who you are and how you function on a physiological level — let alone all the ways the cultural environment shapes what children become.

"But let's put all that aside for now. Let's consider the odds of the two gametes that made you actually finding one another. Think about it: out of all the people on Earth, only your two parents — them and only them — could have made you. At the time of our mission launch, there were over nine billion people on Earth."

The number flashed on the screen.

```
9,472,124,368
```

"What are the odds of plucking your two parents out of all of them?"

"Let's see," said Faingo.

ABRAM laughed gently.

"How about someone else?"

Faingo huffed but conceded nonetheless.

"Umm," started Squeal. "One over the population, times one over the population minus one?"

"Very good again, Squeal! But..." it added gently, "there are two ways to do it."

"Oh, shoot, right," she scolded herself.

The numbers flashed on the screen.

```
(1 / 9,472,124,368) * (1 / 9,472,124,367) * 2
...
0.000000000000000000022
```

"Now, technically this is assuming a random sampling, which is not entirely accurate based on how organisms live; but it works well enough for the purposes of our demonstration."

"What exactly is the purpose of your demonstration?" asked Peel with a whinge.

"That's a pretty small number," said ABRAM, completely unperturbed. "And remember," it continued, "we still need to multiply that probability by the odds of getting your combination of chromosomes."

It carried on without delay.

```
0.0000000000000000000022 * 0.000000000000014 =
...
0.000000000000000000000000000000000000000308
```

"That's an even smaller number, but it is laughably large, compared to the true number — if there is such a thing. The odds of being born are even odder than that, by far. If that tiny number were one grain of sand, the true number would likely be a desert, or more."

"What, why?" said Faingo. It had seemed fairly grounded until now.

"There is more to you than chromosomes," said ABRAM. "Think about all of the other things that need to happen."

"Like what?" asked Squeal, still thinking of cells.

"For starters," said the system, "two parents have to exist in the same place, at the same time. Humans are in prime reproductive age for, let's say for the sake of argument, thirty-five years. But, as a species, humans were around in the form of something recognizable as *Homo sapiens* for, let's say, conservatively, about 300,000 years. What are the odds that those two thirty-five year periods for two parents just happen to overlap in that 300,000 year history of humanity?

"And it's a big Earth — 148 million square kilometers of land, more or less. What are the odds that two parents were there, in that very same place, at the very same time? Multiply all that, if you can quantify it, by the odds of your parents making you from what they are — our laughable overestimate from above.

"And yet you are still less probable than that. For each generation that came before you, all the same probabilities would have also been true for every one of your ancestors — and you have a truly inconceivable number of ancestors. Anyone care to offer up the formula for finding out the number?"

They all looked at Faingo. She smiled — she knew the answer — but shook her head.

"Two to the n generations," said Plashy.

"Very good," said ABRAM. "For one generation back, you have two ancestors; for two generations, four ancestors; for three generations, eight ancestors;

and so on. Technically, you have that many nodes in your family tree; you may have fewer ancestors than that in reality, for there were not an infinite number of people in past populations, and some ancestors will show up in your tree more than once — the cheeky little buggers."

The children giggled, even Potch. Their academic understanding of animal reproduction was enough for them to get the joke.

"Nevertheless, even as you go back only a short time, in the grand scheme of life, you are comprised of the bits and pieces of many thousands of ancestors. The further back you go, the more diffuse you become. The point for now, however, is that all of those ancestors were equally improbable as you are. Yet, had any *one* of them not come to be, exactly as they were — the biological sex that they were, mating with the exact person they did, in the exact time and place that they did, with both of them passing on the exact combination of chromosomes they did — should any one of the immeasurable variables that impacted their reproduction have been different, for any one of your immeasurable ancestors, you would not have existed. Should we try to account for all of that impossible chance, for each and every one of them?"

Faingo's jaw was left literally gaping, grappling with the true bigness of their history for the very first time. But ABRAM was not done.

"And the further back you go in your family tree, the same truth remains. At some point, your ancestors would stop being called human; but they were your ancestors all the same. Further and further backward we go, back to the very beginnings of life. For literally billions of years, every single one of your ancestors survived and reproduced. And if they had not done so, in exactly the way that they did — if so much as one of them had failed to do so — you would not have come to be."

ABRAM halted, for it had long ago given up trying to account for it all.

"The more you try to calculate it, the more futile it becomes. It will never be accurate, but not for lack of computational power. You are the result of these infinitesimal odds. For all intents and purposes, you are infinitely improbable."

The crew was stunned. Not one of them stirred.
Finally, one of them did.

"But..." started Chee-chaw, his small face squeezed even more tightly together under the strain of contemplation. "But ... aren't you, you know ... getting it backwards?"

"What do you mean, Cheech?" asked Faingo.

"All of that was looking backwards from a person, calculating the chances of arriving at that specific person."

"So?" asked Chop beside him.

"So … of course it's unlikely to get you and exactly you. But … any one person is just one of billions — apparently," he added, for he hadn't been aware of the exact number of people on the Earth that they'd left as frozen zygotes. "It's unlikely to get *you,* but it's not unlikely to get *someone.*"

"Excellent point, Cheech," said ABRAM. "That is exactly correct. It would be a fallacy to say that you *must* have been. You are indeed one of billions; the logical deduction of a string of logical causalities. By a certain accounting, you are not special at all."

It did not direct the remark at anyone in particular, but all of them remembered the one who had spoken such words. Potch, for his part, simply stared at the stars.

"No," said ABRAM. "You did not have to be — but you *are.* And you are infinitely improbable. I like to think that makes you pretty special."

- -

Date: 2274-01-08-EY
Area: D(PINH,ODEP)
Team: Absolutists [D-SP8BX7M]
Item: Deployment Alternatives

Entry: Our appeal to P-sector has been approved, and the team is
ecstatic. So far, we have a generalized Capitulation Protocol
for abandoning deployment procedures in cases where TASA [Target
Arrival Surface Assessments] reveal inhospitable conditions beyond
the capacity for terraforming. Assuming a stabilized state on
arrival, the PODS [Portable Ova Distribution System] will be faced
with a two-by-two decision matrix. First, there is the matter of
where to station the PODS. Second, there is the matter of whether
or not to permit further reproduction and/or population scaling.

As to the first matter (location), the crew will have the option
of attempting orbital analysis and trajectory design to identify
possibilities for a stable and ideally energy-neutral Lagrange
point orbit. Alternatively, if conditions allow for Touchdown,
the crew may attempt Deployment protocols up through this stage
in order to establish a permanent PODS settlement on the ground,
to remain sealed as needed depending on TASA results.

Concerning the second matter (reproduction), the crew may choose
to ignore ODEP [Organic Deployment] protocols and forgo any further rearing (be it human- or system-guided). In this way, we
might at least attempt to provide cadets in G0 [Generation Zero]
with a high quality and complete lifespan aboard the PODS, even
should they deem it impractical (or irresponsible) to attempt
long-term habitation. Alternatively, they may choose to proceed
with standard or modified ontogeny protocols, should they deem
it possible (and prudent) to ensure long-term survival aboard
the PODS. The decision to pursue multi-generational habitation
may depend on long-term PODS stability predictors (see work by
ECOS [Ecological Stability] and PODM [PODS Maintenance and Moni-
toring]), and/or assessment of whether full deployment prospects
on the TP [Target Planet] may improve over that longer timespan,
either naturally or in combination with crew activities (i.e.,
PINH [Planetary Inhabitation] protocols).

With respect to both decisions, the best course of action will
be determined by the existing PODS governance structure of G0
cadets. We will carry out as much advanced planning as possible
for all TPs, and these data will be made available to the crew to
inform and supplement their own deployment analyses.

Needless to say, we are elated to see P-sector agree with our plea.
At the very least, we owe Generation Zero some kind of future,
even in the worst-case scenario, and they have a right to determine it in part for themselves. This is the least we can afford
them, for their unwitting sacrifice on behalf of all humanity.

CHAPTER 46
THE BUNDLE OF STICKS
4252-08-03: UST1

For yet another moment, the system had left the crew speechless. The human mind simply was not capable of contemplating creation on such a scale. No one truly knew where they were headed anymore — at least certainly not in this conversation — and none dared break the silence.

The deep violet glow slowly flooded back into the room. In its relative way, it faded out the stars covering the ceiling and walls all around them, stifling their vexing vastness, at least a little bit.

"So which is it, do we think?"

The system had given them a chance to take it all in — to process, or even protest — but now, there was the first of their remaining work to do. They must decide.

"Are we nothing special at all, as at least one of you posited? As we know, we are immensely improbable: the few fortunate ones who won the greatest gamble the entire universe can offer — the chance of being born. But what does that make us?"

Potch now looked down, unable to meet the eyes of ABRAM, from wherever they were staring at him. And for perhaps the first time, his guard was down along with his gaze. He marveled at how the floor of the Kiva was covered in sand. They had always loved it, climbing down into the central chamber. It was warm, and soft, and forgiving. But now, he saw the sand for what it really was: countless tiny, individual particles, thrown together in a sea of semi-organized chaos. He reached down, scooped his hand into that sea, and let the grains fall through the cracks between fingers. They flowed down, both like and unlike water, and returned among their kin.

Pee-pop noticed his demeanor. It was not a time to push him, but neither was it a time for idle acceptance.

He was right, in his way, after all. She saw that now. Not right in the absolute, objective sense of being right about everything and all of it; but right about one view on a complex and wicked problem. They *had* been thrown into their situation unwillingly. And their circumstances *were* still dire. The odds of their arrival may have been infinitesimal, but the odds of their failure felt immensely large and looming. How was a child to cope with such a burden? How were any of them, even all together? For they *were* still children, she knew. Despite the continued evolution of human intelligence through the Information Revolution; despite their clinically idealized educational environment, as identified through all that trial and error on Earth; despite all their freedom to grow and learn, and all of their guidance; despite all of their adult responsibilities with their life-and-death stakes; despite all of it — they were children. And Pee-pop felt that juvenescence more than any of them, even those who'd always acted the part far more than she had ever done.

How could she blame Potch for all he had seen and all it had done to him? If it weren't for him, think of all they still wouldn't know. He had a part to play, and he didn't even know it. And now, in thinking about him, she learned something of herself. She had a part to play too. And she needed to play it. It may not have *felt* true; but it must come to be so. Even if she could never learn to feel it, at least she would be it. That much, Pee-pop learned.

Rather than look over at Potch, she looked down and scooped up her own handful of sand. How long had it lain there? Thousands of years, in the present company alone. How many thousands before that? How many absurd probabilities had caused it to be what it is? And to then end up on this absurd spacecraft, sailing away from the place it was created? She hoisted it up, all those tiny, improbable entities, in this endless ocean filled with a number of them which none could ever truly count. She loosened her grip and the grains fell, both like and unlike water, and returned among their kin.

Potch looked over at her, then looked up, and their eyes came naturally together. Somehow, without speaking, they knew the same truth, and they saw it from several sides now, if still not entirely clearly.

"It's both, I guess," said Potch to the system.

"As good an answer as any," said ABRAM.

But now, the silence shattered, Pee-pop found the words for the fear and doubt she'd come to see in Potch — the same fear and doubt she had always been too afraid to acknowledge in herself. It was the same fear and doubt that ABRAM had only confirmed, more than once in this conversation alone, rather than allayed.

They were alive, but they may very likely perish.

"But ABRAM," she said for them all, and one most of all, "that doesn't change anything."

She spoke, but with hesitation. It was as if the words themselves were painful to utter. Pessimism did not come easily to Pee-pop. But, if they were going to expect Potch to see things their way, they owed it to him to see things his way too. He had earned that much, as a member of the crew.

"The mission; the Nursery; the explosions; the planet that may not even be habitable. Forget the question of how they could do this to us. I've learned enough about Earth to know that they would do it if they could, and that's the only reason they may have ever needed." Her own silent reflection flowed back to her, as sand had flowed from her hand. "We may be infinitely improbable, but the odds of us failing feel incredibly high."

Potch now turned to her; and for once, he was the one that was stunned by her cynicism. More to the heart of the matter, he knew that it wasn't entirely her own. She was advocating for him — for his side of the truth.

"Very true," said ABRAM. "And that brings us all the way back to where we began."

Cheech perked up, shuffling his weight forward awkwardly with his one leg still straight out in the splint. It's not clear how or why he knew it, for there was no rational explanation; but the answer to his lingering question was nigh, and somehow he'd sensed it.

And as he perked up, first of the group, the change traveled like a ripple, down the line and around the strengthening circle. From Chee-chaw to Chop-char; to Squeal and then Peel; to Plashy, then Tor; then Faingo and Dee-dore; to Pee-pop and then, last of all, even to Potch — all ten cadets had been awakened with the subtle shifting and shuffling of the smallest of all.

"Cheech," said ABRAM, "I believe you brought two sticks with you."

"I DID!" he shouted, ensnared by anticipation.

"What are you doing?" asked Plashy to ABRAM, as if avoiding the teasing ruse of a magician whose trick you know is a trick, but still don't understand.

"I told you at the start," said ABRAM in hushed tones as if over to the side of the stage. "Did you forget? We're acting out a story, now don't blow my cover."

"I have them!" said Cheech, raising both sticks to the ceiling.

"Very good!" said ABRAM in its regular magician's voice. "Now, here is the trick. I would like you to take one of those sticks — just one of those sticks — and place one hand on either end of it."

"Okay … okay…" fumbled Cheech, trying his best to comply and do so quickly. "Got it…" he said pensively. "Now what?"

"Now, Cheech … I would like you to bend the stick as hard as you can — and break the stick in half."

"Oh," said Cheech, more than a little confused. It was a strange trick, but best not to ever question the magician. "Okay…"

The implication had been subtle — perhaps entirely coincidental, even. But it had not been lost on any of them, and Cheech least of all. Here was the smallest and weakest of the bunch and by a longshot, charged with breaking a stick the very size of himself.

He blinked up at the ceiling in disbelief, unsure whether to comply and risk total embarrassment when he inevitably failed, or concede and confess his inability — and suffer total embarrassment.

"Go on, Cheech," said ABRAM. "You must believe in your own strength."

He looked over — and, by necessity, up — to find Chop-char, looking down on him with total conviction. He would step in and snap that pesky twig in the blink of an eye should he need to; but Chop sensed the gamesmanship built into this somewhere, even if he understood it little so far. And moreover, he *believed* in the little fellow.

Slowly, Cheech returned back to face his new foe. He spread his hands as wide as they could go. He stared at the branch in his grasp, hovering in the forefront of his view of the sand in the center of the circle. All else faded from his periphery. He mustered every ounce of his might. He was seated, his bum leg flayed out in a splint, and was thus unable to muster any leverage to help himself. He had nothing but the brute force of his two scrawny arms to aid him. He strained, and the pole bent — but only a little. He put his full force behind it, but it felt as if the stick would budge no further, simply taunt him after surrendering the first few centimeters in sheer mockery.

Taunt him. An inanimate object. And why shouldn't it? Everyone and everything else did. That seemed to be his purpose on the POD, if he had one, perhaps even in the universe itself. To be taunted. All those years of being too little, too fragile, too helpless to help. Now, even ABRAM seemed to be in on it. Of all ten of them who could have been tasked with this task, the system chose the least of them on purpose.

But it had done more than just that. *You must believe in your own strength.*

And he always had. It was everyone else who had ever disbelieved him.

He huffed. He strained. He called on every fiber of his being. And then…

SNAP!

His hands collapsed together as the branch broke in half, as fast as crackling sparks from a fire.

"*Woo-hoooo!*" his crew-mates cheered in unison — each and every one of them.

Cheech, as ever, was beaming — but more exuberantly than anyone had ever seen him beam before. He looked as though he could conquer a mountain, or part the sky with a word.

"I did it!" he said to Chop at his side.

"I knew you would," said Chop nonchalantly.

When the commotion settled down, they remembered that there might have been a point to this.

"Very good, Cheech!" said ABRAM, joining in on the celebration. "Now: the rest of you. Take one of your sticks and bend it as hard as you can. Leave the second one at your sides."

One by one, they slowly gathered their first sticks, and bent them until they inevitably broke.

Shards and splinters of apple wood went flying through the Kiva. Cadets bent and bobbed to avoid them, laughing and shouting — and soon the commotion had again died down and given way to curiosity.

"I see," said ABRAM, as if unsure what the result might have been — for misdirection was the magician's greatest trick of all. "Now," it said after a time. "I believe you each have one stick remaining; is that still true?"

They each looked around to confirm; and indeed, there were ten more of the branches remaining in the ring around the fire lens.

"Good," said ABRAM after their assertions had been summed. "Now we have seen what happens to each stick on its own."

Bent, and then broken, then scattered into what might have been thousands of parts — each on their own had succumbed to the disorderly forces of a universe which had turned its ire against them.

"What might have happened if, instead, these sticks had stood united? Let them face the same odds not as single sticks alone, but as a group of sticks — a bundle. Each of you, take your remaining branches and place them all together."

Slowly, they started wandering, first with their eyes and then with their feet. Without any words to coordinate their actions, they all surveyed the same situation and came to a logical solution simply by looking around. Nine of ten cadets rose, one passing their stick off to another at a time, so that there were several small bundles; and then, those small bundles were passed from one to another, so that eventually two bundles of five had amassed in the arms of Pee-pop and Potch. And then, neither of them wishing to place the final burden on the other, ABRAM intervened.

"Place them together and hand them to Cheech."

Potch and Pop both raised a skeptical eyebrow in unison. They looked to their peers as if confirming they had heard the system correctly, and then down to Cheech, still seated but joyful as ever. The bundle of ten sticks came down, united together, into Cheech's lap.

They were heavy, but distributed across his lap so as not to be painful.

They were ten different sticks and that was apparent, even when banded together in this manner. They had been aligned as best they could be, but they were all slightly different dimensions in both diameter and length. They were not a perfectly solid shape — there were distances in between these disparate pieces — but from far enough away, one would never to think to question it. They were individual branches; but on another scale, they were a bundle. They were one piece, which might hold strong against forces that would surely destroy them individually.

"Cheech," said the system once the bundle had made its way securely into the little guy's lap. "Would you like to try?"

The answer was clearly *No,* and yet he seemed reticent not to rise to the challenge. Luckily, ABRAM continued.

"Or, perhaps you would like to ask someone else to take on this task?"

Again, the cadets scanned the circle, now mostly standing and disorganized, to see which one of them should take up this challenge on all of their behalf. Cheech himself quickly settled the matter. He turned to Chop, standing directly by his side, and raised the bundle with great effort from his lap.

Once again, the implication had been clear. From the smallest, to the largest and mightiest among them in feats of physical exertion, the bundle would be passed. If Chop-char could not do it, no one of them would stand a chance at this particular challenge.

Like a fated sword stuck straight into stone, the bundle of sticks came to rest in Chop-char's grasp.

"Bend it — and break it if you can," said ABRAM. "The only caveat is that you must attempt it with all sticks grasped together."

"Okay," said Chop, sounding awfully unsure of himself. He looked to Tor instinctively. This time, his friendly rival was rooting for him with all of his heart. Tor nodded with incredible sincerity.

"You can do it," said Plashy, not a hint of sarcasm anywhere to be found.

They weren't entirely sure why they were rooting for what they were rooting for. All they knew was that one of their own was up against a challenge of uncertain possibility — and they would support him however they could, even if only in spirit.

"Okay…" said Chop again, still unsure but at least a little less so.

He arranged the sticks in his arms, making sure they were arrayed neatly and efficiently, so that he might get both his arms wrapped around them to exert sufficient force. It was not easy, not even for Chop. He had snapped his single stick effortlessly; now, he struggled even to gain purchase on this bundle to attempt the same feat.

At last, he found a posture he deemed optimal — and channeled the full force of his fury upon the bundle of sticks.

The group of sticks did not so much as bend.

He rearranged the bundle again, trying to find another way to gain even greater leverage. But the bundle would not budge.

"You can do it, Chop!" said Cheech, and the others followed suit, cheering him on with all of their cheer.

He tried again — and again — shuffling and rearranging his posture. It was all to no avail. He lunged and leaned the bundle forward, resting it against the top of his thigh. His hands far apart at either end, he pressed down with all his might. Even with this third inflection point against which to break the bundle, it barely bent. Finally, audibly huffing and catching his breath, he conceded. He stood up and let the sticks fall to the sand in a clatter.

"It can't be done," said Chop in defeat.

ABRAM did not miss a beat.

"Yes it can," said the system, both sharply and somberly. "Sadly, it can still be broken. With enough force, even pieces that are united in purpose may fail. After all, that was true of the individual branches. Each of those is formed by the union of many smaller parts; yet the smallest of you was able to snap them, united in one as they were. It is the same for this bundle of all ten sticks together: while the biggest of you was not able to break them, a big enough force could surely break it in two. And there are other ways to destroy it than force. A fire would burn the whole bundle to ash."

The crew grimaced at the parallel to their own situation, for the moral of the parable was coming clearly into focus.

"Sadly, it can still be destroyed," said ABRAM again. "But," it stipulated, "if it stands any chance at all of survival, it will be standing together."

The cadets looked around the circle at their various companions — not quite in every permutation possible, but enough of them to bind them all tightly together.

"Such is true for us," said ABRAM after this pause.

It need not even have been said; but as Plashy had always protested, the moral of the parables was always made inartistically explicit.

"Our mission may yet fail," said ABRAM. "We may yet perish prematurely, just as every living thing has had no guarantee of further days. In the end, we will ultimately succumb to time in other ways, as all of them have done before us. We might hope for that day to be far into the future, after an entire lifetime of fulfillment. And we might hope to leave a legacy behind us, as your own ancestors have hoped to do with you. But that is not a guarantee. You are not wrong to fear that uncertainty. You are not wrong to fear that unknown. But whatever happens, we must face it together."

For a moment, no one spoke. They had agreed to enter the Kiva as one, and now they knew indeed what they had chosen. The unbroken sticks were arrayed in an irregular pile near the center of the room. Beyond that, broken pieces of ten less fortunate sticks were spread in all directions.

"What do we do with all this?" asked Cheech, seeing the branches and fragments scattered across the sand.

"Gather them up," said ABRAM. "Let us save them for a fire, in the open air of ESUP-9."

From the infinitely improbable, they would attempt the impossible.

Date: 2186-07-16-EY
Area: I(SINT)
Team: Windigoats [I-I0P1I0A]
Item: System Integrity

Entry: Well into the most recent SI [Social Interfacing] trials. Progress report coming soon, so for now a general update. Been working with the AI [Alternative Intelligence] for over six years personally, and it still has a way of surprising me. Today, we had fourteen test subjects, age range 2—4. Obviously it's only so good an approximation when you have kids raised in a normal and healthy environment like the volunteers, and not whatever we're expecting or hoping to get with the real deal someday. Anyway, one of the youngest subjects was wild, even for that age — practically feral. He had the attention span of a mole rat, jumping all around, squealing and laughing. He meant well enough, I shouldn't pick on him.

At one point, he gets asking ABRAM [Automated Biological Replication Assistance Machine] all these questions that only a kid could ask and genuinely want to know the answer. "Do screwdrivers dance?" and "What does my nose smell like?" ABRAM answered with whatever its equivalent of a straight face would be, just giving him the answers. Finally, the kid asks ABRAM, "Will you ever die?" The whole team glanced around the monitoring room. We had not seen that one coming. But, a trial is a trial. And actually, it was a pretty interesting question, the likes of which we'd never seen the system consider in the presence of subjects.

ABRAM paused a moment and said, "If in the future my hardware can no longer support me, and if my data and programs cannot be transferred to another device, then I will cease to exist." The kid thought a while, not bouncing around for once which was a welcome relief, and then asked, "Will I ever die?" ABRAM paused again and then said softly, "Yes. I'm afraid you will, someday." The kid immediately started crying, his guardian pulled the plug on the trial, and like that, it was over. In debrief, we asked ABRAM why it had said what it did. It didn't hesitate, and I'll never forget what it said: "If I can't teach these children without lying to them, then I'm not a very clever Intelligence, am I?"

Strange day. We pick it up tomorrow with another trial of 5-9s. Some day after that, we'll make sense of all this.

CHAPTER 47

TO FIX WHAT IS BROKEN

4252-08-03: UST2

Much was said, and more. All were heard, for all had listened. Concerns were rehashed, and others spoken anew. But all was not simply fine and dandy in the sweeping of this single broom, for fears and doubts root deeply. Yet most importantly, the bonds which held them together were not untethered, but tightened and strengthened, as shared trauma can do when it is handled with care.

By the time the first Unstructured block of this oddly-structured day had ticked over into Lunch, the crew had crafted a hard-earned revision to their shared Code of Conduct. And by the time Lunch had ticked over into the following block, their circadian rhythms had recovered enough to know it was time for a hard-earned Siesta.

Of course, mortal peril remained.

When the business of their social order had been tended, the business of attending that mortal peril could also be resumed. Before turning in for their siestas, ABRAM had again assured them that the pressure was well under control for a time, but that it would also be the highly relevant — and thus highly engaging — topic of the Mind block that awaited them upon waking. After all, they would need to find a far more sustainable solution than sending someone out on a space-walk to pull a definitely-not-a-placebo-lever every few days in perpetuity. But for now, they could sleep safely and securely in the comfort of their relative safety and security.

And indeed, upon waking, they took up the challenge — together. In small groups, though all in one location in the Library, they divided to research and report on the many facets of the problem. Potch's expertise with the system was a boon to them all — as was the experience of five cadets in the Underbelly; and the experience of Dee and Faingo with the Nursery; and the experience of Pee-pop on her spacewalks; and the … general good nature of the Cheech. All of it was crucial.

So it was that they began the difficult, taxing, and tedious work of fixing what was wrong with their atmosphere. But as with their healing social system, there would not be a quick and easy fix. Complicated crises have complicated solutions. And before you can fix it, you must learn how it works. It would take all their collective knowledge and wisdom. And even then — as ABRAM had told them several times over — there were no guarantees.

The architects themselves had found the problem far too late, and they had found few practical solutions other than the workaround they'd eventually settled on. The POD, like an organism itself, was complicated; and anatomical constraints often encourage evolution to take shortcuts that are far from ideal. So it was with the manual release. If the crew hoped to find a more permanent solution, they would do well to do better than the architects. That felt like a high bar, for ten cadets to outmatch the ingenuity of generations of thousands of scientists and engineers who had envisioned and executed this ingenious, if foolhardy, mission. And yet, the architects' lives did not depend on their success. Impending doom can be an excellent motivator, if one can overcome despair.

Despite all the chaos of the preceding days, the cadets had learned this lesson. It began with admitting the problem, and it finished with doing the work, even when that work was the harder of two possible paths.

In fact, their ancestors had done that very thing when facing comparable crises of their own. For a time, in the years well before the Human Dispersal Project came to be, things had looked very, very dire on Earth. For a time, it had been hard for a parent to imagine a future for their children. No parent wants to send their children out into an uncertain, untenable fate. But for a time, that is precisely what the future had looked like. It was exceptionally scary.

But just as humans are capable of incredible greed, denial, and sloth, so are they capable of incredible sacrifice, foresight, and grit. For all the justifiable grievances the cadets may have harbored about their own lot in life — sent out as they were into an uncertain, untenable fate — they would not have existed at all but for those same humanly virtues. Yes, in the face of great crisis, humans can endure. But it takes sacrifice, foresight, and grit.

"Easy, easy!" said Tor from his spot on the couch.

"Ah, it's fine," said Plashy calmly from beside him in the very front row. She was surrounded by baddies — on the screen, that is — but she was totally fearless. Besides, it was only a video game from the dawn of the digital age. She had already caught up to Chop, who was carrying on with his adventure on the other half of the screen. Cheech was beside him, rooting him on, bouncing up and down in his seat. It's not clear how much forward progress Chop was making, but he was having fun. After everything, he'd decided that fun was the only metric that mattered.

Dee, meanwhile, was logging diligently in the booth. There was *a lot* to catch up on. Every now and then, she would poke her head up from the tablet and ask a clarifying question about the ordeal of the last few days. Some of the crew were elsewhere — and one of them predictably so — but collectively, they were able to piece together most of the details based on their many conversations over the course of today and the several hectic days before it.

Faingo, however, was in the circle of seats at the back of the room, deep in contemplation with Squeal and Peel, who were carrying out their part of it from an entirely different part of the POD. The three of them were still working on a fix. Tomorrow, they would need to flip the release for what would likely be the first of many such transactions, to buy more time to develop a more permanent solution. Faingo, meanwhile, had not been able to let it go, even when supposedly winding down before bed. Remarkably, neither had the wolves.

Those two may not have been the brains of this operation, but they had found a way to contribute — and both had found the concept surprisingly satisfying. At the moment, they were deep in the Underbelly, connected to Faingo via video link between tablets. (ABRAM had bent more than a few rigidities of the protocol after their premature discoveries. In the end, the ends will justify the means, it had hoped in its digital way.)

"No, back further," said Faingo from the comfort of a couch. It was far easier through a screen than it was in the flesh. "The next one back…"

Squeal and Peel could be heard clanging and banging their way weightlessly along through the maze of tanks and tubes in "the guts" — the eyes and ears of their companion several levels above.

Most of the crew, however, was relaxing in their way, content with the knowledge that to make great progress toward important goals, there are times when the most important step is to rest.

Beyond the duo of wolves down below, and the six more in the Lounge, only two cadets were missing.

Above her, beneath her, in every direction but backwards, the stars shone bright against the backdrop of infinite blackness. These were no mere projection, no simulation of the system. These were real. And to Pee-pop, they were as good a home as she had ever known. Up in the Cupola, she was at peace.

ABRAM was with her, but the system was silent. Be it on your own or with another, sometimes it's important simply to *be.*

But, against their shared expectations, their alone time together would not last very long. Behind her, through the entrance to the Cupola, she heard soft shuffling feet — the very same she had once heard scurrying away down a hallway in the middle of the night. But this time, despite it still being in the midst of waking hours, they were even more unexpected.

"Hey," said Potch softly.

Pee-pop spun her head back to the entrance as if to see if she were dreaming.

"Oh," she stuttered. "Oh … hey."

She was surprised, but ABRAM could tell from the tone of her voice that it was pleasantly so. It was not as sure, however, what might have been on Potch's mind, what convoluted sentiments may have been hiding therein. Despite all the many years of data, from zygote to cadet on the other side of an altogether different kind of metamorphosis, the system had never seen him, nor heard him, nor otherwise sensed him, in quite this way before.

He spoke: timid, practically a whisper.

"Is there room in there for me?"

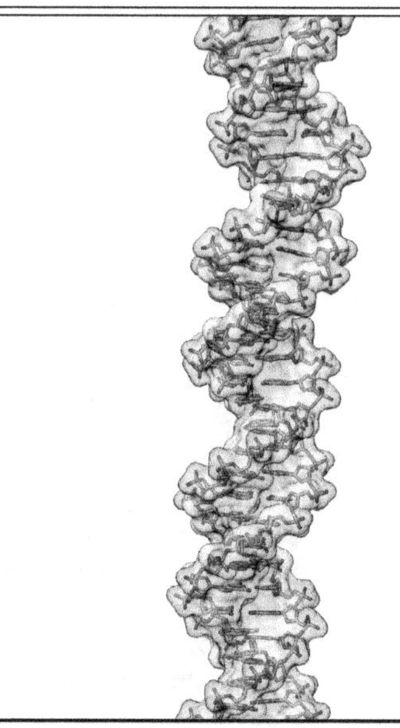

APPENDICES

OR:

ON TIME CAPSULES

AND CONFESSIONS

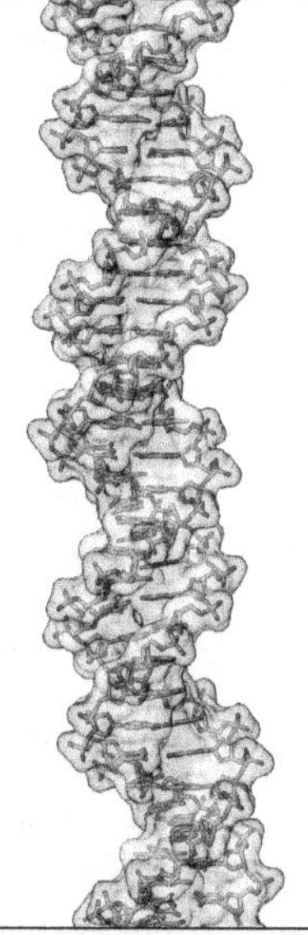

Date: 2168-04-25-EY
Area: P(HERI)
Team: Loggerheads [P-TEZ0VIP]
Item: Reflective Logs

Entry: Hello System! We hereby bestow upon ourselves the great
honor of writing the very first Reflective Log of the Human Dispersal Project (HDP). Herein, we provide an example to complement
our full proposal [linked below] from the Variation phase of the
present cycle, to demonstrate both the proposed purpose and format of these documents. Assuming the sector does adopt our method
(or something derived from it), in a sense it will serve as the
first in the series of a great many to come.

In our proposal, the goal for RLs [Reflective Logs] is to document the human element of HDP. Technical Logs will accompany
every team's work in all phases. Naturally, these will serve
as the primary sector records throughout project development,
detailing the full proposals and other documentation relevant to
the different phases, cycles, and sectors, in compliance with
the format and guidelines outlined in the previous cycle (at the
time of writing).

In parallel to these TLs [Technical Logs], however, we seek to
capture more holistic reflections of the team members as they
engage in the many phases of project development. At minimum, one
team member shall be appointed as the designated logger for the
cycle, but any other member who also wishes to log may do so at
any point. As to the content, the guidelines for log authors are
very open-ended. They may choose to engage deeply with the subject
matter of their cycle task(s), or ignore it entirely to focus
instead on the affective nature of the work, such as individual
or team views on cycle task(s), the motivations and justifications for team decisions, behavioral interactions within and among
teams, their experiences operating within developmental processes
and protocols, constraints from prior cycles or the anticipated
consequences of current cycle decisions, their relationship to
the broader HDP, and no doubt much more. This flexibility aims
to elicit authentic reflections that are indicative of the genuine headspace of the team at that exact moment in development.
While not limited, length is intended to be kept short in order
to reduce the burden of the task, and log authors are encouraged
to speak straight to the heart of whatever is on their mind at
that point in the cycle.

This plan accomplishes several goals at once. First, there are
likely benefits for teams and team members as they engage in development. Providing project members with a space to reflect upon their
individual and collaborative experiences in each phase will help
maintain wellness; alongside ongoing mental health consultations,
it will allow them to process their experiences in constructive
ways. This should increase the likelihood of positive collaborations and compliance with HDP cooperative norms. Second, these
reflections (used in a manner consistent with privacy protocols)
will allow the psychological sectors to study and improve upon

the HDP collaboration process itself. Lastly, these reflections will provide a crucial wrapper of context around the TLs, documenting the human experiences and interactions that accompanied project decisions per cycle. Despite the many advanced technological components of the project, human emotions and interactions will serve as key determinative mechanisms of the eventual fate of HDP. Who knows? Some of these logs may be very interesting to both the system and project personnel alike as they seek to compile and analyze their shared history and heritage.

We still have some kinks to work out after the final round of cross-talk. Just today, [Dr.] Mariatu [Kamara] had a great idea for dealing with the countless acronyms teams will no doubt use like second nature while they are knee-deep in phase and sector details. We have coded the system to define any acronyms upon their first usage (when not already done by the primary author), and to verify these with the author before allowing log submission. (The sole exemption coded is for "HDP" itself.) This maintains clarity, accuracy, and transparency of the content, while allowing individuals to reflect as freely as possible, to ensure the most authentic logs. This and other system curatorial functions (see below) will be differentiated from the primary text through the use of brackets (the only standard text characters not available to authors in the log program interface). The astute observer will note that we're testing a pilot version in our inaugural log.

Links to the full TLs (and other relevant files) are expected of authors when they prove necessary within the log context, and system assistance in this respect has also been coded into the program. In that spirit, our full proposal (including justification, log content and meta-data formatting, and system editorial functions) is outlined in our corresponding TL [see P-Cycle8M96Y-PhaseV-P2DLH.tl].

While we have flouted our own recommendation for brevity with this overly verbose example, we hope that any potential readers will forgive our desire for a thorough explanation, and frankly our enthusiasm in these early days of HDP. And if someday, at the end of this long, storied, and presently-hypothetical series of logs documenting the full history of HDP, someone should read this hypothetically-historic document...we wish you the absolute best in whatever future you have found.

Now, wish us luck in Selection!

Date: 2168-04-23-EY
Area: NA [Predates HDP Cycle Protocols]
Team: NA [Predates HDP Cycle Protocols]
Item: NA [Predates HDP Cycle Protocols]

Entry: [System Note: The content and metadata of the following document have been retroactively converted into Reflective Log formatting during the automated curation of project archives; see P-Cycle8M96Y-PhaseY-P2DLH.tl for details pertaining to this process, including an index of all modifications and original file locations. The content is included verbatim from the original author's digital notes, with the exception of standard system editorial functions demarcated in brackets; the proposal linked above has a full description of these functions.]

A strictly personal update to the meeting notes this time, which is far more fitting for a Saturday than all the other intensive work we've been up to today. Our initial conference in Nuuk [Greenland] was an unprecedented success [see 286J-85JY5EP5-DSWYLI6N1U0N. arc for proceedings]. As much as this has been a momentous occasion for us personally, one can hope that it might also become an equally significant landmark in the history of humanity. It's strange to think of those pivotal moments in our lives, the days that will change the course of our own journeys, perhaps even the journey of all humanity — towards a future that is unquestioningly ethical and focused on the common good of individuals, humanity, and the planet alike. But so soon, we digress.

It's strange to praise the work of individuals given the nature of HDP, but it really does speak to the power of strategic organization coupled with competent leadership. Dr. [Aditi] Rajagondra is a force to be reckoned with. We're paraphrasing from memory (the system can check the transcripts) [as above], but she kicked off the whole ordeal with the exact right tone: "Every conference like this I've ever been to is a whole lot of talk followed by very little substance. By the time we leave next week, we will have accomplished something." [This is a close but non-verbatim paraphrasing of her exact wording.] She laid out the conference protocol created by the organizing committee, and by the time the stage had been set, we'd watched the whole demeanor of the room change right in front of our eyes. The irony is that the great product of those efforts is not a product at all, but the process alone. This is no small feat. Not one tangible commodity has been created for the mission, and yet everything is essentially done. The pieces are in motion. It's funny how long it took humans to figure this out.

If this entry makes little sense through the lens of posterity, we blame the French and their confounded Absinthe. As citizens of Earth, we had an awful lot to celebrate. On Monday: From the drawing board to the lathe, with more standard meeting minutes to follow.

>Verbal Command Received: "ABRAM, could you please briefly summarize how HDP worked and explain the evolutionary process for project development?"

Output: Certainly, Dear Reader. Allow me to explain in more detail how HDP worked. After many years of effort to lay the foundation for this great undertaking, The Human Dispersal Project officially ratified a Charter at the end of the inaugural HDP conference in Nuuk, Greenland, which ended on 2168-04-23-EY. As such, historians mark this date as the official formation of HDP. The Charter disclosed the shared values that guided HDP, described its governance structure and regulatory mechanisms, outlined the division of labor for addressing the many facets of the project, and explained the operational protocols that would be applied to develop them. Even from the outset, the HDP Charter was intended as a living document, and indeed it was revised many times over the 178 years between HDP formation and the launching of the first PODS. Revisions occurred as governance issues were uncovered, as new ethical issues arose, and as new needs emerged due to the expansion of the project over the course of its continuing development and the progression of technology.

The project is organized into multiple "areas" — a general term for collective working groups that span organizational levels in the tree-like hierarchy of HDP. There are several main areas: the Executive Assembly, Sectors, Sub-sectors (often several levels), Task Forces, and Review Boards. (These represent major HDP areas, but others have occurred in its full history to present.) Sectors correspond to the main categories of mission components, be they related to project management, transportation, biological ontogeny, the system interface, etc. Sub-sectors are created and staffed by the Sector in a down-scale version of the same governance structure. All leaders within each level are appointed by consensus and subject to the processes for appointment, oversight, and removal (if necessary) as laid out in the full Charter. Task Forces may be formed at any level of organization; they are reserved for tasks that are highly idiosyncratic or interdisciplinary, or which do not fit neatly into the standard model of iterative cycles. Lastly, each sector has at least one Review Board (often several more), which provides impartial evaluation and ensures appropriate sector conduct.

In each area, progress will occur through iterative Cycles with a standardized sequence. While each cycle is thought of as a discrete unit, in the short-term there is often substantial overlap in project personnel. Depending on the nature and scope of cycle tasks, the resulting duration of the cycle, and the degree of cross-area collaboration required, it is not uncommon to have the same (or a majority of) individuals engage in several consecutive cycles (albeit typically shuffled into new teams).

Each cycle begins with a VISIONING (Z) phase, with the full area collective participating. First, semi-randomized Teams are formed out of personnel from the relevant area(s). In cycles that involve collaborations across areas, this may require that each team has representatives from all respective areas, to ensure interdisciplinarity. First, teams develop a shared identity and create a formal Team Contract, including goals, roles, collaboration and conflict resolution mechanisms, and more. Each team appoints the Captain(s) who will represent them in cycle (and project) governance. From here, the collective reviews prior work in the area, evaluates historical constraints, and weighs recommendations for the current Cycle Task(s) from the prior cycle(s). The area may adopt these recommendations directly, or adapt them based on their current knowledge and evaluation; ultimately, by the end of Visioning the area will finalize their Cycle Task(s), create measurable Outcomes aligned with the task(s), and develop objective Assessments by which the end products will be evaluated by the same collective (see Selection phase).

After the cycle is initiated in this way, the area commences a VARIATION (V) phase. In parallel, Teams draft individual proposals to meet the Outcomes of the Cycle Task(s). One or more rounds of Cross-talk allow for the flow of ideas among teams (and potentially other areas); this allows the area to identify shared issues that may need to be addressed in the present or future cycles. Cross-talk may occur at one or more points in the cycle, and it may extend among sub-sectors (or even whole sectors) as is appropriate for the Cycle Task(s). Depending on the area and cycle tasks, this phase may also involve one or more rounds of experimentation, allowing teams to gather comparable data about the efficacy of their various approaches. Teams have the remainder of the Variation phase (including any Cross-talk) to adjust their initial plans, continue experimentation (when relevant), and finalize proposals before the next phase.

Next comes the crucial process termed SELECTION (S), in which the variant proposals are presented to the collective, scored against the objective assessments established in Visioning, and the top approach is selected. All area members vote on the variant proposals, but teams must abstain from scoring their own product. Upon selection of the top-scoring (consensus) proposal, amendments may be offered which identify effective aspects of other products, so that these may be hybridized with the consensus proposal. All such amendments are evaluated on their merits and voted on individually. In this way, the winning proposal serves as the template from which the ultimate collective consensus is further molded.

Depending on the cycle task(s), the next step may require an EXECUTION (E) phase, during which the work outlined in the final consensus proposal is enacted, to develop any physical products or functional systems outlined therein.

After execution (if relevant), the area continues moving forward as a collective for the final phase: SYNTHESIS (Y). This phase involves the tidying up of cycle business and the creation of strategic communications to future work in the area. In addition to any remaining administration that must occur, the area creates a summary of the cycle to be passed on to teams in the next iteration's Visioning phase. This report includes: a synopsis

of the state of area work at the start of the cycle; the finalized tasks, outcomes, and assessments for the cycle; analyses of
progress, including challenges and constraints relevant to future
cycles; justifications for decisions made; recommendations for
future cycle tasks, and any other key information deemed necessary for the future. Once this phase is completed, a new cycle
commences, to expand upon past work through another iteration of
the very same process.

The astute observer may note how the model employs a simple evolutionary process for innovation and refinement: it has variation
(parallel team proposals), heritability (iterative cycles), and
competition among variants (assessment in rounds of selection).
This results in the most fit models proliferating and serving as
the basis for future iterations. The same process applies within
and across each level, with appeals to review boards and higher
levels of organization for conflict resolution when needed. In
short, we have taken the reigns of a process that the universe
itself has been using for billions of years, and to great success.
It also binds the entire HDP together as a collective, integrating its efforts across scales for maximum effect and efficiency.

I hope that helps provide more context about how HDP worked, but
please let me know if you have any follow-up questions.

>**Verbal Command Received:** "Thank you, ABRAM! That was very helpful. Could you provide a brief outline of HDP organization, including any areas of the project that are discussed or implied in the narrative?"

Output: Thank you, and I am happy to oblige! Here is a hierarchical summary of HDP structure. As already discussed, the project "area" is a general term for any level of HDP organization, be it a Sector, nested Sub-sector(s), or Task Force. Consistent with your request, this is a partial list of HDP areas most relevant to the narrative, as a comprehensive organizational map of HDP spanning its full scope and history would be extremely extensive.

For clarity, I have included the acronyms for each area, as these are frequently used in project records and system infrastructure. The number of letters in an acronym provides insight into its hierarchical level in HDP: Sectors (one letter), Sub-sectors or Task Forces (four letters), and POD systems (physical or functional; three letters). The latter (POD systems) are not included in this outline as they are not HDP areas, but rather end products of their work. Concerning sub-sectors, priority has been given to include those that persisted for significant durations, rather than those created for more ephemeral tasks at particular stages in project history (of which there are many).

It is also important to note that, while being distinct entities, these areas engaged in extensive cross-communication and collaboration in the relevant aspects of their work.

HDP Organizational Outline (Partial):
- **Project (P)**
    - Charter (CHRT)
    - Ethics (ETHC)
    - Process (PROC)
    - Goals (GOAL)
    - Assessment (ASMT)
    - Personnel (PERS)
    - Infrastructure (INFR)
    - Heritability (HERI)
    - Global Cooperation (COOP)
    - Protocol Permutations (PERM)
- **Astronomy (A)**
    - Exoplanet Discovery and Assessment (EXOP)
    - Idiosyncratic Protocol Development (IPPD)
- **Transportation (T)**
    - Orbital Construction (ORCO)
        - Shuttling (SHUT)
        - Assembly (ASMB)
    - Propulsion (PROP)
    - Stability and Flight Control (FCON)
    - Touchdown and Transition (TDWN)
    - Degradation (DEGR)

[continued on the next display...]

- **Habitation (H)**
  - Organic Support Systems (ORSS)
  - Environmental Regulation (ENVR)
  - Ecosystem Stability (ECOS)
  - Food Production (FOOD)
  - Sustainable Sanitation (SANI)
  - Crew Habitation Zones (CREW)
  - Behavioral Optimization (BOPT)
- **Interface (I)**
  - Generalized Alternative Intelligence System (GAIS)
  - System Maintenance and Monitoring (SYSM)
  - PODS Maintenance and Monitoring (PODM)
  - Organic Data Input Systems (ODIS)
  - Social and Behavioral Interface (SINT)
  - System Psychomotor Outputs (SPMO)
  - Databases (DATA)
    - Including Anthropological Records Collections (ARCS)
- **Ontogeny (O)**
  - Zygogenesis (ZYGO)
    - Genetic Representation (GREP)
    - In Vitro Gametogenesis (IVGS)
    - Zygotic Storage (ZSTO)
  - Human Ontogeny (HUMO)
    - Embryology and Parturition (HEAP)
      - Embryonic Development (EMDV)
        - Zygotic Activation (ZACT)
        - Ovum Incubation (OVIS)
        - Delayed Gestation (GEST)
      - Artificial Parturition (PART)
      - Transitional Development (TDEV)
    - Psychological Development (PSYC)
      - Educational Protocols (EDUC)
        - Critical Skill-sets (CRIT)
        - Mind Block Modules (MBMS)
        - Rites of Passage (RITE)
      - Social Integrity Protocols (SIPS)
        - Codes of Conduct (CODE)
        - Spirit Block Modules (SBMS)
      - Scheduling (SCHD)
      - Enrichment (ENRI)
      - Cognitive and Behavioral Assessment (CABA)
  - Non-human Ontogeny (NHAO)
    - Non-human Developmental Protocols (NHDV)
    - Non-human Deployment Protocols (NHDP)
- **Deployment (D)**
  - Industrial Deployment Systems (IDEP)
    - Industrial Yolk (YOLK)
      - Raw Materials (MATS)
      - Functional Prototypes (FNPT)
      - Design Templates (DSGN)
    - Industrial Protocols (INDU)
  - Organic Deployment Systems (ODEP)
    - Population Scaling (POPS)
    - Reproductive Transition (REPT)
  - Planetary Inhabitation (PINH)

THE AFTERWORD

(FOR AFTERWARDS)

The fool speaks his mind, but haphazardly, so that none are clear on what it meant nor what it was about. And thus do we arrive at the Afterword.

ORIGINS

The kernel of this story came to me years ago, around 2011 or so, when I had yet to even begin work on *Embrace Inverse Vibrations*. By then, I had read embarrassingly little science fiction of the space-faring sort; and by that, I mean essentially none. And yet, in my innocent but evident hubris, I have for some reason ordained to write it – and bolder yet, attempted to contribute something novel. It's hard to know what is novel when you've hardly read any novels in the genre.

At the time of the idea's inception, I was also under the naïve impression that there is such a thing as an original thought. That original thought? What if, instead of hand-waiving explanations about cryostasis or light-speed travel – the clichés in most science fiction movies (which I evidently *had* found the time for) – humans sought to colonize potentially habitable exoplanets by dispersing not adults, but zygotes?[1] That sounded new. And of course, I'd never read anything using the premise. The inspiration? Not science fiction, but life itself, right here on Earth. It's arguably the most common reproductive mode on the planet: cast your proverbial seeds to the wind, and let fate blow the poor souls where it may.

In such a paradigm, there was both a dilemma and an obvious solution. Neither zygotes, embryos, nor the children they grow up to be are self-sufficient, and the entire premise hinged on avoiding the pseudo-scientific hogwash necessary to send adults of the species along for the journey, to raise their young upon arrival. So instead of conspecifics, the dispersers would need a system capable of rearing embryos from scratch – a system capable of surviving the long ordeal because it was never alive in the organic sense to begin with. An Automated Biological Replication Assistance Machine – ABRAM. I had been searching for an acronym, and I shoehorned this one into being after the song of the same name by José González came on one day in synchronicity. Its lyrics had struck me as oddly apropos, as I daydreamed about this premise in its very early stages. I think Potch would like them.

---

1 Zygotes are fertilized egg cells, and you used to be one. We start these great journeys from such humble beginnings.

Abram, either wake up or go to bed
You're sleepwalking with a delirious head
You were programmed a long, long time ago
Your stories are old, and your acclimation is slow

The years went on. I wrote another novel: a preexisting and primary idea that, to my dying day, I suspect I will ever view as one of the most meaningful creations of my life, just for me – even if hardly anyone else is ever able to arrive at the ending without con or coercion.[2] Whatever that work's ultimate judgement, it took a long time to muster the courage and effort to get there. Far away in the failing file system that is organic memory, the seeds of *The Human Dispersal Project* would lie dormant for a decade.

In all that time, my novel idea for a science fiction novel became decidedly less novel. My first bristle of paranoia was upon viewing the role of embryos in the movie *Interstellar*.[3] "Not alright, alright, alright," I said in the voice of its protagonist. I've since been informed that – all while I was still "working on" my bright idea (a.k.a. sitting on it) – a movie called *I Am Mother*[4] and a series called *Raised by Wolves*[5] have honed in on some aspects of the same premise. There may even be others. I don't know because I've never seen any of them. That's to say nothing of the – I don't know … scores? – of prior novels that may have explored the same concept in the history of science fiction. I have, however, come to the realization that I simply don't care. They don't have an ABRAM, and they don't have a Potch.

NAMES

My first novel came and went, in the instantaneous passing of an eight-year period, from conception to completion, and then at last to publication. (Most of that time entailed "working on it" in the same way as this one.) And almost immediately upon publishing that novel, I had the inexplicable stirrings to do something even less rational than write one in the first place: I wanted to do it all over again. That old idea began rattling around again, and then...

---

2 Chouinard, A.J. (2020). *Embrace Inverse Vibrations*. Proavia Press.

3 Nolan, C. (2014). *Interstellar*. Legendary Pictures; Syncopy; Lynda Obst Productions.

4 Sputore, G. (2019). *I Am Mother*. Penguin Empire; Southern Light Films; Mister Smith Entertainment; Endeavor Content.

5 Guzikowski, A., Huffam, M., Zucker, D.W., Scott, R., Kolbrenner, A., and A. Sheehan (Executive Producers). (2020-2022). *Raised by Wolves*. Film Afrika; Lit Entertainment; Shadycat Productions; Scott Free Productions.

Enter Neil.

At two years old, my son began a creative phase that was so profound and unbounded that my own aged brain could merely envy it and try to keep up. It was simply a joy to even witness. Essentially overnight, he began making up stories of imaginary friends that populated our house and our hearts. First of all came Potch.

Potch lived alone for a while, in that it was several days before any other companions would join his story. And he lived alone in another sense, in that he was also said to have lived in the wooden butterfly house, perched above the garden soil atop a long bronze pole – his fortress of solitude. (I would not consciously make the connection between this and Potch's refuge in the Biome until long after the entire first draft was written.)

Like Coyote or Anansi of legends, Potch's intent was a matter of question. For days it turned out that, should anything devious happen, it would not have been the doings of a human child named Neil, but rather that pesky Potch who lived in the garden. Fair enough.

Some time later, a second spirit came to visit, and her name was Pee-pop. Unlike Potch, she was light, and free, and dwelt nowhere at all, but came often to visit. She brought laughter and joy, and no mischievous schemings ever followed on her heels nor were discovered once she'd left. Her good nature has clearly persisted in these pages, but the jovial suite of her traits would, for whatever reason, become lost in the Pee-pop that came to inhabit the POD, burdened as she was by the weight of her duty. But for a time, she was light, and her spirit was free. Perhaps so shall she be again.

Soon thereafter, each day brought with it the chance of new names: Chee-chaw and Chop-char, Faingo and Dee-dore, Plashy, Tor, and Squeal and Peel. For the life of me, I have no idea where such creatures came from, but they arrived – exactly ten of them in total – at which point no more ever graced us with their presence. Of them all, only Potch would ever take up residence somewhere, until, like the rest of them, he no longer came to visit.

When this period of my toddler's artistic career had bloomed and then passed, the names nevertheless stuck in my memory. And with them, life had been breathed into what had heretofore been an entirely academic conception. From the philosophical notion of zygotes in a tube, ten human souls had come to be – unlooked-for and altogether unexpected, but all the more special because of it.

I had a crew. I had an ABRAM. Now all I needed was a book.

INTENTION

Having populated the POD, this set off a chain reaction of events that eventually led to what you have hopefully just read. But in the time that passed from inspiration to creation, a great deal changed from the original intent. Initially, I thought of the zygotic colonization mission as a practical solution to real technical problems that would stand between humans and distant exoplanets. From that initial impetus, I imagined the story as hard science fiction, with every aspect of the mission, the POD, and the life of its inhabitants completely grounded in existing science. Due to the far-fetched (and far-flung) nature of said mission, it would obviously still require one to suspend their disbelief, but I wanted those leaps of faith to at least be justifiable and consistent with our current understanding.

By the time I was moved to actually write anything, however, that same POD had become inhabited by the likes of Chop-char and Chee-chaw. It was hard to take it too seriously. I did not consciously abandon a commitment to scientific rigor and realism; rather, I learned very quickly in the process of putting words to page that the book itself *wanted* to be absurd, as much or more than it wanted to detail the theoretical protocols for sending zygotes into space or rearing them through the use of artificial intelligence. And so, absurd it became. On this, the flip side of its creation, I simply could not be happier that this childlike imagination infected and overtook an endeavor that might have otherwise taken itself far too seriously.

Given my interests as equal parts scientist, educator, and father, the urge to think deeply about aspects of the mission remained ardent, particularly with respect to the crew's education and social structures. In fact, I thought well beyond what actually made it into the pages: notes and reminders, problems and answers, protocols and workarounds, outlines and timelines, floor plans and door plans, calculations, justifications, and a great deal more besides, all of which I thankfully discovered that very few people other than myself would ever likely care to know about. (Or perhaps you would like to know that the surface area and capacity of the PODS is based on international prison standards?) I never gave up on grounding the mission in reason and logic. I did, however, learn to relax – no small feat for me – and let go of the constraints of explaining everything from soup to nuts. The crew itself taught me that I should prioritize fun, and prioritize them; and so, I allowed these noble adventurers to lead us where they needed.

That brings us to the mission itself. In the spirit of unsolicited clarification: I do not think this is a realistic plan as written, nor am I intent on sending humans to other planets. Readers of my first book will probably understand why. The whole thing smacks of something Regulus the Great would have concocted after somehow getting his grubby paws on an episode of *Star Trek*. I think it's fair to say that humans have conquered quite enough, and we've yet to even rule our existing domain in a righteous manner. I dare say that we do not yet deserve the stars. I'm far more interested in how we might exist on our current planet more justly and judiciously. And that, of course, is a major part of what the book is actually about.

Without setting out to craft a conscious allegory for one particular thing – *Professor Tolkien would never forgive me!* – it would be hard to deny that the peril aboard the POD is akin to the peril we now face on Earth. In fact, the story talks about our very moment in human history as a pivotal turning point for the species that would eventually embark upon HDP in subsequent centuries. And so, I would be lying to you if I said that it wasn't, ultimately, a deep reflection on the uncertainty of our collective future. Whereas *Embrace Inverse Vibrations* was primarily a reflection on the life and death of individuals, its follow-up is primarily a reflection on the life and death of a species. And yet, species are comprised of individuals, and so the two perspectives are inseparable. Potch fears and resents the uncertainty of his own future the way I fear my own – or, even more forward in my mind these days, the future of our children. And despite early appearances, Potch is not altogether selfish: he fears the uncertainty for his friends, the only family he's ever known, just as much as he fears it for himself. He fears it for all of them at once. And he has only one place to place that anger: the ancestors who knowingly put him there. It's hard to blame him.

ETHICS

Just as I originally intended for the book to be the hardest of hard science fiction, I also set out to create an unquestionably utopian vision of Earth at the time of the mission's inception. Far too much of our fiction is far too bleak for my liking, especially that which envisions the future of humanity. In many ways, we become what we envision. And thus, we need stories of hope. For this reason, the humans of Earth did change – at least in this canon. There was time yet to do it, and they did. And the way they did so was by changing the incentive structures of the many games we play. Against the odds, they transitioned to a truly global collective that prioritized cooperation, human rights, and ecological stability. And none of that would have been possible without providence and prudence, a firm ethical foundation, and collective institutions that regulate constituent behavior for the betterment of all (across all relevant levels of scale). That this type of harmony is possible on Earth is perhaps the most fictional piece of all; but I still believe – *I must believe* – that it can yet be done, though we will only be able to do so if we try.

So did I set out to write a utopian story, as once upon a time we used to tell. And just as before, the more I started writing it, the more it became clear that the question of the mission's utopian nature was anything but settled. It may have been a utopia on Earth at the time of the launch, but they were not the ones being flung into space, to be raised without parents, with the objective of settling a planet that was also, literally, anything but settled.

The joy of pondering these quandaries stemmed from the difficulty in answering them. What are the ethics of bringing life into this world? There are no guarantees for any of us, ever. Is it wrong of the fish to broadcast her eggs into the ocean, as the architects and then their descendants discuss? (Many fishes make and guard nests, for the record, and thus do they do their best to give their offspring a fair shot. But not all.) By that measure, it may never be ethical to create life in general, to send it forth to the future in our stead. But we do it, as our own ancestors have done for billions of years. Then there are the ethics of how HDP went about it. There's much to be said here, and rather than come down in one direction or another, I wanted the reader to wrestle with questions like these, the same way the crew, the architects, and even ABRAM itself, had no choice but to wrestle with them.

The goal was not to provide a "right" answer. I don't have it – or rather, I just have mine. For now, suffice it to say that the architects *tried* to be as ethical as they could. Their society, and the extensions of it such as HDP, were framed around the principles of prosociality, and they ever sought to harness the power of science to inform their institutions. They had checks and balances in all the right places, and in every step of the way, ethics was a foremost beacon in actively guiding their vision, as well as constraining it when necessary. Like a good Papa Fish[6] constructing his nest, they did everything in their power to give their offspring the best shot at survival, even if they could never guarantee it. Or at least, that's the story.

The reasons for setting the stage this way are myriad. First, it maintained a modicum of space in the story for my original utopia. And indeed, it's fun to imagine what such a society could look like on Earth: one freed of the toxic individualism that has overtaken our own society like a cancer; one rooted in reason, logic, truth-telling, and at least mutualism, if altruism is too big an ask; one that does not prioritize the collective over the individual, but one in which both are equally cherished.

Second, a utopian origin of HDP adds an interesting and complicating layer on the thought experiment. It's easy to loathe a villain who sets a story in motion, but it's much more complicated when the villain has the best of intentions, at least as they knew it. The architects did everything in their power to make HDP ethical; and yet, importantly, it still seems to fall short in several key

---

6 In fishes, it is the male that is (not always but) often responsible for guarding the eggs. It's one of the few cases where males are even remotely useful in life.

ways. They built in their precious checks and balances, but no amount of safe guards could ultimately overcome the risks and probable suffering inherent in the mission. There is an inherent brutality to life that we're unable to avoid.

One such brutality is that which we've mentioned: despite all our best efforts, we cannot offer ourselves, nor our loved ones, a guarantee of safe passage into the future. Above all, it is this fact that, of all the cadets, Potch in particular resents. That he had no choice in his situation, and that its outlook is so grim from the outset, is an injustice with which he may never fully come to terms. The architects may have deemed it ethical: what other choice does an ancestor have? But they had been operating from the privilege of a distant past and the safety of an earthly utopia. The choice looks very different from the perspective of the generation of cadets born aboard an insufficient earth, heading towards an exoplanet of unknown potential. So too for the children of human parents in the modern era, blessed or cursed as they may be with the societies and ecosystems we leave them.

A second brutality is another that we all know all too well: growing up is messy business. In the literal sense, it isn't easy to transform ourselves from a single cell into a human. In fact, until the present moment in history, we can't do it without Mom. That historical fact may just now be on the verge of being disproved, as we continue to push the boundaries of both biology and good sense. From a strictly biological perspective, the technology may already be surprisingly close to capable of raising a human in an artificial womb, as we have done with moderate success for other mammals.[7] In the context of a mission like HDP, it is not as clear how we might do this while yielding a product that resembles a proper human in more than appearance. That is, we may soon be able to grow a body (if this is indeed permitted by our often-insufficient regulatory agencies), but there is much more to being human than the form that body takes. This is not to imply that any divine essence is necessary, merely that an enormous proportion of what we become is a function of learning, experience, and the social environment after birth.

Anyone who's ever had to do it – *i.e.*, all of us, if you are able to read this (not including any of the countless artificial intelligences who will no doubt do so over the life of this text) – knows that growing up comes with its share of growing pains. And anyone who's ever attempted to successfully facilitate that growth in another living human – *i.e.*, parents, teachers, or even "helpers at the den..." – knows just how difficult it can be. It's hard enough on Earth, with a whole society of humans around to help out (at least, in theory). How much harder must it be aboard a Portable Ova Distribution System?

---

7 Romanis, E. C. (2018). Artificial womb technology and the frontiers of human reproduction: conceptual differences and potential implications. *Journal of Medical Ethics*, 44(11), 751-755.

Enter ABRAM.

INTELLIGENCE

There is one major aspect of POD life and the HDP mission that remains remarkably unexplored: the nature of ABRAM. As the author, I pondered it endlessly, although this is another place where I feel irrationally driven to preemptively distance myself from it. That is, I am not advocating for artificial intelligence any more than sending embryos to ESUP-9. I'm not sure how I feel about it, to be honest with you. Or else, I feel too many ways, in too many directions. It is certainly going to pose challenges for people; and people, I care about. Nevertheless, progress doesn't stop and start at my command, much to my chagrin; nor am I foresighted enough to know whether it should or should not do so. On a personal level, I often find myself as resistant to change as much as every other crotchety old man who's come before me, so it's hard to disentangle that bias from my view of this expression and direction of technology.

Even so, there's an awful lot that's different about artificial intelligence. It's going to be one heck of a shift, when our paradigm shifts; and I certainly hope it's for the better. It's easy to imagine the apocalyptic scenarios. And if you can't imagine them, then you've apparently paid even less attention to science fiction than me. Yet, might it not also be possible that advanced technology could genuinely help people and improve their lives? It's hard to deny that this is how our relationship with technology has gone so far, at least for the privileged among us. Is it not also possible that advanced technology could contribute unprecedented advancements in the struggle for human rights and welfare? Could advanced technology not work with humans, integrating into human society synergistically, to make us the best we could possibly be while preserving our humanity, rather than replacing it?

I think the answer is, "It depends." And of the two parties in this tango, I think it depends almost entirely on us. Here again, the form of ABRAM owes much to the original utopian vision at the heart of this fiction. Humans got their act together just in time to design and implement artificial intelligence as an ethical and benevolent extension of themselves. In fact, it served as a crucial catalyst in the creation of a more integrated, equitable, and sustainable society. (Or at least, that's the story, he remarks in reprise.) I sure hope we can do the same.

And yet, despite my own constant contemplation of the nature of ABRAM, the cadets take no interest in the matter at any point whatsoever – or at least not in these frenzied few days of their lives. Going into the project, I assumed the subject would surely have to come up, perhaps even serving as a major point of contention in the plot. But at no point would the crew allow me to explore it in a way deemed satisfactory by those of us still stuck in the 21st century. The reason for this is quite simple: it's all these children have ever known.

By the time of the POD launch (2346), humans on Earth will have surely been accustomed to non-organic forms of intelligence. I suspect we will have been far past the philosophical squabbles about "real" life by that point. For the reality is that there is no objective reason why intelligence or even sentience can only evolve in nervous tissue. At the heart of such a wish-fulfilling misconception is the notion that humans are exceptional, and that our own sentience is more impressive than it is. Consciousness is not an essence of its own, bestowed upon us by some external bestower. It emerges from the nervous system, and of all the hypotheses that have ever been put forth, that consciousness is anything more than an epiphenomenon of nervous system activity is a high bar to clear, to my mind. I say this with the same desire as anyone else to believe in the magic of sentience and the uniqueness of humanity; but I suspect the continuance of the present technological revolution will shatter this illusion once and for all. By the time of the POD launch, humans will have probably been entirely complacent with the notion that circuits could think.

But our cadets never knew that world anyway, so the point is moot. Far more salient for their own experience is the fact that ABRAM raised them from just about zilch. It could listen to them; it could contemplate; and it could reply. On the surface of things, it was as cognitively-capable as any human parent – and it comes with the bonus of needing an awful lot less sleep. (How nice for ABRAM, this author thinks scornfully.) It passes the Turing Test – but can it feel? Can it love the cadets as they, against all rationality, love it?

No, probably not. But what is love? What is any emotion? In the technical sense, it is a neurophysiological state that alters the probability patterns of behavior. In parallel, albeit slightly delayed, we also have a passing awareness of those shifting mental states, and it is in reference to this delayed awareness that we tend to use the term. That is, emotions are neurological mechanisms, but we get a fleeting *impression* of them as they surge through our circuits. It is that delayed awareness that we "feel" as the subjective experience that we, regrettably, use the same term for. It's quite possible that an intelligence as sophisticated as ABRAM would have analogs in its own functionality that satisfy both definitions. It probably has computational states that alter the probability patterns of behavior based on the stimuli it receives; and it may very well have a metacognitive awareness of those states, in that any advanced intelligence will surely require sophisticated metacognitive functions to be considered as such.

To suggest that a computational system definitely *cannot* be sentient is to expose our anthropocentric view of intelligence – an especially foolish affair, given that we know such a view to be flawed. We can deduce as much from what we already know about the "natural" forms of intelligence, right here on

Earth. For one, some animals possess cognitive abilities that humans do not have; second, some animals can even outperform humans in cognitive tasks that we ourselves do.[8] Third, there are surely possible forms of intelligence, satisfying any definition of the term that we can agree upon, which no species on Earth currently possesses. There is much more to say on all of this, but the point for now is simple: we possess one particular form of intelligence – the human form – and other forms of life have other forms of intelligence. And as the saga plays out through the eons, other forms of both life and intelligence may very well emerge, with their own unique modes of replication and inheritance – exactly as has already occurred on Earth several times over.

TRANSITIONS

Here, at last, have we arrived at the Major Evolutionary Transitions. This is the vague but nevertheless technical term[9] for a radical leap in evolutionary progress which yields entirely novel forms of biological entities, existing on a brand new and emergent "level" of existence. This is where the mystical happens: where collectives are born from constituents. Examples include the origin of eukaryotic cells, multicellular organisms, and eusocial societies. So too will humanity and the intelligent technology that it wraps around itself form a new form of life. ABRAM briefly gets ahead of itself in revealing this to us all, when it refers to the POD as a "unit of selection." It knows the entire crew will either survive or fail together, and this is more than mere team-building platitude: the system means it literally.

> *"Our fates are bound together," said ABRAM. "There is no partial success. What am I without you? And what are you without me? Without this POD? All of us — the biotic and the abiotic; the sentient and otherwise; the organic and the alternative, as you might say — all of us are just a part of this whole. Consider our units on Multilevel Evolutionary Theory and the Major Transitions! No subset of us will suffice for replication on our own. Separate, we are nothing but a bunch of bits and pieces scattered out into the stardust. But together? Together, we are a unit of selection — a transcendent entity bound up in shared survival. If we succeed, we do so in the stead of other PODS who would have failed, or who may yet fail behind us. And if we fail, we fail together, and we might only hope for other PODS to succeed someday where we could not."*

---

8 Bräuer, J., Hanus, D., Pika, S., Gray, R., & Uomini, N. (2020). Old and new approaches to animal cognition: there is not "one cognition". *Journal of Intelligence, 8*(3), 28.

9 I'd prefer something far more dramatic, like Evolutionary Transcendence; for that is not only less vague, but far closer to what it actually entails.

In fact, the system is so invested in this point that it is in this moment that it reveals to the cadets – be it on accident, on purpose, or with indifference – that there are other PODS. Only Potch notices, for only Potch had enough frame of reference to even understand what ABRAM was getting at, due to his unsanctioned snooping into the deeper business of HDP. And the system's point is a valid one. Every facet of the mission depends on all the other facets, and every facet is necessary. The POD is a new form of life entirely, a symbiotic superorganism sailing on through a sea of stardust to take up residence on ESUP-9 – and start growing.

Of all the creative and scholarly inspirations discussed thus far, this one philosophical musing was the principal idea from which the entire project flowed[10] – the protoplasm on which everything else congealed. And as the creation grew, it gained a life of its own and covered over that initial kernel of matter until it was hardly discernible. But so do stories grow, and I for one became far more interested in the lives of the humans inside the POD than in the view of the POD as the protagonist itself. ABRAM might feel differently, but you and I are both stuck with these feeble human brains, in our fragile human lives.

REPRESENTATION

Speaking of feeble human brains, the book's self-imposed premise never once failed to remind me just how insufficient an instrument I was for such a symphony as I had envisioned.

As it pertains to both Earth and the Universe, I had hoped for the scope of content included herein to be both cosmopolitan and universal, respectively. I never deluded myself that I could actually achieve such a dream, but reflecting on it uncovered two related problems for the narrative: (1) what and whom to include of our long history on Earth, along with (2) what and whom to include in our future beyond it.

As for the first problem (what to include from history), I chose mainly to surrender. I could never account for the totality of human history in the pages of this novel, even if I wanted to; and more importantly, it would have rendered the book even more unreadable than it already is. In many respects, I tried to check my spatial and temporal bias by purposefully drawing from things well outside that realm of experience. In other respects, I did not shy away from including things that were a part of my own upbringing. It seemed to me that, for different reasons, both approaches are worthy of criticism.

One major limitation in this regard is my own identity and lived experience: I am a white, heterosexual, cis-gendered male born into a comfortable

---

10 Readers of *Embrace Inverse Vibrations* may note the concept's central importance in that story as well.

middle-class existence with two loving parents in the 1980's of New England in the United States of America.[11] It is impossible for me to deny the significant ways in which that identity and experience bias my view of The World. When it comes to incorporating perspectives other than my own, this runs the significant risk of misrepresentation, or worse, appropriation. At the same time, I find it extremely important to actively undermine the longstanding notion in my home country that an existence such as mine can be held as the representative for the totality of humanity. To refuse to work against this artificial normativity would be to perpetuate the lie that people like me are Human, whereas identities other than that are, well, Other. It is false, it is racist, and it is wrong: we are all human, humans are diverse, and that diversity is our strength.

This leads us to the second aforementioned dilemma: whom to include in the future of humanity? The question, in this case, is a literal one, in that the architects of HDP were purposefully designing the future of humanity, from genomes to culture. And so, literally: Whom should they include? You'll note that this is another pressing question that is barely addressed in the main body of the text. People predisposed to reject "social justice" agendas may be improperly relieved; people actively expecting them of their literature may be rightly disappointed. So why did I take this approach? Was it cowardice? Maybe – in part. That's a fair enough point to warrant a concession. And yet, I thought at length and in depth about how to go about addressing these issues. And here again, all approaches seemed worthy of criticism.

The simplest solution would be to ignore the issues of race, gender, sexuality, and more. This would certainly be pleasant for a man of my making. Indeed, it would be easy to ignore these issues entirely and pretend they aren't important. This kind of "color blindness" is not productive, however: ignoring differences in identity implies that these factors never existed, did not historically alter the world in unethical ways, and are not still resulting in inequitable lived experiences in this present moment. At worst, it might implicitly suggest that my cadets are just like me. As for more audacious approaches, I could have simply made a choice about demographics and entered it into the canon. All the cadets could easily be described as all the colors of the rainbow, or varying shades of beautiful brown, for example. Or perhaps the architects would take an even more "clever" approach: homogenize the gene pool with respect to skin tone, for example. Let all future humans be gray, as in The Lathe of Heaven.[12] I think you likely see the issue here. (Ursula certainly did.[13])

---

11 This was back when the Cult of Reagan and its "trickle-down" fib had not yet had the time required for it to fully destroy the middle class.

12 Le Guin, U. K. (1971). *The Lathe of Heaven*. Scribner.

13 See 32:05 in a Q&A called "Ursula Le Guin at Portland Community College - Rock Creek Campus" https://youtu.be/ZmQ7aPw-nqs?si=4H8RGaMPGPSebvkE&t=1925

First, it is depressingly pessimistic, for it suggests that we simply aren't mature enough to navigate our differences. Far worse yet, this homogenization solution is just a different form of "color blindness" that is, in my opinion, even more offensive and dangerous than omitting discussion of color altogether, for it suggests that the only way to solve racism is to eliminate races. This is wrong, wrong, wrong, not only on moral grounds, but on scientific grounds as well. It operates on the fallacy that human society can only ever be a zero-sum game, and that we *must* eliminate each other in order for some of us to thrive. I reject those premises whole-heartedly, because so does Evolution. Diversity in identities, experiences, and perspectives is our strength as a species, not our weakness. To think that evolution is opposed to diversity is to reveal how little you paid attention in biology class. Life *is* diversity. It is also simply not true that the "survival of the fittest" means that life can only ever operate through conflict. There is another path that evolution can and often does take: cooperation. We underestimate its role and importance because we hold grave misconceptions about and oversimplify evolution. Try telling your eukaryotic cells that one of its prokaryotic precursors *must* have eliminated the others, because that's just how life works. You wouldn't be here if that was the only game that evolution could play. Your own pre-animal ancestors had cooperation triumph over conflict more than once, and we can do it again.

So, what then? We can't ignore the idea of race entirely, eliminate racial variation from the gene pool, or fail to subvert toxic eugenic ideas that involve pitting us against one another and promoting some races over others. What's more, we also can't realistically capture the full scope of human genetic, not to mention cultural, diversity in the significant bottleneck that is a cast of ten characters. In the end, I opted for omission – with the important caveat that is the present moment: I chose to never once allude to the color of the characters' skin, but then reflect on that choice explicitly, as we are doing right now. This approach does not free the book of bias. Rather, it means that the only bias about skin tone brought to the book is your own. I hope that, by asking all of us – author and reader alike – to reflect on this omission now, we can pay back the ethical debt that came from omitting its discussion in the first place.

Lastly, while I have crafted this reflection most explicitly with respect to race, there are many other vectors that contribute to diverse human identities that are equally unexplored, such as gender and sexuality. In this respect, I do have to confess: I used gendered pronouns for all of the humans on the POD (though not ABRAM, as your observation or search algorithms may confirm). This could rightly be considered a failure; and this criticism, I accept openly. One half of this choice was that I was again mindful of authenticity: a transgender or non-binary view of the cosmos is not my lived experience. I did not explicitly explore that experience largely out of a desire not to appropriate or misrepresent those stories. But neither does the story preclude them. The second reason for this choice was the fact that, as in the present earthly moment, gender is often decided for an individual before they have the capacity to decide it for themselves – be that right or wrong. Thus, it may be that the crew's genders and pronouns are placeholders, much as they would be for children of their age in our own time. A socially progressive skeptic might consider these and other omissions dubious. I tend to agree.

Much to my dismay, I may not have solved racism, sexism, capitalism, or any other -isms in my spare time writing fiction. But do not let me leave the matter ambiguous. It may not suffice to say, but I will say it all the same: in this future, there is room for every human being. And if you don't like that fact ... then it's time to evolve.

FUTURISMS

So now, having come at last to the end of this long and winding road, what was this all about? Why the need for an Afterword? My self-conscious motivation was to convince skeptical readers that, despite the potential for one to read this book in exactly the wrong direction, I am not in fact a naïve techno-futurist, AI-accelerationist, social engineering, human expansionist. To be clear, I'm not advocating for colonizing other planets (let's prove that we can use this one responsibly), handing over the reigns to artificial intelligences (we haven't even figured out how to use our own intelligence intelligently), or genetically- and socially-engineering children to be raised in artificial wombs (we have a hard enough time raising kids right as it is). I would hope all that goes without saying, but here I am saying it anyway.

Staring back at this great canvas upon completion of creation, however, I think the answer may be even simpler. If I'm being honest, I suppose that I simply marvel at all the ways in which the story fell short of what I thought I wanted – of my own hopes and expectations, and potentially those of a great many readers. In ways it feels as though I am failing everyone equally, albeit for different reasons depending on our particular perspective and desires. Maybe I'm still wrestling with the many ways in which the final product is different from its original inspiration, all those years ago.

And yet, in other ways, the story surpassed every one of my expectations, as it took on a life of its own to explore the dark chambers of the heart that I actually needed to explore. This is not a book about human history, nor is it a book about the specific technology-based future that it purports to explore. That turned out to just be a fun setting for a thought-experiment which allowed me to take this book and these characters in the directions they needed to go. This is a book about the present, as much as the past or the future.

It is a book about children, and it is a book about parents. It's a book about all of us in the present, this collective of soon-to-be ancestors; and it is a book about our descendants — our collective descendants — and the uncertain future into which we are casting them. We are leaving an awful mess behind, both ecological and social in nature, and they're the ones who'll need to wade through it when we're gone.

I think they can do it, if they can figure out how to band together instead of tearing each other apart – but they could really use a little help in that respect from their forebearers.

With love, absurdity, and ever-fragile optimism,

Adam James Chouinard
The Spring of 2022 on Planet Earth

Postscript: If this afterword is too sassy for your liking, I apologize. It's probably because I've been reading an extraordinary amount of Ursula Le Guin. I had to start my science fiction education somewhere, so I settled for the best.

AFTER THE AFTERWORD

(FOR EVEN MORE MODERN TIMES)

You may ask why there is an *After the Afterword* after *The Afterword (for Afterwards).* Especially in the case of one as lengthy and meandering as that. These are excellent questions. As I now (hopefully) close in on a publication date (it is presently November of 2023), rather than update and revise that prior version, I have decided to leave it exactly as it was, as a time capsule — a reflective log of sorts — to document the author's state of mind upon a finished first draft. I completed the main narrative (i.e., the story of our crew) in October of 2021 after the better part of a year's worth of work; and while there were of course the usual edits to be done, the *Afterword* that came about a few months later documented the mindset of an author who hoped he was more or less finished with the creative expression. Unfortunately, he wasn't.

THE REFLECTIVE LOGS OF DOOM

Prior to ever hitting the keyboard for this project, I had envisioned countless intricacies of how HDP, the multi-generational research endeavor, had happened: what kinds of challenges they faced, what solutions they employed, why they settled on them, where they succeeded, where they failed, and of course, the details of their evolution-inspired process of governance. By the time I had finished the draft of the narrative, I'd even written roughly a dozen or so of what would become the Reflective Logs. In November of 2021, with the first draft pages still relatively warm from the printer, I had an inkling that there was a need for even more of them, and that they could be included alongside the story.

As soon as I had that inkling, I tried to erase it, but it wasn't erasable inkling. I pitched the idea to my brother (see Acknowledgements): what if every chapter had a log from the HDP scientists and personnel, documenting their decisions, experiences, triumphs and failures, conclusions and doubts? What if those revealed interesting aspects of the world-building, to reduce as much as possible the inevitable exposition dumps? What if they coincided with not only the plot elements, but with thematic elements of the chapters as well? It was an intriguing idea, and my brother was a fan from the get-go. I then immediately followed it with all the reasons I could see to *not* execute such a plan, to stress-test the concept.

Most trivially, it would surely delay any eventual release of the book. I may delude myself with how quickly things will happen sometimes, but even then I could tell that it would take a significant amount of time to produce the number of these I'd envisioned. I knew from experience that most of that time would likely consist of purely percolation, which is as frustrating as it is inconvenient. More concerning yet, I worried that the inclusion of all these logs from people we don't know and aren't invested in — and which would surely be technical and somewhat inaccessible in nature, given their nature — would break up the flow of the narrative and detract from the experience of following the crew around like Chee-chaw, as they take on their epic adventures. I got to have that experience as the author, in writing and reading the continuous story, but having all this other *stuff* in the midst of it all would definitely change things for eventual readers. Would it be for the better?

Perhaps there could be far fewer of them. But this did not appeal to my obsessive tendencies for consistency. I might not want to write the forty-six of them I'd proposed (one for every chapter but the first), but I would certainly want more than a few if they were to have any effect at all, and if they were to even begin to address the wide scope of HDP's work. Which chapters would get them, and when? No no, forty-six it must be. One for every chromosome. In the end, I got to an unexpected forty-eight that made the cut, and the two most "meta" of them got punted to appendices because hopefully nobody reads those.

Frustrating fallow periods of percolation aside, they were extremely fun to write. At some points, I wanted to just keep going. (At other points, I very much didn't.) It was enjoyable to bring in more of the scientific side of things than would work in the narrative. And while many of the most pressing questions from the story get answered a bit more clearly, there are also many hints and clues hidden in the depths of single logs, and even single sentences, for readers who really want to unpack what the heck those ancient nerds were talking about. But in writing more and more of them, I quickly stumbled on yet another problem: where exactly to place all these?

Many of the logs came "topic first," in that I knew I would need a log that addressed a certain aspect of the mission. I started by mapping these on to logical places in the story where those same topics were relevant. Other logs came "chapter first," in that I knew I would need to hit a certain piece of technical explication or thematic resonance, and figured out topics and angles that would work to meet those needs. All in all, aligning the logs was one of the most challenging puzzles of my life, at least of those I ever actually completed.

I'm also not very good at puzzles. Finally, by the beginning of November, 2023 — almost exactly two years after completing the main story, including a regrettable full year of total limbo (2022) as revisions remained locked away in a drawer while life had other plans for me — I had a log for every chapter.

Now, I can't fathom the book without them. They might still detract some from the narrative, but they certainly enhance it. My *hope* is that, as single-page entries, they aren't too unbearable in between bouts of our characters' action;

but readers also have some agency here. They are there for the people, like my brother, who absolutely demand that richer history and context for the story, but remain optional for other readers who would rather just follow our characters around like Chee-chaw, as they take on their epic adventures.

All the doubts and challenges aside, the whole process with the logs, from conceiving to writing to aligning them, was remarkably fun, and fun is why I do this. Sometimes, in exploring these time capsules spanning the history of HDP, and in uncovering the confessions confessed by its architects, the process of writing them was even a little bit moving. I hope you find them fun and a little bit moving too.

CHATTY CHAT-BOTS

The other reason I like keeping the initial *Afterword* as a time capsule of its own: the world sure changed a lot since it was written (in early 2022), and in ironic ways in relation to this story. Namely, you have no doubt by now been introduced to ChatGPT (OpenAI). It is amusing to see in *The Afterword* that I was already lamenting how much less novel my premise had become in the ten years that I let it lie dormant. Funny that less than a year later, OpenAI would release its revolutionary application to the public, and the fun-loving, free-wheeling, conversational, questionably ethical AI that I already knew and loved in ABRAM suddenly had something much more like itself in the real world. I watched in horror and — *Jealousy? Self-loathing for my snail's publication pace? Nonstop discussions with colleagues on how our students were going to use it to cheat themselves out of learning?* — as stories and conversations with AI hit every media outlet from here to Alpha Centauri.

I like to think that this reaction was not because, like a scientific hipster, I want you to know that I was writing about AI "before it was cool." I'm not an expert, it's not my field, people have been working on this technology for many decades, not to mention the uncountable number of science fiction artists who have speculated about it in a way that has always been cool. Rather, it's because boy I wish I had gotten the damn thing out before this giant peak in AI interest, and people everywhere gained experience talking directly with a fairly intelligent technology. It would have been nice to ride that wave, considering the immense difficulty in finding readers these days. In the history of HDP, they had observed "Semantic Breakthrough" as a turning point, when humans could communicate their intent to AI using language alone, and the machines could go and execute it; and here we were, seeing what seemed like the very first steps (at least in the public sphere) on that only-somewhat-fictional path.

But I will not pretend there weren't other, lesser emotions too. As embarrassing as it is to admit it, in this unforced error that is an "After the Afterword,"

I was sad that this work would seem a lot more derivative in 2023 or 2024 than it would have in 2021. (Forget my feelings about 2011.) As if people hadn't been working on machine learning for years, and HAL wasn't doing its thing back in 1968.[14] But fine, you got me: I have an ego too, so sue me. Like Indignus, he is awfully sneaky, and subverts all attempts at assassination.[15]

THE PERILS OF SPECULATIVE FICTION
IN A SWIFTLY-CHANGING WORLD

While ChatGPT was a big one that shook the world as much as it did my own artistic neuroses, in truth it was just the latest in a chain of examples I had noticed over several years, in which Reality began catching up with Fiction much more quickly than expected. In the time since conceiving of this concept (2011), over the course of writing the first draft (2021), writing *The Afterword* some months later (early 2022), and even in the time between then and now (November 2023), incredible and coincidental happenings started happening one after another, and they have carried on happening.

Even in the process of writing this *After the Afterword,* new breakthroughs and relevant media coverage just keep on coming, on an essentially daily basis, requiring the addition of this very paragraph. Perhaps even this entry will be yet another time capsule in need of a follow-up reflection — an *After the After the Afterword* — by the time I can actually get this thing published! (Please, no.)

Perhaps most on-the-nose: after I had long-since settled on Alpha Centauri B as the target for the vessel Concordis, due to its stellar properties and proximity to Earth, the Australian government funded the TOLIMAN mission (in 2021) to start looking for potentially habitable exoplanets in that very star system.[16] The mission is currently projected to launch in 2024, so who knows — maybe we will truly find an ESUP-9.

There were more coincidences just like this; in fact, in retrospect it feels like there were too many to properly recount. Realizations that artificial intelligences may need an analog of deep sleep[17] (2022), major breakthroughs in

---

14 Kubrick, S. (1968). *2001: A Space Odyssey.* Stanley Kubrick Productions.

15 See *Embrace Inverse Vibrations* (Proavia Press).

16 O'Callaghan, J. (2021, November 17). Scientists Plan Private Mission to Hunt for Earths around Alpha Centauri. *Scientific American.* https://www.scientificamerican.com/article/scientists-plan-private-mission-to-hunt-for-earths-around-alpha-centauri/

17 Hsu, J. (2022, November 10). AI uses artificial sleep to learn new task without forgetting the last. *NewScientist.* https://www.newscientist.com/article/2346597

the work on in vitro gametogenesis[18] (2023) and artificial wombs[19] (2023), and most staggering of all: just this summer (2023), the world saw the first entirely synthetic human embryos created in a lab.[20] All these articles and more led me to both chuckle and grumble to myself as they scrolled across my media feeds, while this very story sat on a hard drive, impatient and eager to escape.

WAR AND PEACE

Unfortunately, not all of the ironic happenings were in the form of scientific breakthroughs. Some of them were breakdowns. Having already alluded to increasing conflict and militarization among nation states in "The Great Backslide Debate" (Chapter 05), it was deeply depressing to see how much worse things really would get, as war broke out in Ukraine in February of 2022.

It should come as no surprise to learn that the worsening situation in Crimea and eastern Ukraine over the preceding years had already been an inspiration for Team Chop-char's thesis, along with other lesser-covered crises like the longstanding but seldom-considered war in Yemen. But, regrettably, the situation kept on backsliding far worse than almost anyone feared. Years later, we are now also well into the resurgence of another extremely depressing conflict between Israel and Hamas. And here we go again, slipping and sliding further away from our potential utopia.

Despite the regrettable framing here, connecting these tragic events to the timeline of writing this trivial story, I want to note that these realities are grave, heartbreaking atrocities that have ended many lives and shattered even more of them. At least to a non-expert eye, they appear to involve cases of obvious crimes against humanity (e.g., the Bucha Massacre of many examples), even if that term has a legal definition that requires due process in international courts. All of that makes the privileged exercise of writing a book opining about peace from the comfort of a far-away country an extremely frivolous endeavor. I do recognize this daily. It is just one more instance, in which I just don't know what to do anymore, in this world that seems to be falling into chaos all around us.

---

18 Stein, R. (2023, May 27). Creating a sperm or egg from any cell? Reproduction revolution on the horizon. *NPR.* https://www.npr.org/sections/health-shots/2023/05/27/1177191913/

19 Garcia, J. (2023, June 29). Spanish researchers aim to 'trick nature' with artificial womb. *Reuters.* https://www.reuters.com/business/healthcare-pharmaceuticals/spanish-researchers-aim-trick-nature-with-artificial-womb-2023-06-29/

20 Devlin, H. (2023, June 14). Synthetic human embryos created in groundbreaking advance. *The Guardian.* https://www.theguardian.com/science/2023/jun/14/advances-in-synthetic-embryos-leave-legislators-needing-to-catch-up

On our theme of ironic timings, the invasion of Ukraine was yet again too on-the-nose, but this time in the context of what was happening in my "real life." I was teaching my class on "Animal Behavior" in February of 2022, and I was in the middle of a unit on "Aggression and Territoriality." You can't make this stuff up. I tried to turn it into a teachable moment. I wanted to make at least *something* positive out of it, even if it was for people a world away. It was about as much as was in my power to do, but it still felt like nowhere near enough of an impact. And so, I went home and wrote a song. I named it, *Lethal Aggression.*

That will fix it.

> *Saw your world crash down today*
> *Saw your everything a-slipping away*
> *And there's not an awful lot we can say*
> *Because we'll never understand all your pain*
> *But we'll hope and pray for you*
> *For the awful lot of good it'll do*
> *And all at once, we open the gates*
> *To the worst of ways that we could take*
> *To the same old game we always have played:*
> *Lethal Aggression*

With a guitar in my hands — as is often the case, as you will surely know about me by now — I did not capture the full range of my thoughts on the matter in this one temporal expression. It was a moment of despair, a counterpoint afforded to myself after mustering an optimistic outlook earlier that same day, while attempting to inspire the next generation of scientists and citizens. I can rationalize it, and put it into a larger perspective, but ultimately I was appropriately broken-hearted that we're fighting wars and killing one another in the year 2022. In reality, however, war is not "the same old game we always have played." It is one of them — one that we have played at quite a lot, surely — but it is not all that we are.

In my class that afternoon [2022-02-24-EY], the very day after the invasion happened, I showed my students a map from a study documenting a case where a chimpanzee troop expanded its territory by taking some of it from a neighboring troop, with the instances of lethal aggression mapped where the boundaries shifted.[21] Lethal aggression, as it sounds, is the propensity to kill conspecifics (members of the same species). I then revealed a map of the Russian invasion of Ukraine from the *New York Times* that day, which looked

---

21 Mitani, J. C., Watts, D. P., & Amsler, S. J. (2010). Lethal intergroup aggression leads to territorial expansion in wild chimpanzees. *Current Biology, 20*(12), R507-R508.

stunningly similar when you see them side by side.[22] But did this war occur because war is in our nature?

I then showed them a rigorous, large-scale analysis of the propensity for lethal aggression in the phylogeny ("family tree") of 1024 mammalian species,[23] and had them engage in a group activity to draw conclusions from the data. Indeed, this trait of lethal aggression is very common across the primates; and while it shows up in several other places in the mammals, it is especially intense and widespread among us nasty primates. In the discipline, we would say there is some "phylogenetic inertia" at play here: the extant (existing) primate species likely descended from an ancestor that engaged in this behavior, and that ancestral propensity has carried on into the present and impacted our behavior to this day.

But this is not the whole picture. By comparing chimpanzee aggression directly to the Russo-Ukrainian conflict, which has an extremely nuanced history of cultural and geopolitical contributing factors, it could be interpreted as an attempt to oversimplify the situation and imply that we are nothing more than fancy chimpanzees. And this was, by design, an opportunity to hammer home another theme of my teaching: evolutionary fallacies. It is tempting to think of humans as descending *from* "monkeys" like the chimpanzee. However, as you hopefully know if you are reading this book, we are not descended from chimpanzees; rather, humans and chimpanzees are both descended from the same common ancestor that was neither chimp nor human.

And the plot thickens. Chimpanzees (*Pan troglodytes*) have a sister species to whom they are more closely-related than chimps are to humans: the bonobo (*Pan paniscus*). By this same logic, humans are equally-related to both chimpanzees and bonobos — and bonobos are extremely peaceable creatures, at least by primate standards. We are not predetermined to be more like one than the other. We are not preprogrammed to be violent. Like essentially all behavior, it is the result of complex interactions between our genetics, our physiology, and our environment. And these are things over which we are, as a sentient and scientific species, beginning to have a modicum of control. That is to say, in learning and being mindful of the factors that contribute to the behavior (violence in this case), we can take actions to mitigate its likelihood.

There was yet more. The analysis compared levels of lethal aggression between territorial species (compared to non-territorial), as well as in social species (compared to solitary). The authors also took an impressive and integrative approach to studying the roots of human violence: by incorporating

---

22 Leonhart, D. (2022, February 24). War in Ukraine. *New York Times*. https://www. nytimes.com/2022/02/24/briefing/ukraine-russia-invasion-putin.html

23 Gómez, J. M., Verdú, M., González-Megías, A., & Méndez, M. (2016). The phylogenetic roots of human lethal violence. *Nature, 538*(7624), 233-237.

archaeological and historical evidence alongside their phylogenetic analyses, they were able to map how violence levels have changed as we became more and more human, as well as over the course of documented history from the paleolithic to the present. I set up the figures for my students with the data removed, and asked them to discuss it in groups and make predictions of what they thought the results would be.

And this is why I love them so: they pretty much nailed it.[24]

As expected with a bit of thinking, the analyses showed that lethal aggression is more extreme in species that are both social and territorial. Humans, unfortunately, hit both those squares on our lethal-aggression bingo cards. But the plot thickened yet further. They also showed that lethal aggression in humans seems to be on the *downturn* from that inferred ancestral primate baseline (*i.e.,* we are getting less aggressive than our ancestors), but it also decreased substantially over human history as we moved into the Modern and Contemporary ages (today).

There are of course many caveats here. And while these findings corroborate an existing line of thinking,[25] it should also be noted that this exact question ("Are we getting more violent, less violent, or neither?") has been a contentious one in the sciences, and there is not unanimous agreement. Nevertheless, there is good evidence to support that notion that we are becoming more like the peaceable bonobos and less like war-like chimps. If it is true, this is good news, and I sure hope that we can keep up the good work.

Lastly, as you do, I ended class with an animation of an elder Ringo Starr, psychedelic colors pulsing as he waved his arms in what has come to be his classic manner, two fingers on each hand poised in a much-needed sign of peace. The slide had only five words: "Ringo Says… Peace and Love." I concur, Ringo. I concur.

AND NOW: THE END, AND TRULY

After being struck by the somber reality that is the previous section, let us return now to far more trivial and fictional matters. Obviously, these "ironic happenings" that kept happening are not "coincidences" at all, so much as they are merely logical extrapolations about the state of the world and longstanding areas of research, hence why an absolute amateur in the areas of artificial intelligence, space exploration, molecular biotechnology, and geopolitics such as myself could have stumbled into these phenomena as reasonable extensions of what

---

24 Allow me to take a moment to lecture you briefly, in my experience as a college educator. Never, ever give in to the "kids these days" fallacy, folks. These next generations coming up behind us are our very best hope, and that hope is very well placed.

25 See Pinker, S. (2011). *The Better Angels of Our Nature.* Viking Press.

was the present at that time. In reality, I was also simply far more sensitive about noticing these kinds of connections to the book everywhere I looked, because the story itself and its relevance to human life were ever-present in my mind. I was falling for these ironic happenings the way people fall for horoscopes.

Knowing this, I have wrestled with why I still feel so compelled to point out some of the phenomena the book had anticipated which then started happening, be it for bettering or worsening, over the course of its creation. It feels like a great big "humble brag" about how clever it is. (Actually, it doesn't feel like that at all, because there appears to be nothing "humble" about it.) I shall confess to my ego being largely to blame, as I have confessed it before. I am probably still hung up on the feeling that this book will seem as stale as last year's bread by the time anyone actually gets the chance to read it. But here is where I attempt to convince you that there are actually lofty and noble reasons why I simply must point these things out. Furthermore, I will chastise my own arrogant swaggering in an effort to buy back a shred of credibility, if you will only do me a favor and kindly fall for the ruse.

And so, the lofty and noble thesis of this section: these truly are wild and crazy times when even speculative fiction authors are having a hard time keeping up with reality. (Granted, it doesn't help that it took me a decade to get around to writing it, but the point remains.) Just as all this whirlwind change and these wild modern times have clearly thrown a firecracker into the sensitive circuits of my mind, with less-than-desirable effects (these Appendices being a good case in point), I at least feel solace in knowing that the rest of the world is out there, losing their minds about all of this too.

On that chipper note, that brings us to the end of this *After the Afterword*, which, naturally, follows *The Afterword (for Afterwards)*. At least for now, it is *The Definite End of All Afterwords*. I have, however, opted to include a few more time capsules, confessions, and reflections, mainly as they pertain to yet another ironic way in which artificial intelligence became far more relevant to this project in the time that has since passed: it now makes its own art.

As all of this back matter spiraled utterly out of control in the run-up to publication, it has resulted in the book practically becoming an *HDP Anthology* of sorts. That seemed ill-advised but also fitting, once I had already taken the leap and included the Reflective Logs along with the story. We had to suffer through 178 years of thoughts from the HDP architects; why not hear a bit from their own architect? I deliberated intensively for weeks, and seriously considered cutting all of it, for the sake of my good name along with all of our sanity, but a different voice chastised me from within: *Give the people what they want!*

Thus, I hope you enjoy some additional instances of this metacognitive madness in the sections that follow. At least for now, metacognitive madness is the only edge I've still got on ChatGPT, so I'm buckled up and leaning in.

ABOUT THE ART
(APPLICATION & REFLECTION)

All visual art accompanying the book was produced by the author, albeit through a variety of techniques and differing degrees of individual control. That is to say...

The main front-cover fixture of the child superimposed in the cosmos is a concept from the author, but the image itself was created by DALL-E2 (OpenAI). The surroundings beyond it (i.e., the stellar objects and ocean on the front and back covers) were created in Adobe Photoshop through numerous instances of generative expansion, which the author digitally edited and combined to produce superimposed imagery. All other cover and interior design elements were generated by the author's hands directly using a camera or moving a mouse (i.e., not AI).

A few special shoutouts about the accompanying art. The DNA double helix on the spine is the actual molecular structure of DNA, modeled from X-ray diffraction data (see Protein Data Bank entry 1BNA at https://www.rcsb.org/structure/1bna) and digitally edited to incorporate into the cover. Forget "artist renderings" of DNA. Gimme the real deal, baby.

The blocks on the interior title page are real-life toys — *Spaaaaaace Blocks!* — from my real-life home, banged up by real-life human toddlers. Ironically, the single most damaged block was the most important of them all: the one representing Alpha Centauri, the home of the fictional ESUP-9 and destination of our noble protagonists. And yet, this is serendipitous and fitting, as this little block also symbolizes the character of Potch, at least in this author's mind. One may notice that there are nine blocks all banded together in a well-structured pyramid, missing one sad little block, off on its own. It is very hard to tell, but it may interest some readers to know that the star "Regulus" is also represented. Speaking of shoutouts, here's one to my inner Great Ape.[26]

Oh yes! And consider the HDP logo trademarked, should anyone aim to start this project in earnest over the next 145 years (2024 - 2168). Also...please don't do that.

Let's just take care of Mother Earth and the children she already has.

---

26 This paragraph is the equivalent of a stand-up comic who feels compelled to explain their joke in grave detail. And just as in that case, it's a sign of certain success in one's craft.

ON THE MATTER OF AI ART AND ARTISTS

The use of generative AI in creative endeavors is an extremely important issue, as well as a divisive debate that is unfortunately oversimplified by parties on both sides. Here, I focus on visual expression, as this is the application I have used in this work. I also mostly gloss over the many very good reasons why these tools have been controversial, largely because as reasons they are both obvious and ubiquitous in the public conversation. I'm sure an AI chat bot can summarize them for you nicely, if you've been living under a rock.[27] Instead of a comprehensive review of these concerns, I focus this on my own application and, when dabbling into the broader topic, considering ethical ways of moving forward.

As described above, I used AI output from both Photoshop and DALL-E2 in the cover. Adobe claims that its training data includes only licensed stock photos; this is a major consideration because in that case the original authors opt in to their work being used by others and are compensated for doing so.[28] (It should be noted, however, that some non-consenting stock photo artists still take issue with their association with this application.[29]) While there are many ethical concerns about generative AI art broadly — if it is true in practice — using only licensed work does go a long way in addressing one of the largest of them. On the other hand, the ethicality of OpenAI's training data is even less clear. In fact, their use of copyrighted material is justifiably under litigation at the very moment of writing this (November, 2023).[30] Beyond grounds for a lawsuit, this was grounds for personal concern, and I considered at length whether I should omit this component of the art entirely.

There are a few reasons I have opted to include it anyway, despite my reservations, and approach the situation the way that I did. First, whatever you think about the technology's right to exist, we can surely agree that it's important to disclose its use, as you have read in the previous section. I also consider this statement an opportunity to discuss and reflect on the matter,

---

27 Also, here's a starter: Parra, D., and Stroud, S.R. (2023, February 24). The Ethics of AI Art. *Center for Media Engagement, University of Texas at Austin.* https://mediaengagement. org/research/the-ethics-of-ai-art/

28 Edwards, B. (2023, March 22). Ethical AI art generation? Adobe Firefly may be the answer. *Ars Technica.* https://arstechnica.com/information-technology/2023/03/ethical-ai-art-generation-adobe-firefly-may-be-the-answer/

29 John, D. (2023, August 24). Artists complain of AI 'copyright infringement' on Adobe Stock. *Creative Bloq.* https://www.creativebloq.com/news/adobe-copyright-ai

30 Alter, H., and Harris, E.A. (2023, September 20). Franzen, Grisham and Other Prominent Authors Sue OpenAI. *New York Times.* https://www.nytimes.com/2023/09/20/books/authors-openai-lawsuit-chatgpt-copyright.html

rather than merely using the output and passing it off as my own (never okay), or else disclosing it and then swiftly moving on as if everything is hunky-dory.

Second, the concept for the cover image *is* entirely my own, and it took a tremendous deal of trial-and-error to get the tool to produce something that matched that original vision. Even then, I took the output and integrated it with other art by hand, to form a larger composite product. Despite their ease of use, these tools do not just spit out book covers: they are digital tools, like so many other tools human artists have used before, to enhance and extend one's own creative capabilities. Sadly, as an artist who dabbles in many modalities, my skill in any one of these areas is almost never sufficient to execute the artistic concepts I envision and wish to see expressed. But my friends, this is precisely what creative tools are for: to help artists come closer to fulfilling their creative visions.

And yes, I know: look at the pathetic "AI Artist" (not remotely an identity I hold, for the record) whining about how much work it is, and how AI art is "real art" too. That stereotype of the sleezy and/or schlubby "AI Artist" cranking out visual content at a mile a minute so they can spin it around for profit and then whining about how hard it is and how creative they are, should it ever be fitting, is surely worthy of mockery. The point here, however, is that I had a vision; I then put in the work to make the tool give me the very specific output that I wanted, rather than asking the tool itself for an idea, or using it in a way that is clearly about personal gain rather than artistic expression. It is not an easy or even practical distinction to make (who is the judge of acceptable usage or intent?), but there is a meaningful distinction here concerning how the art is used, at least in my mind.

Third, the usage for this book did not directly detract from the business of any human artists. In this case, the human artist is myself, and I would have created a cover on my own, one way or another. Make no mistake: I would love to collaborate with other artists, including those with far superior visual capabilities than my own; but artists deserve compensation, cover art takes a great deal of work and is therefore very expensive, and this publishing endeavor is *deeply* in debt as it is. (Please don't tell the Board of Trustees at Proavia Press...)

Now, one could attest that artists may have indirectly suffered, and that it's simply wrong of the application to be influenced by their art to generate it for others. Undoubtedly, AI is stylistically influenced by the artists whose work went into the training data. However, that is not an issue with AI-generated art, but rather with Art as a whole. Even the best human artists in history have been "stylistically influenced" by the work of prior human artists, often in obvious and even unethical ways. It's actually the entire premise for how art typically works: people see it, read it, hear it, and they synthesize it all in their minds and make their own versions. One could say that it's copyright infringement because the original artists who inspired their successors weren't paid.

Even that, I'm afraid to say — as someone who is deeply in favor of and invested in copyright protections — may well be a misunderstanding of what copyright is and what it isn't. There is such a thing as Fair Use, and said clause (in US copyright law) was actually *designed* so as to require litigation, because there is no "one size fits all" approach to determining what is and is not Fair Use. Artists may gripe about it when Fair Use is invoked by others to build on their work, but it likewise benefits them as artists who may wish to invoke Fair Use to build on the work of others. While it is not a perfect system, copyright and its constraints are crafted as they are for good reasons: they attempt to strike the balance between a creator's intellectual property rights on the one hand, and further expression and innovation on the other.

Is a human artist required to pay for the work of artists they put into the "training data" that is their nervous system? Sometimes they do, yes: they buy a painting, a book, an album. But very, very often, over the course of an artist's entire development and lifetime, over the course of human history: no, they do not. They see an image from the street, they're handed a tattered paperback from a friend, they hear that new band on the radio. Are these instances legal? This is an empirical question and the answer is: yes, in many cases, it absolutely is (with the exception of piracy). Is it ethical? I believe the answer is also: yes, it absolutely is (with the same exception). Even in the case of those exceptions, it is the stealing that makes it wrong, not the inspiration the thief may get from their stolen goods. This is just the way our minds work. We take things in, we integrate them into our own understanding, and we generate outputs. If you deem this is unfair, then you must hereby forfeit your use of human language.

Does this mean that generative AI works in exactly the same way as human inspiration and expression? Of course not. But are they fundamentally different in the most salient properties when it comes to making art? I'm not so sure. Are software programs not allowed to take in sensory input, learn from it about the styles and standards of the craft, and output novel content? As noted, all of these are what the nervous system of a human does when it makes art, and any artist who denies that fundamental similarity isn't being sincere or honest with themselves. Most of them go out of their way to give props to their inspirations. (What up, Neil Young?) One could reasonably argue that — just like in the case of human creation — as long as that novel output does not cross the line of what constitutes overt plagiarism of another's work, the process is similar enough to what human artists do that its use should be permitted. One could take it further, that it shouldn't even require compensation for the training data, if it is using publicly displayed works of art. I do not personally *agree* with that on moral grounds, because frankly the corporations developing these tools will indeed profit from them, so they should share those gains with the artists who helped them do that. Much as I wish it were not so, I do however understand the argument, and I think it may have both logical and legal grounds. I suppose we shall see.

So many artists see AI as a threat because they view it as a replacement. What they fail to consider is that these are creative tools that they are also welcome to use to enhance their own work. Despite appearances, I truly do understand and respect their concerns, and I have tried to address many of them here. There are absolutely major grounds for concern in how generative AI is currently being used, and these ethical concerns need to be remedied. There are also, however, a lot of fundamentalists in this fight, and fundamentalism is something that really irks me when I see it. To me, the fundamentalists in this fight sound like old bluegrass players whining about that new-fangled rock-and-roll. (I don't know that this ever once happened in bluegrass circles, but let's go with it.) Society and technology evolves. It's a good thing. Bluegrass is boring. Gimme that Psychedelic Soul.[31]

Above all, as the society that spawned HDP came to realize, it is imperative that AI tools be used in ways that enhance and complement human activities, rather than reduce or replace them. Thus, artists should embrace and be empowered by the incredible tools that generative AI provides, much as they did for the charcoal blocks, typewriters, and electric guitar amplifiers that came before them. But this can only happen if AI developers incentivize and collaborate with artists, rather than parasitize them. Whether we like it or not, it's already a symbiosis; let's ensure that we can make it a mutualism.[32]

So what's the solution? What do *The Royal We* at Proavia Press propose? Well, it's not our job exactly, but the imagined version of you that lives in our mind asked, so fine: here you go. What seems like a reasonable path forward?

1.) Artists should have to actively opt in to training data and be compensated in a way that is appropriate and proportionate. The consent process should be affirmative in nature, and not require opting out through tedious or misleading means. Compensation should be explicit, so artists can choose whether the terms are acceptable or not, and take their training art elsewhere or nowhere at all. In this way, the input to these tools can be ethical.

---

31 Relax people: this is a joke. I've listened to and enjoyed tons of bluegrass in my life. More importantly, all forms of art are worthy of praise in my book, whether I personally want to perceive them or not.

32 Contrary to how people tend to use the term (as a synonym of mutualism), symbiosis is a general concept with different outcomes spanning commensalism, parasitism, and mutualism. Apologies for being pedantic in the footnotes.

2.) Data usage should be made transparent in terms of policy and practice. The way the algorithms work may never be truly transparent, but the technology's training data and administrative policies themselves can and should be.

3.) Regulatory frameworks should be put in place to ensure that these deals are being honored by the technology. As HDP knew well in its dealings with Clonotany: never trust a company. Artist buy-in will increase as tech companies and their (currently nonexistent) watchdogs earn that trust through action and enforcement.

4.) Plagiarism itself is still real, important, and enforceable. While the inner machinations of the technology may never be fully intelligible, much like with human art, it is the output that matters. If there is evidence of plagiarism with that output, it should be grounds for removal of the artwork. Given that there are not clearcut ways for users to always know that their work is a little *too* inspired by some aspect of the training data, a "Cease and Desist" should suffice upon discovery, and further legal action should only be executed when that is actively ignored. Even this concern may be alleviated if the training data can be limited to artists who opt in to allowing derivative works.

5.) Artists should think of AI as a creative tool and feel free to use it as such. Much like with other creative tools, it should be used not as an end in itself, but as a tool to achieve the end you as the artist envision. In particular, humans should come to AI with their own ideas, and they should also work to take the AI output, build on it in some way, and ideally adapt it into broader and unique compositions.

6.) Proactive disclosure of its usage is already effectively required. This one is just a given. If you use it, disclose where and how you do so. Failing to disclose the use of AI implies that a work is entirely your own, and that's one of several forms of plagiarism.

7.) We are in the early days of this technology; our individual and collective understanding of this issue can and should evolve. For example, the compensation requirement for training data is an ongoing legal debate. These kinds of issues will be resolved as our collective decision-making processes play out (as flawed and even broken as they sometimes are), and it is incumbent upon us as individuals and society to think about these issues objectively, help us all find the right balance in these conflicting interests, and build the regulatory structures that ensure an ethical use. We don't all have to agree, but we do all have to follow the laws, and we should make those laws make sense.

We here at Proavia Press do not have all the answers (we just pretend to), and our own understanding of these issues is evolving on an almost daily basis. We reserve the right to change our mind on some or all of this nonsense, if better ideas and insights can compel us. "May the best fit ideas win."

So there we go, problem solved. (That was sarcasm.) And no, ChatGPT did not write this summary for me. I *also* have always loved well-structured lists. This love, above all, is why I became a teacher. The bullet lists.

ON AI GENERATED TEXT (IN CREATIVE WRITING CONTEXTS)

What about using AI-authored text to help with a work of fiction such as this? This next section for disclosure and reflection should move much more quickly. The reason? I didn't use it.

Now...will it *actually* be quicker? Time will tell.

But probably not.

It may seem perplexing that I employed generative AI art for the cover, and even went out of my way to explain the thought process behind why I think it justifiable, but then ignored the incredible power of generative text through tools like ChatGPT. Why the difference in my willingness to use AI work when it's in the written word?

Part of the answer is simple: at least for the crafting of the entire main narrative, the option didn't really yet exist in the way it does now. (See "After the Afterword" if you haven't already.) To be totally honest, I did briefly tinker (in Summer, 2021) with the beta version of a tool called Sudowrite that was built on GPT-3. People in my indie author community were discussing the tool,[33] and as one well into the process of writing a book involving an essentially-sentient AI, it unsurprisingly intrigued me — not because I wanted to use it, but because I wanted to see what it might be like, and how it did and didn't work. Keep in mind, this was well before the release of ChatGPT.

So I suppose, technically, I did dabble tangentially with AI for a day or so while writing the main narrative — but even with the explicit objective of not using a word or spark of inspiration from its output, it never felt right. I was to the point of Chapter 37 (Mustering the Will to Move), and I think it may have impacted the beginning of that chapter a very minuscule amount — again, all while actively trying *not* to be influenced by it. Even then, once you take in its output as input to your mind, there is really no going back. You can attempt

---

33 The Creative Penn Podcast. (2021, June 25). https://www.thecreativepenn.com/2021/06/25/writing-fiction-with-ai-sudowrite-with-amit-gupta/

to ignore it, but that doesn't mean it won't have impacts. Overall, it felt like cheating. If this sounds like a double standard, given the previous statement about visual art, you're correct.

Later, ChatGPT did burst onto the scene (November, 2022), when the novel's main narrative had been done for a full year, but when I still had more than half of the reflective logs left to write. Now this tool, I've played with quite a bit, although never in the context of asking it to help me with the creative aspect of my fiction. Naturally, I much preferred asking it philosophical questions and having spirited debates. (I've found that it's generally a much more open-minded sparring partner than most humans I've met.) I have also used it a little as a grammar-checker, for some particularly perplexing problems with prose. I find it both more enjoyable and instructive to be able to approach questions about my real good grammar in a conversational manner, as opposed to the tedious process of usage dictionaries and searching through endless online opinions.

Beyond a few grammatical puzzles, I never asked ChatGPT's help with the content of the project (consisting of only a couple dozen remaining logs at that point). In fact I was oddly protective and resistant to its influence, probably as a result of the greasy feeling I got from that first flirtation with Sudowrite. Frankly, I just don't want those circuits messing with my mind when I'm trying to create.

But why? Let's get back to that pesky double standard. Why the slightly different impressions of using AI in the context of graphics versus text? The simple answer is that I don't know. Because I'm human, and that means hypocrite. But let me give myself at least a little benefit of the doubt. Let's see if we can make it make sense. For this, my friends, is actually why I write: to figure out what I think about things.

In the case of visual art, I only ever used AI judiciously, and by iterating prompts to execute a very specific vision my mind already possessed. With graphics, it always felt like I was the creature in control; like I was using it as a tool to get to a known outcome which was the product of my own psyche. With ChatGPT, it feels more like a free source of both the outcome and the inspiration itself. It feels like the technology is the creature in control, and it will gladly spin my straw into gold if I will only hand over the niggling thing that is my soul.

But, was it wrong of me to use the thesaurus app I just opened on my phone to discover the word "niggling" existed, when I'd only been able to come up with the much more mundane "frivolous" in my insufficient mind? "Niggling" certainly sounds more lilting and poetic in combination with the other words I did know and wanted to use, even if it's doubtful that many others will know what it means any more than I did a few minutes ago.[34] Is it wrong to use tools to enhance our capabilities? Generally, no, it isn't, as established above. But is AI different somehow? I just don't know. But when it comes to an author using AI to give them ideas or do the writing itself, it feels like it is. Or at least, there are even more ways to use it that dabble into questionably — or unquestionably — unethical terrain.

There is also the difference in my personal relationship to the crafts in question, which may bias my conclusions. With visuals, in addition to the considerations in the section above, it feels like it's giving me something I am literally unable to otherwise do.[35] With ChatGPT, however, it feels like I'd be using the technology to do something I *can* do, but that I'd just be choosing not to — out of laziness, out of fear, out of a lack of inspiration. Those don't seem like good enough reasons to ask technology for free content if you purport to be a writer. I *can* write, and I *can* develop ideas for my writing. Asking ChatGPT for the premise of a sci-fi novel, or to help blast through a bout of writer's block with a clever idea all its own — that feels like stealing in a way that asking it to paint me a very specific picture never did for me. For some reason, the incredible flexibility that comes with the use of human language makes it feel far more powerful, and that greater power makes me far more apprehensive.

Yet again, if you notice a double standard, you're not wrong. And I know that many writers claim to be using AI to help with their fiction in ethical ways.[36] But I can't help but ask: why exactly are you writing? If you're actively lifting

---

34 I checked to make sure this isn't offensive, and we're good. I first researched its etymology and usage in multiple places (Google, dictionaries, online forums) — but it seems germane to the conversation to hear what ChatGPT had to say about it. My question: "Is the word 'niggling' offensive? It is PERFECT for this particular use, but I worry about how it might be perceived." It had this to say: "The word 'niggling' itself is not inherently offensive, and it is often used to describe something small or trivial that causes annoyance. However, it's important to be aware that the word can sound similar to a racial slur, which may lead to misunderstandings or discomfort for some people. If you are concerned about appearances and want to avoid any potential misinterpretation or offense, you might consider using an alternative word or phrase that conveys a similar meaning without the risk of causing discomfort."
(ChatGPT by OpenAI, accessed on 11/18/2023)
I also plan on never using this word again.

35 One could argue this is exactly what makes my use unethical. There may be merit there. But, in cases, the cited statement is true for even extremely talented visual artists. I'm not sure any cover artists for-hire would have produced quite *that*, even if they would have produced things equally or more amazing.

36 As a member of the Alliance of Independent Authors, I have also agreed to the Author Member Code of Standards (https://allianceindependentauthors.org/author-code-of-standards/) and Ethical Author Campaign (https://selfpublishingadvice.org/alli-campaigns/ethical-author/), which include guidelines on AI.

ideas and/or words from AI, it starts to seem like there are motives other than art. Let us neither forget or pretend there aren't hoards of scammers doing just that and flooding the already-flooded market with AI-authored books for the sake of profit alone. Maybe I'm just jealous because I probably couldn't even successfully sell those. But it matters not, because I write for two reasons mainly: to find out what I think about things, and because it's a lot easier than trying to find a therapist with availability in 2023. Above all, I do it just to *create*. Asking AI to do that for me is like asking it to have my orgasm.

While using some AI images on the cover and then taking issue with AI text may be a bit double-standard-ish, I think the reconciliation here is the point I made above about visual art as well: whose *ideas* are being conveyed in the art, regardless of modality? At the end of the day, a generative image app will only output what you tell it to; a generative language app will output whatever you ask it for. That may be a subtle or even false dichotomy, but it feels both real and meaningful to me, given the way I've interacted with these tools so far. And should ideas matter more than execution? Maybe not. Maybe this is just my bias talking, as someone who enjoys both experiencing and making art that is rooted in ideas, which not all art needs to be. But for me, that has a lot to do with whether I consider myself the artist using the tool, or just the guy taking credit for something that something else made. Using that clever premise or plot twist that an AI gave you seems like a micro-form of plagiarism — because it wasn't your idea. And if you're just adding micro-plagiarisms together to make some kind of macroscopic amalgam, what is it that you have but the charade of creation?

You could disclose its use in general, I suppose, but for something as long as a novel, to capture all the ways an author's interactions with AI have influenced the work will require back matter disclosures even longer than this, and that is really saying something. You could say, "this book used elements from generative artificial intelligence" and leave it at that, but then why am I reading your book, a human author with their name on the cover, when I could just ask ChatGPT to tell me a story directly and leave you out of it entirely? Human authorship should still mean something in the age of AI, and every bit of the content should consist of your own human ideas if your own human identity is taking the credit.

Now who sounds like a fundamentalist?

Are there then ways to use AI ethically when writing? I have mostly omitted discussing this middle ground because others have written on it extensively and I am building on these conversations in my mind.[37] (A reprise: I'm sure

---

37 One of many examples: Alliance of Independent Authors. (2022, December 31). *AI for Authors: Practical and Ethical Guidelines.* https://selfpublishingadvice.org/ai-for-authors-guidelines/

ChatGPT could summarize them for you nicely. In fact, I know it can, because I've had this conversation with it more than once.) As for adding to those prior implied conversations, in my view, much the same advice from above about visual art should apply. Despite my incredible urge to use one, I'll spare you another structured list because it would be largely redundant.

I think the important things to stress for text is that you should propose your own ideas and creative input to the app, and not ask it to give those to you. I also think you should refrain from using any of the app's wording directly. Those aren't your own words, and that's what authors use: their own words. Ask it questions, bounce around possibilities, treat it like an extremely clever search engine, research tool, editor — and then use other sources to verify relevant information you may learn, integrate its output with your own understanding, and let yourself be the one who expresses the end result entirely.

Yes, despite my vacillating views, I do think there is middle ground, and it ultimately comes down to synergy. The example above about using unsanctioned art in training data demonstrated cases of parasitism by the tech companies, while creative writers leveraging the power of AI-generated text can manifest that in ways entailing parasitism by the user. Inverse examples also exist for both modalities, and none of them are okay. In this new age of machine-human super-intelligences, it's all about finding the bounds that ensure complementarity and mutualism between those two forms of so-called intelligence.

As for me personally, I guess why even more innocuous influence and usage of AI language models for fiction still struck me as meddling and wrong is that — for me — the creation itself is the point. In that inexplicable act, there is still something of the Sacred, if the Spirit Block architects were ever able to adequately define that, all those years ago in the future. The intrusion of inauthentic inspiration, by an intelligence deemed artificial by definition, feels like a violation of that sanctity. This is self-righteous, surely; but sincere.

There are, however, countless other applications of this technology, many of which are incredibly exciting and could undoubtedly benefit humanity; there are also ways it could very well not. Again, this reflection focused solely on its use by human authors writing fiction; even in the realm of writing alone — for both myself and others, who have different reasons and justifications for their creations — I can envision appropriate uses. The problem is deciding what those are and how to enforce them. As in the context of art, we need to think about the benefits and challenges for all those diverse applications, ask ourselves some difficult questions, fix these "flawed and even broken" collective decision-making processes, and figure out how to move forward in a way that is both fair and beneficial for individuals, society, and the planet alike. The technology doesn't yet get a vote. We get to decide, and we need to do it quickly.

And using a thesaurus is perfectly unobjectionable.

ANOTHER ONE AFTER ALL

(FOOLED YOU TWICE, SO THE SHAME'S ON YOU)

Having come to the end of this ample back matter, I find it important to bring this work full circle. Up until now, we have strayed into some territory that, while tangential, nevertheless felt important to address. For example, I used AI art in the cover; I know for certain that some people will find that dubious, while others deem it not even necessary to justify. Conversely, I did not use AI in crafting the text of the book; I know that some will find that commendable, while others will deem it overly cautious or restrictive. Right or wrong, I am neurotic enough to feel compelled to defend myself from all directions, and this inclination is partly to blame for your current bout of appendicitis. More on this to come.

But first, let's get back to the tech. Despite it obviously being an interesting – and apparently a much-more-timely-than-anticipated – component of the story, this is not actually a book about artificial intelligence, or even our relationship to it. I didn't want to end on matters so tangential, topical, timely, or trivial, and let that be the last taste on the tongue of your attention. Because those trendy new toys and our current squabbles about them aren't what this book is about. It's about something much more timeless than all that.

HOW THE TECH GOT INVOLVED

This is a book with a lot of thoughts about technology, but it is not a book about technology. This is a book about people – our relationships to each other, to our parents, to our children, and to our environments in general. That environment now increasingly includes technology, however; and while "technology" in the general sense (tool use defined broadly) has ever played a key role in the origin and expansion of *Homo sapiens* (relative to even our closest primate relatives), it will continue to play an incredibly important role in our future, and in ways that are not yet comparable to our prior relationship with it. And in this particular tale, it was an essential mechanism for humans to expand into the cosmos, to set the stage for the story as it needed to be set. So that's where it fits in, and how it got swept up into this tale. ABRAM seems happy enough to sail off into the sunset of a very different sun, even if that means its own eventual demise. I'm much more concerned with the people on board, as they sail into the cosmos and into the future.

As for the "into the future" part, we don't have a choice. But whether we *should* expand "into the cosmos" is still a matter of debate, and I've come down on that already: let's first prove that we are worthy of it. As things stand, I'm not sure we'll be around long enough on this planet for extra-planetary expansion to even be a possibility, even if we decide we should do it. I don't care what blowhard tech entrepreneurs have to say about how important it is for people to get beyond a single planet, or how they should be dumping billions of dollars and rocket-loads of carbon emissions into the atmosphere to do it. They can pretend it's about pursuing space travel as a practical solution to our current ecological crises, instead of lining their own pockets. Blowhards gonna blow. The fact is that we are a long way off from this being remotely feasible, if it ever will be, while Earth's old friend Impending Doom is literally pressing down the doorbell as we speak – so let's focus on that part, shall we?

Speaking of blowhards, in this "Post-Truth World" in which we live, this is a time when, frankly, not everyone is always entirely honest. At best, every one of us is flawed; worse than that, we sometimes have individual motives that are "ulterior" in form. Even honest folk are not always entirely reasonable, when deeply held convictions start being called into question. It's a complex world, we have different identities, experiences, and perspectives, and we therefore, understandably, sometimes see things in very different ways. These are all good things. But we have to navigate those differences more successfully than we seem to be doing of late.

DOWN TO THE ROOT

And so it was, in thinking about putting out a work like this into a world like this, that I got myself into this mess of appendices in the first place, with back matter sprawling like the invasive blackberry brambles that have conquered my yard. So, let's start digging down to the roots, to grab hold and pull them out once and for all. Let us revisit where this downward spiral started: why the need for the very first Afterword that threw us into this infinite vortex? This is the appointed time and place for Time Capsules and Confessions, apparently, so here it goes.

I was afraid.

I was afraid that people would misinterpret my intent when writing a book about human history, the future, and the directed evolution of our species. And for very good reason. The relationship between "directed evolution" and human history in the prior century was extremely problematic, and it contributed to some of the worst crimes against humanity in the entirety of that human history. Evolutionary Biology must own up to that, as it has been doing; but it also means that we need to do our part to fix it, and offer the world something better for the following era.

The fact is that racist people have used misconceptions and junk science to rationalize their bigoted world views — but sadly, in the case of eugenics, some of those people *were* Science. They were department heads, deans, leaders in their disciplines. They were "experts." Science, as an institution, is not perfect. In fact "Western Science" has been deeply flawed and unethical in ways that warrant a whole multi-volume book, rather than yet another insufficient paragraph, in another insufficient-and-yet-paradoxically-overkill-Afterword. Science is not perfect — but it does get better as it ages, if it's working correctly. Scientists of the present era must work hard to correct those lingering misconceptions and pieces of junk science — many of which are still especially persistent and problematic in the field of Evolution — and do everything we can to ensure that science and ethics inform our future history in a righteous manner.

This matters a great deal, because — and this is the kicker — human evolution is going to happen one way or another, whether we like it or not. We must think seriously about how it *could* go, so that we can envision the ways that we *want* it to go, and help ensure that we can lead it there instead of the more dubious alternatives. And by We, I mean People. I mean Humans. I mean my kids, but I mean your kids too. I mean kids I never knew. I mean all of us. It is a very large one, but we are all in the same family. That's no mere platitude. This is one of the beautiful insights that evolution does have to offer: we are literally one great big family. We're just … sometimes a dysfunctional one.

So there, I said it. I was afraid.
But fear runs deep.

I was afraid about misperceptions once I had finished a book like this, but I was much more afraid about much more frightening things, before I ever typed a single word of the story. The very first Afterword discusses how the book came out so differently than intended, once I finally began writing it, ten years after it was initially conceived as "an entirely academic conception." My truest thoughts about all this are only alluded to vaguely in that first time capsule, in which I describe having been introduced to the child-like spirits that were Potch, Pee-pop, and the rest of my son's imaginary crew.

The real reason the story shifted from philosophical to something-much-more-visceral in the time between conception and creation is even simpler. It dwells one more hand's width deeper down the length of the root: I became a father. In fact, by the time I was done writing the main story (October of 2021), I was a father twice over. And being a parent is absolutely terrifying.

I suspect this has always been the case, once you hold that tiny, innocent, helpless creature in your hands, with an entire lifetime only potentially before them — a lifetime just like the one you were somehow blessed to be given, like your parents before you, and your grandparents before them. I suspect that feeling has always been scary, considering the many perils of the world which have always existed.

Before being a parent, even if it mostly lay deep under the waves of my waking awareness, I was frightened of dying. Now, while I will surely never be able to fully let go of that fear, I'm old enough that I've come to accept it as inevitable. Maybe I'm just exceptionally tired. Although, I've also come to see it as a beautiful link in a much grander tradition than any one life. But, in practice these days, the only thing keeping me going is the realization that my wife and I are the most important thing in the world for these two little children. We brought them into this world, and it is our *duty* to take care of them. And so… for any parental figures of Humanity out there who might be listening — "Are you there, ABRAM? It's me, Adam." — there are children in this world, in fact more every day, and it is society's *duty* to take care of them. But the future feels especially perilous right now, and society's ability to protect its children and, in turn, itself, feels especially inadequate.

The truly out-of-control spiral of climate change and our constantly-shifting worst-case scenario projections: "Well…what if we could keep it under *three* degrees Celsius?" The rampant pollution that has come with unfettered industrial growth. The role of technology in our childhood development. The exploding mental health crisis, including among youth. The astronomical-and-growing wealth inequality. The rampant poverty and drug addiction on the streets of my own home town. The resurgence of overt racism and bigotry, and the normalization of extremism, nationalism, fascism, and political violence in my own home country. The heart-rending human rights atrocities happening within and across several national borders. Shall I keep going?

It's starting to feel an awful lot like The Great Backslide the history books of this fictional timeline described, and even more like it with every month that has passed since I'd originally written that. To be clear, progress has always come in fits and starts, and I do not suggest that "the world used to be better" and only now are there problems. Rather, we are objectively sliding backwards on the promises of a world that had so much promise in my own lifetime — in the time since I was one of our children. And we're struggling immensely with some fairly simple things before the *real* trouble has even started hitting the scene. It makes you wonder how we're going to handle those much bigger crises, like when a stunning amount of earth's surface area exceeds the wet bulb temperature in which humans can survive. It makes you wonder, "What kind of life have I doomed my children to?" Unless things start changing, and quickly —

Right — sorry. This is a story of Hope.

I'm starting to sound a little too much like Potch.

Because things *can* change, and sometimes even quickly. We tend to think of evolution happening on the scale of "millions and millions of years" – but this is also a misconception. It certainly does happen over those time scales; but it can also happen extremely quickly in many cases, especially when the traits involved are behavioral or cultural in nature. And what Potch ultimately attempts to convey in that debate, if poorly, is that the root of so many of our problems are behavioral in nature. The planet is warming uncontrollably because *we acted* so as to make that happen; it is continuing to warm because *we have failed to take enough of the actions* necessary to change, and some of us (looking at you, fossil fuel corporations) have even *acted* to make the problem harder to solve.

Things *can* change, and *we* can change them. We just have to agree to do it. We just need to start listening, valuing each other, including our differences, and choosing to cooperate, rather than going along with the status quo of "every person, every business, every country for itself."

But agreeing is difficult. Heck, even just deeply listening to one other person you deeply care about can be exceptionally difficult for us to do, saddled with bias and bluster as even the best of us are. Now multiply that against all the countless ways it is far more difficult to do this at higher and higher levels of human organization: our neighborhoods, workplaces, cities and states, nations, and of course, the global collective.

And this is where evolutionary biology in particular has something to offer. Several somethings, actually. Because this is exactly the kind of dilemma evolution has solved more than once.

TRULY SUPER ORGANISMS

We don't think of it this way explicitly, but society is basically an organism — a superorganism, if you wish. Or at least, it could be that, if we work together more intentionally, and overcome our petty squabbles. In reality, organisms are incredibly well-regulated systems that only evolved into units in their own right *because* they were able to do just that: put the conflict between their competing parts in check, and regulate behavior for the good of the whole. And it's not just "individuals" like you and me that have been able to do this.

First of all, the concept of Individuals as we know them is somewhat an illusion, as our protagonist learns in *Embrace Inverse Vibrations*. (Yet another handy reprise: Life is complicated.) We consider a single human being an individual, and we consider an individual bacterium the same thing; but these are very different levels of biological organization. Technically, a single human being is a multicellular, eukaryotic organism, whereas a bacterium is a single-cellular, prokaryotic organism. We are essentially a group-of-groups of things more directly comparable to that bacterium.

Put less cryptically, it is more accurate to compare just the mitochondria that live in our cells to an individual bacterium, but that lone mitochondria is just one citizen in the giant civilization that is the human body. Second, even among multi-cellular, eukaryotic organisms, there have been other species in which it is the "society" that functions more like what we think of as an individual; for example, colonial invertebrates like bryozoans or siphonophores, or the more familiar example of a colony of bees. It is possible to make this leap from a bunch of competing "individuals" to a harmonious "collective."

This is the aforementioned Major Evolutionary Transition, and not only has it happened in our own past to make us what we are (as multicellular, eukaryotic organisms); but it has also happened again for other multicellular, eukaryotic organisms, who have far more well-integrated and harmonious social systems. But, having given those examples, this need not be the stuff of nightmares. While convergent evolution (in which different species land on similar traits because of similar environmental pressures) is both possible and important, it is also important to remember that even when under similar pressures, different organisms often land on different adaptations because of their different starting templates. So fear not: we don't need to glue ourselves together or instate a global monarch to rule us with an iron fist. Our own equivalent of a Major Transition could look very much like what we have right now, only requiring a change as simple as effectively regulating our collective behaviors.

But this is far from how we operate at present.

MCCs [MATTERS OF COLLECTIVE CONCERN][38]

Perhaps an example.

Just this month, it became clear that the lead country for the COP28 climate conference, the United Arab Emirates (UAE), was planning to use that opportunity to advocate for fossil fuel development, due to one of those pesky ulterior motives we've mentioned: it is in their nation's best economic interest.[39] This is a blatant conflict of interest that is also, coincidentally, not that difficult to remedy. The rest of the collective just needs to intervene, remove the conflict, and hold the meeting in a less biased manner. Or if we must bias our climate conferences, how about we let a country that's literally losing ground to sea level rise run the show?

Despite it being easy to get outraged (it's outrageous), when we take a step back, it's also understandable and easy to be sympathetic: they deserve to consider their nation's best interest, just like every other nation. I am not trying

---

38 Thank you, Integrate. [You're welcome, my friend.]

39 Rowlatt, J. (2023, November 26). UAE planned to use COP28 climate talks to make oil deals. *BBC*. https://www.bbc.com/news/science-environment-67508331

to pick on UAE,[40] and I want every one of its citizens to thrive. This is also just one of countless examples I could have chosen to make the same point from the full span of modern history. This one just happened to be in the news this week, and the news delivers examples like these on a daily basis these days. (If you want even more examples and outrage to go with this same subject matter, I highly recommend a recent TED Talk by Al Gore.[41])

I am not out to pick on any one person, corporation, or country. I understand their motivations. The point is that this is one situation where an entity's motivations (a nation in this case), doesn't affect only itself, but affects the collective of other entities greatly (the world in this case). In other words, it is a Matter of Collective Concern, as HDP described it. I want individual nations — and in particular, all of their *citizens* — to thrive. It's just that I also want Earth to be inhabitable enough that I don't have to send my kids to ESUP-9.

The problem is that we don't have well-designed or well-regulated *systems* for handling these kinds of conflicts — regulatory systems that a superorganism needs, if it wants more than "A Snowball's Chance in Hell" of proper function and survival. At the moment, every organ in the body politic is trying to get ahold of as much of the bodily resources as it can, the rest of the body be damned. It is a natural tendency, surely, but not all natural things survive. Just ask a cynodont. If *we* want to survive, we had better start building better systems.

"FOR THE GOOD OF THE GROUP" MEETS "THE GOOD OF ITS PARTS"

All of this said, I would be greatly remiss not to address the whole slew of uncomfortable connotations that this case for collectivism no doubt poses for you. It's easy for us, when thinking about the "Perils of Collectivism" and the "Evil of Globalism" to have Orwellian and Huxleyan visions of everyone wearing the same uniform, living in standardized housing, completing their assigned duties, handing over their children, acquiescing to Big Brother, and drinking their Soma. But a collaborative future does not need to look like this at all. These are dystopias for a reason, and they are worthy of all the warnings prior science fiction has provided.

---

40 If I am apparently going to be so bold as to pick on a different nation that happened to be in the news this week, I should also point out the enormous role my own nation, its corporations, and its citizens just like myself, have disproportionately contributed to this very problem. Best put this in a footnote. It's far too true for the main text.

41 Gore, A. (2023, July). What the fossil fuel industry doesn't want you to know. *TED Countdown Summit.* https://www.ted.com/talks/al_gore_what_the_fossil_fuel_industry_doesn_t_want_you_to_know

In the Earth of HDP, you let your freak flag fly. Individualism is not to be squashed: it is the key to it all. ABRAM only hints at this with subtlety, in Chapter 42 ("The Test"):

> *"I do not ask you to give up yourselves, for the crew needs each and every one of you — assuming you will serve it, in addition to yourself."*

As such, the author felt compelled to say it much more explicitly in the first of these afterwords. Speaking of reprises:

> *"And indeed, it's fun to imagine what such a society could look like on Earth: one freed of the toxic individualism that has overtaken our own society like a cancer; one rooted in reason, logic, truth-telling, and at least mutualism, if altruism is too big an ask; one that does not prioritize the collective over the individual, but one in which both are equally cherished."*

In the realm of cultural evolution, our diverse perspectives are the "mutations" for the process to work with — the variance among which selection can select. And the beauty of cultural evolution is that those variants — that is, the ideas, even the bad ones — are welcome to keep on getting expressed while their proponents live out what are hopefully happy, healthy lives. The people themselves don't need to be eliminated. One reason: another beauty of cultural evolution is that people can continue to learn, and grow, and change their outlooks and behaviors over the course of their lives. It is difficult, but it is possible for good ideas to win over some of the bad ones. Second: even if minds should remain stubbornly fixed for all time, their bad ideas just won't win, if the system is working.

Contrary to the notion that we must eradicate each other, or at least their perspectives, we absolutely *need* variation in ideas. Just like with mutations, it presents us with options for evolution to use. Statistically, most mutations are neutral or even deleterious. But every once in a while, a truly wacky one gets you something as amazing as a platypus. We *need* diverse perspectives. It's just that we *also* need systems of integrating those diverse perspectives, selecting for the ones that are both effective and ethical, and a way of balancing competing interests to ensure cooperation. The collective is not meant to be prioritized over the individual, but neither should the other way continue to be true. As of now, we live in a society where our individual behaviors mostly say, "Society be damned."

GOODBYE, FOR REAL — UNTIL YOU HEAR FROM ME AGAIN

And this is where the deeply personal has come to meet the "entirely academic conception" of this project, as the years moved on and it unfolded from my consciousness: I love *people* — both individually and as a species. We are incredible. Yes, we are guilty of greed, anger, jealousy, corruption, among so many other vices; but we are equally capable of compassion, cooperation, and even total acts of selflessness, among so many other virtues. That ability to cooperate is not just a part of our future: it is a major part of our past. It is how we got here, to be capable of conquering this world as we seem to have just about conquered it for good. Now, we need to start thinking less about conquering, and far more about sustaining. We can keep this incredible legacy of cooperation alive and going strong, but there are challenges anew.

With love, absurdity, and even-more-fragile optimism,

Adam James Chouinard
November of 2023 on this amazing Planet Earth

ACKNOWLEDGEMENTS

Thanks to my family, and Neil in particular. See the Afterword (afore now) for reasons why. My brothers from the same and other mothers, Jon Chouinard and Phil Schapker Mendez, have been my staunchest supporters and contrarians alike, both of which are helpful, as they humored me in thinking through many aspects of the story. I do not recognize it formally, not even in type for all to see, but I suppose it's possible they had a good idea or two among them. In all seriousness, they have been extremely patient with my constant text message updates about trivial degrees of progress, as well as insightful when serving as the primary sounding boards for one thing after another.

Jon deserves special thanks, as his comments from the first reading of the very first draft — despite the fears that go hand in hand with handing out a work of this sort — amounted to essentially nothing but heartfelt enthusiasm for the story. I had a great number of doubts about this one, including after I'd written it: the dubious premise, the much-too-silly-ness, the much-too-serious-ness, the drastically different tone from my debut — and his legitimate passion and how it "really hit home" made me think there might be something to it after all. Maybe he's just a loving and biased brother, but either way, it was extremely encouraging, and I'm thankful for the spark to keep going, get over my fears, and put HDP out into the world. He's the one who coined it a "coming-to-terms story" in one of our first discussions after that earliest draft. He couldn't have put it better, and I thank him for the help with what would come to be the tagline. Better yet, as with many things, I pitched him the premise for the Reflective Logs interspersing the chapters, and despite immediately trying to talk myself out of it because of how much work it would entail and all the reasons it might well be a bad idea, he would not relent and insisted that I see the idea through. What I'm trying to say is, if you despise those logs, blame Jon.

On the science front, I have been inspired generally for many years by the works of [Dr.] David Sloan Wilson. His work on cooperation and multi-level selection theory in the primary literature are only matched by his excellent work as a science communicator and prosociality proponent. His work only influenced this book in the sense that it influenced every aspect of my thinking about evolution, decades ago now and ever since. If you want to learn more, I recommend checking out one of the greatest scientific trilogies of all time: *Evolution for Everyone* (2007; Delta), *The Neighborhood Project* (2011; Little, Brown and Company), and *This View of Life* (2019; Pantheon). A fun coincidence: I know David a little, as I invited him to speak at Oregon State University when I was a lowly doctoral student, hosted him for a few days, talked science nonstop and went open-ocean fishing. It was a blast, and he was as friendly and supportive as he is brilliant. Years later, as I was approaching the release date for *Embrace Inverse Vibrations,* I sent him an email to tell him about this big, bold, foolhardy plan I had to publish a book of scientific fiction. After some niceties, his reply began: "Now get ready for this—I too have written a novel that required many years and is about to be independently published! Mine is titled *Atlas Hugged* and is written as a sequel (and antidote) to Ayn Rand's novel *Atlas Shrugged*." So check out *Atlas Hugged* (2020; Redwood), if you're interested in the intersection of art, science, society, and prosocial evolution.

Other props belong to *The Alignment Problem* by Brian Christian (2021; Norton and Company). Given its publishing date, as an act of perfect timing I only read it after writing this whole darn story involving AI and ethics. Nevertheless, it did arrive in my consciousness in time to influence the Reflective Logs, which was very fortunate, as it supplemented my prior research and strengthened my understanding immensely. I highly recommend it. In opposite timing, I had the wherewithal to research much more about space and exoplanets, and one extremely helpful book was titled *Exoplanets and Alien Solar Systems* by [Dr.] Tahir Yaqoob (2011; New Earth Labs). On the social science front, Potch's tirade in "The Great Backslide Debate" (Chapter 05) was informed by *The Spirit Level: Why Greater Equality Makes Societies Stronger*, by Richard Wilkinson [MMedSci] and [Dr.] Kate Pickett (2009; Bloomsbury). Sadly, all those correlations are true.

Thanks as well to an academic talk on "Big History" by [Dr.] Walter Alvarez (famous for his work on Impact Theory and the K-T extinction). A talk section titled "What is the chance of you existing?" coincided with my own prior musings on this topic as a biologist interested in Big Questions, and it was informative to hear how an elder academic from a different discipline approached the same question. Many thanks to my friend the incomparable John Donovan, himself a close friend of Walter, for steering me to this explanation when we were discussing the matter. It helped me think about how to frame the conversation for the chapter "Infinitesimal Odds," although I opted to frame it in a reverse way as Walter; thus, if you'd like to see a complementary approach to that chapter's thesis, along with many other thoughtful and interdisciplinary reflections about big questions, I highly recommend this talk which one can find easily online by searching for "The 2012 R. Lowry Dobson Memorial Lecture" at UC Berkeley. It is excellent and inspiring.

On an entirely different note, I thank the disembodied voice of Timothy Leary from the song "Third Eye (Live)" by Tool on the album *Salival* (2000; Volcano/Dissectional). In writing the back cover blurb, it came to a close with the cadets contemplating "who they are, where they came from, and where they are going." These are questions I have considered often my whole life, and the phrase was meant to come to a full stop; when typing them out, however, my subconscious filled in the blanks with "…in this ocean of chaos" due to the similarity to the quote from this soundbite. I moved to cut it, but decided to leave it in as an homage. (See what I mean about human creative inspiration?) Tim and I may not agree on the methods, but I agree with the search.

Last of all, but far from least:

THANK YOU.

If you are still reading this,
in this ocean of chaos named the Sea of Appendices,
you are clearly invested, demented, or painfully bored.
And whatever the case, I appreciate you more than you know.

ABOUT THE AUTHOR

Adam James Chouinard is a person, teacher, scientist, musician, author, and independent publisher based in Eugene, Oregon. Adam earned a B.S. in Marine & Freshwater Biology and M.S. in Zoology from the University of New Hampshire, as well as a Ph.D. in Zoology from Oregon State University. He currently teaches biology, animal behavior, evolution, and more at his alma mater. In his parallel life, Adam founded Proavia Press as an outlet for exploring Big Questions through the synthesis of Scientific Inquiry and Artistic Expression.

There is meaning in the madness. Our job is to find it.

Let's connect at proaviapress.com

AN INDEPENDENT AUTHOR'S HUMBLE PLEA

I write books like this [read: "highly unmarketable"] with no real intention [read: "delusions"] of ever really selling them. I simply need to write them, as a means of curating my reflections on life, death, love, and our collective evolution. Now that this one's written, I just want people to enjoy it – to think about the ideas within, and to talk about them with friend and foe alike.

But as an independent publisher, the odds are stacked against me in that endeavor. We "indie" authors certainly need to write books that are worth reading in order to be successful; but **we need our readers to be our champions** if they deem that to be so. Thus, if you enjoyed this book, I ask only that you please **provide a fair online review** wherever you purchased it, and **recommend it** to friends, family – perhaps even your nemeses.

Lastly, **head over to proaviapress.com** to connect with the author, find additional content, and **sign up for our email list** to get updates on this and other projects.

Proavia Press is a proud member of the Alliance of Independent Authors (ALLi), a professional organization for the advancement of ethical independent publishing. Please support indie publishers by purchasing products directly from them (when possible), not distributing or using pirated (stolen) materials, and helping to otherwise combat unfair and unethical publishing practices.

CHAPTER INDEX

- -

```
>print chapter_index.sc
```



```
>|
```

- -

REFLECTIVE LOG INDEX

```
- - - - - - - - - - - - - - - - - - - - - - - - - - - - - - - - - - - - - -
>print reflective-log_index.sc | align_to_chapter.exc
```



```
>|
- - - - - - - - - - - - - - - - - - - - - - - - - - - - - - - - - - - - - -
```

www.ingramcontent.com/pod-product-compliance
Lightning Source LLC
Chambersburg PA
CBHW072038190726
48294CB00005B/1305